MINE

THE IRELAND SERIES
BOOK 4

SUE LANGFORD

To those who loved Irish Eyes, and those who love spice with their romance. A love story from Ireland.

"You only need one man to love you. But him to love you free like a wildfire, crazy like the moon, always like tomorrow, sudden like an inhale and overcoming like the tides. Only one man and all of this." C . Joybell C

SUE LANGFORD

Chapter 1

"Katie, just come and sit down. Let the boys handle it," Mia said.

"He's not worth throwing fists over Mia."

"Ronan was cruising for a damn fight with that lad Katie. I could see it in his face. Let him handle that guy."

"I mean, his ex is out there too," Katie said.

"Then she's about to get a tongue lashing too. Just sit and when they come in, I'll get the information out of Kian for you," Mia said. Katie shook her head and Pat, the bartender, brought over an espresso martini for Katie and a pint for Mia.

"At least the lads took it outside. I don't need that in here," Pat said.

"I just don't understand why," Katie said.

"Because he's defending your honor Katie. Whoever that guy was, hurt you in some way and he dealt with him. Most lass's would be impressed." Katie shook her head and when she saw the pub door open, Ronan and Kian came back to the table.

"What were you doing," Katie asked.

"Dealing with him. He's not touching you or coming anywhere near you ever again," Ronan said.

"Meaning what?"

1

"Meaning we handled him," Kian said.

"Ronan, what did you do?"

"Told him that if he came near you again, or parked outside my damn house, he was done for. He doesn't get to hurt you and get away with it."

"Then why is Anna staring at you from the bar?" Ronan looked over and shook his head. When Anna walked towards him, he got even more irritated.

"What?"

"Can I speak with you for a minute," Anna asked.

"Lass, leave the man alone. He's with his girl. He doesn't need your stupidity," Kian said. Ronan kissed Katie and got up.

"What do you want," Ronan asked as Anna sat down at the bar.

"You did that to defend me," Anna said.

"I did that after what I found out that he'd done to Katie not you. He's not a decent guy Anna. You want to date him, go ahead. Just don't bring him anywhere near me."

"But you did..."

"I did that for Katie."

"What did he do that was so damn bad," Anna asked.

"He hurt my girl. That's enough."

"Ronan."

"Goodbye Anna." He walked back over to the table with Katie, Mia and Kian and sat down.

"Change of topic. So, what's this I hear about you two moving in together," Mia asked.

"Nice try," Kian joked.

"What did you do," Katie asked.

"He said you were still his. Had to set the bloke straight."

"Ronan."

"He nailed him between the eyes and when he started to get up, I punched him," Kian said. Katie's arm slid around Ronan's, and he snuggled her to him, instead sliding his arm around her shoulders.

"You shouldn't have done that Ronan."

"He deserved it. Anyone that hurts you is dealing with me. I told you that." Katie was almost trembling. "Do you want to go home," Ronan asked. Katie shook her head and drank down her martini. Pat went to get her another, and Ronan shook his head. "Pat, can I borrow your office?" He nodded and handed Ronan the key and he walked Katie back there.

He walked her into the room and closed the door behind them. "Why did you do that," Katie asked.

"Because he was convinced that you were his. I don't want him anywhere near you or me. Hell. I don't even want him near Anna, and I can't stand her."

"Ronan, throwing a punch? Seriously?"

"He would've done it if I hadn't. I don't want him parked outside my house making you shaky all night. We're supposed to be enjoying the time we have. Not stressing about him coming after you again."

"Ronan."

"No. I don't want you shaking like you did all night. You saw that car and were shaking like a leaf Katie. That's why I said we weren't doing anything last night. Not that I was exactly in the mood, but after you getting shaky, I wasn't pushing anything. You needed a night to make you feel like you were safe. Like you were okay, and nothing could hurt you. I don't want anyone making you feel like that again." She kissed Ronan. "What," he asked.

"No more throwing punches."

He kissed her and pulled her to him, snuggling her to him. "Someone ever threatens to hurt you, I'll put them into the ground."

"Still think you didn't have to punch him."

"Only took one punch. I guess it must be all the gym time."

Katie smirked. "Ronan, promise me. No more throwing punches." He nodded and kissed her.

"No more stressing. You get worried, talk. That's part of that whole dating thing that you dared me into." He kissed her and devoured her lips until he heard Pat coming down the hall.

"Do you want to head back to the house or stay?"

"Stay and visit. Get all of it off my mind so when we get home, you can do anything you want," Katie replied with a smirk ear to ear.

"So, are we talking anything at all or just the teasing?"

"Tie." He kissed her and snuggled her tight to him.

"Anna and that guy are back. I figured you'd want to know," Pat said as he came into the office.

"Can we get rid of them?"

"Already tried. He said he wanted to talk to you," Pat replied.

"Can you get Kian?" Pat nodded and left them to talk.

"Don't go out there," Katie said.

"I'm getting him to leave."

"Ronan, please. I don't want you in another fight."

He kissed Katie. "I'm handling him." He slid his hand in hers and they walked out into the pub.

"And what do you want," Ronan asked as Katie stood beside him.

"Can we talk without her?" Ronan kissed Katie, and Mia got her to come and sit down. "Pat, can you get Katie a drink?" Pat nodded and Ronan walked outside.

"Whatever you have to say, do it here. You'll be leaving anyway." Kian followed and Devlin wasn't impressed.

"What," Ronan asked.

"You do realize that we never actually broke up right?"

"Let's just say you are from now on since I'm dating her. Leave the girl alone," Ronan said.

"She's my girl," Devlin said.

"If you really want another punch to the damn face, by all means keep going."

"I'm taking her back."

"Over my dead body, and I highly doubt you could pull that off," Ronan said.

"She's mine," Devlin said. Ronan threw a punch and knocked him to the ground.

"She doesn't want you. It's done. Leave the lass alone or you're dealing with me," Ronan said.

"And me," Kian chimed in.

"She wants me back Ronan. She doesn't want you."

"And that's why you were parked outside my house this week? Because she told you to and she wants you?"

"Yes."

Ronan kicked Devlin, breaking Devlin's nose with his foot. "You show up ever again and a busted nose is gonna be the least of your damn worries. Leave Katie alone."

"And you think she doesn't still want me? You watch. She'll come running to me," Devlin said.

Ronan wanted to hurt him. He wanted to pulverize Devlin. Kian stopped him. "Go Kian."

"No. You aren't throwing another punch."

"She still misses me. You'll see. When I bend her over and screw her right in..." Ronan punched him, and he hit the wall. Ronan walked back into the pub and got a shot. When Katie went to get up, Kian stopped her.

"Pat, can you call the police and get that scum out of here?"

"You threw punches Ronan."

"Just eliminate him. Please."

Pat went outside. "You're out of here lad. Don't come back."

"It's a pub."

"And I own the pub. I'm saying you and Anna are out of here. You're banned from the pub."

"Fine, but what I said stands. Katie is still my girlfriend."

"Between us, she's long gone from you lad. She's Ronan's girl. She's staying his girl."

Pat came back inside and nodded to Ronan. "Talk," Katie said.

"About what," Ronan asked.

"Just tell her what she said," Mia said.

"He said you two never broke up and that you were still his girlfriend."

"Because I left. I took off in the middle of the damn night or I'd never have been able to leave," Katie said. Ronan shook his head and went to get up.

"Ronan," Kian said. Ronan got another drink. When Katie went to get up, Mia shook her head.

"Just give him a minute," Mia said.

Ronan tossed back two more shots, and Pat handed him a pint. "Sit down lad. He's gone." Ronan paid his tab and Pat shook his head. "Sit down with your lass. She's burning a hole in your back right now," Pat said quietly. Ronan took his pint and sat back down.

"Ronan," Katie said.

"What?"

"Talk to me."

"I should've beat..."

"Ronan," Kian said.

"That little piece..."

"Ronan, stop," Mia said. Katie looked at him.

"So now you're mad..." Ronan got back up and walked into the mens room.

"I'll handle it," Kian said.

"What did I say," Katie asked.

"Just give him a few to calm himself down. To be honest, I haven't seen him throw a punch since high school. He was protecting you. That's obvious," Mia said.

"But he can't even look at me," Katie said.

Mia nodded. "He's in protector mode. Let him come down from it," Mia said. Katie turned and watched the mens room door.

"What did i say," Katie asked.

"If you throw a punch at the mirror, I'm out of here," Kian said.

"She had to run away in the middle of the damn night? Seriously? And he thinks that she belongs to him? He's lucky I didn't beat him senseless."

"Ronan, you're freaking the lass out."

"I can't. Who in the world could do that to her of all people? I know what he's done Kian. I don't want him near me or her."

"Then come back out, take a damn breath and be with your lass before she worries that you're walking away from her. She's upset," Kian said.

"How could he do that to her of all damn people?"

"Breathe."

"I swear, if I see him again, I'm kicking his backside to the moon," Ronan said.

"Just take a breath. She's upset now. What are you gonna do," Kian asked.

"Just give me a minute to calm myself down."

"Ronan, take it out on who deserves it. Not her. She's scared that you're literally pushing her away." Ronan took a deep breath and walked back into the bar with Kian.

Ronan sat down with Katie and Mia and Katie looked at him. "Do you want to go?"

"Depends on whether you're still mad or not," Katie said.

"Mad at him. Not at you."

Katie took a sip of her drink. "Are you sure you're okay?" He nodded. "Ronan."

He kissed her. "Are you okay," Ronan asked. Katie nodded and Ronan slid his arm around her. "I'd protect you with my life if I had to. You know that right?" Katie nodded. He kissed her again and he made a decision. "We'll get together tomorrow night. Hopefully it'll be less drama," Ronan said as he took Katie's hand and helped her out of the booth.

"Just take it easy tonight," Mia said. Ronan nodded and headed out with Katie. When they walked outside, thankfully, Devlin was gone. They walked back over to the house and Ronan walked Katie inside and locked up behind them.

"Are you okay," Katie asked. He pulled her to him and kissed her. He deepened the kiss until he had picked her up, wrapped her legs around him and was walking up the stairs to the bedroom. He leaned her onto the bed and leaned into her arms. "Ronan." He kissed her again.

"What?"

"Are we gonna talk about it?"

"No." He kissed her again, peeled her shirt off then her jeans.

"Ronan, stop."

"What?"

"Tell me what happened."

"Not now."

He peeled his sweater off and Katie kissed him. "Tell me."

He shook his head and peeled her bra and lace panties off then kissed her neck and just as he was about to kiss down her chest, she stopped him. "What love?"

"Are you okay?" He looked at her and ignored what she asked. "Ronan, answer me."

"We're not talking about it. We're busy." He kissed down her chest and licked and nibbled at each breast until she was moaning.

"Ronan."

"What," he asked as he kissed and licked down her stomach and then nibbled at her hip.

"Mm."

"Good answer." He kissed and licked his way to her inner thigh and her toes curled. "Katie."

"What," she asked almost breathless.

"Still want to talk or do you want this," he said as his fingers teased, and he licked and nibbled and sucked at her wetness.

"Ronan," she said as he could hear her moaning.

"And this," he said as two fingers slid deep inside her.

"Shit."

"Yeah, that's what I was hoping you'd say." Her body throbbed around his fingers, and he kept teasing.

"Ronan, come."

"Not done yet lass. Your legs aren't shaking."

"Ronan." He smirked and kissed her as his fingers continued to tease.

"Yes love."

"I need to taste you."

He shook his head. "I'm getting my way tonight," Ronan said.

"Meaning what?"

"Meaning no dessert."

"Ronan." He pulled his hands away from her and slid his jeans off. "Ronan."

"What?"

"Come here and let me help."

"No."

"Ronan." He kicked his jeans onto the chair and peeled his boxers off. "Come here."

"Tell me what you want lass."

"I want to taste…"

"Katie."

"Come here."

He walked over to her, and she slid him into her mouth. "Katie." She slid him deeper into her mouth and he shook his head. "Katie."

"Mm."

"Babe, stop."

"Mine." She kept going, sucking and licking until he pulled away from her. "What?" He kissed her and pinned her onto the bed, sliding deep inside her. "Aah," she said as her breath hitched.

"You're mine Katie. Mine."

"Yours," she replied as he kept going deeper into her, then harder, then more and more intense. "Ronan." He kept going as her legs wrapped tight around him.

"What?"

"Harder." He kept going and when she found her release, he kept going. "Aah. Ronan." He kissed her and kept going until he climaxed. He slid to his back and Katie slid over and leaned her head on his shoulder. "Are you okay?"

"Katie, leave it."

"I want to know what happened. Just tell me."

He shook his head and got up, walking off into the bathroom, determined to wipe it out of his mind. He cleaned up a little bit and when he walked back into the bedroom, she was curled up and waiting for him. "Katie."

"All I asked was what he said. I get he ticked you off Ronan. Him breathing ticks me off. Just say it." Ronan pulled boxers on, put his jeans onto the hanger and went downstairs. He got himself a drink, got one for Katie and walked back up to the bedroom, handing her a drink. "Well," Katie asked.

"He said that you two never broke up. That you were his. That he was taking you back."

"What?"

"Now you know why I was mad."

"Ronan, you do know that I'd never walk back into his life right? I'm here with you. I don't want to be anywhere else."

"And if he thinks that you're his, it means him coming after me. I don't need his crap."

"If he was on a date with your ex, then obviously we aren't together. He was doing it to get on your bad side."

"And it bloody well worked Katie. After what he did to you when you two were together, all I saw was red. He doesn't deserve to have you in his life, and he doesn't even deserve to breathe the same air as you."

"Ronan, he's trying to cause a damn breakup. That's what he wants. He even said that nobody else would ever want me because I was used up."

Ronan looked at her. "What?"

"We broke up months ago. I figured me leaving a note saying we were done and walking out and moving would be enough to make him understand that we were done."

"Katie."

"What?"

"I love you, and I know you're attempting to calm me down, but I'm ready to pulverize him right now."

"He's not worth the effort Ronan. We're together. I'm not leaving."

"After everything that man did to you. I can't sit here and pretend that it's nothing."

"It's history. He doesn't get to have me back." Ronan pulled her into his arms and her legs slid around his hips.

"Nobody is ever hurting you again. You know that right?" Katie nodded and kissed him.

"He's not worth it Ronan. He really never was."

He kissed her, put his drink down and put hers beside his. "Promise me that if we don't work out, you still tell me if he's coming after you."

"Ronan."

"Promise me."

"I promise you that no matter what, we're gonna work out even if we have to have another fight to do it. I'm not going anywhere." He kissed her and pulled her tight against him.

"I don't know what I'd do if he ever tried to hurt you again."

"I'd hold onto you."

"Katie."

She kissed him. "I don't want you fighting him on the street Ronan. I want you beside me."

He kissed her, devouring her lips. "Okay," Ronan said as he held her tight. Somehow, she managed to do the one thing he couldn't seem to do. Calm himself down.

Just as he was about to curl up with her, Katie's phone rang. One look at the screen and he could feel her shaking. "I'll handle him," Ronan said.

"Just ignore the call. He'll go away." Ronan kissed her, grabbed the phone and pressed answer and speaker.

"When I said that Katie was off limits, were you not listening or did you need a knock to the head again?"

"Katie, I don't know what you told him about us, but you know dang well that we never broke it off."

"I walked away. I broke up with you in that note. You know why I left."

"And you know that a note isn't a breakup. Come home."

"I'm gonna say this once and only once. You contact Katie again, come near her, hell, breathe the same air as her, you'll be in a body bag. Understood," Ronan said.

"You're the one with my girl," Devlin said.

"And you're the one who's gonna end up being a puddle on the cement." Ronan hung up the phone, blocked Devlin's number and called his friend at the police.

"Ronan."

"Need your assistance. My girl's ex is stalking and harassing her. He's pissing me off on top of it all and he's scaring her. Anything you can do?"

"Depends. Did you try talking to him?"

"I did. He called her phone to harass her after I said to stay away from her," Ronan said. "She can get a protection order I think. Just don't go starting a fist fight with him. The guy probably deserves a Ronan butt kicking, but don't start a problem," his friend said.

"He already did," Ronan replied.

"Then I'll handle things. What's his phone number?" Ronan sent it to him in a text and Katie shook her head. "Alright. Consider it handled. If we're able to get you set with a protection order, I'll let you know what you need to do."

"Thank you," Katie said.

"Most welcome Katie." Ronan hung up with him and she wrapped her arms around Ronan's neck.

"See, even your police friend said to not get in a fist fight with him." Katie kissed Ronan and he shook his head.

"He calls or finds a way to contact you, you're telling me." Katie nodded and hugged Ronan. "Tell me what happened."

"Ronan, I'm not making all of this worse."

"Tell me. He's gonna hold it over my head, and if I don't know…"

"Okay. He wasn't that bad at the start. Then he started trying to force me into doing things in bed with him and doing what he told me to. One time I didn't do what he asked, and he pushed me into the wall. That was the least of what he did."

"Katie."

"Once he decided that I wasn't doing what he wanted me to in bed and almost choked me. He wasn't a good person. I tried to leave a few times, and he'd hunt me down and find me."

"Just like he did when we got home from Paris and you had just moved in."

Katie nodded. "I know that your first instinct is to kick his butt, but I need you with me Ronan. Please."

He shook his head and leaned her onto the bed. "If I ever do something you aren't comfortable with, tell me."

Katie kissed him. "We haven't done anything I didn't want Ronan."

"Promise me." Katie nodded and kissed him. "I just can't understand why he'd do that. That's never happening with us. You know that right?" Katie nodded and kissed him. "What," Ronan asked.

She kissed him and slid her arms around him. "I don't want to talk about him."

"Katie." She looked at Ronan and he pulled her legs around him.

"What?"

"What do you want to do?"

"Talk about anything else but him."

"And?"

She looked up at him. "Come here."

He kissed her, devouring her lips until he managed to let her up for air.

"Tell me." He smirked and kissed down her neck.

"Ronan."

"Tell me what you want."

"I need you inside me."

"More?" She nodded. He kissed her and nibbled and licked and teased each breast until she had goosebumps.

"Ronan."

"What," he asked as he kissed down her side.

"Stop."

"Stop what sexy?"

"Teasing."

"Not planning on teasing lass. I'm just warming you up." His hand slid between her legs and started teasing. Before she could say another word, he kissed her again and slid two fingers inside her.

"Aah."

"That's what I thought."

"Ronan, aah."

"All turned on already."

"All you," she said as he kept teasing and going until her body was throbbing around his fingers.

"Ronan."

He kissed her. "Tell me what you want."

"You inside me."

"Now?" She nodded and he grabbed something from the bedside table and tied her hands.

"Don't move them." She nodded and he slid deep into her.

"This what you wanted?" Katie nodded and he started sliding in and out, over, and over, harder then deeper then slowly sped up until she was moaning his name.

"Ronan." He kept going then stopped to kiss her.

"Tell me what you want."

"More." He kept going until she was ready to explode. She crashed around him, and he followed a matter of seconds later. "You're way too addictive," he said as he untied her hands. Her heart was racing in time with his and he slid to his back. Katie slid to his side and rested her head on his shoulder.

"Now what were you saying about addictive," Katie teased.

"And all yours, lass."

"Good. I refuse to share that of all things."

"Good. Same goes for me," he replied as his phone buzzed, and he put it on speakerphone.

"It's Chase. My police friend. Chase, what's up," Ronan asked.

"She has to come to court to get the order. They said they can do it on Monday."

Katie nodded.

"Can we make It early," Ronan asked.

"8am?"

"Please," Ronan replied.

"See you Monday then. Just stay as far away from him as you can."

"Will do my friend. Thank you." Ronan hung up with him and Katie kissed him.

"I'll let work know I'm coming in at 10. I'll get you to work after."

"Ronan."

"Honestly, I'd rather that you were safe here instead, but you have work."

"I wish I could just stay here in bed with you instead of work," Katie joked.

He kissed her. "Unfortunately, I have meetings Monday afternoon. Just make sure you stay out of sight until he gets the papers. I don't want him showing at your work."

Katie nodded. "I think I'm working in the office next week anyway. Closed doors."

Ronan kissed her. "Good. Now, back to what we were doing."

"Which was what," Katie asked.

He kissed her, devouring her lips. "We need to get sleep."

"Says who," Katie teased.

"We need sleep love."

"No work tomorrow."

He kissed her. "Still have a workout to do love. We still need to sleep."

"And if I say that I'm making breakfast tomorrow and you're sleeping in?"

He kissed her. "Katie, I love that you want to, but I'm still getting up and doing a workout."

"Ronan."

"If I'm up before you, I'll make breakfast. Deal?" Katie kissed him and leaned into his arms, straddling him on the bed. "And what do you want lass?"

"I'm making breakfast and you're staying in bed." He kissed her, devouring her lips and pinned her to the bed, flipping her to her back.

"And how did you think that you were gonna be able to do that when I tie you to the bed?"

"And how did you think you were gonna be able to do that," Katie teased. He reached over and grabbed the handcuffs from the bedside table and held them up. "You wouldn't dare."

"Tie or rope?"

"Ronan." He put the handcuffs down and grabbed the soft velvet rope and tied her hands to the headboard.

"Ronan, untie them." "You want to tease and start something again, I'll finish it, and your legs will be shaking for the rest of the night."

"I wasn't starting..." He kissed her, devouring her lips and deepening the kiss until she was sprouting goosebumps.

"You were starting something lass. I am just reminding you of what happens when you start and don't finish."

Katie shook her head. "I never said I was starting anything." He kissed her again and pulled her legs around him.

"You were starting something, and you know it," Ronan said.

"Because I was sitting on top of you and you were getting all turned on?"

"Because I know you and those hands."

"Untie them." He shook his head. "Ronan."

He kissed her again. "What?"

"Untie my hands."

"No."

"You do realize that if I wanted to, I could find a way."

"I know you can. That's why I tied them."

"Ronan, untie..."

He kissed her, devouring her lips until she was tightening her legs around him and pulling him to her. "Tell me what you want Katie."

"You."

"Nope. Answer me."

"I want to taste you."

"I know what you're up to and the answer is no."

"Why? Because you'd be at my mercy?"

"Because you're not getting your hands untied until I decide to."

She kissed him and he shook his head. "Please," she asked.

"Katie."

"That's what I want."

"You're behaving." Katie smirked and nodded. "And when I say stop you're stopping." Katie smirked.

"Maybe."

He shook his head. "Katie."

"Okay." He untied her hands and kissed her.

"Behave."

"Never." Her hand slid to his length and he shook his head.

"Katie."

"On your back."

"Katie."

She pushed him onto his back and slid on top of him, taking his length into her mouth. He shook his head. He knew it'd be too much. "Mm."

"Katie." She slid her mouth up and down until he was past being turned on. She licked and teased and kept going until he was deep in her mouth and she was looking up at him.

"Katie stop." She kept going, taking him a little deeper until he was almost ready to explode.

"Mine."

"Katie." She kept going and going until he pulled her to him and he pinned her back onto the bed. He re-tied her hands.

"Ronan."

"What?"

"I want you."

"I bet you do lass." He pulled her legs around his ribs and slid deep into her.

"Aah."

"That what you wanted?" Katie nodded and he kept going. This time, it was harder, rougher and even more intense than usual.

"Shit Ronan." He kept going until she was moaning. Until she was begging for more. Until she was spent and pulsating around him over and over. "Ronan."

"Mine," he said almost purring into her ear.

"Shit." He kept going, hard and fast until she exploded around him again then he followed a matter of seconds later, pouring into her.

"Untie them," Katie asked. He did and kissed her, devouring her lips all over again.

"You are such a damn bad influence," he said.

"And?"

He shook his head. "We're going to sleep." He went to get up and she shook her head.

"What?"

"Stay in bed."

"Two minutes," he replied as he walked into the bathroom and cleaned up. When he walked back into the bedroom, she was asleep. He smirked, slid on a pair of boxers, and slid into the bed beside her. Just as he was closing his eyes, his phone buzzed:

> *Tell me that you miss me and I'm yours Ronan. - Anna*

It was from an unknown number, and he knew exactly who it was. He deleted the text and put their phones on the charger. "No phones allowed," Katie said with her eyes closed.

"Charging." He kissed her and she curled up with him, falling asleep on his shoulder with her arm wrapped around him. He shook his head and nodded off a matter of minutes later.

The next morning, Ronan woke up at 5 and Katie was still out cold. He got up, gently sliding out of the bed. "Where are you going?"

"Workout. Have to look good for my girl," Ronan said.

"Come back to bed. You look good enough already," Katie said.

He kissed her, freshened up and saw her back asleep. He walked downstairs and did his workout then came back upstairs to see Katie still asleep. "Get back in bed."

"Food lass. I'll make it."

"Get back in bed Ronan. I know what I want for breakfast and he won't get back in bed." He shook his head and kissed her again then walked downstairs and made a quick protein shake. He put breakfast on for them and smirked. He went from an empty bed to one with a lass begging him to come back to bed. From an empty house, to one where she loved him. Where they made good memories. It all hit him at once as he flipped the bacon. He scrambled the eggs and plated them for them both. He got some fresh juice from the fridge, got them each a mug of coffee and carried it upstairs to bed complete with cutlery.

"I thought I was making breakfast," Katie said mid-yawn as she smelled the coffee.

"Like I said, you'd have to get up before me."

"I tried." He kissed her and handed Katie the coffee.

"What did you make?"

"Scrambled and bacon." He handed Katie the tray, taking his off of it and putting it onto the bed. He ate and Katie got a grin ear to ear. "Whatever you're thinking, stop," Ronan said.

"Just thinking that somehow every Sunday we end up having breakfast in bed and you never ever sit beside me."

"Katie, just eat." She smirked and had her food, and Ronan took a deep breath. He finished his food, and his coffee then walked over to the bed, sitting down beside her. "What," he asked.

"It's Sunday right?"

"Yes."

"Do we really have to go?"

"To what? Church or the pub?"

"Church." He kissed her. "We're going love. Someone I wanted you to meet."

"Like who, Ronan?"

"You'll see when we get there." He kissed her and took the dishes downstairs, cleaning up. Just as he was putting the last dish in the washer, her arms slid around him from behind. "And what can I do for you lass?"

"Turn around." He shook his head and turned to face her.

"Yes love." She went up on her tiptoes and kissed him.

"And what's that for," he asked.

"Breakfast. Coffee mostly though." He nodded and picked her up, sitting her on the countertop.

"Tell me what you want lass."

"What I want is standing in front of me in joggers and a tee."

"And?"

"Come back to bed."

"Why?"

"Because I have something I needed to do."

"Katie."

"Please."

He shook his head and kissed her, devouring her lips until she was pulling at his drawstring of his joggers. "Katie."

"Now."

"Sofa." She shook her head.

"Bed." He picked her up, wrapped her legs around him and carried her back up the steps and leaned her onto the bed in the main bedroom.

"Now, what did you want?"

"Take the joggers and the boxers off."

"Katie."

"You don't have work. We have time to do whatever we want to."

"Church."

"It can wait." He shook his head and Katie looked at him.

"I'm waiting."

"We have to be there in an hour."

"Then you should hurry up."

"Katie, we need to get ready."

"Come and get over here or else."

"Or else what lass?"

"Or else you're gonna end up having a super long shower."

"Katie." She peeled his joggers off and pulled him close.

"Determined?" She nodded and kissed him. He kicked his joggers and boxers off and slid into her arms. "Tell me what you want Katie."

"I want you. I want to taste you."

"That's not happening right now."

"Really?"

"Katie." She tried to slide him onto his back, and he stopped her. "You're not getting your way with that lass."

"Oh, I will." He slid deep inside her and her breath hitched.

"This what you want?"

"Yes," Katie said as he kissed her and kept going, sliding in and out, harder then faster then deeper. "Ronan."

"Yes lass."

"Mm."

"Good answer," he replied as he kept going until he could feel her throbbing around him. He went harder.

"Aah."

"Good girl," he said as he pinned her hands to the bed and kept going.

"Let go."

"Nope."

"Mm."

"Yes lass. That's what I wanted," he teased as he kept going, harder and faster.

"Ronan," she moaned.

"Mine," he said. She crumbled around him, and he exploded into her a matter of minutes later. "Now about that whole long shower thing," he teased.

"I can't move."

"Good." He kissed her and got up.

"Where are you going?"

"To shower so I can get ready for church." He kissed her again and walked into the main bathroom.

Chapter 2

Ronan flipped the water on and let it warm up as he freshened up. He finished and stepped into the shower, washing his hair and cleaning up. Just as Katie was about to step in, he shook his head and stepped out. "Ronan."

"Go ahead lass. Have your shower."

"Ronan."

"I told you. If that's what you want, it can wait until later."

"You are such a party pooper."

"You're the one that said you could barely walk." She shook her head and showered and when she stepped out, he was already getting dressed. She wrapped herself in a warm towel and walked over to his closet. He was standing in his boxers.

"Ronan."

"Yes lass."

"What are you wearing?"

"To church?" She nodded. "Suit pants and my dress shirt and tie. Why?"

"So, if I went naked would you be mad?"

"Didn't feel like getting out of bed today did you?"

"Not exactly. I was kinda hoping the robe would be enough to talk you into staying in bed with me." He kissed her and devoured her lips.

"You still have to get dressed lass."

"And what should I wear?"

He shook his head. "A dress."

She smirked. "Okay then." She walked over to her closet and saw the dresses that had been added to it. She slid on the sexiest bra she had, the skimpiest thong she had and slid the dress on with the highest slit. She slid her heels on and went and dried her hair, putting on a little makeup.

"Katie."

"What," she asked as he walked in and saw her then leaned against the door frame.

"You do realize it's church, right? It's not a sexy dinner thing." She nodded and smirked. "Oh, I know. I thought it would work though."

"And why is that," Ronan asked. She motioned for him to come closer. "I'm not falling for it."

"Do you want me to show you then?"

"No."

"Give me your hand."

"Katie."

"Give me your hand Ronan."

"I know exactly what you're up to. We have to go." She grabbed his hand and pulled him to her.

"And what might I be up to?" He shook his head.

"Katie, we have to go." She slid his hand to the barely there thong and he shook his head again. "You're determined to tease today."

"Because I know what you actually want to be doing instead of church."

"Damn you."

"Still think we'd have more fun here."

"Katie."

"What?"

"We're still going."

"Ronan."

"That will be dealt with when we get back."

He took her hand and walked her down the steps. He walked her outside and she saw the waiting car. He locked up and they left to head to church. "And why did we have to leave so early?"

"So we could get there after my folks did."

"What?"

"They were 3 rows in front of us last week. I'm aiming for more," Ronan teased.

"Did you want me to meet them," she asked as she turned to face him.

"That's up to you, to be honest, but later works too."

"Ronan, do you want me to meet your mom and dad?"

"They wanted to meet you."

Katie looked at him. "And what about you?" Just as she said it, they were pulling up to the church.

"Well, I guess the answer is yes since they're right there." Ronan hopped out, helped Katie out of the car and his Dad smirked.

"Couldn't sneak in the back way," his dad teased.

"Trust me. I tried," Ronan said. "Dad, this is Katie. Katie, my Dad."

"Your mom's already inside. Nice to meet you Katie."

"As long as you didn't bring all the cousins and relatives."

"She'll want to meet you too," his dad said.

"I'd love to meet her," Katie said. Ronan shook his head, and they walked inside.

"Are you sitting with us or hiding out," Ronan's dad asked.

"We'll be back here," Ronan said as his mom got up and came back to them.

"You must be Katie," his mom said.

"Mom, Katie. Katie, my mom."

"Nice to meet you," Katie said.

"You two are coming and sitting with us," his mom said.

"We're fine here mom. We can talk after. Go get your seat," Ronan said. She went and sat down, turning around to watch Ronan and Katie throughout the service. When it was done, Ronan was determined to sneak out before they caught up to them. "Ronan," his dad said.

"Yep."

"What are you two doing this afternoon," his dad asked.

"Pub with Kian and Mia. Why?"

"Why don't you two come to the house for lunch before you head over," his mom asked.

"We sort of have plans. We can..."

"Ronan," his dad said.

"We can't stay for long. I promised them we'd come around 1," Ronan said.

"Good. We'll meet you at the house," his dad said. They got into the waiting car and Katie almost laughed.

"Couldn't say no to your mom," Katie teased.

"Fine, but we're out of there at 1."

They made it to his mom and dad's and went inside. "I'm almost surprised that we talked you into it," his mom said as he came into the kitchen with Katie.

"So, you're still doing the sports day at the pub," his dad asked.

"I promised them we'd come. We haven't been in a while," Ronan said.

"And why was that," his mom asked.

"Defending Katie last time we were there."

"Well, you weren't actually defending me, you were more like removing the trash and taking it out," Katie interjected.

"I do like the sound of that better," Ronan said.

"So, where did you two meet," his mom asked.

"We were both at a lounge at a hotel. He was at a meeting and so was I. We just sort of started talking and then we ended up having another date the following week."

"And my boy found the prettiest lass there was," his dad said.

"Well thank you," Katie said as she blushed. Ronan kissed her cheek.

"We can't really stay for long. I promised Katie that we'd get there early," Ronan said attempting to get out of having her at his mom and dad's.

"We just wanted a little visit. I don't know why you're never over here," his mom said as she handed Ronan a drink and handed one to Katie. "Mom."

"What? You aren't."

"It's called work. I was working almost 6 days a week during that merger. I haven't had a ton of spare time. I just got back from a meeting in Paris," Ronan said.

"And did you take Katie with you?"

"She was there," Ronan replied as Katie sipped her Ice water.

"And what did you think of Paris," his mom asked.

"It was beautiful. We had a great time," Katie said. Ronan's dad looked at him.

"And did you take her to that restaurant that your mom always wanted to go to?"

Ronan nodded. "I surprised her with that one. She wanted to go to the top of the tower, and we stopped at the restaurant and went up to the top when the lights started."

"That must've been beautiful," his mom said.

"It was romantic," Katie said smirking at Ronan.

"We really should head out. We have to get changed and head over," Ronan said as he pulled Katie to him.

"You're coming for dinner next week. Promise?"

"I have a meeting on Saturday. So does Katie. I promise we'll come up with another option," Ronan said.

"Then we're getting together on Wednesday for my birthday," his mom said.

"Fine. We'll come for dinner," Ronan said. He gave them each a hug and so did Katie, then they headed out.

They got into the waiting car and Ronan shook his head. "We could've stayed," Katie said.

"I have plans."

"I bet you do," Katie said as she kissed him.

"Don't start," he teased.

"Oh, I get to start whatever I want Ronan."

"Katie, I love that you think so, but if you start, you know exactly what's gonna happen," he said undoing his tie.

"Go ahead and tease Ronan. I can do whatever I want to." When they got to the house, he hopped out, helped Katie out of the car, and walked her inside.

"See, now I get..." He kissed her and pinned her against the back of the front door.

"You were saying," he teased.

"And what are you gonna do Ronan?"

He slid the tie off. "Upstairs."

"And if I said no?"

"Walk or I'm carrying you," he said as she slid her heels off and kissed him.

"Or what," she teased.

"Upstairs Katie." She went up the steps and he followed.

"Ronan."

"You don't move, I swear I am gonna chase you into the damn bedroom." She got upstairs and ran into the bedroom. He followed, catching her and pinned her to the bed.

"What," Katie asked. He kissed her and peeled the top of her dress off, then slid the skirt part up her legs.

"What are you up to," Katie asked as he went for the zipper of her dress. "Ronan." She undid the zipper and he pulled it off, seeing the sheer little thong she had on.

"Had to didn't you," he asked.

"Was attempting to get your attention." He kissed her and pulled the bra off then the little thong. "Ronan."

"What?"

"You're overdressed for what I want to do to you."

"And you're perfectly dressed for what I'm about to do," he replied.

"Shirt off."

"Katie."

"And the boxers and the pants."

"And what are you gonna do when you're tied to the bed?"

"I'm getting what I want first."

"You are so very bad."

"Take them off Ronan." He threw his shirt onto the chair, slid his dress pants off and threw them onto the chair with his shirt then Katie looked at him.

"What?"

"Come here."

"Katie."

"Come here Ronan." He slid his boxers off and walked around the bed to her.

"What would you like lass?" She got up and kissed him. "You're teasing." She nodded and he felt her hand on him. "Katie." She kissed him again and then he shook his head and felt her mouth on him. Licking and sucking and teasing until he was hard as a rock and she was enjoying every second. "Katie."

"Mm."

"When I say stop, you stop." She shook her head.

"No. Mine." She went back to licking and sucking and he shook his head.

"Stop Katie."

"No." She kept going.

"Katie, stop." She looked up at him and he stopped her.

"Why," Katie asked.

"Come here." She kissed him and he leaned over and had her pinned to the bed.

"Ronan."

He slid deep inside her and her breath hitched. "Shit."

"Are you done teasing lass?"

"Aah."

"Good girl."

"Ronan."

"Yes love," he said as he slid deep into her over and over. It got more intense, harder then she pulled her legs tight around him and he went faster. When her body started to throb around him, she was moaning his name. "Mine," he said.

"Mm."

"Katie."

"Ronan, please."

"Please what lass?"

"Mm. More." He kept going until he could feel he was close. He exploded into her and leaned into her arms.

"Shit," Ronan said.

"Much better," she teased as he kissed her again and slid to his side.

"Lass, you are determined to make me collapse on the damn bed."

"Staying in bed on Sunday. Much better plan," she teased.

He shook his head. "We're still going."

"And what else do you have planned while we're there," Katie teased.

"You mean since you and the skirt are coming?"

"I'm not wearing a skirt. It's not exactly warm out."

"Katie."

"No skirt Ronan."

"Then don't be surprised when I slide my hand down the front of your jeans."

"Ronan."

"You want to start then so will I lass."

"Fine, but don't start."

"Start what? Teasing you until you're bent over the counter at the pub?"

"That and no fighting."

He shook his head. "If he shows up, I'm handling it." Ronan got up and went and cleaned up, sliding on fresh boxers and his jeans.

"We really have to go now," Katie asked.

"Game starts at 1:30," Ronan said.

"Ronan."

"All I'm saying is that if he's there…"

"You're keeping your hands to yourself until I get the protection thing tomorrow. I need you to stay with me instead of walking out and handling him." Ronan grabbed one of his rugby shirts and slid it on then slid his sweater over it.

"You're seriously going now," she asked.

"Kinda ruined the mood lass."

"How?"

"I don't want to talk about him. If he shows, he'll be removed from the pub. Pat already told him to leave."

"And," Katie asked.

"And I'll do my best lass."

"Meaning you're staying with me and not going outside and picking another fight."

"Can you get dressed?" She got up and went into her closet, sliding on the jean skirt and a sweater.

"Why can I not wear one of your jerseys," Katie asked.

"That what you want?" She nodded. "I'll get you one."

"Thank you." He kissed her and she finished getting ready. They headed over a few minutes later and as soon as they were through the door, Kian walked over to them.

"And what took you two so long," Kian asked.

"Mom and Dad caught us at church and demanded we came over. What's going on," Ronan asked as Katie hugged Mia and slid into the booth.

"They were here. Pat kicked them out and called the police on the guy. He said he was here to talk to Katie."

"Well, he won't be able to tomorrow. She's getting a protection order."

Kian shook his head. "At least it'll make for less blood during rugby."

Ronan got drinks for him and Katie and brought them over. "Thank you," Katie said.

"Did you two need another round," Ronan asked.

"We're good. So, what did you think of mom and dad," Mia asked.

"Super nice. We're going over this week for dinner I think," Katie said.

"I can tell you that mom likes you. That's kind of obvious," Ronan said.

"Are you actually going to dinner with them," Kian joked.

"Since Katie got roped into it too, probably. The Spanish Inquisition all over again. Just be prepared for a million and one questions," Ronan said.

"I think that they're happy you're with someone," Katie said.

"Since they never met the other one, I'm not surprised," Ronan said.

"You managed to sneak that through without them knowing?"

"She refused to come to church with me. They knew she existed, but they never met her. We were only together a couple months," Ronan said.

"She's being called that after a few months?"

"After she cheated, yes." Katie smirked and took a sip of her drink.

"Did you two talk about the idiot guy," Kian asked as Ronan kicked him under the table.

"Yeah, we did," Katie said.

Ronan shook his head. "Can we stay off the topic of the psycho," Ronan asked.

"You mean since she's not allowed back in here," Kian said.

"Good," Ronan said.

Katie shook her head. "Who's winning the game," Katie asked determined to get off the topic.

"We're winning so far. Even though someone forgot his jersey," Kian said.

"Under the sweater." He slid the sweater off as she saw a peek of the abs she loved.

"Happy," Ronan teased.

"Very," Kian said as he could see the tension all over Ronan. Katie shook her head.

"What," Ronan asked.

"We need to talk."

"Pat, can I borrow your office?" Pat threw him the key, and he walked Katie back there.

"What," he asked as he closed the door. "You call her the damn Devil."

"And?"

"Ronan."

"She fucked someone in my house when I was away at a business meeting. I came back early to surprise her, and she was screwing him on my sofa. That's why I can't have her anywhere near me. She is the damn devil. She ripped my heart out, shredded it and threw it in my face."

"And it can't be the guy's fault right?"

"Meaning what? He got his butt booted from the house after he tried to throw a punch at me."

"Do you know who he was?"

"Katie."

"Ronan, you want to be mad, then be mad. You want to kick Devlin to the moon, leave it alone. Take me home before you throw another punch. You want to be mad, take me to bed and do what you want. I don't want you all aggravated. She didn't deserve you Ronan. You didn't deserve what you got from her either. Just let it..."

He kissed her, pulling her to him. "I don't want to talk about her. It's me and you or nothing Katie."

"No more Devil stuff."

"I don't want to talk about it."

"If we ever broke it off, would you do that to me?"

"No." He kissed her again and sat her on the desk.

"Ronan, be serious."

He kissed her, devouring her lips until he wanted to take advantage. "Not in here," Katie said as his hand slid up her leg. He locked the office door. She shook her head.

"Not here Ronan. Home." He kissed her again.

"Here." She shook her head.

"No."

"Katie." She shook her head.

"Not in here." His hands slid up her legs. She went to shake her head yet again and he kissed her, and she felt his fingers starting to tease.

"Ronan."

He kissed her again and his fingers slid inside her. "Shit."

"That's what I was hoping you'd say," he teased. She undid his jeans, and he shook his head. "Teasing you."

"And I want you," she said.

He slid his boxers down and slid into her as her breath hitched. "This what you want," he asked. Katie nodded and they had fast and hard sex.

"Ronan, we..." He kissed her and he kept going until he could feel her throbbing around him and he exploded into her.

"Ronan."

"Yes lass."

"Pat's gonna be mad at you."

He kissed her. "No, he won't." He kissed her again and devoured her lips as he zipped his jeans back up.

"Better," Katie asked.

He nodded. "No more talk about her. We're having fun with them."

Ronan nodded again and kissed her. "I'm sorry."

"No more bad mood. You start again, I'm taking you home and tying you to the bed," she teased.

"You wish."

"I will. No more bad mood." He nodded and kissed her.

"By the way, I'm not done with you."

"Not in here."

He smirked. "Nope."

"Good." Katie went to slide off the desk and he kissed her.

"You know why I was mad."

"And I also know that it's you and me now. She's history."

"She's messaging and texting and emailing Katie."

"What?"

"She thinks I was fighting him for her."

"Now I want to kick her butt."

"I set her straight. I promise you. I know what I want."

"Good. If you didn't, I'd start to wonder what this was."

"Meaning," Ronan asked.

"I want you and just you. Only you. If you still want to be with someone like that, I don't know that I could stay beside you."

"Good thing that you don't have to."

He slid his arms around her and kissed her. "No more talk about it." Katie nodded and they headed out of the office, locking up behind them and Ronan handed the keys back to Pat.

"Everything good," Pat asked.

Ronan nodded. "The lass needs a refill when you get a moment," Ronan said.

"I swear, you're trying to get me tipsy."

"Succeeding," Ronan teased. He sat down and finished his pint as Pat came over with a refill for him and Katie.

"Thank you," Ronan said.

"Welcome," Pat said, patting Ronan on the back.

"Everything good," Mia asked. Ronan nodded.

"Let's just stay off the bad topics for once," Ronan said. Mia nodded in agreement. Just as she did, the team they were rooting for scored and everyone was put into a better mood.

When the game was finished, Pat brought over dinner for everyone. "Thank you," Ronan said.

"Thought 3 pints should include dinner. Enjoy," Pat said.

"So, what's the next game," Katie asked.

"Involves me taking you home," Ronan said.

"And here I thought we were hanging for a while," Katie said.

"You are," Kian said as the next game started.

"We're gonna head home," Ronan said.

"Nope. One more game to go," Kian said as Mia smirked.

"We're gonna head back. We have two games next weekend. I'm getting Katie a lucky jersey. We're heading out." Ronan took Katie's hand and helped her up, paid the tab for everyone and headed out after a quick goodbye to Pat.

They walked down to the house, and for once, nobody was parked outside the house. They just came home and within a matter of 2 minutes of locking the door, Ronan kissed Katie.

"What," she asked. He kissed her again, pulling her to him and devoured her lips. "Mm."

"Upstairs."

"Ronan."

"Go." He followed her up the steps and she walked into the bedroom.

"All determined to get me..." He kissed her and leaned her against the wall by the door. He undid her skirt and slid it off, then her shirt, getting her naked.

"You're overdressed," Katie said as he let her up for air for a split second.

"Nope." She went to slide his shirt and sweater off of him and he pinned her hands to the wall.

"Ronan, don't."

"Don't what love?"

"Hands."

"And what are you gonna do if I don't tie them to the bed?"

"Take the pants off Ronan."

He picked her up and carried her to the bed, leaning her onto it and tied her hands with a tie from the drawer. "I'm not done," he teased.

"Meaning what?"

"Meaning you don't get your way right now," he said as he started teasing her with his fingers.

"Ronan."

"Nope. You want something you have to say it lass. I get my way until you do."

"Take them off." He kneeled down and licked at her wetness, teasing and kissing and nibbling until she was moaning.

"I'm waiting," Ronan said as he kept teasing and his fingers slid inside her.

"Take them off and come here."

"And?"

"I want to taste you."

"Nope."

"Ronan." He kept going until he could see her toes curling and could feel her legs tightening around him. He slid his jeans off and kept going.

"Ronan, come here."

"Nope."

"I want you inside me."

"Not yet lass."

"Ronan please." He kept going until she was throbbing around his fingers then pulled her to him and kicked his boxers off, sliding deep into her.

"Aah."

"Katie."

"Mm."

He leaned over her and kept sliding inside her. Hard, fast and deep. "Tell me what you want," he said as he kept going.

"More," Katie said. He slid her legs over his shoulders and went deeper. "Shit Ronan."

"More?"

"Aah."

"Say it."

"Mm. Please." She exploded around him again and he kept going, flipping her to her stomach as the tie around her hands tightened.

"Ronan, please."

"Please what? Not enough?"

"My legs." He pulled her to him and kept going until her body gave in and crashed around him again. He followed a matter of seconds later and fell to her side, untying her hands.

"Shit," she said.

"What," he teased.

"I can't even move."

"Good. You won't be teasing me tonight."

"Ronan."

"What love?"

"I swear, if you get up right now and walk into the damn shower, I'm gonna handcuff you to the bed."

"I'd love to see you try love." He kissed her as she slid to his side.

"Stay in bed."

"Or what?" Her leg tangled around his.

"Just stay." He kissed her again and she curled up to him.

"That what you wanted?"

"I can't even move."

"And that's a bad thing?"

"That's an insane thing. We have that thing tomorrow."

He kissed her. "I know we do love. You needed a distraction."

He kissed her again, pulling her to him. "What," she asked.

"You okay?"

Katie nodded with a smirk. "You're staying in bed."

He kissed her. "I'm getting up and getting us a drink."

"Ronan." He slid the phones onto the charging pad and got up. He went and showered, slid on fresh boxers and walked downstairs to get them each a drink. When he came back upstairs, Katie was in one of his t-shirts.

"Nice shirt."

"Thanks. I thought it looked good," Katie joked.

"You have lingerie from Paris, and you still choose that?"

"Comfort," she mewed as he handed her a glass of Jameson's.

"And how are we feeling about tomorrow?"

"You mean if I can walk?" He nodded and kissed her. "You know he's gonna bring up what happened at the pub."

"This is to protect you. Nothing happened between you two."

"Still." He kissed her with the taste of whiskey on her lips.

"He's gonna have to stay away love."

She nodded. "I'm just a little worried." Ronan finished his drink and got up to close the curtains and saw that same car sitting in front of his house. Ronan grabbed his phone and called his officer friend.

"Ronan."

"He's parked outside my house again."

"We'll send the police round. Don't go outside and confront him please. If he's arrested she won't have to face him in court. Just his lawyer. He was served 3 hours ago."

"Just handle him before I have to please." Ronan hung up with him, closed the blinds and walked back over to the bed.

"Were you serious that he's outside?"

"Surprised he couldn't hear you moaning," Ronan joked trying to lower the stress level.

"Ronan, seriously. He's out there?"

"He'll be handled soon enough. Just relax."

"Ronan."

"Police are on the way love." Ronan came and sat back down on the bed and curled her into his arms.

"Ronan."

He kissed her. "Let them handle it. You did say that," he replied. She slid into his lap and kissed him. "And what are you starting?"

"Nothing. Just glad you're here instead of running outside to start a problem. You heard me."

"Not that it isn't tempting to deal with him myself, but you asked love."

She kissed him and he leaned her back onto the bed. "Tell me what you want."

"I have what I want," she said. Just as he was about to lean in and kiss her, his phone buzzed. He reached for it and saw his friend's name on the call display. "Yep."

"Handled. He said he was trying to talk to Katie and resolve the whole protection order thing," his friend said.

"And I specifically told him not to come anywhere near her ever again. Even the thing he was served said it."

"He's being arrested. I just wanted to keep you updated."

"Thank you," Ronan said.

"Just let the lass know that she's safe for tonight especially."

"Thank you. I'll let her know." Ronan hung up with him and put the phone back on the charger.

"And," Katie asked.

"He's been arrested."

"Good. No more distractions."

"Katie."

"He's not my problem anymore."

"You sure you're alright?"

She kissed him. "I don't want him ruining another night Ronan."

"What did you want to do then?"

"I have a few ideas."

"Katie."

"What?"

"We need sleep if we are going to court tomorrow."

"Then sleep. I have other plans," she teased.

"Such as?" She kissed him and he pulled her to him, deepening the kiss until her legs were wrapping around his hips.

"Katie, you're behaving tonight." She shook her head.

"We're not..." She nodded.

"Katie, you need sleep."

"I need you more."

"Baby."

"What?"

"We just..."

She kissed him.

"I want you."

"Katie, you've done..."

"Not enough."

"Oh really?" Katie nodded again and he felt her hand slide down the front of his boxers. "So that's what you want."

"That's what I want," Katie said as he stopped her.

"You aren't starting that."

"Yes, I am," Katie said. He shook his head. "Don't make me tie you to the bed," she teased. He shook his head and grabbed her hands, pulling them above her head. "Ronan."

He kissed her and Katie tried to flip him onto his back. "Don't start lass."

"Mine."

"Katie, you're not getting that tonight."

"And why not? You're tired?"

"It's almost 10. You need sleep."

"I want that first."

"Katie." He kissed her and she wriggled a hand free.

"Move over," Katie said.

"You aren't starting that."

"Yes, I am Ronan." Her hand wrapped around him, and he shook his head.

"Don't start."

"Already am," Katie said as she pushed him onto his back.

"Katie, don't."

"Why?"

"Because I said so." Her hand slid up and down his length and when he felt her warm mouth cover it, he moaned. "Katie, stop."

"Mm." She kept going, taking him deeper and he shook his head.

"Please." Katie kept going. Finally, he was almost at his breaking point, and he pulled her to him, devoured her lips and had her pinned onto the bed in what seemed like one move.

"Ronan."

"What," he asked as he kicked his boxers off and slid deep inside her.

"Shit." He pinned her hands to the bed and tied them with his tie.

"You start that and I'm finishing it," he said as she tried to wriggle her hands from the tie.

"I know you are. Untie them." He shook his head and kept going, teasing and going harder and faster until her body burst around him. He kept going, determined to make her legs cramp up. When he finally exploded into her, she was a mess and could barely move. "That what you wanted," he teased.

"Shit, I can't even move."

"Good. You won't be teasing me tonight then." He got up, cleaned up, slid his boxers on and slid back into bed.

"You aren't ever willing to play fair are you," Katie asked. He untied her hands, and she curled up with him.

"Fair? Fair like you keep going even when I say stop?"

"That's just payback handsome. You when you keep going even when my legs are giving way."

"That's only because you ask. You want your legs shaking, I'll make it happen."

"Ronan."

"Get some sleep lass. You'll need it for tomorrow."

"Ronan."

"What love?"

"I didn't mean that I wanted you to make my legs shake."

"And what did you want lass?"

"I wanted you. Every single inch of you."

"Katie."

"I got part of what I wanted."

"You are so bad. Just close your eyes and get sleep instead of pouncing on me."

"Pouncing."

He nodded. "You know exactly what I'm talking about and you know it."

"Then you aren't working out tomorrow."

"Yeah, I am love. You'll be fast asleep."

"Then I'm making breakfast."

"If you're awake."

"Ronan."

He kissed her. "Just sleep. You want to make breakfast, I'll wake you up," he said curling her into his arms.

"And if I wake up before you, you're mine in the morning." He kissed her.

"Sleep."

The next morning, he slipped out of the bed and slid on his workout gear, heading downstairs to get in his workout. When he came back upstairs, she was still asleep. He smirked and kissed her then went and put the coffee on and started breakfast. When he saw arms slide around him, he smirked. "Nice of you to wake up," he teased.

"Thank you for waking me up." He turned around and kissed Katie and she made the bacon.

"I'll do the eggs," he said.

"At least you woke me."

"Very subtle. Wasn't sure if you'd actually wake up."

"I was gonna try and make you come back to bed." She flipped the bacon and kissed him.

"That was the plan. Breakfast in bed," he teased.

"I wanted you."

"Well, you can wait until after we eat. We have to be in court by 8:30."

"Ronan."

"It's 6. We have time. We just have to leave here by 8."

"Then hurry up with the eggs." He shook his head, plated them and she added the bacon to the plates. They sat down to eat, and she couldn't stop staring at him.

"You can stop staring any time now."

"Was just thinking." He ate his breakfast and shook his head.

"And what were you thinking?"

"Upstairs."

"Katie, come on now lass."

"Hot shower, curl up in bed and just be."

"Right."

"Not my fault if you think I meant go upstairs and get my legs shaking so I can't walk."

"Make them permanently shake."

"Ronan."

"Make them shake so all day you're thinking about what I did this morning."

"Well, you haven't done it Ronan. I'm still walking," Katie joked as she finished her food and grabbed his plate and got up to clean up the dishes.

"What are you doing," he asked.

"Dishes. Cleaning up," Katie said as he brushed her hair off her neck and kissed it. "Ronan."

"What?"

"You hate dishes in the sink when you leave for work. Stop." He took them and put them into the washer then turned her to face him. "What," she asked.

"Starts now."

"What does?" He kissed her, picked her up and leaned her against the counter as he wrapped her legs around his hips. "Ronan." He kissed her again and went to sit her on the counter.

"Not here."

"Why?"

"Because." He shook his head and carried her back upstairs to the bedroom and leaned her onto the bed, pinning her hands down. "Ronan." He pulled her legs tighter around him, peeled his shirt off and leaned into her.

"Don't move your hands or I'm tying them," he said. He peeled her shirt off and kissed her.

"Ronan."

"What?"

"You're overdressed." He kicked his joggers off and Katie smirked.

"You don't get your way today lass."

"Says who?"

He got up and walked over to the bedside table, took the tie out and tied her hands, tying the other end to the headboard. "Says me."

"Ronan, come here." He shook his head.

"I know what you want. No." She wriggled a hand free and grabbed the waistband of his boxers.

"Katie."

"Come here."

He shook his head. "I'm gonna have to rethink how I tie that."

"Ronan." He kissed her and felt her hand slide around him.

"Shit."

"Come here." The minute he felt the warmth of her mouth on him he shook his head and untied her other hand.

"Shit Katie, stop."

"Mm." He shook his head again, sucking in a breath. She took him deeper in her mouth and he looked at her.

"Had to." She nodded and he pulled away from her.

"Ronan."

"I can't take anymore," he said as he turned her to face him and slid deep inside her.

"Aah."

"Good girl," he said. "Had to start something." She nodded as she moaned. He kept going, harder then deeper then faster until she was moaning and begging for more. He kept going until he could feel her body reaching its climax.

"Shit Ronan."

"Oh, I'm not done with you," he said as he kept going until her body was tightening around him all over again then exploded into her.

"Damn you lass."

"What," Katie said trying to catch her breath as he leaned into her arms.

"Had to go and mess with my plan," he said.

"We both got what we wanted," she teased.

"You're so damn bad."

"Only fair," she teased as she leaned into his arms.

"You are bad. Couldn't have just let me devour every single inch of you. Had to go and do that."

"I'm your kryptonite Ronan. Always will be." He kissed her, devouring her lips. "Don't even think about getting up."

Ronan kissed her again. "We have to get ready," he said.

"You can wait," Katie said. He shook his head and got up. "Ronan."

"I'll meet you in here."

He walked into the bathroom and turned the water on in the shower, freshening up. He turned and slid into the hot water, face to face with the steam. He washed his hair and by the time he was about to wash up, she stepped in and took the oversized sea sponge and washed his back for him, kissing across his back muscles. "Katie."

"What?"

"Don't start that."

"Not doing anything," she joked. She turned him to face her and kissed him.

"Katie."

"What?"

"Hands."

"Just helping."

"Yeah. I see that."

He kissed her and took the sponge away. "Under the water lass." He rinsed off and she slid under the water. He washed her hair for her and just as she was rinsing out the conditioner, he slid out.

"Ronan."

"Finish up. I'm going to get dressed." He wrapped a towel around his waist and disappeared into the bedroom.

Katie finished in the shower, stepped out and wrapped herself in a towel then freshened up and came into the bedroom to the scent of his cologne.

"Damn it," Katie joked.

"What love," he asked emerging from the closet in his dress pants and undone dress shirt.

"Smelling all good and everything."

"Well thank you lass. How was your shower?"

"Uneventful and unfair."

He smirked and kissed her. "Go get ready. We have to be out of here in a half hour."

"No time to be nervous about this right?"

"That was the plan. Distracted you for as long as I could." She shook her head and kissed him.

"Well thanks for that, but you're still a party pooper."

"I love you back lass." She smirked and went and got dressed. When she emerged from the closet, she was in a sweater dress and heels.

"Katie."

"What?"

"The sweater dress?"

"Warm since it's raining."

He shook his head. "Had to do it."

"And it works for later."

"Meaning?"

"Either pub or home."

"And then what," he teased.

"I guess you'll find out tonight."

"Tell me that you didn't do something silly."

"Check your texts." He looked at her then felt his phone vibrate. When it said that the toy was powered on, he shook his head.

"So, I get to tease you while you're at work. Good plan," he joked.

"For tonight."

He shook his head. "While you're on your way to work."

"Ronan."

"While we're on our way to the courts." She shook her head.

"I swear, you start something in the car and I'm getting rid of it." He slid his phone in his pocket and pulled his suit jacket on.

"You ready then lass," Ronan asked. He helped her with her coat, and they headed out together.

"How long until we're there," Katie asked as the car headed off.

Chapter 3

He slid his hand into his pocket and ran his finger across the screen to unlock it. "Don't start." He grabbed his phone, logged into the toy and ran his finger across the screen as her nails dug into his hand. "What did I say about that?"

"Just making sure it was on."

Katie shook her head. "Sure you were."

He ran his finger over the screen and Katie looked at him. "Oops."

"I'm taking that phone away when we're in there," she said.

He smirked and kissed her. "Can't tease you while we get there," he whispered.

Katie shook her head. "Not unless you really want to go there while we're in the courts. Don't start."

They pulled up to the courts and headed inside, finding the way to the room they needed to be in. "We're sure he's not gonna be here right," Katie asked.

"Since he was arrested, if he is it'll be a surprise to me too." He held onto Katie's hand. When they were called up, the judge went through the paperwork and thankfully Devlin didn't show. She got her order, and they went to head out when Ronan slid his hand in his pocket and ran his finger over the screen to tease her.

"You're seriously starting that now?"

"Celebrating." Katie shook her head, and they made their way out to the car and hopped in.

"You coming with me," Katie asked.

"Going back to the house so I can get my car. He'll take you in and pick you up to bring you home tonight."

"Ronan."

"Yes love?"

"No teasing while I'm at work."

"Call me at lunch then," he teased.

"Depends on what you have planned." He ran his finger over the screen, making it that much more intense. "Ronan."

"Something like that."

"Quit." He did it again intentionally and her nails dug into his leg.

"Mine," he whispered.

"Then quit it before I can't move." He kept going as she squirmed in her seat.

"Having fun with that little thing."

"I bet you are...mm."

"Leave it there. Promise me?" She nodded and he smirked just as they were pulling up to his place.

"No more teasing," Katie said. He kissed her and he headed off. Just as he got into his car, his phone buzzed with a text:

> No teasing until lunch.

He replied:

> If anything happens, call me and tell me love.
> Hopefully it's an uneventful day.

Ronan got to the office and his assistant followed him in. "Messages," he asked.

"None. Quiet all morning. Your meeting starts at 10. Coffee," she said handing him a cup.

"Thank you. If Katie calls at all, come get me out of the meeting. That situation this morning has me on edge about her safety. If you hear anything about some sort of disturbance at the hospital. Anything." His assistant nodded.

Ronan got going through his emails and found one from Katie:

> Thank you for coming with me this morning.
> Kinda glad you were there. Hopefully this means
> no more cars parked outside your place. PS
> Lunch is at 12:30. Call me. Love you

He smirked and got his paperwork together and headed into his 10am meeting. When he walked in and saw Declan, he almost laughed. "And what are you doing here," Ronan asked.

"You decided to invest. We expanded like we talked about back in the day. If you're investing, it's a new division. Expanding to Canada and Australia. We already did the expansion for the European end. We just wanted your input on the investment for the new locations."

"Well then," Ronan said as he got the meeting going.

By the time lunch came, he had already started teasing Katie. He slid his finger over the screen, teasing and making it more and more intense. When his phone buzzed, he smirked and slid his AirPods in. "Yes."

"Stop."

"Why?"

"Because you're drawing too much attention. I can't even move."

"Oh really."

"Ronan, cut it out."

"You did offer that fun."

"I didn't expect it to be on high. Cut it out."

"But this is okay," he said gently running his finger over the screen.

"Ronan, unless you're planning on showing up and resolving this situation, stop."

"That turned on?"

"Understatement."

"So, if I did this," he said as he made it intense all over again.

"You're meeting me at the house. Now."

"Can be arranged."

"Ronan, I have meetings."

He smirked. "And where are you now?"

"In the office."

"Alone?"

"Depends on what you're doing."

"Somewhere alone Katie." He heard the click of a door and then kept going.

"Shit."

"Just remember something. You can't touch."

"Ronan."

"How bad do you want me there."

"Right now. I need you inside me."

"Good girl."

"Meaning what," Katie asked. He ran his finger over the screen again until he could hear her moaning.

"Shit."

"Meaning what," he asked with a smirk ear to ear.

"Ronan, stop."

"Nope."

"Aah."

"Much better."

"Stop." He stopped and got a grin.

"Or what," he asked.

"Or else I'm seriously making an excuse so I can leave and you're gonna be having sex in your office."

"So that's your plan is it."

"What time is your next meeting Ronan?"

"45 minutes."

"Then quit making my legs shake or you're gonna miss your meeting."

"We're staying home tonight by the way."

"Doing what?"

"Bending you over every damn counter and going until you can't move anymore."

"That a promise or a threat," she joked.

"Do you really want to know," he replied.

"Ronan, I need to be able to walk."

"Says who?"

"You aren't funny."

"Then we're having a fire," Ronan said.

"Pillow pile," Katie said.

"Bending you over the table."

"Ronan."

"And I get to do what I want to until you beg me to stop." His finger ran over the screen again, teasing and taunting until she was ready to explode.

"Ronan."

He smirked. "Spent yet?"

"You are so getting it when I get back."

"Counting down the minutes lass."

"I have to go back to work."

"Then you should probably go before my hand twitches."

"So bad."

"All for you love."

"See you tonight." They hung up a few minutes later and Ronan finished his lunch.

By the time he got home that night, Katie was still at work. He smirked and started a fire. He ordered in some food for dinner and when she showed, she walked into candles and a pile of pillows in the tv room. "What is all of this," Katie asked as she slid her heels off.

"Dinner and a movie plus that other thing that we talked about at lunch."

"Oh really." Ronan nodded and kissed her. "I'm sorry I was late."

"Since I got back early you mean."

"What time did you get back?"

"A little before 5. Come and sit," Ronan said as she saw the pillows and blankets ready.

"You actually did the pillow pile."

"That's what you said you wanted love."

"Well, all things considered, there was something else that you wanted that you mentioned during lunch."

"And that's happening tonight."

"And just when did you plan on that happening," Katie asked.

"Depends on how fast I can get that dress off you."

"Ronan, food first."

"If that's what you want love."

He walked her into the kitchen, and she saw the food sitting on the table.

"You seriously got Irish stew?"

"Thought you might need real food since we're having such an exhausting evening."

"And just what did you really have planned?"

"Eat then you bent over the table with me behind you."

"And then?"

"You'll be begging me to let you up."

"Ronan."

"Eat." He handed her a glass of wine, and they had their stew. He slid his chair closer to her.

"You are starting to resemble a panther ready to pounce on his prey."

"Because tonight you are lass."

"That's your plan is it?" He nodded and finished his stew.

"Planning on making you forget what day of the week it is."

"Distraction. Good plan." He got up and cleaned up the dishes and Katie slid in behind him.

"Ronan."

"Yes lass."

"Do you want a refill of your wine?" He shook his head.

"I'm good. I have something else planned."

"Such as?" He smirked and turned to face her.

He kissed her and slid her wine glass out of her hand. He put it down on the counter and picked her up, sitting her on the counter beside it. "Ronan."

"Yes love." He slid her dress up her legs.

"What are you doing?"

"Getting you naked." He kissed her, devouring her lips as she felt her dress slide to her waist.

"You're not being serious."

He peeled her panties off then slid his hand in his pocket and flicked his finger over the screen.

"Aah." He held his finger down on the screen, intensifying the teasing. "Shit Ronan. Stop."

"And if I don't?"

"Ronan."

He slid his hand out of his pocket. "Take it out." He shook his head. "You're not playing fair."

"You did this to yourself lass. I didn't ask you to."

"Take it out."

"You sure?" She nodded and slid her legs around him. He picked her up and carried her into the sitting room where he'd set up the pillows and the fire. "Take it off." She slid the dress off and slid the toy out intentionally. "Katie."

"No more teasing me with it tonight. I want you."

"Katie, what did I tell you."

"And what are you gonna do Ronan?" He bent her over the table and slid his tie off, tying her hands to the table and pulling him to her so her back was across the table with her backside right near him.

One lick and her legs were shaking. "You were bad."

"And so were you all the way through lunch."

"You're still bad. You did the one thing I said not to."

"I don't want to be teased anymore."

"Tough. You're getting teased then you're not gonna be walking back upstairs. That's why I set up the pillows."

"Then untie my hands."

He licked again, teasing until she was moaning. He smirked and saw her trying to undo the tie. "New knot. Don't even think about it."

"Ronan." He slid his fingers inside of her as he licked and teased until her knees were trembling. "Please."

"There's so much more I could do right now," he teased.

"Ronan, you aren't being fair."

"And you taking it out when I said not to was fair was it?"

"No more teasing."

He kept going until her legs were shaking then slid his dress pants off and pulled down his boxers. "Ronan." He leaned into her and slid deep inside her, hard then slowly went faster until she was throbbing around him.

"Shit."

"You going to behave?" Ronan kept going until he couldn't hold himself back and exploded into her.

"Untie my hands."

"On one condition."

"Ronan."

"Next time I say don't touch it, you obey me."

"I'm not your toy Ronan."

"You either do what I ask or you're getting punished."

"Meaning what?"

"You really want to know?"

"I don't know if I do. What was the punishment?"

"Tying you to the bed or to the table and I keep going until you're begging me to stop."

"Are you untying my hands?"

"Are you gonna behave?"

"No."

"Then I'm not untying them."

"Ronan, you can't just leave..."

"Yeah, I can." She tried again to slide her hand out of the tie. "Katie."

"Undo it." He shook his head. "Ronan." He undid her hands, and she turned to face him.

"Tell me what you want," he teased.

"You."

"You have me."

"No more tying my hands."

"And if I do?"

"Then I tie yours."

"Not likely lass." He pulled her legs around him and she slid his boxers right off.

"And what are you doing?"

"Taking advantage of you."

"Katie, don't make me tie your hands." He felt her hand slide around him and he shook his head. "Stop."

"Then come sit down on the pillows with me."

"Not when I know exactly what you're up to." Her grip tightened around him, sliding up and down.

"Katie."

"You want me to whether you say it or not."

"Don't start." When she slid off his lap and wrapped her lips around him, he shook his head.

"Katie, stop."

"Mm."

"Katie." She took him deeper in her mouth and kept going over and over, deeper until he shook his head and pulled her away from him.

"Ronan." He kissed her, devouring her lips and pulled her to him, sliding deep inside her.

"Aah." He pulled her tight to him. "Ronan."

He kissed her. "What," he asked as he pulled her legs around him and got up, leaning her onto the pillows. He started slowly, teasing and then slowly went harder, deeper until she was moaning. "You're getting your way," he teased.

"Not quite," she said almost moaning. He kept going, pounding into her over and over. "Shit." She throbbed around him, and he went deeper. "Ronan."

"I'm not done with you."

"My legs."

"Should've thought of that before you tried untying your hands." She moaned again. "Mine," he teased. "Aah."

"Tell me what you want," he said.

"More."

"Good answer." He kept going and just as she exploded around him again, he climaxed.

"Shit Ronan."

"What?"

"My legs are shaking."

"Good."

"You're so not fair."

"Now we can curl up in the pillows," he joked. She kissed him.

"Had to tease again."

"Teasing is the least of your problems tonight lass. You not being able to make it up the stairs is one of them."

"What else were you planning on doing?" He slid the blanket over them and kissed her.

"You do know that you're still in for it right?"

"Considering that I can barely walk you mean."

He kissed her again. "I'm not done with you."

"Ronan."

"You're still in trouble. You remember me saying not to touch it right?"

"And I remember saying no more teasing."

"Katie."

She kissed him. "I just wanted to have a night where we could relax. No stupid pub, no friends. Just you and me by the fire."

"Then you should've left it where it was."

"Ronan."

He kissed her. "What?" He leaned her onto her back and pinned her hands to the floor.

"I want you and me alone. Is that allowed right now?"

He kissed her. "Determined to keep me to yourself."

"After what's happened with him, yeah. I'm still a little worried that something's gonna happen."

"He was arrested. He's in jail love."

"Still a little worried." He shook his head and snuggled her.

"He's not coming near either of us. I'm not about to let that happen. You know that."

"And what happens when he does Ronan?"

"The police deal with him. You want me staying with you, I'm right here. He's not getting out Katie, and he's not coming near you."

She kissed him. "Distract me."

"Love, if you're worried, it's fine."

"Just distract me."

He shook his head and kissed her. "Babe, I love that you think that I can fix this, but I can't."

"I just want to keep my mind off it for one night."

He kissed her, snuggling her to him. "You're really that worried?" Katie nodded. "We just went to court to handle it love. Why are you still..."

"Like I said, distract me."

He kissed her and snuggled her to him. "Tell me what you want to do then," he teased.

"Get my mind off it." He shook his head and curled her into his arms.

"You do know that you're safe right?"

"Ronan." He kissed her.

"Just relax then. Nobody is getting in here. That's why I have the alarm."

"Distraction."

"Then ask me what you want."

"Promise me that you don't go after him."

"I'll send the police instead."

"I know I'm being irrational." He kissed her, devouring her lips until she curled into his arms.

"You want a distraction then get up."

"Why," Katie asked. He kissed her, put the fire out and walked her upstairs. "What are you doing?" He kissed her as they reached the top step, kissing the back of her neck. He walked her into the bedroom and leaned her onto the bed.

"What?"

He kissed her. "Two options. Soak in the tub or just curl up in bed." She slid onto the bed and pulled him to her.

"I take it that means curling up in bed." She nodded and kissed him.

He curled her into his arms and did his best to distract her the rest of the evening. By the time she nodded off, he was more than pissed. He couldn't let her see it, so he did his best fake all night. When his phone buzzed around midnight, he grabbed it so she wouldn't wake up. All it took was a text:

He's getting out.

Ronan shook his head and gently got up, looking out the front window. So long as he stayed away, Katie would never know. He slid back into bed and did his best to rest. Now he was just irritated. Her watching over her shoulder wasn't fair, and it wasn't something that he wanted for her or for them. He nodded off soon after and woke up at 5 to an empty bed. He got up, slid his joggers on and walked downstairs to see Katie pouring a mug of coffee.

"What are you doing up," he asked.

"I couldn't sleep. I kept thinking that I was hearing things."

"Katie."

"I know it's ridiculous. He's not out. He's not coming in here. I know."

"You need sleep."

"I tried."

"Katie."

"You were tossing and turning too Ronan. Tell me why."

"Because I could sense that you weren't comfortable. That something else was wrong."

"The real reason."

"Because of a text I got late last night from my police friend."

"He's out."

Ronan nodded. "Getting." Katie shook her head, and he pulled her into his arms. "He's not coming near you."

"Ronan."

He kissed her. "He's not."

He picked her up and carried her back upstairs to the bedroom and leaned her onto the bed. "I can't..."

He kissed her, slid his shirt off of her and kicked his joggers off. "What," Katie asked.

"You wanted a morning in bed, you get a morning."

"Ronan."

He kissed her. "You're staying in bed for a while. You need sleep love."

"How am I..." He kicked his boxers off and wrapped her legs around him.

"How are you what?" He slid inside her and her breath almost instantly hitched.

"This what you need," he asked.

"Mm."

"Yes," he asked as she wrapped her legs tight around his hips. She nodded and he slid in and out until he could feel her throbbing around him.

"Mine," he said.

"Ronan."

"Yes lass."

"More." He kept going, harder, faster, deeper until she was moaning over and over again. Until she was spent and so was he. Until he collapsed into her arms and devoured her lips.

"No more worrying. No more tossing and turning. Sleep."

"Stay in bed with me then." He kissed her and nodded. He got up and cleaned up a little then came back to bed, sliding boxers on. She curled up next to him and looked at him. "What?"

"Really that easy?"

"Meaning what?"

"To get you to curl back up with me."

"When you're up before I am, yeah." She kissed him and curled into his arms.

"Katie, whatever is going on you can talk to me."

"I know. I just don't think we need to add more to the drama."

"Meaning what?"

"He's not doing it again. It doesn't matter."

"Meaning what love?" She shook her head. "Secrets."

"Ronan."

"Fine. You get some sleep, and I'll get going on my workout. Maybe you'll..."

"Ronan."

"Talk." She looked at him. "Fine." He walked off and went and got in a workout, made breakfast and brought some up to her then went to go have a shower alone.

He flipped the water on and slid in, determined to try and get her off his mind. Whatever she was hiding now had him irritated. Even more irritated. He rinsed the shampoo from his hair and felt her slide in with him. "Katie, not now."

"Ronan."

"Then tell me what the hell he did. Just say it."

"He forced me into doing something."

"Katie."

"I like doing it with you, but not when he forced..."

"Say it." He almost growled as he said it, spinning and pinning her against the tile wall of his oversized shower.

"You know what."

"Then don't. I tell you not to half the time anyway."

"But I like to when it's us."

"Katie." She kissed him.

He picked her up and she slid her legs around him. "You can't keep up with the secrets. Tell me all of it love."

She kissed him. "I told you everything else."

"Bruises?" She nodded. "You know about that."

"I still want to kick..."

She kissed him. "Not anymore. Just you and me." He kissed her again and they had sex in the shower. He could care less about being late at that point. He had barely slept all night anyway. When he exploded into her, her body was throbbing around him.

"You're gonna end up being late."

"I can't concentrate."

"You calling in sick," he teased.

"And if I did?"

"You really want to come to the office, you can."

"Sofa?"

He nodded. "Just no messing around." She kissed him.

"Then we should finish our shower." He nodded and kissed her, sliding her to her feet. They finished in the shower, and he stepped out, wrapping a towel around him and wrapping the other around Katie.

"You sure you want to come sit in my office all day?"

"After yesterday, yes."

"He's not gonna come after you."

"Just for now."

"If you're that convinced that being at my office will help then fine love."

"I'm worried that he's gonna cause an even bigger problem Ronan. I'm worried that he's gonna end up outside again. That he's gonna show at my work and security won't be able to do anything."

"You're just as safe at work as you are here or at my office. You know that right?"

"Just for today?" He kissed her and got dressed. "What," she asked.

"Slide the dress on. I have to be in a meeting at 10," he said.

"You sure you're okay with me coming?"

He nodded and kissed her. "I hate that he's making you feel like this, but if being at the office helps then I'm good as long as you're feeling better."

Katie got dressed, and when he stepped out of his closet, she was already in the dress. "No more teasing with that little toy today either lass. Promise me."

"But that wouldn't be any fun," she teased.

"Not in the office."

"Lunch." He shook his head. She took it off the charger and smirked.

"Lass, don't you start."

"Making up for yesterday," she said with a smirk.

"And you do realize that you can't beg for mercy in the office either right?"

"I'll just slide onto your lap."

He shook his head. "Not there."

"And if I said I'd sneak under the desk instead."

He shook his head. "Don't start with me."

"And if I said I could just lock the door of your office?"

"I'd say you aren't getting away with anything. Bring it if you want, but you still can't do anything."

"So, you get to tease me, and I have no recourse?" He nodded as he buttoned his shirt.

"Tease."

"You're the one that wanted to bring it lass." He grabbed his tie and Katie looked at him.

"Tie?"

"In case I need it this afternoon."

"Mm." He slid his suit jacket on and walked over to her as she slid her heels on.

"Don't start that."

"What?"

He kissed her and backed her up against the wall of the bedroom. "That's all it took?"

"Funny lass. Don't start or you're gonna make me late." He kissed her again, devouring her lips then backed away.

"Fine. No more teasing."

"Back at you." He shook his head and grabbed their phones off the charger. He walked her downstairs and saw the car outside waiting. Katie grabbed her laptop bag and her purse and looked at Ronan. "What," she asked.

"No teasing at work." She kissed him and nodded. He helped her with her coat, and they headed off, locking up behind them.

He helped her into the SUV and slid in beside her. "Sir."

"My office please."

"Not two stops?"

"No. Katie's coming into the office with me."

"Yes sir."

"You sure about that rule you made?"

"Positive. You're behaving while you're at my work," he said.

"I have foundation stuff to do anyway."

"Don't you think you should call your boss?"

She kissed him. "Yes."

Katie fished her phone from her pocket and called work. "Katie."

"Hi. Remember that conversation that we were having about me taking today off?"

"I do," her boss said.

"Are you okay with me working from home?"

"As long as I can reach you if we need you. Take the day lass."

"Thank you," Katie said. "I'll be into my emails in about a half hour if you need anything."

"Thank you." Katie hung up and Ronan looked at her. "What?"

"Were you that worried at work yesterday?"

"I was watching over my shoulder all day. Only time I wasn't was when we were talking."

"You do know that you're as safe at work as you are with me at home or at my office right?"

"I just couldn't stop thinking about it. It's a piece of paper. It doesn't stop him from doing anything."

"It does lass. I promise you that it does. He's not coming near us. He does, they can handle it."

"Still would rather stay with you today." He kissed her forehead and within a matter of 20 minutes, they were pulling up to his office.

He slid out, helped her out of the SUV and headed into the office. "Katie, this is Marsha. My assistant."

"Nice to meet you," Katie said.

"Sir, is Katie working from your office with you today?"

"Yes."

"Would you like a coffee?"

Katie nodded. "Two milks and a sugar for her please," Ronan said as he walked Katie past reception and down to his office. She walked in and saw the view first, then the fancy glass desk.

"This is bigger than my first flat," Katie said.

"Sofa is there. If you need anything just ask Marsha."

"Ronan."

"Yes lass."

"Thank you."

"For what? Letting you come with me?"

She nodded. "I oddly feel better being here than at the hospital."

"Surely they have security."

"They do. I just don't think they have enough people to warrant the crap that we went through."

"Sir," Marsha said as she came in with their coffees.

"Thank you," Katie said.

"Most welcome. If you need anything, I'm right in the hall."

"Can you make sure that we order enough of that Irish stew for us both," Ronan asked.

"I'll make sure there is sir. Your messages. Your meeting is starting at 9:45. They wanted to get an early start on it. Did you need anything else," his assistant asked.

"Thank you." She nodded and headed out.

"You do realize that if I wasn't here, she'd be batting her eyes at you right," Katie teased.

"She's been my assistant for years. She knows better," Ronan said.

"So, you didn't notice everyone staring when we came in."

"I'm the boss. Second, they've never seen anyone come with me," Ronan said.

"And part of me thinks that there's more to it."

"Katie."

"What?" She looked up at him. He locked his office door.

"Professional," he said.

"You're the one that locked the door. He walked over to her and kissed her, devouring her lips and leaned her against the edge of his desk. "What," Katie asked.

"My staff has been here for years. Nobody is making a pass Katie."

"And if I said that you just don't see it?" He almost growled and kissed her again, devouring her lips as he picked her up and sat her on the edge of the desk.

106

"Ronan."

He shook his head and kissed her again. "What?" "I'm telling you, if she had the chance, she'd be on her knees for you."

"She wouldn't get the chance," he replied.

"And why's that," Katie asked as he pinned her hands to the desk.

"Because I have what I want right here," he said as he released one of her hands and inched the hem of the dress up her legs.

"And here I thought you were so determined for us to not be messing around in your office."

He kissed her again and Katie's hand slid to the waistline of his dress pants. "Katie, no."

"You started it."

"Not in here."

"Nobody will know."

"Katie, I said no."

"Then tell me what you want me to do."

"Get it and put it in."

"What?"

"You know what. You're gonna squirm through that meeting." He kissed her again and let go of her other hand.

"How about this," she said as she stood and went and grabbed it from her purse.

"What?" She walked over to him, flipped it on and handed it to him. "You put it in."

He looked at Katie. "My office."

"Only takes a second." She sat back down on the edge of the desk and slid the dress up when he saw the black lace thong.

"Katie."

"What?"

"You do realize that you are supposed to behave right?"

"You want it there, put it in." His hand slid between her legs and teased.

"Shit."

"Had to go and start something," he teased.

"Ronan."

"Couldn't have just behaved."

His fingers slid inside her and her hands slid to his chest. "Ronan, stop."

"Not done yet." He kept going, sliding his fingers in and out and teasing until she climaxed practically into his hand.

"Shit." He slid the toy in and removed his fingers, licking them off.

"You are so bad."

"You're the one that decided to wear that to the office," he said.

"You're the one licking his fingers after he taunts me." He kissed her.

"Now, let me get work done before I have to go off to that meeting."

"I'm you're distraction now?" He nodded and kissed her. She slid off the desk, shaky legs and all, and went and sat down on the sofa as he unlocked the door. Just as he got to his desk, his phone buzzed.

"Yep."

"Your meeting starts in 5. Did you need anything else," his assistant asked.

"Nope. Just keep an eye on Katie if you would. She needs anything, get it."

"Yes sir," his assistant said.

"Thank you." He kissed Katie, she brushed her lipstick off his lips, he grabbed his laptop and papers and went to his meeting.

Katie sat back on the sofa and smirked, sliding her laptop into her lap and going through emails. She got most of the way through them and felt the toy buzz. "Shit." He had it going for a good ten minutes before she texted:

> Mercy. Please. Not playing fair.

A few minutes later, the toy was unrelenting and getting more intense and she saw a message:

> You started it this morning lass. Reminding you that you need to concentrate on something else.

Katie shook her head and sent a text back:

> Please

Just as she saw read on the message the buzzing stopped. She shook her head and got a few more emails done then saw a message come up on her screen:

> Mine.

It was from a number she didn't recognize. She started getting shaky. When Ronan came back into the office a half hour later, Katie was curled up on the sofa, still shaky. "Too much," he teased. Katie shook her head.

"What?"

"I told you that he wasn't gonna go away. That it was just a piece of paper."

"Katie, tell me what is going on." She showed him her laptop with the text message still open. He wrote down the number and made a call.

"Sir," his tech guy said.

"Can you trace a number for me?"

"I'll be in your office in a few minutes." The tech guy hung up and within a few minutes, was walking into Ronan's office. "What's the number," the tech guy asked.

Ronan gave it to him, and he did a search. "It's a burner phone. I can block it so it doesn't happen again," the tech guy said.

"Please," Ronan said. He took a screenshot of the text and sent it to his police friend. When he got a reply back 2 minutes later, he shook his head.

"What," Katie asked.

"You wanted me to let them handle it and I promise I will."

"Ronan."

"The number is blocked and handled. If you see anything from an unknown number again, or even an unknown email, just screen shot it and block." Katie nodded and the tech guy headed out.

Ronan closed the door and sat down with Katie, sliding her into his lap. "Why," she asked.

"Because he has no damn control. Nobody is getting near you, love."

"He's trying to find a damn way. I told you that piece of paper wouldn't make him go away."

"The police have the information. If they decide to bring him in, they have the power to do that."

"Now do you understand why I wanted to come with you?"

Ronan kissed her and pulled her into his arms. "Katie."

"I mean, is it safe at your place? I kept thinking all night that he'd find a way to get in."

"Love, there's a security alarm that's linked to the police. He's not getting in the house."

"Then can you just get me away from here?"

"One meeting left and we can go wherever you want to."

"He knows where my work is. He knows where you live for goodness sakes."

"Are you gonna let me handle him myself?"

"No."

"Katie."

"I want you with me," she replied.

"Tell me what you want me to do."

"Get me away from here." He nodded and kissed her. He got up and called his assistant.

"Sir."

"Cancel the meeting for this afternoon or change it to a video call. I'm heading home."

"Yes sir." He packed up his laptop and put his papers into the laptop bag then walked over to her.

"Let's get your things."

"Ronan."

"We're getting out of here. I know you hate the damn hotel suites, but we'll be safe."

"Ronan, just take me home." He kissed her, took her hand, grabbed her bag and walked her out, walking downstairs and hopping into the waiting SUV. "How did they know we were…"

"My assistant." They got in and he pulled her into his arms. "You're okay love. We'll put a few things together and go," he said.

"Where?"

"Just pack some clothes for a few days."

"Ronan."

"If you're not comfortable and you're worried, then we go somewhere that we don't have to worry." He sent off a quick text to his officer friend:

> *Taking Katie to a hotel. She's not feeling safe. Can you get someone to keep an eye on the house?*

When he got a reply back from his friend, Katie almost jumped:

> *I'll get a car posted. They haven't found him. He was released and all but vanished.*

Ronan called him. "What do you mean vanished," Ronan asked.

"They've been trying to figure out where he was since you sent that message to me. He's not at home, his work or his regular haunts. An officer is on the way to your place to make sure that it's secure."

"Thank you for that. We'll be at the house in a few minutes." They pulled up to Ronan's and he hopped out, helping her out.

"We'll be back in 15. Just wait please." They went inside, reset the alarm and got a bag together for each of them.

"Where are we going to go," Katie asked.

"Presidential suite."

"The one from when we got in that fight."

"The one you were never in. That I use for work."

"Ronan."

"We're going lass. Like it or not." He finished packing and saw her getting things together and called the hotel.

"Your suite will be reserved for you. How long will you be staying," the reservation attendant asked.

"A week."

"Yes sir."

"A week," Katie asked. He nodded and Katie went and got more of her work clothes. Ronan went and packed his things into his suit bag and heard a knock at the door.

He walked downstairs and saw the officer there. "Thank you," Ronan said.

"We'll keep an eye out while you're away until he's found. Just keep us up to date if anything else comes through on phones or emails." Ronan nodded. He walked back upstairs and got the bags, taking them down to the waiting SUV.

"I'll keep you notified of the updates," the officer said. Katie walked downstairs and Ronan took her hand.

"You ready," he asked. Katie nodded and they locked up, flipped the alarm on and headed off.

Chapter 4

When they walked into the suite, flowers were waiting along with a bottle of Jameson. "And what's that for," Katie teased.

"Thought we might need a drink after all of this." He kissed her, devoured her lips and wrapped his arms around her.

"Do you feel better?"

"Safer."

He kissed her. "Good." He set his laptop up at the table and went into his emails. When he saw one from his assistant that it would be a call instead of a meeting, he breathed a sigh of relief.

"What," Katie asked.

"Call in meeting instead of having to be there. Not until 2 though."

"Ronan, I know that you..."

"I want you to feel safe love. If being here, so nobody knows where we are makes you feel that way then fine. I want you to be able to sleep."

"I just don't understand why he's doing this."

Ronan hugged her. "Come set up your laptop and we can both get some work done." Katie put her laptop on the table and Ronan saw her still shaky. "Are you okay," he asked.

"I just don't understand."

"He's trying to get your attention. That's obvious. I guess he doesn't realize that breaking the order means jail."

"What time is it?"

"Noon. I was going to get us lunch once we were set up."

"Can we eat up here?" Ronan nodded and kissed her.

"Just tell me what you want."

"Honestly, you."

He kissed her. "Lunch."

"Oh. Whatever you want to get." He kissed her again, devouring her lips.

"I want you more." He smirked and made a call. "What did you order?"

"Easiest thing to get. Fish and chips."

"You and your fish..." He kissed her, picked her up and carried her over to the bed.

"What," Katie asked.

"Half hour for lunch. We have time."

"Ronan."

He leaned her onto it and kissed her. "I'm distracting you."

"I bet you are," she teased. He slid her dress off, slid the toy away from her and kissed her.

"You're overdressed Ronan." He kissed her again and she undid his dress pants and slid his boxers down.

"Katie."

"You started it," she teased. He slid out of his dress pants and boxers and just as he was reaching to pull the last of her lingerie off, her mouth was on him.

"Shit Katie."

"Mm."

"Lass, you do know you're gonna have to stop." She shook her head and kept going, taking him deeper in her mouth. He almost growled the more she did. "Katie." She shook her head, and he pulled away from her, pulling her legs around him and sliding deep into her.

"Aah."

"Katie."

"Mm." He kept going, pounding in and out until her body was throbbing around him.

"Good girl."

"Ronan."

"Yes, sexy woman of mine," he said as he kept going.

"Aah."

He kissed her and kept going until she reached for him. "Roll over"

"Ronan."

"Roll over." She did as he asked, and he slid deep into her over and over as he pinned her hands behind her back.

"Mm."

"My lass," he said whispering into her ear as her body reacted and burst into goosebumps as her body throbbed. When he finally climaxed and exploded into her, Katie collapsed to the bed with him on top of her as he slid to his side. "I can't move."

"Good," Ronan teased. He smirked and Katie slid to his side.

"What about lunch?" He kissed her then got up.

"Where are you going?"

"Getting changed."

He cleaned up, slid on boxers and his jeans and just as he came out of the bedroom, there was a knock at the door. He smirked and went and answered as room service brought in the food for them. "Thank you," Ronan said as the attendant left. When Katie came in with Ronan's shirt on, he smirked.

"Always stealing my shirts."

"It was there." He grabbed his hoodie from his bag and came and sat down, eating a quiet lunch side by side with Katie.

"Not as good as the pub," Katie teased.

"Now you know why I go there."

"What time is your meeting," Katie asked.

"We have time. I have another hour. Besides. You have work to do too," he teased. Katie refreshed her emails and saw 10 messages she had to reply to.

"Can't really leave work for a few hours."

"Katie."

"I just want to breathe."

"Are you feeling better now that you're here," he asked.

"I am, but I still just need to relax. I don't understand why Ronan."

He kissed her. "Because he's a fool. He's determined to get your attention love. He knows that stupid texts are gonna get him in trouble, but he doesn't care."

"But what am I supposed to do Ronan?"

"Don't let him near you first off. Don't look at messages if they're not from one of your contacts."

"I just can't understand why he doesn't accept that we aren't together. That you and I are. I think that's what bugged him so damn much. Seeing you and me together."

"Katie, he's gonna do whatever he wants to. He doesn't want you happy away from him. That's all that it is. You deserve to be happy even if you do steal my shirts."

"I steal them because they smell like you."

"Oh really. So, what else did you want that smells like me?"

"Kinda hinted at it when we were in the bedroom."

"Katie."

"Just saying." He shook his head and kissed her as she got up and slid into his lap on the chair.

"You do realize that I have a meeting and need the shirt back."

"Then take it off of me." He shook his head and got up, picking her up and walked into the bedroom, leaning her back onto the bed and sliding her out of his shirt.

"What did you need the shirt back for?"

"In case I have to call into the office."

"Then I'm stealing your hoodie."

"Katie."

"What?"

"I saw you pack workout clothes."

"I like yours better," she teased.

"I bet you do love." He kissed her and she wrapped her legs around his hips. He shook his head.

"And if I said more," she asked almost mewing. He leaned in and kissed her.

"You're insatiable. You realize that." She kissed him.

"I know."

"And it's not just avoiding going on your laptop."

"Am I not allowed to want you when we're supposed to be working?"

"Distracting you."

She nodded and kissed him. "You want something."

"You."

"Something else love. You want me to permanently get your mind off it." She nodded with a grin ear to ear. "Katie."

"What?"

"I still have work to do and so do you."

"Just a little while," Katie teased.

He kissed her, devouring her lips until he felt her legs curl around him. "Katie."

"You're the one that said we had time."

"And you are just trying to avoid your computer."

She kissed him. "And I want you."

"I bet you do lass." She looked up at him and felt her undo his jeans. "Katie."

"What?"

"I know what you're doing."

"Good." When he felt her hand slide under his boxers, he stopped her and pinned her hands above her head. "Ronan."

"Not doing it. We're getting..." She kissed him again and he devoured her lips, deepening the kiss until he was turned on.

"Please." He shook his head and kicked his jeans and boxers off.

"You're intentionally taunting until I give in."

"That was my plan," Katie said.

He slid deep inside her until her breath hitched. "That what you wanted," he asked.

Her legs tightened around him as she nodded her reply. "Shit Ronan." He kissed her and then went harder, faster and deeper until she was panting. Until she was moaning and couldn't catch her breath. He kept going until her body was tight against him and she was moaning his name. When she throbbed around him, he kept going. He continued until she was begging and throbbing a second time. "Ronan."

"You're mine." She nodded her reply. When he exploded into her, Katie's body throbbed.

"Shit," she said as he pulled her tight to him and kissed her again.

"That what you wanted," he teased.

"Yes," she said catching her breath.

"You okay?"

She nodded and kissed him. "Promise me something."

"Name it," Ronan said as he slid to his back, and she curled up against his side.

"I don't want to ever lose this."

"Lose what?"

"You and me doing this."

"Katie."

"If it ever gets to the point where you're not happy..."

"You're talking crazy, love."

"If I'm not enough..."

"Katie." She looked at him and his arm slid around her.

"If I'm not, just tell me."

He shook his head. "You can't be serious right now. Love, you wouldn't be living in the house if you weren't enough. I wouldn't be with you at all if there was even a tiny doubt in my mind. Don't you see that?" She looked at him. "Katie." When he saw tears in her eyes, he shook his head. "You're serious?" She nodded and brushed the tears away.

"Ronan."

"He actually said something like that to you?"

"Ronan, he said a million things like that."

He took a deep breath and got up. "Where are you going?"

"Shower then getting dressed so I can do the meeting."

He had to remove himself from it. He was about ready to snap and hunt Devlin down himself. He had a quick shower to clean off and stepped out, wrapping a towel around him then came out and slid his boxers and jeans on with his dress shirt.

"Ronan."

"You know that him saying that doesn't mean anything right?"

"That's why I walked away from him in the first place."

"And you're never going near him again. Personally, I'd like to wipe the damn floor with him for even making you think that."

"You promised me."

"I said once to tell me everything. You didn't Katie." She looked at him.

"What else did you want me to say?"

"That he said that to you. That he made you doubt yourself and your worth."

"He screwed with me intentionally."

"You actually believe that he was saying the truth."

"Ronan."

"I can't Katie. I can't sit here and hear that and not want to kick him. Not want to rip his throat out. If you actually believed what he said, then you need to get that out of your head. He was trying to force you into doing what he wanted and stay no matter what crap he spewed. I'm never doing that. I'm not that stupid. If you don't want to be with me, then say it. I'm never putting you down. Honestly, I want to use him for boxing practice."

"Ronan, please just come here."

He walked back over to the bed, and she slid closer to him. "I know that what he did was wrong. I know it wasn't true. I just don't want to find out at some point that I'm not enough."

"That day isn't ever coming lass." She kissed him and he got up, handing Katie his hoodie.

"For this afternoon only," he teased. Katie kissed him and slid into the hoodie, getting up. She slid her joggers on, and he walked into the living room area and went to look through his emails:

> *Update: Still haven't tracked him down, but the cell information helps. We're tracking his phone and the burner he texted Katie from. House is safe and under watch. Any other tips that you two came up with?*

Ronan replied:

> *He was out with my ex when he started the fight. They may be together.*

Ronan closed the email and his phone buzzed with a reminder that the meeting was starting in 5 minutes. "Everything okay," Katie asked.

"Meeting in 5 minutes. You alright?" Katie nodded.

"If I need to take a call I'll go in the bedroom until you're done." He kissed her and she smirked. "I love you too Ronan."

He called into the meeting and got it done and out of the way while he watched Katie get her work done. "What," Katie asked silently as he was finishing up. He motioned for her to come closer. "Send the email over and I'll get back to you by the end of the day," Ronan said in reply to one of the people on the call. He hung up a matter of minutes later and kissed her.

"And how was your meeting?"

He smirked. "Went better than planned. How are your emails?"

"Too many of them. Way too many."

"You okay," he asked.

"No crazy emails or messages." He kissed her again.

"And how are you feeling?"

"If you're asking if I still want to curl up in bed instead of going through emails, the answer is yes."

"I still have work to do love." She kissed him and he pulled her into his lap.

"Emails?"

"Too many, but none from him."

"I got one from the officer I talked to."

"And?"

"They haven't found him."

"He would never think to look in a hotel like this. I'm still worried that he's gonna try to break into your place."

"Police are posted at the house. If you want to go back to the house, say it." She shook her head.

"I'm good so long as I have you with me."

"And you want to stay the rest of the week?"

"I just don't want to have to jump with every creek in the house."

He hugged her. "That's why you couldn't sleep?"

She nodded. "I was tossing and turning anyway."

"Next time you can't sleep, just snuggle in tighter. Deal?"

Katie kissed him. "How about you just hold onto me all night," Katie teased. He kissed her, snuggling her tight to him.

"Or I just make sure you get your mind off it." She smirked.

"That works," Katie teased.

He kissed her again. "Alright. Up before I end up having to finish these emails in bed. Up."

"And if I said..." He kissed her again and shook his head.

"Work."

"Party pooper." He kissed her, devouring her lips and her arms slid around his neck.

"You sure you want to get work done?" He nodded, kissed her and slid her off his lap.

"Get the emails done and we can do dinner."

"What if we went to a pub over here?"

"What if we had dinner downstairs then dessert up here?"

She smirked. "I like that idea," Katie said.

"Then finish the emails love. You get a fancy dinner tonight." She kissed him.

"And if I don't do the emails?"

"Then you're gonna be tied to the bed."

"Kinda like that idea."

"And you don't get dessert."

"Ronan."

"Then go work on the emails." She kissed him and got up, then went and worked on her emails.

"Such a party pooper." He smirked and sent her an email:

> *Behave and you get your dessert.*

He went through the rest of his emails and saw a reply:

> *What if I behaved and didn't wear anything under the dress?*

He looked over at her and she smirked. "Behave."

"Not as much fun," she replied. He finished up his emails and got up.

"Where are you going?"

"To get changed."

"Ronan."

"Get the emails done." He walked into the bedroom and made a call, getting a reservation for dinner for the two of them. He slid into the shower and just as he was about to rinse his hair, Katie slid in behind him. "What are you doing," Ronan asked.

"Having a shower with you."

"Emails."

"Done." He turned to face her and picked her up, wrapping her legs around his hips and pinned her against the wall of the shower.

"What," he asked. She kissed him.

"Mine," she teased. He kissed her and slid deep inside her. "Mm."

"That what you wanted?" She nodded and they had sex in the shower. Hot, intense sex that had her knees shaking and her body throbbing in his arms.

"Shit," he said.

"What?"

"Damn addictive." She kissed him and he carried her out of the shower, sitting her on the bathroom counter. "How did the emails go," he teased.

"Finished for today anyway. Thought you needed company," she teased.

He kissed her. "Get dressed."

"What time are we doing dinner?"

"5. Early. I have plans for tonight."

"And what plans are those," Katie asked as he wrapped her up in a towel.

"Involves you and me and a tie."

She smirked and slid off the counter. "I kinda like that plan Ronan."

"Good. Which dress are you wearing to dinner?"

"The black one," she replied.

"The one with the high slit on the side."

"The one that you love."

"Good pick." She kissed him and went to get dressed. He freshened up, came out of the bathroom and saw the dress on the bed. "The sexiest dress you have."

"Not necessarily. I did bring the red one you liked." He shook his head.

"Had to do it." She nodded and he saw the lace lingerie.

"Katie."

"What? I thought you liked the lace."

"I do. Looks even better on the floor." She smirked and towel dried her hair.

"That where you want it?"

"That's where it's gonna be when we get back."

"Promises, promises," Katie teased. He shook his head and slid his dress pants on. He put on her favorite cologne then slid his dress shirt on. When he turned around, the lingerie was on her and she was zipping the dress up.

"Temptation in heels," he teased.

"Looking handsome there yourself sexy."

Katie finished doing her hair and makeup and when she came out of the bathroom, Ronan got a grin ear to ear. "You smell too good," he teased.

"Meaning?"

"Meaning we may have to do dinner up here."

"We're going to dinner Ronan." He looked her up and down.

"Then you better get going before that dress ends up on the floor." She slid her hand in his and they went down to dinner. When they were seated at a booth in the back, she smirked.

"I know exactly what you're up to Ronan."

"And what's that love," he asked as the waitress brought over their drinks.

"Hands to yourself." He shook his head with a smirk. They ordered their dinner, and the waitress left them alone. Ronan slid closer to her. "And what do you want," Katie asked.

"You look beautiful."

"Thank you." She took a sip of her drink and Ronan kissed her neck. "I know what you're doing."

"I bet you do." He shook his head.

"What," she asked.

"What am I gonna do with you?"

"I have a few ideas, but we should kind of have dinner first," Katie teased.

"And if I decided to tease you through dinner?"

"Ronan."

"You did start this earlier."

"With what," she teased.

"The lace."

"Ronan."

His hand slid to her thigh. "Yes love."

"Don't start."

"Start what," he teased as he kissed her. His hand slid up her thigh.

"Ronan."

"Yes lass."

She stopped his hand. "Stop teasing."

"I haven't even started yet. I'm almost surprised that the little pink thing didn't get added into what you were wearing."

"It did." He slid his phone from his pocket and ran his finger over the screen. "Ronan."

"Mm. I can almost tell how turned on you're getting," he whispered.

"Ronan, stop." He kept going until her legs were almost shaking. When he stopped, her hand clamped down on his leg.

"Not fair."

"And you didn't tell me that you were wearing it."

"No more teasing."

"Then you shouldn't have worn it."

"Ronan." He kissed her shoulder.

"You started it," he whispered. Katie shook her head.

"You do realize that I can take it out."

"Or I can when we get back to the suite."

"Ronan." He ran his finger over his phone screen again to tease as her hand clamped down on his. "Stop." He shook his head. "Ronan." The food showed and she got her break. "You and that damn toy," she teased.

"You're the one that started it," he teased. They had their dinner together with silly smirks between them. "What," he asked.

"Remind me not to bring it next time."

"Or we do something else completely."

"Meaning what," Katie asked as she had a bite of her steak.

"Next time, I get to tease you with something else," he replied. Katie shook her head, and he smirked.

They finished their dinner and headed up to the suite. When they got in, dessert was waiting for them. "What's this," Katie asked.

"Dessert," he replied.

"Ronan."

"What?"

"Chocolate covered berries?" He nodded. He walked over to her and picked her up, wrapping her legs around his hips and sliding her dress up.

"What," he asked seeing the smirk on Katie's face. He slid his hand in his pocket, running his finger over the screen until he could feel her throbbing.

"You're not..." He kissed her, devouring her lips then slid his hand up her leg and slid the toy out.

"Aah."

"What?"

"You're teasing is making me..."

He kissed her and unzipped the dress. "What?"

"No more toys."

He kissed her. "I haven't even got started yet."

"Meaning what?" He picked her up and carried her to the bed.

"Dress off." She stood up and slid it off revealing the sexy black lace lingerie under it. "Off." She undid the bra then slid the lace panties off. He pulled her into his lap and leaned her onto the bed.

"Don't move."

"Ronan." He grabbed a tie from his bag and tied her hands to the bed. "What are you up to," Katie asked. He got up and slid his shirt off, then his dress pants then grabbed something from his bag.

"Getting something else to tease you with."

"Which is what," Katie asked.

"Close your eyes."

"No."

"Do I need to get the blindfold?"

"Ronan, tell me what..."

She felt something vibrate against her and she shook her head. "Something distracting you," Ronan asked.

"Mm."

"And that's on low. Hm. I wonder what high is like," he teased as he slid it against her and ran it up and down her warmth.

"Ronan, stop teasing."

"Nope. I get to tease you until you beg," he teased.

"Shit Ronan. Stop."

"Not until you beg." He kept going, teasing and running it over her over and over again.

"Stop. Ronan, stop please."

"Why?"

"I want you inside me. No more toys."

"And if I said not yet?"

"Ronan." He slid the toy to the side and licked and teased and nibbled as he felt her body grinding against him.

"Mm."

"Mine. All mine," Ronan said.

"Aah." His fingers slid inside her and he kept going.

"Ronan."

"Yes love."

"Come here." He licked and nibbled then kissed up her torso.

"What," he asked. Katie kissed him.

"No more teasing."

"Tell me what..."

"I did. I want you inside me." His fingers slid out of her, and he pulled her legs around him and pounded into her. "Aah."

"That what you wanted?"

She nodded. "Mm." He kept going, in and out until he could feel her throbbing around him. "Aah. Ronan."

"Say it," he said.

"Undo them."

He shook his head. "Nope."

"Ronan."

"You think that you can slide that little toy in and not tell me and think that you're gonna get away with it," he teased.

"I was gonna tell you."

"When?"

"When we got upstairs."

"Here." She nodded.

"Just remember something lass. You slide that toy in and I'm the only one that can remove it. Understood?"

"And if I take it out instead?"

"Then you get in trouble." He kept going intentionally making her body throb over and over then exploded into her.

"Shit."

"Ronan."

"Yes love."

"Untie them." He untied her hands and slid to his side.

"Dessert?"

"I don't know that I can move," Katie joked. He kissed her and got up.

"Where are you going?"

"Clean up then getting dessert."

"Ronan, come here." He cleaned up, pulled on boxers then brought the strawberries in. He laid down beside her and she curled up next to him.

"What are you really up to?"

"You wanted distractions. You get distractions. End the day with something romantic."

"You realize that my legs are still shaky."

"That's why I brought dessert to you." He kissed her, grabbed a strawberry, and fed it to her.

"Mm. Thank you."

"Feeling better?"

"I needed today. I know that sounds ridiculous, but I needed this."

"I know this is what you needed. You don't need to worry about him for a while. I may go down to the gym for a workout in the morning so don't get worried alright?"

"Are you gonna leave me sleeping alone again?"

"Yes, but not for long," he teased. She kissed him.

"Am I allowed to say that I want to come with you?" He shook his head.

"Because you don't want to be up here alone?"

"I just feel better when I'm with you."

"You're fine up here. When I get back, we can have breakfast then I'll take you to work."

"But don't you need to get into the office?"

"I told them I'd be in before 10. Making sure you're okay is my first priority."

"Ronan."

"Just relax and sleep. You'll get a better night's sleep tonight. We're safe up here."

"I still think..."

"Katie."

"Part of me still worries about your place."

"The officers will let me know if anything happens. We're good love."

"I know we're gonna go back, but I'm worried." He snuggled her to him and pulled the blankets up around them.

"Nobody is coming near you. You can go back to work without any problems tomorrow. He's not dumb enough to show up at your work. If it weren't the hospital offices, I'd get a security guy for you."

"Ronan."

He kissed her. "Here's the deal. You start worrying and watching over your shoulder, call me. I can get the car to come pick you up."

"Ronan."

"I mean it. The car will come pick you up when you start worrying. The driver has protection in case something happens."

"Now you're scaring me."

"He's ex military. He's been my security for years."

"And who's gonna keep you safe?"

He kissed her. "In my office? Surrounded by my security staff."

"And if it's too much at work then I can come up to your office right?"

"If that's what you want. You can come back here."

"If I want to come up to the office with you?"

"I have a couple meetings tomorrow, so you'd have my office to yourself part of the day. Just try to stay as long as you can at work. You can't hide love. You need to walk with your head up high. He can't hurt you anymore."

"Doesn't mean he won't try." He snuggled her to him and took a deep breath.

"Let's get some sleep. It's gonna be an early morning."

"And why's that," Katie asked as she leaned her head on his shoulder.

"Because I'm waking you up when I'm done in the gym." They curled up together and managed to nod off.

After tossing and turning part of the night, Ronan was up at 5. Katie was out cold. He gently got up, changed into his workout gear and went down to the hotel gym to get a workout in. He was just finishing up when a woman came in and looked at him.

"And what on earth are you doing here of all places," the woman said.

"Sorry?"

"Samantha. We met a couple months ago."

"Don't remember sorry."

Ronan grabbed his towel and left the gym, ordering breakfast for him and Katie on the way up. When he got into the elevator, the woman jumped in with him.

"Did you really think that was gonna work? I know you remember me," Samantha said.

"Nothing personal, but I don't recall."

"Ronan, we had sex."

"Like I said, I don't recall."

"Then come with me and I'll remind you," Samantha said as the elevator doors opened on her floor.

"My girlfriend is waiting for me. Sorry," he said as he closed the doors and pressed the upper floor to the suite.

He got in and Katie was still asleep. He walked into the bedroom and smirked, kissing her forehead. "How was the gym?"

"Interesting. Still kinda prefer the gym at the house."

"Bump into someone you know or something?"

"Sort of."

"I was joking," Katie said.

"Let's just leave it at I hope she's gone by tonight."

"Remember when I said that I didn't like going to hotels when I knew that you'd been there before?"

"I haven't been in the suite. Second, this is the safest hotel. You slept well last night and everything."

"What did you say to her?"

"That I had my girlfriend with me and was heading up to my room."

"Ronan."

"That's what I said love."

"And?"

"And what? She has no idea where we are, and I want it that way. She's obnoxious." Katie smirked. "What?"

"Another one-night stand?"

"One. An hour actually. I couldn't..."

"Ronan."

"I found what I wanted love. Past is the past."

"Nice try."

He kissed her and she slid her arms around him and pulled him into the bed with her. "And what might you want?"

"Did you order breakfast?" He nodded and kissed her, devouring her lips. Just as she was about to peel his shirt off, there was a knock at the door. He kissed her again and got up. He checked through the peephole and let the room service attendant in.

"Thank you," Ronan said as the man brought the food in then left. Ronan left the covers on it to keep everything warm and walked back into the bedroom.

"Are you gonna come and eat before it gets cold or are we doing breakfast in bed," Ronan asked.

"What time is it?"

"7."

She kissed him. "Up then we are coming back to bed for a little while," Katie teased. He handed Katie his hoodie and she got up, wrapped herself up in it and came and sat down with Ronan to eat.

"Did you really think that I was gonna tell her where we were staying?"

"Partially."

"Katie. We are a couple now. History stays history. I wouldn't have done anything regardless."

"And," she asked.

"And what?"

"You weren't even tempted?"

He kissed her. "No. Not when you were up here waiting."

"And if I wasn't?"

"Still wouldn't have gone near her. I actually tried to leave in the elevator before she got in."

"Ronan, you can tell me the truth."

"I'd rather come up here and slide into bed with you then go near her." Katie finished her breakfast and sipped her coffee. "What," he asked.

"Nothing. Do you want to stay here the rest of the week or go home," Katie asked.

"That's kinda up to you love. I don't want you losing sleep being at the house. Give us a few days to relax before we head over."

"If that woman is staying here..."

"What would you prefer I do love?"

"Something to make her leave you alone."

"Which would be?"

"I was gonna give it to you for your birthday."

"Katie, what did you do?"

"We're doing this right? We're staying together?"

He nodded. "Why?"

She got up, grabbed something from her bag and handed it to Ronan. "What's this?"

"Woman repellant." He opened the box and saw a ring.

"Katie."

"It's one of those rings that monitors how you sleep and stuff. Since you workout all the time, it's silicone so you can workout with it on."

"And when were you gonna tell me that you got this," he asked.

"When I decided the time was right. I'd say after this morning, the time is right." He kissed her and picked her up, carrying her back into the bedroom and leaned her onto the bed. "What," Katie asked.

"Remember something when you start worrying that I'm gonna find someone else. I'm here in bed with you every single night and I wouldn't have it any other way."

She kissed him. "Are you sure that you don't?"

"I'm positive."

"Ronan."

"What love?"

"You're overdressed." He undid the zipper of the hoodie and slid it off her, pulled his shirt off then Katie went to help him slide his joggers and boxers off.

"Katie."

"Helping."

He shook his head. "No, you aren't love."

"Then take them off." He kicked them to the floor and Katie's legs slid around him.

"Tell me what you want love."

"You know what I want," she replied. He slid deep inside her and Katie almost moaned.

"That what you wanted?" She nodded and he kept going as she grinded against him.

"Mm."

"Damn," he said as he kept going. "Katie."

"What?"

"Tighter." She pulled him tighter as he went harder and deeper and kept going in and out until she was throbbing around him.

"Ronan."

"I want you throbbing for hours," he teased as he kept going harder and faster.

"Mm." He flipped her over and kept going until he could feel her exploding around him again. "Ronan." He kept going, harder until he crashed into her and exploded, collapsing on top of her and rolling to his side.

"I can't even move," Katie said.

"Good," he teased. Katie shook her head and slid over to his side, wrapping her arm around him and leaning her head on his shoulder.

"Ronan, you sure you don't want company at work?"

"You have work to get to love. They need you almost as badly as I want you."

"Oh really?"

"You don't need to hide out at the office. If something happens and you start feeling like you aren't safe, then call me."

"And if I get there and feel like something is really off?"

"Then get some work done and count the hours until I come to get you."

"Are you really gonna come in?"

"If that's what you need, yes." She kissed his chest.

"And if I say I want to show you off to all my co-workers and I want you to come in?"

"So now I'm your toy to parade around?"

"A little," Katie teased.

"Katie."

"What?"

"You realize that I've been in that hospital a million times."

"Never when we were together."

He kissed her. "You want me to walk you in?" She nodded. He kissed her again. "Then we should probably get up and get showered."

"Do I have to," Katie joked.

He kissed her. "Yes, love you do." He got up and walked into the bathroom, flipping the shower on. He freshened up and stepped into the shower with Katie sliding in behind him as he shampooed his hair. "I know what you're thinking."

"I didn't do anything," Katie teased as he turned to face her and kissed her. He rinsed his hair, and she slid her arms around him.

"What," he asked.

"Nothing." He washed himself off as she washed her hair. "I would've but I know that you would've ended up more than distracted," Katie said.

"Exactly what I meant," he teased as he rinsed off and kissed her again.

"You sure you really want to come to my work?"

"If that's what you want love." He kissed her and stepped out, letting her get washed up.

He walked into the bedroom and slid into his suit pants and his dress shirt and heard her come out of the bathroom. "You do know I can smell that cologne from here."

"And you love it, so I do it." Katie kissed him and he picked her up and sat her on the edge of the bed in her towel. "And what else do you want?" She smirked.

"Thank you."

"For what?"

"Coming with me. The hotel. Making me feel better," Katie said.

He kissed her. "I'd only do this for you, love."

"I know. Maybe we should go back to the house."

"If that's what you want. I'm good either way."

"I don't want to put you out and make it feel like a mistake."

"And what do you mean by mistake," he asked.

"Having to go through this. We just got together and already we're hiding out in a fancy hotel."

He kissed her. "If you want to go back to the house, we'll go, but the police are still keeping an eye out."

"What if we stayed here another night then went back on the weekend?"

"In other words, staying here two more nights."

"It is kind of nice to be here though."

"And none of this has anything to do with me bumping into that woman this morning."

"Fine. It does, but I still like being here." He shook his head and kissed her.

"Alright love. Get ready and I'll take you to work." One more kiss and he went and finished getting dressed.

Katie got dressed, then walked into the living room and grabbed her laptop. "You ready," Katie asked as he packed up his laptop bag.

"Looking sexy as usual," he teased.

"Well thank you handsome."

"Are you ready to head down?"

Katie nodded and she grabbed her purse. They made their way down to the waiting SUV and went off to her work without a single look from anyone. "You're really walking me in." He nodded. He slid his hand in hers and kissed her hand. "Ronan."

"Yes lass."

"We okay after this morning?"

He nodded. "I know you didn't want to hear about what happened at the gym," he said.

"Let's just hope she's gone from the hotel and doesn't show up tomorrow."

"And if she shows?"

"Then just come back up. It's not like you need…"

"Katie."

"You don't."

"If I took a day off, I'd feel like crap. Too much energy," he teased.

"I can fix that."

"I'm sure you could love."

"You don't need to."

"Hard to explain, but I do. Gets all the frustration and irritation out so I'm nicer."

Katie smirked. "Sexy, yes. Nicer?"

He kissed her. "Leave it at the workout stays." She nodded and kissed him as they pulled up. "You ready," he asked.

"Sir," the driver said.

"Be back in 15. Just walking her into work," Ronan said. He helped her out of the car and walked her inside.

"Ronan."

"What?"

"Tell me that I'm safe," she asked as they stepped into the elevator to head to her floor. "You start to not feel safe, call me and I'll get the driver to come get you."

Katie gulped and nodded. "You're that worried?"

"I just have a bad feeling."

Chapter 5

The elevator dinged and he walked her to her desk.
"You're good," Ronan said.

"I will be I guess."

"Katie, this must...Ronan," her boss said.

"Good morning. Just wanted to make sure Katie got in
alright. How are you," Ronan asked.

"Good. Just a surprise seeing you here. Normally it's only
at those meetings."

"You set," Ronan asked. Katie nodded. "Alright. I'll see
you tonight," he said as he headed back to the elevator
and went back down to the waiting car.

"Sir."

"Let's go," Ronan said as they headed to his office.

"If she starts getting worried again, just head over here
and pick her up. She can come work from my office
again."

"Yes sir." Just as Ronan was going through emails, he saw
one pop in from Katie:

> To the handsome one who walked me into work.
>
> Thank you. Moira was a little stunned. She said if
> I started feeling worried again then I was fine
> working from home. I guess seeing you does
> that. I also saw a few nurses watching you walk

away. Got a few questions. Kinda happy to say that we're together. Miss you already.

K

He smirked and replied:

To my lass.

The car will be outside if you need it. I'm glad I could get you a smile today. Hopefully all good things were said. Happy I have you too. See you tonight love.

R

He made his way into the office and it felt like the day dragged on. Meeting after meeting. When he came back to his office at 4, there was another email from Katie:

Hey handsome. Working until 4:30. Wanted to let you know in case you feel like coming back up to meet me so everyone can stare again. Miss you.

He got a smirk ear to ear then there was a knock at his office door. "Yes," Ronan said as his driver knocked. "I thought you were waiting at the hospital for her?"

"Did you want to go pick her up or should I just go back down and wait?"

"I'll go. I need to stop at the house for something," Ronan said.

"Officers are still on the premises."

"Thank you for checking," Ronan said as he put his papers together, slid his laptop in his bag and let his assistants know he was heading out.

"Sir, you may have one more call."

"I'll do it from the hotel." His assistant nodded. "Just send me the info."

Ronan headed out, stopped at the house, and picked up what he needed, doing a quick check and flipping the alarm back on, then headed to her work to pick her up. When he showed up at her desk, she was laughing with a co worker. "Hey handsome," Katie said.

"Hey yourself lass. Are we ready," he asked.

Katie nodded and got up, putting her laptop in her bag. "See you tomorrow," Moira said.

Katie nodded and they headed down to the SUV.

"And what did you do after you left the office," Katie asked as they hopped in and headed to the hotel.

"Stopped at the house to grab a few things. Why," Ronan asked.

"If you want to go back we can."

He kissed her. "It's fine. Weekend," he replied.

"What did you need?"

"You'll find out when we're back," he teased.

"Ronan." He kissed her and not long later, they were pulling up to the hotel.

"Are you gonna tell me?" He smirked and helped her out of the SUV then they headed through the lobby and up to their suite. "And," she asked. He slid her bag off her shoulder and put it on the sofa. "Why do I get the feeling that you're up to something," Katie asked. He slid his bag onto the sofa beside hers and pulled out the one thing that he'd grabbed from the house. "Ronan."

"Yes love," he said as he walked into the bedroom.

"What did you do," she asked.

"Picked something up."

"Which was what?" She saw the handcuffs and the key and shook her head. "Tie not enough," she teased.

"For tonight, no."

"Meaning what?"

"Meaning you're at my mercy tonight."

Katie shook her head and smirked. "And what else did you have planned," Katie asked.

"You handcuffed. Me teasing until your toes are in knots. You begging me to be inside you. Teasing until you're at your breaking point. Me going more and more until you can't move."

"And the fact that you just made my toes curl?" He kissed her, devouring her lips and slid her dress off, walking her backwards to the bed.

"Food," Katie asked.

"Depends on what you're gonna be eating, because I know exactly what I am." He leaned her onto the bed.

"Ronan, dinner first."

He kissed her again, then got up and grabbed his phone. "What," she asked.

"Room service." He ordered them dinner, requested that it was in the room by 6, then wrapped his arms around her and leaned into her arms.

"Ronan."

"Yes love," he said as he unbuttoned his shirt.

"What did you order?"

"Am I making you nervous," Ronan asked.

"You're on the prowl."

"And?" He kissed her again and devoured her lips. He slid his shirt off and felt her arms slide around him.

"I might've missed you today," Katie said.

"And I craved you all day," Ronan said as he undid the waistband of his dress pants.

"Ronan."

"What?"

"What did you want to do?"

"Starts with you naked on the bed. Sorta like you almost are now."

"And then what," Katie asked.

"Handcuffs. You begging me to let go. Kissing down your chest." Just as he said it, his phone buzzed. He kissed her and grabbed his phone. "Good," he said.

"What?"

"Meeting was cancelled." He kissed her neck and kicked his dress pants off.

"You were saying."

"Nibble at your breasts. Tease until you're aching then kiss down to your hip." He kicked his boxers off and peeled her lace panties off.

"Ronan."

"Then lick and tease and suck and nibble at you until you're exploding over and over again. Dining on you. Licking until you explode then my fingers sliding inside you and teasing until you can barely contain yourself." He slid her bra off and kissed down her chest.

"Shit."

"What?"

"My legs are shaking already just thinking about it."

He devoured her lips. "And then I make you throb inside and out until you can't take anymore."

"Ronan."

"What?" He kissed and nibbled at each breast until they were aching.

"Ronan, please."

"Please what," he asked as his phone buzzed a second time.

"You're really gonna start this now?" He looked at his phone.

"No. I'm gonna keep going until you beg me to stop."

"What's wrong?"

"Don't move." He read the text:

> *We caught him. He tried to walk up to your house. He's in custody for violation of the protection order.*

Ronan kissed down her torso then licked and nibbled at her hip. "Are you gonna at least tell me what that was?"

"No." He kissed it then slowly trailed the kisses to her inner thighs.

"Aah."

"All wet. Just the way I like it," he teased.

"Ronan come here." He shook his head and licked at the wetness between her legs.

"Mm." He kept going until he felt her hands in his hair.

"Katie."

"Come here." He shook his head and looked up at her.

"I told you I have handcuffs."

"Come here." He looked up at her.

"You want me to stop?"

"For a second," she mewed. His fingers slid inside her and she moaned. He moved up and kissed her.

"I know what you're doing," Katie said.

"Good thing lass. Am I allowed to continue."

"I want you."

"Oh, but I haven't even started the teasing yet."

"Ronan."

"Am I pulling out the handcuffs?"

"No."

"Then I'm gonna keep going until you can't breathe."

"Food."

"Coming."

"When?"

"6."

"Ronan." He kissed her again, devouring her lips and she felt something slide around her hands. "What are..."

"Tie."

"Ronan." He kissed her then pinned her hands to the bed.

"Don't move them."

"Ronan." He kissed her again and kissed back down her torso until he made his way back down to the wetness between her legs and teased and licked and nibbled until she was moaning his name then slid his fingers inside her again and teased until he felt her throbbing. "Ronan, please."

He kept going, intensifying the licking and teasing. Intensifying the vibration of his fingers inside her and her legs started to shake. "Good girl," he teased.

"Please."

"What?"

"I want you. Please." He kept going until she exploded around his fingers and her stomach started trembling. "Ronan." He kissed her inner thigh and kept teasing. "I need you."

"How bad do you need me," he asked as she moaned and exploded again.

"Ronan." He slid up her torso and slid deep inside her.

"This what you wanted," he asked.

"Aah." He kissed her and went harder, deeper and more intense until she was throbbing around him over and over again.

"Shit," Katie said.

"What," he asked as he kept going until her legs were shaking. She moaned and he flipped her onto her stomach and kept going until he couldn't hold himself back anymore and exploded into her.

"Shit," Katie said.

"And," Ronan asked as he leaned onto his back and undid the tie around her hands.

"I may need dinner in bed."

He smirked. "Could be arranged."

"I can't move my legs."

"Sore or I killed your legs?"

"Aching. I can't move."

"Good."

"Ronan."

"What?"

"What was the text?"

"Nothing love."

"Ronan, just tell me what it was. I know it was something."

"They arrested him." Katie stopped and rolled over, looking at him.

"What?"

"He was walking up the driveway of the house and the cops got him. It was part of the protective order that he couldn't go near us or the house. He was arrested."

"That mean we're going home?"

He kissed her, devouring her lips. "It means that tonight we have all night to relax."

She kissed him. "And to pack."

He kissed her. "Won't take long. We'll stay tonight then go home tomorrow after work."

"If I can even walk."

"I could always carry you into work. Your friends will get a laugh out of that."

Katie smirked. "You had that planned out all day."

He nodded. "Among other things," he teased.

"Such as," Katie asked as her arm slid around him, and she curled up beside him.

"Among other things. Tying you to the bed with the handcuffs. Using that other toy you had for when we weren't together."

"Really."

"It's in my bag."

"I don't know that I can even move," she teased.

"And that's a good thing." He kissed her and got up.

"Where are you going?"

"Cleaning up and putting something on so we can get dinner." He kissed her then went and had a quick shower, slid his joggers and hoodie on and handed Katie her robe.

"I'm serious. I don't know that I can move." He kissed her, leaning into her arms.

"When you see dinner you will."

"And what did you order?"

"Lobster Ravioli and Blue Lobster," Ronan said.

"Sounds so good."

"From the chef at the fancy dining room downstairs."

"Steaks were out I guess." He smirked.

"I just chose the two most amazing sounding things and ordered two."

He kissed her again and heard a knock at the door. "Back in a minute. Put the robe on." He walked into the living room, checked the peephole and saw the chef. "Chef, thank you again."

"I wanted to make sure you were both happy with the dinner. I also brought up a bottle of wine I paired with the meal."

"Thank you. I appreciate this." The chef nodded and left them to eat. Ronan walked into the bedroom and saw Katie sitting on the edge of the bed in her fancy satin robe that he'd bought her.

"You coming to eat?" She smirked and he grabbed her hand, helping her up.

"I swear you do this intentionally."

"Making your legs shake until you can barely move?" She nodded. He poured them each a glass of wine and they sat down to eat.

"Oh, my goodness," Katie said.

"Pretty damn amazing right," he asked.

"Ronan." They finished the appetizer and then had their entrees. All of it was above and beyond anything she'd ever had, and it was to die for. They finished the food and had another glass of wine.

"Ronan."

"Yes love."

"We kinda need to pack."

He kissed her. "Lots of time. I thought you'd want round two."

"I can barely walk. You're not that funny." He kissed her again.

"And how was your wine," he asked.

"So good. Did you really plan all of this out today?" He nodded.

"Most of it anyway."

"And what part didn't you plan?"

"Dinner." He kissed her and got up, walking over to the sofa. She got up and came and curled up on the sofa with him. "You do realize that I might not be walking tomorrow right?"

"Then I'll carry you back into the house."

"We should pack."

"That's really what you want to do right now?"

"No, but I don't know that my legs can withstand round two."

"Shall we test them out?" He kissed the back of her shoulder then up her neck.

"Ronan."

"Bad influence." Katie nodded. She turned to face him and kissed him. "And what do you want lass?"

She kissed him again and straddled him. "You."

"And here I thought you wanted to pack." He pulled her legs around him, picked her up and carried her back into the bedroom, pinning her down to the bed.

"I think we should maybe pack, but I want you more."

"You sure your legs can take it," he teased.

"I'm sure that I'm gonna be a damn mess walking into work tomorrow, but..."

He kissed her, devouring her lips and deepening the kiss until she had goosebumps. He peeled the satin robe off and she shook her head with a smirk ear to ear.

"What," Katie asked.

"This time you get the handcuffs."

"Ronan."

"What?"

"No handcuffs."

"Why?"

"Because I don't want them." He kissed her and felt her hands slide to the waistline of his joggers. "Don't you start that."

"Don't start what," she asked as he felt her hand wrap around him and start sliding up and down his length.

"Katie."

"Mine." He shook his head and Katie kissed him.

"Roll over," she said.

"No."

"Ronan, it's only fair."

"I said no lass. Let go." She kept going, feeling him harden in her hand. "Katie."

"What?"

He grabbed her hand, freed himself from it and grabbed the handcuffs, locking her hands to the bed and away from him. "Ronan."

"Now, back to where I was," he teased as he slid his boxers and his joggers off.

"You realize that you're a party pooper right?" He kissed her, devouring her lips and deepened the kiss until her legs were coiling around him.

"Party pooper?"

Katie nodded and kissed him. He shook his head and kissed her with a kiss so hot she forgot her protests. "Something you have to say," he teased.

"Undo them."

He shook his head. "You can't be trusted to keep your hands and those nails to yourself love."

"Ronan." He kissed her again and trailed his kisses down her neck, then down her torso until she was fighting the handcuffs. "Undo them."

"Not on your life lass." When he reached her hip and nibbled, Katie shook her head and almost moaned. "And I'm not even warmed up yet," he teased.

"Because you're taunting me."

"Call it payback."

"For what?" He kept going, licking, and kissing her inner thigh then moving to her warmth.

"Mine."

"Ronan." He licked and her toes curled. He slid her legs to his shoulders and kept going, teasing, and licking and kissing until she was moaning again. "Shit Ronan." His tongue slid over her and teased until he felt her body exploding right onto his tongue.

"Ronan, please." He kept going until he could feel her almost shaking in his arms.

"Please what," he asked.

"I need you."

"To do what love?"

"Inside me." "

You sure you don't want more of this," he asked as he licked and teased again.

"Ronan." He kissed back up her torso then licked and kissed each breast until he felt her legs wrap around him. He kissed back up to her neck then devoured her lips until she was trying again to wriggle her hands free.

"They aren't coming undone love," he said as he briefly let her up for air.

"Undo them." He shook his head and kissed her again.

"Please," she said. He slid deep inside her and her breath hitched.

"Please what love?"

"Mm."

"That's what I thought you said," Ronan said as he slid in and out over and over, harder, deeper until he could feel her body exploding around him. He took his time, but he wasn't letting up until she begged him for mercy. They kept going, harder, faster then more intense until he could feel her legs shaking. "Tell me what you want love."

"Just you." He kissed her and kept going.

"Roll over." She shook her head, and he turned her to her stomach then slid deeper into her and kept going until he couldn't hold himself back and crashed into her.

"Undo them." He grabbed the key off the counter and undid the handcuffs. He slid to his back and Katie curled up with him.

"You alright love?"

Katie smirked and nodded. "Better than okay."

"Good." She snuggled into his arms, and he went to get up.

"Where are you going?"

"Shower. Give me a minute."

"Ronan."

"Back in a minute." He went and cleaned up and when he came back into the bedroom, she was curled up under the blankets.

Ronan slid boxers on then slid under the covers with her, and she snuggled up to him. "You good love?" Katie nodded and kissed him.

"I was cold," Katie said.

"I can imagine. You're all naked." Her leg slid around his.

"I know," Katie said as he kissed her.

"Love."

"What?"

"You sure you're okay?"

"I love you."

"And I love you. What's wrong?"

"Why do you always get up and shower after?"

"Because I was hot and sweaty."

"And?"

"I never go to sleep all hot and sweaty love."

She kissed him. "Then I'm getting up with you." He shook his head.

"If that's what you want." She snuggled in closer to him and he looked at her.

"What's wrong?"

"Just feels like you're trying to wash me off of you." He kissed her forehead.

"It isn't about you, love. I've been this way for years." She nodded.

He shook his head. "Do you want me to sleep on the sofa?"

"No."

"Then why do I get the feeling like you're upset?"

"Just want more time to curl up together before you shower and vanish."

He was quiet. Irritated and quiet. "Katie."

"What?"

"Something bugs you then just say it."

"I want you in bed with me. No getting up." He shook his head.

"Fine." He went quiet.

"What," Katie asked. He shook his head and put the phones on the charger. "Ronan." He checked his watch and made sure that it was charged then flipped the light off. "Turn it back on."

"I'm not having a fight with you Katie. You said your piece. Done."

"So now you're mad."

He shook his head. "No."

He attempted to get comfortable. "What happened to not going to bed mad?"

"I'm not mad."

"Ronan."

"Lass, just get some sleep." They both nodded off and Ronan ended up tossing and turning half the night.

Ronan woke up the next morning after the rough night. She had been just as bad and unable to get comfortable all night long. He gently slid out of bed and changed into his workout clothes, grabbed his phone, room key and AirPods and went down to the gym. He got started on his workout, happy to have the gym to himself. When he was done, he went to head up to his suite when he saw the woman in the lobby. He quickly dove into the elevator and went up to the suite, ordering breakfast on the way up. When he walked into the suite, Katie was still asleep. He went and made coffee, taking one in for her and put it on the bedside table. "How was the gym?"

"Good. Breakfast is on its way up."

"Come back to bed."

"Katie."

"Come back to bed."

"Breakfast is coming. I'm just gonna check emails."

"Ronan." He kissed her and went back into the living room. He went through the emails making sure he didn't have any morning meetings. When he saw his first wasn't until 11, he breathed a sigh of relief. Katie came in a few minutes later and walked over in nothing but her satin robe and slid his laptop from his hands, putting it on the table.

"Katie, I was working."

"No morning emails. My time," she said.

"And what did you want love?"

"You." She slid into his lap and kissed him as he tasted the minty toothpaste.

"Katie."

"What?"

"What are you doing?" When she straddled him, he shook his head. "Don't start that."

"Not starting anything." When her hand slid down the front of his joggers, he stopped her.

"Don't love."

"Why?"

"Because the food is literally on its way up." She did it anyway and he stopped her again. "Katie."

"Then come back to bed."

"No."

"Why..." Just as she said it, there was a knock at the door.

"Like I said, breakfast."

"It can wait." Ronan got up, sliding her to the sofa and got the door as they brought in the food and set it up at the meeting table.

The attendant left a few minutes later and Katie walked over to Ronan. "Sit down and eat."

"So, you're still mad."

"Katie, I'm not mad. Last time I'm saying it."

"I'm sorry for putting you in a bad mood before bed."

"Just open the cover of the food before it gets cold." Katie did and saw the heart-shaped omelet.

"Ronan."

"I wasn't exactly in a good mood last night. I'm sorry."

"Did I tell you that I love you today," Katie teased.

"Love you back." They ate and finished their coffees when Ronan got up to check emails.

"Ronan."

"Yes love."

"No emails before work."

"Was just getting some out of the way before I take you to work."

"I have a better idea."

"It's after 7. We have to get ready for work and head in," Ronan said.

"We have time."

"For what love?" She walked over to him and kissed him, sliding her hand in his and walked him into the bedroom.

"Katie."

"Mine," she said.

"You really want to start this now?"

Katie kissed him and nodded. "We have to pack and get ready for work."

"Ronan, get back..."

He kissed her and leaned her onto the bed. "Tell me what you want."

"You." He kissed her, leaning into her arms and pinned her hands above her head.

"Don't you even think it."

"Then leave them there." He slid her out of the satin robe and kicked his joggers and boxers to the floor. She peeled his shirt and hoodie off and he kissed her, sliding his arms around her until her legs wrapped tight around his hips.

"What do you want love," he asked.

"You know what," Katie said.

"We don't..."

"Ronan." He kissed her and devoured her lips and slid deep inside her.

"Aah." Her breath hitched and he kept going, harder, deeper and more and more intense until she exploded around him. He kept going, making it more intense until he practically exploded into her and rolled to his side. "Mm."

"What," he asked.

"Much better," she replied.

"What?" He kissed her.

"Tomorrow morning, I want you to stay in bed with me."

"Workout."

"Bed. Cardio," she teased. He laughed and kissed her.

"We need to pack love."

"Such a party pooper." He got up and walked into the bathroom with her and her shaky legs two steps behind him. He flipped the water on and stepped in and she stepped right in behind him.

"Katie, shower."

"Meaning what?"

"No funny business. We have to get dressed and pack."

"Ronan." He washed his hair and rinsed then washed up while she washed her hair.

"Can't even enjoy this can I," Katie joked.

"Not if you're up to something. I know that look," he teased.

"I'm not doing anything," she said as he rinsed off. He kissed her and stepped out, leaving her to finish getting showered. When she stepped out of the shower, she wrapped herself in a towel and walked in the bedroom to see Ronan in his dress pants, packing his bag.

"We could just stay tonight," Katie said. He shook his head.

"We're going back. You're not in danger. The house is safe."

"Or we just stay tonight and stay in bed." He shook his head.

"I already let the hotel know that we're going home today."

Katie kissed him and went and got dressed, then packed everything up to head back to the house.

"You sure you have everything," Ronan asked as he saw Katie wheel her suitcase to the door.

"Everything except what I'm wearing," Katie said. He kissed her.

"Good. We have to leave in the next 15 minutes."

"What time is it," Katie asked.

"Almost half 8."

"Do you have everything?" Ronan nodded as he zipped up his bag and went and put his laptop and papers into his work bag. They headed downstairs, checked out and went out to the waiting SUV. They slid in as the driver put the bags in the back.

"Did you want me to take them to the house," the driver asked.

"Please," Ronan replied as Katie slid closer to Ronan.

"Did you want me to walk you in again," Ronan asked.

Katie smirked. "You don't have to. Honestly, I feel better knowing he's been handled." Ronan kissed her.

"Still walking you up." Katie smirked.

"Thank you." He kissed her again.

"We should be there in about 5 minutes," the driver said.

"Thanks," Ronan said. When they pulled up to Katie's work, Ronan hopped out and got her door for her.

"You know you don't have to right?"

Ronan nodded. "Come with me," he teased.

They walked in and went up the elevator, as he kissed her again. "He'll come get you after work. I'll meet you at the house."

"What are you planning?"

"You'll see when you get home."

He walked her upstairs, said hi to a few of her co-workers and headed off to the office. When he showed, his coffee was in his office, his messages were on his desk, and his assistant was following him into the office. "What's up," Ronan asked.

"Is Katie coming into the office today?"

"No. I just took her to work. Why?"

"Well, I wanted to make sure that she was comfortable if she was."

"I know that all of you like her. Just say it," Ronan teased.

"She makes you smile. That's all. You're always in a good mood when she's around and you may need it."

"Meaning?"

"You got a call from the officer you talked to."

"I'll call him back."

"Your coffee is on your desk."

"Thank you. Can we confirm that meeting for this morning?" She nodded and went to her desk.

Ronan sat down and took a gulp of his coffee. Just as he put it down, a text came in from Katie:

> *Thank you for walking me up to work. I'm thinking that we should definitely have a do-over from last night. I tried this morning. You're such a party pooper. I'll see you tonight handsome. Love you – K*

He smirked and replied:

> *And how do you know that isn't part of my plan for tonight love? We have the entire house to ourselves, no crazy people. The question is will it start in the living room, the kitchen counter or the stairs? See you tonight love. – R*

Ronan went through messages, returning them by email as much as he could, then got a pile of his emails done so he could relax a little. When his assistant came back in, she smirked. "What," Ronan asked.

"The 11am meeting was cancelled. You somehow resolved it with an email. The only meeting you have is at 2pm. Should be short. What did you want me to get you for lunch?"

"The stew. You know it's one of my favorites. And I think after that meeting, I'm gonna work from home. No need to be in the office until 6."

"Alright. Is there anything you need me to do?"

Ronan shook his head. "No, but thank you."

By the time that Ronan finished his meeting, he headed off and went to the house. He walked in, threw in laundry and cleaned up, seeing the fresh groceries put away by his housekeeper. He took something out for dinner and went upstairs to change out of his work clothes. He came downstairs in jeans and a tee and started a fire in the fireplace. When Katie got home, she walked in and saw him tending to the fire.

"What are you up to," Katie asked as she came in and locked the door behind her.

"Come and sit love."

Katie slid her heels off and walked over to the living room as he got up. "You really did all of this?"

Ronan nodded. "Thought you needed a little home-cooked dinner and some time to relax."

"You did hear that there's a meeting on Saturday right?" Ronan nodded.

"Not that I really want to spend another Saturday at a foundation event."

"It's a meeting only. Probably only an hour or two. We can go to the pub after."

"You sure that's what you want to do?"

Katie nodded. "I thought you'd like to see Kian and Mia."

"I do, but are you sure?"

Katie kissed him and slid into his arms. "I'm sure," Katie said. He kissed her and devoured her lips, sitting down on the sofa and pulling her legs around his hips, sliding her skirt up.

"Are you cooking?"

"It can wait."

"What were..."

He kissed her again. "What is it?"

"Fish and salad."

"Ronan." He kissed her then leaned her against the sofa, leaning into her arms.

"Don't..."

"It's waiting." He slid the dress up and off of her then kissed his way up her torso.

"Ronan."

"What?"

"Upstairs." He kissed her again and slid the dress to the floor.

"Here," he replied.

"Ronan."

He shook his head. "Upstairs." He got up, picked her up and flipped her over his shoulder and carried her up the steps to the bedroom then leaned her onto the bed.

"Better?"

She nodded and he slid the lace bra off, then went for the lacy panties. "You're overdressed," Katie said.

He kissed her and felt her go for the button of his jeans. "Don't start that love."

"Then take them off." He pulled his shirt off and kissed her.

"Off." He kissed her and felt his phone buzz in his pocket.

"Don't you even think it," Katie said. He slid his phone from his pocket and saw his assistant's name.

"Yes," Ronan said.

"There's a 10am meeting tomorrow. Just got added to the schedule."

"I'll be there," Ronan replied as he hung up. Just as he put the phone on the table, Katie undid his jeans. "Katie."

"No answering the phone when we're busy."

He kissed her and his hand slid to her warmth and started to tease. "Shit."

"Then stop going for what i know you are. You're mine lass. All mine."

"And?" He grabbed her hands and pinned them over her head with one hand.

"Ronan."

"Don't touch."

"Or what?"

"Don't make me get the handcuffs." She smirked and he shook his head, getting up.

"What," she asked. When she felt something cool wrap around her wrist and click, she shook her head.

"Ronan." One piece wrapped around a side of the bed and wrapped around her other wrist.

"You asked for it."

Ronan kissed her and kicked his jeans to the floor.

"Now, what was it that you wanted," he teased.

Katie shook her head. "You know what I want Ronan." He leaned up against her and pulled her legs around him.

"This," he teased as he kissed down her neck and kissed her shoulder. "Or this," he said as he kissed and nibbled and licked at each little peak of her breasts.

"Aah."

"Or maybe this," he asked as the kisses trailed down her torso to her hip, then down to the heat between her legs.

"Mm."

He licked and teased and nibbled until she was almost moaning. When he slid two fingers inside her, Katie's breath hitched. "So that's what you wanted."

"Almost," Katie said breathlessly.

"Tell me."

"Take the boxers off."

"And then what," he teased as he kept going.

"I want you inside me."

"Mm. You sure about that," he asked as he continued to lick and tease her as he kicked his boxers off.

"Aah. Yes."

"Katie."

"Yes."

"How turned on are you right now."

"Bad enough that I need you." He kissed his way back up to her hip, then to her breasts again until she moaned, then kissed back up to her lips and slid deep inside her.

"Shit."

"What," he asked.

"You feel so good."

"Now that you have me."

"Undo them."

He shook his head. "Nope."

"Ronan." He kissed her again and started slowly speeding up his pace until she was throbbing around him over and over again. Until he could feel her exploding around him, he took his time until her legs were almost shaking. Then he slowly sped up, going harder then faster. "Undo them." He grabbed the key and undid the handcuffs and kept going until she exploded around him again and he followed. "Shit," Katie said.

"What?"

"If that's what being home means, I may have missed being home," Katie joked.

He kissed her again. "Now to cook you dinner," he teased.

Chapter 6

They had dinner together then curled up on the sofa as Ronan pulled a blanket over them. "And how was dinner love?"

"Amazing. Thank you."

"You're most welcome. So, what did you want to do next," Ronan asked.

"That's kinda up to you. Pub?"

"If we go, skirt."

"And what we just did wasn't enough," she joked.

"Never."

"Do you want to?"

He kissed her. "Since the fire is almost out, it's kind of up to you, love." She kissed him and he deepened the kiss until they were making out on the sofa.

"Where's your phone?"

He slid it out of his back pocket. "See if they're over there. If they are we can go."

He kissed her and slid the phone to the table. "What?"

He devoured her lips and undid the belt of her satin robe. "Not down here."

"Why?"

"Because someone could see."

"Nobody can see in love."

"Not down..." He kissed her again and pulled the blanket up over them.

"Ronan."

"Yes or no?" She undid his jeans.

"That wasn't an answer."

"Take them off." He slid his boxers and jeans to the floor and pulled her legs around him.

"Katie." She looked up at him and kissed him as he sunk himself into her again.

"Mm."

"I guess we aren't making it to the pub," he joked. They curled up together and had sex on the sofa, determined to wipe away the bad memories of the past weekend. Even when they both climaxed, they still curled up together, watching the flames from the fire slowly burn out.

"You alright," Ronan asked.

Katie nodded and snuggled into his arms. "Ronan."

"Yes love."

"You didn't run for the shower."

"Because you're coming with me."

"Now?"

"Or did you want to soak in the tub?" She kissed him, devouring his lips and snuggling tighter to him. "Upstairs?"

Katie shook her head. "Fire isn't out." He kissed her. "It's almost done unless you want to stay down here for a while." Katie kissed him. He slid out of the blanket, pulled boxers on, and grabbed his jeans and shirt. "Where are you going?" He picked her up and carried her upstairs to the bedroom.

"Are you coming with me or no," he asked as he leaned her onto the bed.

She got up and followed him into the bathroom and he flipped the shower on. "This mean that you're hopping in with me?"

"Depends. Do I get to taunt you back?"

"No. Shower. Period." He kicked his boxers into the laundry and slid in, and Katie slid out of her satin robe and slid in with him.

"Do you want me to wash your back?"

He turned to face her. "Katie."

"What?"

"I know what you're thinking."

"Washing your back."

"And the hands aren't going to wander?"

"Never said that." He kissed her and finished washing up then stepped out of the shower. "Ronan."

"What," he asked.

"Where are you going?"

"Bed." Katie finished showering and slid out of the shower, drying off and wrapping herself up in her satin robe. Ronan slid his boxers on and slid into the bed.

"Phones?"

"On the charger," he teased.

"And what exactly are we doing in bed this early?"

"Watching a film. We can go to the pub tomorrow."

"Ronan." He motioned for her to come closer.

"Get in bed sexy. We're having an us night love." He flipped the tv on and found an old movie. Katie slid into the bed with him, curling up with him in the bed.

"So, now that you got what you wanted tonight, what else did you want," Ronan asked.

"Just you. Always you."

He kissed her. "Now you're just sucking up."

"You made me dinner Ronan. First, all of the crazy that we had up here, then downstairs with the fire. It's already been an insane night. I just wanted us."

"And you got what you wanted."

"More."

"Oh really," he teased.

"Definitely more." He kissed her and curled up with her as they watched the movie.

"So, you wanted to do this instead of going to the pub?"

"Like I said. I wanted a night with you away from the hotel and away from people. You needed a night to relax."

"So, this was all for me?"

He nodded and kissed her. "You kinda had a rough few days, love. It's called making you feel better."

He kissed her again and smirked. "Thank you."

He nodded. "Now watch the movie." They watched the movie and half-way through, he looked over and saw her asleep with her head on his chest. He kissed her head, flipped the TV off and checked his phone. He had a ton of work emails, but there were a few unexpected ones. Ones that Katie would be livid if she saw:

I'm in town. Do you want to meet up?

Lonely tonight if you want company. Meet me at the hotel.

Ronan deleted them and put his phone back on the charger. He snuggled into the bed with Katie and flipped the light off, nodding off not long later.

The next morning, Ronan was wide awake at 5am. He slid out of bed and slid into his workout gear. He grabbed his phone and AirPods and went down to the gym and got a workout in. Just as he was finishing, he looked up and saw Katie watching him. "You're awake."

"Rolled over and you were gone."

"I wasn't far away love."

"I was gonna make us breakfast."

"I can do it. Just give me a few minutes."

Katie walked over to him. "What?" She motioned for him to come closer. He pulled her onto his lap. She kissed him and he wrapped his arms around her. "And what would you like?"

"You." He shook his head. "Ten minutes."

She nodded and kissed him again. "Katie."

"I'll make coffee." He kissed her again and she got up and went back towards the door. He got back to finishing his workout and Katie smirked. She went and put the coffee on and came back up to see him finishing his workout.

"Good timing," Katie said. He got up and walked towards her, picking her up and sitting her on the counter.

"I know you're up to something. It's not even 7 yet."

"Taunting my man."

"I bet you are." She slid her legs around him, pulling him closer to her. "And what would you like love?" She kissed him and he deepened the kiss, picking her up and carrying her to the bedroom, leaning her onto the bed.

"Now, you were saying," Ronan teased as he slid his shirt off.

"I want you," Katie said.

"I bet you do love." She kissed him and he undid the satin robe. "Had to come down in this."

"You said no stealing your t-shirts." He shook his head and slid the robe to the floor. "Ronan." He kissed her, devouring her lips until he could feel her toes curling. "You're overdressed."

He kicked his joggers and boxers off and slid deep into her. "Aah."

"That what you wanted?"

Katie kissed him. "Always."

He slid in and out, harder then deeper then slowly speeding up his pace as she started moaning.

"Shit Katie."

"Mm." He kept going until he could feel her explode around him more than once.

"I can't," Katie said.

"Can't what love?"

"Mm."

"Can't what?"

"Aah." She crashed around him, and he kept going. When he finally found his release, she held on and wouldn't let him go. "Lass, what can't you do?"

"I can't keep doing that. Over and over again."

"Meaning what?"

"My legs are dead."

"Good. Means you won't be walking much," he teased.

He went to roll over and she didn't let go. "Katie."

"What?"

"This mean you're getting up with me?" She shook her head and kissed him.

"I don't want you getting up. It's not even 8 yet."

He kissed her. "Love, I have to get up." She shook her head. "Shower."

"Not yet."

He shook his head. "I love you, but we're getting up." He slid out of her arms and got up.

"What time is it?"

"Almost quarter to eight."

"Fine." He walked into the bathroom and turned the shower on, freshening up then sliding into the shower with Katie sliding in behind him.

"You can walk," he teased.

"Funny. Not for your lack of trying so I can't." He kissed her and slid her under the hot water. He washed her hair for her and Katie kissed his chest.

"Don't start."

"I'm not." He shook his head, and she rinsed her hair out, then slid the conditioner in while he washed his hair and rinsed off.

"What?"

"Nothing," Katie replied.

He kissed her. "Finish your shower. I'm going to towel off and get ready."

"Ronan." He kissed her again and stepped out. She finished her shower and saw the warm towel. She wrapped herself up in it and walked into the bedroom.

"What are you wearing to work," Katie asked as she walked into his closet. He was in his boxers and sliding on black pants.

"Are we matching today love?"

Katie walked to him and kissed him. "Maybe."

"Lass, you have to get ready."

"I know."

He shook his head. "Then stop looking at me like I'm sex on a stick."

"You are," she said.

He shook his head. "Go."

"Ronan."

"What love?"

"Black sweater dress or black skirt?"

"Don't tempt me."

"Sweater dress it is." He went and grabbed the little pink toy from his drawer and walked into her closet. "What," she asked.

"You want to tease me, then you're wearing this to work," he said as he handed it to her.

"Am I really teasing you?"

"You're wearing it." He flipped it on, kissed her, and slid it inside her.

"Ronan."

"What?"

"You know this is a lot more fun when we're in the same office."

"And it's even more fun when I make you squirm all day."

Once they both finished getting ready, they grabbed their things and headed out to the waiting SUV. "So, you aren't driving yourself into work anymore?"

"Just until things settle down," Ronan said as the driver headed off, making his way to Katie's work.

"We're going tonight, right?"

Ronan nodded. "I'm sure Kian and Mia will be happy to see you."

"And you'll be happy to hang out with them for the first time in a while."

Ronan nodded. She nudged him. "What?"

"You don't want to go?"

"Just don't want any drama this time."

"The drama is in jail. I don't see any other issues."

"Both of the drama causers are."

"Meaning what?"

"Someone smashed the door of the office yesterday."

"What?"

"They arrested her."

"Ronan, why didn't you tell me."

"Because it was handled."

"Did she take anything?"

Ronan shook his head. "Just caused stress. She smashed the glass, and the door and security handled her."

"Ronan." He shook his head. Katie slid her hand in his and he held on.

"We're almost there, sir," the driver said.

"Thank you. Do you want me to walk you in," Ronan asked.

Katie shook her head. "Are you alright?"

"I will be. They should have the new door and glass installed by the time I get there," Ronan replied.

When the car stopped, he slid out and helped Katie out. "Call me at lunch," she asked. He nodded and kissed her. He slid his hand in his pocket and buzzed the toy.

"Just making sure it's turned on," he teased. She shook her head with a smirk, kissed him and went into the office. Ronan slid back in, and they left for his office.

"Sir."

"I may work from home depending on meetings this afternoon. If I do, just make sure that you're here for Katie."

"Yes sir." They made their way to his office and when he arrived, he went straight in through the brand-new door.

"Sir, your messages," his assistant said as she handed them to him and followed him into his office.

"When are the meetings today?"

"Two this morning then the afternoon is free," she said.

"I may work from home this afternoon. Probably head out around 2."

"Yes sir," his assistant said as she headed out of his office. He slid his hand into his pocket, pulling his phone out and went into the app, running his finger over the screen to taunt her. A matter of minutes later, his phone buzzed with a text from Katie:

> *No teasing when I'm working.*

He ran his finger over the screen and sent a reply:

> *Just making sure it's working. Making sure I have your attention.*

He smirked and slid his phone to the desktop and went through the messages. When he finished them, his assistant knocked.

"Meeting in 5," she said.

"Thank you," Ronan said. He sent off an email or two and headed into the meeting. By the time it got to lunch, he was ravenous, and he could smell the Irish stew. He sat down and ate and sent a quick buzz via the toy to Katie. Within a matter of 10 minutes, he'd ramped the teasing up even more, knowing that it was only a matter of time before she called. When his phone buzzed, he smirked and answered with a grin ear to ear.

"And how is your lunch going," Ronan asked.

"You're doing that intentionally."

"Getting your attention is all love. Something wrong?"

"You mean since I almost jumped out of my chair?"

"Good. You're wearing the dress to the pub."

"Jeans."

"Skirt."

"Ronan."

"Skirt."

He laughed and finished his stew. "And what are you having for lunch," Katie asked.

"Irish Stew. The same stuff we had when you were here. What about you?"

"Soup. Something to keep me warm. Was there something that you weren't telling me this morning?"

"Katie."

"Tell me."

"It's nothing."

"Tell me Ronan."

"Just messages I didn't bother to read and just deleted."

"They're just coming for you," she teased.

"Nobody else that I want to be with love."

"Good comeback."

"I'm working from home this afternoon. When you're ready to head home, let me know. The driver will be waiting for you."

"Ronan, why don't you come?"

"Work."

"Party pooper."

"I'm gonna be getting the paperwork done so I can take my lass to the pub. You good with that or do you want..."

"I want you to come."

"Then I'll come and pick you up. On one condition."

"Which is what," Katie asked. He smirked and slid his AirPods in then went back to the screen that controlled the toy. "You're too quiet." He ran his finger over the screen. "Shit."

"Mine."

"At least warn me."

"Here's your warning," he said as he did it again and made her knees shake.

"Ronan."

"Yes love."

"Stop."

"But I'm not done playing yet."

"I bet you aren't, but I'm at work."

"At your desk?"

"Yes." He did it one more time and he could hear her breath hitch. "Please Ronan."

"When I get there, you'll know," he replied.

"I have a meeting before I leave."

"Then it'll be subtle."

"Then be prepared for what will happen."

"Pouncing on me," he joked.

"Yes."

"Good. See you tonight love." He ran his finger over the screen one last time and heard her say his name again. When he hung up, he smirked, and his assistant knocked.

"Sir," she said.

"What can I do for you," Ronan asked.

"You have one call meeting this afternoon at 2. Shouldn't take long. They have the paperwork. It's just going through the contract. Is there anything you need from me before you leave for the day?"

"Not a thing. Thank you for getting lunch."

"Welcome sir. I'll message you if anything else comes up for the afternoon."

"I'll keep an eye on the emails. Everything should be fine. I'm just working from home. Doesn't make sense for me to be here when there aren't any meetings." Ronan finished lunch, got his papers together and headed home.

Ronan got back to the house and the driver headed off. He walked in and saw the mail waiting. One look and he saw an envelope with his name on it and nothing else. He shook his head and opened it to see a note from his ex:

I know that you don't want her. You always were better off with me. Tell me when you want me to come back Ronan. I miss you. I need you. I miss us together. Call me.

Ronan shook his head and ripped the note up, shredding it and throwing it into the fireplace under the logs then went upstairs to change. He slid into jeans and a shirt and came downstairs, logging back into emails and getting some work done before she made her way back to the house. When his phone buzzed around 3, he looked at the screen and didn't recognize the number.

"Hello," Ronan said.

"Did you get my message?"

"The part where I said that I have the woman I want and to back off meant nothing did it? Second, what's with the burner number?"

"You blocked me. What did you expect me to do?"

"Back off and leave me and my girl alone. You start this, you do realize that I know people on the police."

"And I know that you can do a heck of a lot better than what that girl is. She's a nobody Ronan."

"Enough. You don't get to insult her. Not after everything that you did. I'd rather be with her than anywhere near you. Get it through your head. We're over." He hung up and took a deep breath, grabbing himself a drink.

He came and sat back down, going through emails, then blocked the phone number she'd called from and tried to take a breather. Just as he leaned back, his phone buzzed with a text from Katie:

> *Finished the meeting early. How's working from home?*

He went into the app that controlled the toy and buzzed it. He made it even more intense and his phone rang.

"And how was work," he asked.

"Are you just gonna tease me all afternoon or are you coming to meet me?"

"I'm on my way. Do you want me to come up or just tease you when I arrive?"

"Finger off the phone Ronan."

"And here I thought you were wearing that toy for fun."

"For you."

"I'll be there soon." They hung up and the driver took Ronan down to Katie's work. He walked in and went up to her desk and slid his hand in his pocket, teasing her again. She looked up and saw Ronan.

"Good timing," Katie said.

"Are you ready?" She nodded and he ran his finger over the screen again. She looked up at him and shook her head. "Kinda fun."

"Cut it out." She walked down to the SUV with him and slid in beside him as his finger slid over the phone screen again. "You are so bad right now."

"I like my toy," he teased.

"I'm sure you do." When he did it again, her hand clamped down on his leg.

"What," he teased.

"Don't."

"And if I said that I was gonna make it worse?" She shook her head and grabbed his hand.

"When we get home."

He nuzzled her neck. "And if I said I wasn't waiting," he whispered as she broke out in goosebumps.

"Ronan." They pulled up to the house and he helped her out, thanked the driver, and walked her inside.

"I swear, you touch your phone, I'm seriously going…" His finger ran over the screen, and she turned to face him. "Ronan."

He kissed her and pinned her against the back of the front door.

"Mm."

"Tell me what you want."

"Upstairs."

He picked her up, slid her dress up her legs and carried her to the bed. He slid the dress off when they made it to the bedroom and threw it to the floor. "What," Katie asked.

"That little toy. I have…"

She kissed him. "Toy out."

"Nope."

"Ronan, I want you. Take it out."

"Not yet," he said as he slid his phone from his pocket and started teasing her again. "Aah."

"Much better," he teased as the toy amped up teasing her.

"Ronan, I want you."

"I'm not done playing yet," he teased.

"Yeah, you are." He shook his head and ran his finger over the screen again. "Shit Ronan."

"Mine."

"Then take it out and come here."

"And if I say that I'm taunting you until you start begging?"

"Then I'm taking it out and taking your phone away."

213

He slid his phone to the charger, and she went to remove the toy when he shook his head.

"Leave it."

"Ronan."

"You don't get to touch it remember? Remember what happened last time you did that?"

"Then take it out and come here." He kissed her, devouring her lips as she felt the toy slide out of her. "About time," Katie said as she went to peel his jeans off.

"Katie."

"No more teasing."

He peeled her lace panties off, then the lace bra as he kissed down her neck then nibbled and licked each breast until she was moaning. "Mine," he teased.

"Ronan." He peeled his shirt off and leaned into her arms, licking and kissing his way down her torso until he was at the warmth between her legs.

"Take the jeans off."

"No."

"Ronan."

"I'm teasing you until you beg."

"Shit." He licked then nibbled then felt her legs twitch.

"Please." He slid his jeans and boxers off and kept teasing, sliding his tongue inside her as her breath hitched.

"Ronan."

"Mm," he said.

"Please."

He kissed and licked and teased until her toes were curling. "Please what," he asked.

"I need you inside me."

"Which part?"

"Ronan." He kissed back up her torso and pulled her legs around his sides, sliding deep into her.

"That what you wanted," he asked.

"Mm."

"Is that a yes lass," he asked.

"Aah," she said.

He kissed her, devouring her lips and slid into her again, going slowly intentionally.

"Ronan, you're teasing."

"Intentionally."

"Mm."

"More," he asked.

"No more teasing."

"Harder?" She nodded and he did just that. Harder then faster until she was exploding around him over and over again.

"Tell me what you want," he said as he flipped her to her stomach and pinned her hands to the bed.

"Harder." He went harder and couldn't hold himself back from exploding into her.

"Shit," he said.

"Aah."

"I'm not done with you," he said.

"I can't even move," Katie said.

He smirked. "And you won't be at the pub either."

"Ronan." He slid to his side and kissed her shoulder.

"What love?"

"You're intentionally killing my legs."

"You wanted to go to the pub. We aren't that far away."

"I gather you're carrying me there," she teased. He kissed her.

"Depends. We could just go tomorrow."

"Or we can go tonight like we planned. Mia said they're saving us a table."

"Then you should probably get up." He got up, kissed her, and walked into the bathroom, cleaning up.

When Katie got up, she walked in behind him and slid her arms around him. "Yes love."

"Are you carrying me?"

"Nope." He turned and kissed her, slid her face into his hands and cradled it then kissed her again.

"What," she asked.

"Nothing. We're leaving in 20."

"And?"

"If I said I wanted it back in?"

Katie shook her head. "No. Not after what you did."

He smirked. "What did I do lass?"

"Teased until my knees were twitching."

"I thought that was what we just did."

"Legs shaking. Different thing."

"Gotcha."

"You still want me..."

"Yes."

"Answer is no. I can barely walk as it is," Katie said.

"Such a party pooper," Ronan joked as he kissed her again.

"I'm the party pooper? Really," Katie said as she walked over to her closet.

"Skirt."

She looked at him. "Why," Katie asked.

"Do you really want to ask that question?"

"Ronan."

"Wear the skirt."

He got dressed and walked downstairs. When Katie came down a little while later in her skirt and a sweater, he smirked.

"What's the smile for," Katie asked.

"Nice skirt."

"I was tempted to put on jeans."

He kissed her. "Good choice."

"Are you ready to leave?" Katie nodded and kissed him again. She slid her boots on and walked down to the pub hand in hand with Ronan.

"You good," Ronan teased.

"You mean can I walk? Hard to do," Katie teased.

He kissed her hand. "Seems to me that you're fine."

They got to the door of the pub, and he smirked and pulled her into his arms. "What," Katie asked.

He kissed her. "You ready to head in?" Katie nodded with a smirk ear to ear.

They walked in and Pat smirked. "Pint and one of those fancy drinks," he asked.

"Please," Ronan said.

"Oh really," Katie asked.

"Yes love. No work tomorrow." Ronan saw Mia and Kian and went and grabbed a seat with them.

"I was wondering when you two were gonna show," Mia said.

"We got here as fast as we could. I mean really," Ronan said.

"Considering that you disappeared last week you mean," Mia said.

"Blame that on you know who," Ronan said.

"She still after you," Kian asked.

"Understatement. She went and got a burner phone."

Kian shook his head. "Go figure," Kian replied as Katie looked at Ronan. "I got her to back off, but she's insane," Ronan said as he slid his arm around Katie.

"You didn't tell me," Katie said.

He kissed her. "Nothing to worry about love."

"I thought you were blocking her," Mia said.

"I did. She left a note in the mailbox and then called with that scam phone number." Katie looked at him.

"At least we're somewhere she can't be," Kian said as the boys clinked glasses.

"Do you want anything for dinner," Ronan asked.

"Please," Katie replied as Ronan kissed her and got something ordered from Pat.

When Ronan came and sat back down, Katie shook her head. "What?"

"Nothin," Katie said. He kissed her and Mia smirked.

"You two are just too cute. You realize that right," Mia asked.

"Well gee, thanks," Katie teased.

"I guess you two are doing okay after all of that hideout at the hotel stuff," Kian said.

"Considering how worried we both were, we kinda figured it was a good idea," Ronan said.

"Was it really that bad," Kian asked.

"Worse," Katie said.

"I saw cars parked outside your place all day and night. I was wondering what was going on," Mia said.

"Making sure he didn't try to break in. That's how they actually caught him."

The food came a little while later and they all ate. "And what else is going on tonight," Mia asked.

"Meaning what," Ronan asked.

"Meaning are you two sneaking out or staying around for a while," Kian said.

"Staying for a bit. Having a pint or two with you two then heading home," Ronan said.

"Or we could just hang out a while since we haven't been here in a while," Katie said.

Ronan nodded as his hand slid to her leg. "Up to you, love."

She looked at Ronan and smirked. He shook his head. They finished eating and Ronan got everyone another round. When Katie got up, he shook his head.

"What," Katie asked as she slid up behind him at the bar.

"I give you 5 minutes then you're mine."

"Here?"

He looked at her. "Okay then." He took the drinks to the table and Kian shook his head.

"What," Ronan asked.

"You and that girl of yours." His phone buzzed:

You coming?

Ronan got up and walked back to the bathrooms, walking into the ladies and locking the door behind him. "What," Katie asked.

"Were you planning on teasing me or letting me get my way tonight," he asked. Katie kissed him and he picked her up and sat her on the bathroom counter.

"I'm getting my way," she said as she went for the button of his jeans.

"Katie."

"What?"

"Don't start that." She slid off the counter and went to her knees, sliding his boxers down and taking his length into her mouth. "Aah."

She took him deeper into her mouth and he shook his head. "Determined to do the exact opposite of what I want," he said. Katie kept going and his eyes closed as he almost moaned.

"I don't see you complaining," she said as he pulled her to her feet as her hand slid up and down his length. He turned her towards the counter and bent her over it, pulling her lace panties off and pulling her hand away. "Ronan." He slid deep into her as her breath hitched. "Shit."

He kept going, hard and fast and deep until she was exploding around him over and over again. "Aah."

"Mine," Ronan said as he leaned up against her.

"Stop," Katie said. He did and she turned to face him and kissed him. He picked her up and sat her on the counter and slid deep into her again. He kept going until he couldn't hold himself back anymore and exploded into her. She kissed him and he deepened the kiss until he felt her heart calm.

"Determined," Katie said.

Ronan nodded. "Now we can go home and rest," Ronan said.

"I thought we were finishing our drinks and staying." He zipped and buttoned his jeans and kissed her, sliding her panties into his pocket. "Ronan."

"You're not getting them back lass. I'll meet you out there."

"You're not funny." He smirked and unlocked the door, heading back to the table. Katie shook her head, cleaned up a little and walked back to the table. Ronan let her into the booth, and she smirked as he slid in beside her.

"So, does this mean that you're coming for Sunday," Kian asked. Ronan nodded and slid his arm around Katie.

"This one will just steal another shirt," Ronan teased.

"You did get me one of my own," Katie said. He kissed her.

"And let's hope you wear it," Ronan joked. When her hand slid to his leg, he shook his head. He finished his pint as she was finishing her drink.

"I'm exhausted," Katie said.

"I guess that means we're heading home. You two good," Ronan asked.

"I know how you tired that one out," Kian teased.

"Just a long day at work," Katie said.

"Then I guess we'll see you two Sunday," Mia said.

Katie and Ronan got up, Ronan paid for the drinks and the food for the table, and they headed home. This time there was no fighting, no drama. No exes following them. They headed back to the house, went inside, locked up and Katie kissed him.

"What?"

"I can't believe you wouldn't give them back."

"I have plans."

"Like pinning me to the counter?" He nodded as he walked towards her. "Don't start," Katie said.

"Don't start what?"

She kicked her boots off and backed up to the steps. "You know what." He picked her up and wrapped her legs around him, kissed her and carried her upstairs to the bedroom, pinning her onto the bed.

"You were saying."

"You did enough," she teased. He undid her skirt. "Ronan."

He kissed her, devouring her lips and slid the skirt to the floor. He peeled her shirt off and Katie shook her head.

"Determined," she teased.

"I want you."

"You have me," Katie said. He kissed her, devouring her lips until she felt his hands on her, pulling her tighter to him. "Ronan."

"What love," he asked as he worked his way down her torso.

"You're overdressed."

He peeled his shirt off and Katie kissed him, pulling her legs tight around him. "Still overdressed," Katie teased. He kicked his jeans off along with his socks and boxers and his hand slid between her legs, teasing her. "Shit."

"See, I could've taken my time with this and teased you until your legs forgot how to walk, but you wanted to rush me out of my jeans," he said as his fingers teased and probed her.

"Ronan, stop." He kept going then devoured her lips.

"Aah." She moaned into his mouth, and he slid deep into her.

"This what you wanted?"

"Mm."

"That a yes?"

Katie moaned. "Aah, Ronan yes."

He pounded into her over and over again, making her body throb around him. "Shit."

"That good," Ronan teased. She kissed him and he kept going until she was throbbing around him all over again.

"Mine," he said as he exploded into her and her body clamped around him.

"Yours," Katie said in reply. He kissed her, devouring her lips.

"Don't get up."

"Katie."

"Just stay right here for a minute."

"Why's that love?"

He rolled to his side, and she curled her leg around his.

"Because you're mine too."

He kissed her. "I'm gonna get up and get us a drink."

"Don't you think we drank enough tonight?" He kissed the tip of her nose.

"Bottled water." He kissed her again then got up, pulled on boxers and cleaned up then went down and grabbed them each a bottle of water, guzzling his down on the way upstairs.

He handed Katie the water and sat down on the bed beside her. "Thirsty?"

"After those drinks you need water."

"You mean the ones that you got me so I'd be tipsy and unable to say that we weren't doing the sex in the pub bathroom thing."

"You seem to have enjoyed it," he teased.

"True. Especially the part where your breath hitched when I got you back for teasing."

He shook his head. "About that."

"What?"

He kissed her and leaned into her arms. "Bad girl," he replied.

"So bad you want me to do it again?"

"Bad." He kissed her again and her legs slid around him.

"Didn't like it," Katie asked.

"Oh, I did love. Just bad girl. How did I ever find a lass like you."

"Just don't be surprised if you wake up and I'm doing it again."

"Then you'll be waking up early. I'm working out in the morning."

"Good thing it's not a public gym then."

"Katie, what has got into you?"

"You and all your teasing. Only fair that I get to tease you back once in a while."

"And what else were you scheming to do in that sexy head of yours?"

She kissed him. "So many things," she teased as she smirked.

"You're getting sleep. If you're awake before I go down to do my workout..."

"I'm not letting you get up."

"Good luck trying lass."

He kissed her then leaned onto his side. "And if I get up before you?"

"Then I come downstairs while you're doing your workout and distract you."

"Oh really," he teased.

She slid into his arms. "Yeah, really," Katie replied.

"And you're gonna just do whatever you want to do are you," he teased. Katie nodded. "You mean since I'm always done my workout before you wake up."

"Never know Ronan. I can surprise you." He smirked and kissed her.

"I think starting of with you getting a little sleep would be good. You and all those..."

She kissed him. "Determination. It's a little payback for you teasing me."

"Now when you say teasing, do you mean this," he asked as his hand slid between her legs and started to tease.

"Ronan."

He kissed her. "That what you were talking about?"

"Aah."

"Lass."

"Ronan."

"Want me to stop?"

"Ronan."

His fingers slid deep inside her. "Shit."

"This what you're thinking that you can get back at me for?"

"Mm."

"Lass, you have no idea what else I can do."

"Ronan, stop." He kept going, probing his fingers into her until he could feel her throbbing again.

"Shit."

"And here you thought you could get back at me," he teased.

"Please." He smirked and kissed her as her body exploded around his fingers.

"Ronan."

"Mm," he teased. He almost purred into her ear.

"Ronan, you win."

"It's not a matter of win or lose love. It's me taunting and teasing until you're spent."

"Then you succeeded. I can barely even move," Katie said.

"Good. You'll be tired tomorrow."

"And what makes you think that I won't wake you up?"

He kissed her. "You do, then I'm yours."

She kissed him. "Then you're staying in bed tomorrow morning."

"And how exactly do you plan on making that happen?"

She kissed him. "You want to tie my hands, then I can tie yours."

"If you wake up before I do."

"Or I could just start now," Katie said.

He shook his head. "I need sleep and so do you love." He put the phones on the charger and finished his bottle of water.

"And if I said it was my turn to tease you?"

He kissed her. "Sleep. If you get up before me, I'm at your mercy love."

"And that idea of me sneaking down to the gym and getting you naked?"

"As in me letting you get your control?" She nodded. "Depends on how early you wake up." She smirked and slid over into his lap. "Katie."

"What," she asked as her hands slid to the waistline of his boxers.

"You're not teasing tonight love."

"And if I said I was?"

"Tired. Sleep love." She kissed him and he rolled her onto her back and devoured her lips.

"You aren't tired yet?"

"You aren't."

He kissed her. "I'm more than tired love." He kissed her again and leaned onto his back.

"Sleep love." She kissed his shoulder and curled up in his arms.

"Still say I'm waking you up with my mouth on you."

"If that's what you want to do love." He kissed her forehead and flipped the light off.

"Sweet dreams love."

"I love you too."

Chapter 7

The next morning, Ronan woke up and his hand was tied to the bed. He smirked, undid the knot and gently got up, pulling on joggers and his sneakers, grabbed his AirPods and phone and went down to the gym and did his workout. He finished, went and made coffee and took a cup upstairs to Katie. He put it on the bedside table, and she woke up.

"How did you undo it?"

"Single knot. Wasn't that hard love. I'm going to put breakfast on."

"Come here."

He shook his head and kissed her. "Food will be ready in 20." He kissed her and walked downstairs. When she made it into the kitchen, she walked over to him and kissed his back.

"And what are you doing?"

"Starting something." He flipped the omelet and turned to face her.

"Katie, you aren't starting anything."

"Oh really." He kissed her, picked her up and wrapped her legs around him, sitting her on the kitchen counter.

"And what were you about to start?" Her hands slid to the waist of his joggers.

"Nothing," she said. He took the omelet off the element and plated it. He kissed her and moved out of the way, taking the plates to the table.

"Come here."

"Food's getting cold."

"Come here." He walked over to her, kissing her as her legs wrapped back around his legs.

"What," he asked. Her hand slid down the front of his joggers.

"Katie, eat."

"I will."

"Lass, it's getting cold."

"Why are you so determined to not let me have my way?"

"You wanted me to stay in bed. I got up. You wanted to take advantage while I was in the gym, and you slept through it. Not my fault love." He felt her hand move to the waistline of his boxers.

"And?"

"You can wait until we eat." When he felt her hand slide under his boxers, he stopped her. "Food." He took her off the counter, sat her in the chair and went and got them each a mug of coffee. He refilled her mug and got one for himself, putting them down on the table.

She stared him up and down like it was him on the table. "Stop."

"I don't get it. We could've had fun with all of that this morning, and you just walked away."

"I went and did my workout. That's all love. You were fast asleep."

"Instead of us having fun and just letting me have my way."

"After breakfast."

"Meaning what?"

"It's Saturday. After breakfast we can do whatever you want to."

"Is that a promise," Katie asked.

"Eat." They had their fruit and eggs, and he got up and cleaned up.

"Ronan."

"Yes love."

"Come upstairs." He put the dishes in the washer and walked over to Katie.

"And what might you want," he asked.

"I'll give you a hint."

He kissed her and picked her up, wrapping her legs around him and walked upstairs. "Now what was that hint," he teased as he leaned her onto the bed and peeled her shirt off.

"Come here." He kissed her and pinned her onto the bed.

"What do you want love?"

"You naked." He slid his shirt off and kicked his joggers off.

"Sorta have other plans," he teased.

"Ronan." He kissed her and she felt something wrap around her wrists.

"Yes love."

"What are you doing?"

"Making sure that I make every inch of you crave me."

"Shit."

"Now, what were you saying that you wanted to do," he asked.

"Taste you."

"Really. Interesting since you're at my mercy right now."

"Then untie my hands."

He shook his head. "Mine." He kissed down her neck then down to the little peaks of her breasts and nibbled and licked until her breath hitched.

"Ronan." He kissed down her torso to her hip and nibbled at it.

"Aah."

"Good."

"Good what," she said breathless.

"All mine." He kept going then slid to the heat between her legs and licked and teased and probed her with his lips and tongue.

"Shit Ronan."

"What love?"

"I was supposed to be teasing you."

"Got to you first," he said.

"And what are you gonna do with me," Katie asked as his fingers slid deep inside her.

"Take full advantage of you and make your legs shake until you can't walk."

"It was supposed to be my turn to make you shake."

"Mine." He kept going until he could feel her legs shaking.

"Tell me what you want love."

"I want you in my mouth until you explode. I want my hands free." He slid deep into her and her breath hitched again.

"What," he asked as he leaned in and devoured her lips.

"Shit."

"Mm," he replied. He went harder then deeper. Faster and faster until she was crashing around him over and over again.

"Shit Ronan."

"Much better." He kept going until he couldn't hold himself back and exploded into her.

"Shit," she said.

"What?"

"Hands."

"Oh, I'm nowhere near done with you," he teased.

"Meaning what," she asked. He kissed her again and devoured her lips.

"Untie my hands." He shook his head. "You can't leave me like this." He undid one hand. The minute he did, her arm wrapped around his neck.

"Katie."

"What?"

He slid his arm around her.

"Untie the other hand."

"Depends on what you're doing with it." He untied it and kissed her then got up.

"Stay in bed with me."

"I need a shower love. Workout plus you and I'm a mess." He kissed her again and got up, walking into the bathroom. Katie got up and walked in behind him. "I know what you're up to lass."

"And?"

"Be careful. You could end up tied up in bed again."

"Or I get you back for last night." He turned the shower on and stepped in, intentionally closing the door behind him. He washed his hair and was rinsing it when he felt hands on him.

"Katie."

"Mm." She took him deep into her mouth and didn't let up.

"Shit Katie." She took him deeper then slid her mouth up and down his length. "Mm."

"Stop love."

"Mm."

"Aah."

"Mine," she said as her hands took over. He pulled her to her feet, and he leaned her face first onto the wall of the shower and slid deep into her.

"Shit Ronan."

"Don't start something you can't finish." He pounded into her over and over until her body crumbled around him and he couldn't hold himself back. He exploded into her, and Katie got a smirk ear to ear.

"Happy now," he teased.

"Nope."

"Then you can take full advantage when we're in bed tonight."

"You started it." He turned her to face him and devoured her lips, pinning her hands against the shower wall.

"You do realize who you're teasing right? The one that can make your legs shake so you can barely walk."

"And I know that I get to have my way today." He shook his head and kissed her.

"Shower. That's it. No more teasing." He washed up and stepped out, wrapping a warm towel around his hips.

"Ronan."

"Yes love."

"Get in bed."

"We have to go to the market. We're going out."

"You sure you want to do that after that challenge?"

"Out." He freshened up and she finished her shower. By the time she stepped out and wrapped herself up in the warm towel, he was in his closet in jeans and boxers.

"Ronan."

"We're going out love."

"And if I said I wanted you in bed?"

"I'd say that you should probably get dressed."

"Can't talk you into bed?"

He shook his head. "We need food love. Market then I'm all yours."

"Why don't we just order it then?"

"Put some clothes on love. You'll be cold."

"And if I said that I didn't want to?" He walked over to her, backing her up against the wall.

"Clothes or I tie you to the bed until I come home."

"You wouldn't."

"Want to test that theory?"

He kissed her and she looked up at him. "Fine, I'll get dressed, but as soon as we're done, you're mine."

"Always have been," he replied. She shook her head and after one kiss, she went and got dressed. He put on her favorite cologne and pulled on the one sweater she always tried to steal.

"Can I borrow that..."

"What," he asked.

"Fine. I'll wear my own."

"You want it, you have to get it off of me."

"I'll wear mine." She walked back into her closet and slid into her sweater. When she turned around, he wrapped his arms around her.

"You ready love?" She nodded and kissed him.

They made their way down to the market and got what they needed, with Katie determined to make Ronan dinner that night. He paid for the food then teased. "Do you want to get lunch at the pub," Ronan asked. Katie looked at him.

"Bed."

He smirked. "We could stop in for a pint."

She shook her head with a smirk. "Don't you start that Ronan."

"One pint?"

"No."

"There's a rugby game on."

"Ronan, I swear, you start that..." He kissed her and took her hand walking her back out of the market.

"We're going home. Still say one pint won't hurt."

"You're seriously doing this now," Katie asked.

"Nope. Just saying. We can put this stuff away then go to the pub for a pint."

"Or we can do what you promised."

"Pub it is," he teased as Katie shook her head and hit his backside with the edge of the market bag.

"We're going home." They got back to the house and headed inside, putting everything away. "Ready for the pub lass?"

She looked at him. "You were joking."

"Didn't say I was joking. I'll message Kian and see if they're over there."

"Ronan."

"Ready?" She walked over to him, and he pulled her into his arms and kissed her.

"You're joking right?"

"Jeans. Pub. Works for me."

"Bed."

"Pub."

"Bed Ronan." He kissed her again and picked her up, sitting her on the kitchen counter.

He devoured her lips, and her legs wrapped around his hips. He undid her sweater and saw the black lace bra. "I like the lace," he teased.

"This mean no pub?"

He kissed her again. "You wanted the bed and not the pub remember? I mean, we can still go over there if you want to." Katie took the sweater off.

"Keep going," Katie said. He looked at her and undid her jeans, sliding them off. He saw the lacy thong. The one that made her look like sex on a stick.

"Lass." She kissed him and undid his sweater.

"What?"

"We can have a pint here."

"Or we go upstairs." He shook his head and went to peel the lacy thong off when she undid the button of his jeans.

"What are you starting lass?"

"What I said I was going to when we were at the market. No pub."

"You can't handle what you're starting."

"You can't," she replied. He slid his hands around her wrists.

"Ronan."

"What?"

"Let go."

He kissed her. "You're not getting your way love." She went to pull away from him and he pulled her legs around him, releasing her hands.

"What?" He undid his jeans and slid his boxers down.

"Ronan."

"What?"

"Here?"

He kissed her and slid deep into her. "Here."

"Mm." He slid his hands to her wrists and pinned her to the counter, sliding deep and hard into her over and over again until she was moaning and fighting to get her hands free.

"Let go."

"Not on your damn life." He kept going until she was exploding around him for the third time.

"Aah."

"Mine," he said as she nodded. He devoured her lips, letting go of her hands and crashed into her, exploding into her until he was spent.

"Shit," Katie said.

"Had enough," he teased. Katie nodded and wrapped her arms around him.

"Bed?" Katie nodded a second time and he grabbed her clothes, handed them to her and carried her upstairs to the bed, leaning onto it and right into her arms.

"You are so bad," Katie said.

"I know. Another thing you love about me," he said.

"Ronan."

He kissed her, devouring her lips and holding her face in his hands. "And you think that's why I love you?"

"Part of it," he teased. She shook her head, and his hands slid down her body, pulling her legs tight around his hips.

"Then what is it love?"

"You and everything else."

"Meaning," he asked.

"The sex, the man who fought for me, the one that protected me from everything. All of it," she said.

"And?"

"The one that makes me laugh at myself, the one that laughs with me and knows what I need without even asking."

"Katie, it's called loving every inch of you and your heart and soul."

"You mean that?" Ronan nodded and kissed her.

"I have no idea why it took me so damn long to find you, but I'm glad I did."

"And?"

"And what?"

"No more temptations for one- night stands?"

"I'm not losing you because I want to go and sleep around. I don't really want to. You're more than enough love."

"And you're sure that you don't want more than just me."

He looked at her and shook his head. "Did you really think that I'd walk out one night and have another one-night stand?"

"Part of me wonders if you're tempted to."

"Is that why you're so determined to tire me out today?"

"Ronan."

"You think that I'm insatiable?"

"I think that maybe I'm not..."

He kissed her. "What," he asked.

"Not enough." He shook his head and got up, walking into the bathroom and cleaning up. He kicked his clothes off and slid into the shower alone. When he came out, he went and slid fresh boxers on and a pair of his jeans.

"Where are you going?"

"You're that damn convinced that you aren't enough?"

"Ronan."

"Then I'm going to the pub. You want to come then come."

"Ronan, I'm saying that I'm scared that I'm not."

"What kind of craziness is this Katie? You think that I'm gonna take off with someone else? Is that what you want?"

"Ronan, I can't lose you. I don't want to."

"We're going out."

"Ronan."

"Or I'll go."

Katie looked at him. "Are you sure that I'm enough for you?"

"And everything yesterday and today. That doesn't tell you enough?"

"No."

"Then what will," he asked.

"I need to know. I need to know that you aren't gonna just replace me with another fling. That I'm not gonna end up losing this."

"Tell me what you want me to do Katie."

"I just need to know that when you get sick of me being here that you aren't gonna walk out and end up in another one-night stand with someone else."

"And what I'm saying isn't enough?"

She looked at him. "Get dressed."

"Ronan."

"I'm going to the pub with or without you Katie."

She shook her head and got up, walking into her closet, sliding into jeans and a sweater. When she came back into the bedroom, he wasn't there. She walked downstairs and saw him standing in the hallway. "Ronan."

"That what you want? Me to go out and cheat?"

"I'm worried that I'm not enough Ronan. That you will regardless of me. I'm worried about it every damn time I don't see you."

He shook his head and opened the door. She slid her phone in her purse, slid her purse over her shoulder and walked down to the pub with him in complete silence.

"Ronan, say something."

"Katie, just walk."

She grabbed his hand and stopped him before they walked in, pulling him back to her. "Am I not allowed to be scared that I'm not enough?"

"Is that why you're so damn determined to..."

She went on her tiptoes and kissed him. "I don't want you to think I'm not enough. I don't want to wake up someday and have you walking in the door from a hotel. That's why."

"And that's what you think is gonna happen?"

"Ronan, I just want to know that I'm enough."

"You're the one that dared me to date you. You told me to try. I am and you can't get over what happened before we got together. When we were in the hotel, I could've done anything and you never would've known but I didn't. I walked up to our suite. Isn't that enough?"

"Am I enough?" He went to pull away, but she pulled him back. "Just answer that Ronan. Are you and I enough?"

"If you even have to question that we are, then I'm not enough for you Katie." He pulled away and walked into the pub, ordering a pint.

Katie walked in a few moments later and came and sat down with Ronan. "Do you want a drink?"

"I want to talk." When Pat came over with an espresso martini for Katie, she smirked.

"Thank you."

"Most welcome lass. Let me know if you need anything else." She looked over at Ronan and he was on his phone. She slid it out of his hand and put it down.

"What?"

"Talk Ronan."

"What do you want me to say?"

"Is this enough for you?"

"Katie, if you don't want this then you can move back to your place. You realize that right?"

"I want to be with you. Are we enough?" His phone buzzed and he picked it up and typed in a response.

"Ronan."

"Kian and Mia are on the way here."

"Then answer me."

"If you don't think we are, then we aren't."

"Ronan."

"I'm not gonna sit here and try and convince you that we're enough when you're damn well questioning it."

"Are you still tempted to go back to what you used to do?"

"Does it even matter? If I was, I already would've gone and done it Katie. Every damn night we're together. We talk during the day. What time is in there that I would've been able to run out and randomly met someone? None. That's what. If you don't think that's enough, that's on you, love. Just tell me now if you're staying or going." She looked at him and her eyes were welling up.

"I'm not leaving."

"Then I'll sleep on the bed in the guest room."

"Ronan." He looked at her and she saw the look in his eye. The one that said she'd just screwed up the one good thing in his life.

"That's not what I meant."

"And? Doesn't change that I'm not enough for you Katie."

"You are."

"Then why are you screwing this relationship up and saying that you're worried I'm gonna cheat on you?"

"Because I need to know that I am. That I'm more than enough for you. That you want to be with me."

"And yesterday and today wasn't enough to show you that?"

"No."

"Then I don't know how the hell you expect me to fix it."

Just as he took the last gulp of his pint, Kian and Mia showed. Ronan got up to get a refill and Katie brushed the tears away and tried to breathe.

"Alright. What did he do," Mia said as she sat down opposite her and saw the look on Katie's face.

"Nothing. Just talking." Kian got drinks for himself and Mia and walked over to the table. Ronan sat down beside Katie.

"What are you two doing here in the middle of the afternoon," Kian asked.

"Just wanted a change of scenery," Ronan said as Katie's hand slid to his leg. He moved it. They all chatted and when Katie slid closer to him, he moved away from her. Katie got her phone out and texted him:

Meet me in the ladies.

She slid out of the booth and walked back there. She walked in and tried to get her composure back. When 10 minutes past and he hadn't come in, she shook her head. She walked back to the table and saw Ronan in a fight with Mia.

"Couldn't just leave it alone and keep your nose out of my business," Ronan said.

Katie sat back down beside him, and Pat brought her another drink. "Thank you," Katie said as Pat nodded.

"You alright," Mia asked. Katie nodded and slid closer to Ronan. He got up and went outside, closely followed by Kian.

"What in the hell," Kian asked.

"Just leave it alone," Ronan said.

"She sits close to you and you get up and leave the dang room. It couldn't have been that bad," Kian said.

"It's fine. It's a spat. Even you and Miss high and mighty in there have them."

"Ronan, what happened?"

"She thinks I'm gonna cheat."

"Then tell her you won't. It's not that damn hard."

"What I said to her wasn't enough. I told her that I loved her and she's still convinced."

"Ronan."

"Just leave it alone," Ronan replied.

"Then tell her that she's all you want."

"Already did. That wasn't enough either."

Kian looked at him. "Then convince her."

"Kian, I appreciate you trying, but leave it alone."

"You do realize Mia is like a dog with a bone when it comes to Katie right?"

"Then you two stay with her. I'm going back to the house."

"Ronan." He shook his head and walked in, paying for the drinks. "Everything good," Pat asked.

"Just put whatever she has on my tab." Pat nodded and Ronan walked out.

He got out the door when he felt Katie's hand on his. "Where are you going?"

"Home." He brushed her off and walked back to the house with her two steps behind him.

"Ronan."

"Katie, go back and hang out with them. I need breathing room."

"No."

"Katie."

"Did you not even get my text?"

"I got it. It's not happening." Ronan walked into the house and Katie followed, closing and locking the door behind her.

"Talk," Katie asked.

"About what? That you think I'm gonna cheat on you? The only damn person I've let in my life in years and you're seriously gonna ask me if I'm tempted to walk out on you? Is that what you're seriously asking?"

"I need to know that I'm gonna be enough. For me. I need to know that you're not gonna change your mind."

"And what the hell in the past 3 days has made you think that I would Katie? The marathon sex? The sex three times in one morning? Telling you I love you? What? Enlighten me."

Katie looked at him with tears in her eyes. "I need you to tell me that I'm enough for you. That you don't want someone else."

"If I haven't shown you that in the amount of time we've been together then I don't know what else I can do Katie." He walked into the kitchen and poured himself a drink of Jameson's.

"Ronan." He finished the drink and looked at her with tears streaming down her face.

"What?"

"Tell me that I'm enough for you."

"Why?"

"Because I need to know that I'm gonna be enough 3 years from now. 5 years from now. Ten."

"You're the only lass who's been this damn close in 5 years Katie. The only one who's lived in this house with me. The only one I let this close. That's not changing."

"Do you mean that?"

"I don't say things that I don't mean."

"Ronan."

"You don't think that's enough, then I don't know what I can do." He walked off and went into his office, flipping on his laptop. He went through emails and tried to tune her out completely.

When she walked into his office a half hour later, her eyes that red that they get after crying, he looked up at her. "What," he asked.

"I don't want to lose this Ronan. Fine. You think it's ridiculous that I'm worried. I needed to hear it."

"I can't give you a glimpse of what the future is gonna be lass. All I can tell you is that I don't see this thing between us changing and ending."

"I need to know something else."

"What?"

"Do you want kids?"

"Not right now I don't."

"Future."

"I guess."

"Marriage?"

"Down the road a while, but yeah."

"Okay," Katie said. He went back to going through work emails when she closed his laptop.

"Katie."

She took his hand and stood him up. "Come with me."

"Katie, no." She walked him to the sofa and leaned him onto it.

"What is this about lass?"

She slid into his lap and leaned into his arms. "Katie."

She kissed him. "What?"

"Enough."

"No."

"Katie, stop." She kissed him and didn't let the kiss break until he kissed her back.

"Tell me what you want from me," he asked.

"Love me."

"Then stop assuming that somehow I don't."

She kissed him again and he broke the kiss. "This isn't happening," Ronan said.

"I just need you to hold me Ronan."

"Then stop pushing me. Stop trying to make me say things that you don't want to hear."

"Meaning what," Katie asked. He went to get up and she stopped him.

"Tell me."

"We're in bed together every night. I haven't got up and left with anyone else. I thought that was enough that you'd know, but it isn't. You don't trust that I won't."

"Ronan."

"You don't trust that I'm not gonna cheat."

"That's not it," she said.

"Then what is it Katie?"

"I needed to know that you weren't tempted. That I was gonna be enough. Even if we end up married and having kids, I don't want to be a regret."

"Then stop wondering. The only thing I regret is getting in a stupid fight about this. I don't say I love you to anyone lass. Nobody. You want to be in my life, accept that. You're here. Nobody else is."

He got up and walked back into his office, going through more work emails when she walked in. "What Katie?"

"Can you come here?"

"I've said what I needed to," he replied.

"Please."

"Katie, leave it alone."

"Ronan." He looked at her.

"Come here."

He shook his head and got up. "What," he asked.

She slid her hand in his and walked him back to the sofa. "Katie."

"Sit down." He sat and she slid onto his lap.

"Off."

"No," she replied.

"Katie."

"I love you. I want us to have a life together. A future together. We're gonna fight Ronan. We're gonna have hard conversations. Don't just shut down and walk away from me."

"You can't really sit here and think that..." She kissed him.

"I just want you in my life. I don't want to lose you and sometimes I worry. I've never had this Ronan. I've never had someone who treated me the way that you do."

"Then stop making this a mess. Stop questioning me like I'm automatically doing something wrong." She kissed him.

"I'm sorry."

"You can't just assume that I haven't changed since that first guy you met Katie."

She kissed him again and he shook his head. "Tell me what you want."

"You."

"Even when you are so damn..."

She silenced him. "No more stupid fight."

He moved her hand. "Don't question how I feel Katie."

She shook her head. "I won't."

"Don't doubt any of this."

"Ronan, I was worried."

"Then stop worrying." She kissed him and wrapped her arms around his neck.

"Tell me what you really want Katie."

"To forget this. Move on. Curl up together on the sofa and watch a movie or something." He looked at her and his hands cradled her face.

"When are you gonna get it lass? I am not going anywhere." She looked at him and he kissed her. "No more worrying."

Katie nodded and kissed him as he pulled her tight to him. Just as he did, his phone buzzed.

"Don't you dare," Katie said. He grabbed his phone from his pocket and saw Kian's name and answered.

"You two work out whatever the hell that was," Kian asked.

"Just talking. What can I do for you?"

"Get down here and finish your drinks," Kian said.

"Just having a talk. You two can drink without us," Ronan said.

"There's a game on in an hour. Just get back over here and bring the lass."

"Will try," Ronan said as he hung up with him.

Katie kissed him and he picked her up. "What," Katie asked as he wrapped her legs around him and walked upstairs to the bedroom. He leaned her onto the bed and slid into her arms. "No more second-guessing this."

Katie shook her head. He kissed her, devouring her lips until he was peeling her sweater and jeans off.

"Ronan." He kissed her again as her sweater and jeans slid to the floor. She slid his sweater off and knocked it to the floor.

"No more doubting me."

"Promise," Katie replied as she went to undo his jeans.

"Leave the jeans," he said. Katie shook her head.

"Undo them."

"Nope."

"Ronan."

"You think that I don't want you? Really? Last night wasn't enough, fine."

"Meaning what," Katie asked. He peeled the lacy panties off then slid the lace bra off and kissed her.

"What are you doing?" He kissed her again and she felt the bite of handcuffs wrapping around her wrists.

"Ronan, don't you dare." He kissed her again and kissed down her neck.

"Ronan." He nibbled and licked at each breast until she moaned.

"Shit."

"Exactly. Still worried?"

"Mm." He kissed down her torso, nibbling at each hip then licked his way between her legs. "Oh my god," Katie said.

"Still think I'd rather have someone else?"

"No."

"Good," he teased as he kept going. He licked and nibbled and sucked until she was moaning all over again and exploding right onto his tongue.

"Mine," he said."

He kept going then let his fingers tease and probe her until her body was tightening around them. "Aah."

"Good. I'm not stopping until you beg."

"I want you."

"How badly," he asked.

"Craving."

"Which part?"

"You know which part." He licked and kissed and nibbled his way back up her body and devoured her lips. "Ronan."

"Yes love."

"I need you." He kicked his jeans to the floor along with his boxers and kissed her again.

"Hands," Katie said. He shook his head. "Ronan."

"No love. This time I get to do what I want."

"I need to taste you."

"That what you want?" She nodded and tried to wriggle her hands out of the handcuffs.

"Not happening love."

"Please." He shook his head and got up.

"Where are you going?"

"You want something, you get it," he teased.

"But when I say stop, you stop."

"Ronan." He leaned himself over her lips and she sucked and licked and took him deep into her mouth. Up and down, sucking harder and deeper until he finally pulled away. "No," Katie said.

"Behave lass."

"More." He walked around her on the bed and slid her to her stomach. "Ronan." "You want to tease me, you're not gonna stop coming until I say when," he teased.

"Shit."

Ronan slid deep into her and her breath hitched. "Shit."

"This what you wanted," he said as he slid into her over and over again hard and deep.

"Aah."

"Do you want more," he asked.

"Aah." He kept going faster and harder until she was almost fighting the handcuffs. He flipped her to her back and pulled her legs around his hips and slid deep into her all over again.

"Shit." He kissed her and kept going as she exploded around him over and over and over again. "Harder," Katie said as he pounded into her until he was spent.

"Aah."

"You sure you're done," he teased.

"I can't move my legs and you haven't undone the handcuffs." He reached into the drawer, grabbed the key and undid them, freeing her hands.

"Have you had enough yet," he asked.

"I don't think I could move even if I wanted to," Katie said.

"Good." He rolled over and Katie looked at him.

"Happy now lass?"

"I think my legs are done for."

"Might want to get re-dressed. We're going to the pub." She looked at him.

"That involves walking," Katie teased.

"We're going."

"Ronan, I can't even walk." He smirked and she shook her head.

"Never doubting me again, are you?"

"No," Katie said.

He went to get up and Katie shook her head. "What?"

"I'm coming with you."

"You sure you can walk that far?"

She stood up and looked at him.

"Are you coming?" He got up and walked over to her, kissed her and walked into the bathroom, flipping the shower on. He stepped in and saw her step in right behind him.

"You sure you're okay," he teased. Katie kissed his back as the water trailed down it and grabbed the sea sponge, putting body wash on it and rubbing it down his back.

"I'm good," Katie teased. Her hands reached around his waist and he stopped her before she started something.

"You can't handle more lass."

"Says who?"

"Those sexy shaky legs of yours," he replied as he turned to face her and rinsed off.

"What shaky legs?" He kissed her and leaned her back under the stream of hot water.

"You really want to start that?"

Katie nodded. "Right now, you're waiting and we're going for drinks."

"Pub."

He nodded. "And should I wear a skirt?"

"Just go in your jeans. You start something, they'll be around your knees in the ladies' room and you'll be bent over the counter."

"Promise?"

He kissed her. "Finish washing up."

"Can you wash my back for me?" She turned to face the wall and intentionally backed her backside up against him.

"Katie."

"Mine." He shook his head and kissed her neck then washed her back for her and stepped out.

"Ronan."

"Get dressed love. We're going."

Katie slid out of the shower and wrapped herself in her towel then walked over to the bed. "Do we really have to go," Katie asked.

"We're going love." He kissed her and grabbed his sweater from the floor. Katie got re-dressed and he smirked.

"What," she asked.

"They're gonna laugh when we get there. You know that right?"

"And why would you say that," Katie asked.

"Because we left in a fight and came back holding hands."

"We never fight Ronan. You know that just like I do."

"And fights are short-lived love. Always have been. If it can't be resolved, nobody goes to bed angry."

"That's your rule is it," she teased.

He nodded. "Even if we are short on sleep."

Katie kissed him and he zipped up his jeans. "No teasing allowed love."

She smirked. "Then no fun at the pub," she replied.

"Says who," he teased.

"Oh really? After all of this?" He kissed her and pulled her to him.

"No more fighting today though."

"Deal," Katie replied.

They finished getting ready and headed over to the pub. The minute they walked in, Ronan saw his ex with yet another conquest, or at least that's what he thought. He walked past her and walked over to the booth with Kian and Mia.

"You two make up," Kian asked as Katie smirked.

"We did," Ronan replied as Pat brought two drinks over for them.

"Thank you," Katie said as she snuggled closer to Ronan.

Mia shook her head.

"What's wrong," Ronan asked.

"You two. Get in a fight and it's resolved in an hour and a half. You missed the first game."

"Good thing there's another one then," Ronan teased. They sat back and watched the game then Katie felt his hand on her leg.

"So are we doing game day tomorrow," Kian asked.

"As far as I know yes. Depends on whether you two can handle another Sunday," Ronan joked.

"Funny," Kian said as Mia looked at Katie.

"And if I said that Katie and I were going out," Mia asked.

"You're not missing that game love," Kian said.

"Girl day," Mia said. Ronan's hand tightened around Katie's leg.

"Up to you girl," Katie replied.

"You aren't seriously gonna skip the game to get your nails done," Kian asked.

"We could just go early and be back to watch the game," Mia said.

"It's kind of up to you two," Ronan said.

"Maybe if we go early," Katie said.

"Then we're going at 11. Do you think you can let her out of your sight that long," Mia teased. Ronan looked at her.

"If Katie wants to go."

Katie smirked. "Girl time then I'm all yours," Katie said.

Ronan nodded and Katie's hand slid to his leg. He finished his pint and went to get up.

"Drinks," he asked.

"Please," Kian said as Ronan got up and got them a round. Katie got up and walked over to Ronan. "Are you sure you're okay with me going?"

"Lass, if you want to have a day with Mia then enjoy it. We're just gonna be watching the game. I have emails to finish anyway."

"You sure," Katie asked.

He kissed her. "I'm sure love."

"And?"

He kissed her. "Sit." She went and sat down at the table and Ronan slid into the bench beside her. Pat smirked and Ronan shook his head.

"So, you two go have some girl time and we'll hang out here," Ronan said.

"We'll only be an hour. We'll be done before the half of the game," Mia said.

Katie's hand slid to Ronan's leg and his arm slid around her shoulders. "You sure," Mia asked. Katie nodded.

"We go early, and we may not miss the game at all," Katie said.

"Wouldn't that be convenient," Ronan said.

Katie's hand slid to his thigh. He looked over at her as they all chatted and Katie smirked. He shook his head and Katie very gently nodded. He finished his pint and just as Katie finished her drink, Ronan made an excuse for them to leave.

"I swear you two are just determined to be alone," Mia said.

"I'll see you in the morning. See if we can get in early," Katie said. Mia nodded and Ronan and Katie headed off.

"We didn't even eat," Ronan said.

The minute they were out the door, Katie looked up at him. "What?" She smirked.

"Food."

"I take it we're ordering in." Katie got to the door, and he turned her to face him.

"What are you up to lass?"

"Not hungry."

"For food you mean." She nodded. "And what might you want," he asked as he opened the door, and she backed up.

"You know what."

"Haven't got enough yet?" Katie shook her head. "And here I thought you were gonna start something at the pub."

"You wish I did."

Katie nodded. "Or we went into Pat's office." He shook his head. He took her hand and walked her into his office in the house.

"This what you wanted," he asked.

"Almost," she said.

"And what was your thought love?"

"Your office."

"As in my office in…" She kissed him and he sat her on the edge of the desk.

"Not good enough here?"

"Nobody to catch you."

"That what you really want?" Katie nodded.

"The pub isn't enough?"

"Not today it isn't."

"And what else might you want lass?"

"You." He undid her jeans and slid them off her legs, sliding her boots off with them.

"Katie."

"What?"

"You realize that you're missing something right?"

"And here I thought the pub would've been where you figured that out."

He shook his head and sat down in his office chair. "So, now that you have me, what do you want?"

"To take care of you."

"Katie."

MINE

Chapter 8

She slid to her knees and undid his jeans. "Katie."

"What?"

"Not happening."

"And why is that," she asked as she unzipped his jeans, and her hand slid under the waistband of his boxers.

"Katie." She slid him out of the boxers and slid her mouth over him taking him deep. "Shit."

"Mm." He shook his head as her tongue teased. "Katie, don't start that." She took him deeper into her mouth and his breath hitched. "Lass, come here." She shook her head and sucked harder. "Aah." She kept going as her tongue swirled around him making him even harder. "Lass, on your feet." She shook her head and kept going, sliding his jeans and boxers right off and using both her hands to grip him. "Katie," he moaned. When she got that smirk, he shook his head. "Come here." She shook her head again and sucked him in deeper. "Aah. Katie, stop." She kept going. "Let go love." She refused. "Katie." She kept going until she could feel him building up to his release. "Katie, come here." She slid him out of her mouth and stood up. He kissed her, devouring her lips and sat her back on the edge of the desk. "You are so bad," he said.

"And you like it," she replied as he slid deep into her and her breath hitched.

"Think that you're gonna make me explode," he teased as he pounded endlessly into her over and over again, hard and deep. "Aah."

"So damn bad," he said.

"And you were liking it." He kept going until her toes were curling and he felt her body tensing around him.

"Sorta like you were craving this," he said as she crumbled around him, and he kept going.

"Ronan." He slid out of her and flipped her, so she was bent over the desk and slid into her again, making it even more intense. "Shit Ronan."

"This what you wanted when you started taunting me? To be bent over my desk?"

"Aah." He kept pounding into her until he finally found his release and pulled her onto his lap in his desk chair, still deep inside her. "Ronan."

"That what you wanted lass?"

"More."

"Really?" Katie nodded. "You're gonna have to give me a minute." She went to move, and he stopped her.

"What," Katie asked.

"You really do like being the naughty one, don't you?"

"Only fair since you do that to me every single time. I still don't know that I can walk right now."

"Good. You deserve that," he teased.

"Oh really," Katie said. He let her stand up with shaky legs, pulled up his jeans and boxers and shook his head. "What?"

"Upstairs." She bent over and grabbed her jeans and turned to look at him. "What lass?"

"Sofa."

"Up. Go." She walked to the stairs and made her way up, walking into the main bedroom.

He was two steps behind her, following her into the bedroom and leaned her onto the bed, falling into her arms. He devoured her lips again and pulled her legs around his hips. "Ronan, you said you needed a break."

He pinned her hands to the bed. "To start with, I'm fixing this," he said.

"By doing what Ronan?" He kissed her and she felt something soft wrap around her wrists.

"You aren't starting that again lass. Now you're mine."

"Meaning what? Taunting me until I beg you to stop?"

"Something like that," he teased as he slid his jeans and boxers off and threw his sweater on the chair.

"And just what were you intending?"

"Make you unable to walk for a few days. You may not even make it to your girl day tomorrow," Ronan joked.

"Ronan, don't you start. A girl day for an hour or two."

He kissed her. "Shh."

"Meaning?" He kissed her breast, nibbling at the little peak until she almost ached then moved to the next one. "Ronan, please." He nibbled then let go and kissed his way down her torso, licking and kissing each hip. "Please," she said. He smirked.

"Please what lass?"

"I need you inside me."

"And you think it's gonna be that easy?"

"Ronan."

"You get to taunt me, I get to taunt you until you can't move let alone walk."

"No."

"Yes."

"Ronan." He kept going, sliding his fingers inside her as he kept teasing and making her explode all over again. "Ronan."

"Say mercy love."

"Mercy." He licked his fingers and kissed his way up her torso then slid deep into her.

"This what you want?" She moaned and he smirked, kissing up her neck. "I'll take that as a yes."

"Mm." He slid in and out, over and over. Harder and deeper every time until her legs were shaking. "Mine," he said as she fought against the tie around her hands.

"Undo them."

"Nope."

"Ronan, please." He nibbled and kissed her lips.

"No." He kissed her again and kept pounding into her over and over until he felt her crumble around him again.

"Please." When he finally found his release, she was begging. He kissed her again and untied her hands as her arms almost instinctively wrapped around him.

"Still think that you can walk," he teased.

"I don't think there's a chance in the world." He kissed her and smirked.

"Good."

"My legs are still shaking."

"That was part of my plan."

"You really don't want me to go tomorrow?"

"If that's what you want to do. Just making sure that you aren't pouncing on me first thing tomorrow."

"Might do that anyway."

"If you can walk." He kissed her and went to roll over when she stopped him. "Yes love."

"What happens if I wake you up tomorrow?"

"With what?"

"Me teasing you like I did downstairs. Not stopping when you beg me to stop."

"Katie."

"What?"

"You really think that you're gonna be awake before I am?"

"This thing called an alarm that I have on my watch."

He kissed her. "You can try love."

"Then I do it in the kitchen."

He shook his head. "Bad girl. My very bad girl."

"And here I thought you were gonna say good girl," Katie teased.

He kissed her. "Bad girl and good girl. A deadly pairing."

"Really," Katie said.

"One I like." She smirked and kissed him as he leaned to his side.

"Don't get up," Katie begged.

He kissed her and went to slide out of bed. "Ronan."

"Two minutes." He walked into the bathroom and cleaned up then slid boxers on and walked back into the bedroom, seeing Katie out cold. He slid into the bed beside her, put the phones on the charger, and flipped the light off as she curled up with him and fell asleep on his chest.

Ronan woke up the next morning and Katie was still asleep in his arms. He went to get up and her eyes opened. "Where are you going," Katie asked.

"Get some rest lass. I'm going to the gym."

"Ronan."

"No." He pulled on his joggers and tee and slid his sneakers on and walked downstairs, going and starting his workout. He was done within an hour and looked up to see Katie in the hallway. "Katie."

"What?" He shook his head and got up, walking towards her.

"What are you up to?"

"Making breakfast." He grabbed her hand and flipped her over his shoulder, walking her back upstairs. "Ronan, put me down."

He put her on the bed and pinned her hands down. "Stay here."

"Nope."

"Bringing you breakfast in bed."

"I know what I want and it's not breakfast," Katie replied.

"And what is it that you want," Ronan asked as she slid his sweaty shirt off.

"I'll give you a hint," Katie said as she went to slide his joggers and boxers down.

"Katie."

"Mine."

"Food first."

"Nope." She flipped him onto the bed and pulled his boxers and joggers off.

"Katie." She took him in her mouth, and he almost instantly hardened.

"Mm."

"Katie, please." She kept going, taking him deeper in her mouth until he could feel her sucking and teasing. "Shit."

"Mm." She slid up and down, sucking harder and taking him as deep as she could. "Aah." He saw her smirk. She was getting her way. "Katie stop." She shook her head and kept going up and down, over and over until she could feel him tighten. "Katie."

"Mine," she said as she took him deep again until she could feel him starting to break.

"Stop." She shook her head, and he exploded into her mouth as she swallowed.

"Mm," she said as he shook his head and pulled her to him.

"Had to do it didn't you," he asked.

"I did warn you," Katie joked as she smirked.

"You do realize that it could've been a lot more fun if you'd stopped."

"My turn to make your legs shake," she teased as she went to get up.

"Bad."

"Payback," Katie teased as he got up and walked over to her, chasing her into the bathroom and pinning her to the counter.

"What?"

He kissed her and shook his head. "That was your little plan, was it?"

Katie nodded. "I like my plan. For once it worked the way I wanted it to."

"Lass, you have no idea what you started."

"Wanna make a bet," she teased. He cleaned up and freshened up.

"I'm making breakfast. Try and keep your hands to yourself while I cook." He kissed her and walked downstairs.

By the time Katie came downstairs in her skirt and rugby shirt, breakfast was ready. "And if that isn't the sexiest looking lass," he teased.

"I thought you'd like it," she teased.

He kissed her and handed her plate to her. "I could've made this," Katie said.

"You needed to get ready for girl day love. It's fine." He kissed her and Katie smirked. They sat down and had breakfast with Katie teasing him.

"What," Katie asked.

"Stop teasing lass."

"Meaning what?"

"You know what." He finished breakfast and kissed her.

"I won't be that long. She said they could get us in at 10."

"Missing church."

"Did you want to go or are you going to watch the game?" He looked at her.

"We're going next weekend. Deal?"

Katie nodded. She finished eating and Ronan got up and washed the dishes and finished his coffee. "Ronan."

"Yes lass." "You sure you want to hang out at the pub and watch the games all afternoon?"

"Not all afternoon, but for a while."

"And what else are you planning to do," Katie asked.

"Bring you home and make sure you can't walk into work tomorrow."

"And what if I came to the office with you tomorrow?"

"And you'd be doing that why?"

"Doctor's appointment. I can work from wherever."

"And you're not doing it because you want to have a do-over of what you started here in my office?"

"That too. Sneaking me into your office and us having sex on your desk."

"I did mention that none of that is happening in the office, right?"

"If nobody else is there yet." Katie slid her arms around him, bringing her dishes to the counter.

"Katie, you have a very dirty mind, and I love it, but you aren't getting away with that in my office."

He finished doing the dishes and turned to have Katie kiss him. "And since when are you a party pooper?"

"I told you, not in my office."

"And I can't change your mind," she asked.

"Katie."

"Like if I wore something without anything on under it."

He kissed her. "While I appreciate the naughty suggestion, answer is still no."

"Are you going in early tomorrow?"

"I have to be in the office for 8:30."

"And what time does everyone else show up?"

"My assistants show at 8, love."

"Then we can have a little fun at home first."

"Meaning what?" Katie smirked. "Like we do every morning."

Katie nodded. "Still doing that thing at your office though. The thing I did before you bent me over your desk."

"No, you aren't."

"Says who," Katie teased as he picked her up and sat her on the kitchen counter.

"You aren't Katie. It's my office."

She slid her arms around his neck. "Or we just do it anyway and christen that stuffy office."

"Katie."

"What?"

"Behave."

"You seriously telling me that you've never done anything in your office ever?"

"Why would I," he asked.

Katie shook her head. "Then we're going in before anyone else is there or we go when nobody's there."

"Meaning?"

"This afternoon." He shook his head.

"You're just determined, aren't you?"

"Yes," Katie said as she smirked.

"Why are you so determined love?"

"Because I am. It's fun. Sorta like us at the pub."

He shook his head and kissed her. "Bad girl of mine."

"That mean that we're doing it?"

"That means it's still not happening in my office."

"Still coming with you tomorrow."

He nodded. "If that's what you want love."

"What," she asked.

"You are perfectly fine going to work if that's what you want to do. I have work to get done remember."

"How many meetings do you have to do tomorrow?"

"3."

"Can't do any of them from home?"

"Katie."

"What?"

"In-person meetings."

"Then I'll get work done too."

"You sure you want to come to the office tomorrow?"

"Still coming. And I'm making it happen."

He kissed her. "I love that you wanna try love." He smirked and went to slide her off the counter when she slid her legs around him. "Don't you have somewhere to be," he teased.

"You mean since we aren't going until 10 you mean?" He picked her up and walked over to the sofa, leaning her onto it.

"What," Katie asked. He kissed her and devoured her lips.

"Ronan."

"Yes love."

"Upstairs."

He shook his head. "We're not doing that love."

"Says who," Katie asked.

"You are behaving for once."

"Ronan." He kissed her again and snuggled her tight to him. They curled up and were making out like teenagers until she headed out.

"I'll meet you at the pub."

Katie smirked and headed off with Mia. Ronan walked upstairs, got undressed and slid into a hot shower, the visual of what she'd done that morning still fresh in his mind. The fact that he was getting turned on all over again was just a mild side-effect. He slid his hand around his length and worked himself over in the shower, exploding again like he had with her. "Damn woman." He shook his head and washed up then stepped out and wrapped a towel around him. He walked into his closet, pulled on jeans, boxers and his rugby shirt and went and freshened up. Just as he did, his phone buzzed. He answered.

"And how is the girl day going?"

"Good. Can't decide on a nail color."

"Pink."

"Or French."

"Pink."

"You sure red isn't a good option."

"Katie. Pink."

"Pale pink it is."

"Good girl."

"Say it again."

"You'll hear it tonight. Go have fun with Mia."

"By the way. That thing this morning. I'm doing it again before everyone is in the office tomorrow."

"No, you aren't."

"Yeah I am."

"Katie, for once please just behave."

"No fun," Katie joked.

"Love you too lass." They hung up and he grabbed his wallet, keys and phone and headed over to the pub. When he walked in, his ex was there. He ignored her, walked past and sat down with Kian.

"About time you showed up. I got your pint."

"Thank you. The girlies are having fun," Ronan said.

"You do realize that they only did it so Mia can get the secrets out of the lass right?"

"Meaning what," Ronan asked.

"Meaning she's determined to find out what's really going on with the two of you. She's the first lass you've had around us since the psycho. What do you expect?" Ronan shook his head and took a gulp of his Guinness.

"What," Kian asked.

"I like her. I love her. She's living at my place Kian. What else does she need to know?"

"Probably the one thing she's always wondered about."

"Meaning what? How good I am in bed?"

"Funny. Don't be surprised when she finds that out too."

"Kian."

"She's protective of you whether you see it or not. She's treated you like her brother forever. She's making sure that Katie feels the way you do."

"So that's the whole reason for that so-called girl time?" Kian nodded and took a gulp of his pint. Ronan shook his head.

"Please don't scare the damn girl away alright?" Kian laughed and they watched whatever game was on. Within an hour or two, and a few pints down, the ladies showed up. Ronan took Katie's hand and saw her nails.

"Nice," Ronan said.

"All the better to scratch down your back with," Katie whispered as she bent over and whispered in his ear.

"Tempting." He got up and sat down on the other side of the booth with Katie while Pat brought over drinks. "Thank you," Ronan said.

"Nice seeing you all happy again lad," Pat said.

"I swear. It's like none of you have ever seen me happy."

"We haven't," Mia replied as she kissed Kian and snuggled up to him.

Katie smirked and Ronan shook his head. "What," Katie asked.

"Nothing lass. Divulging secrets I bet."

"What secrets," Katie teased.

"You know what ones."

"I mean, she asked," Katie joked.

"Are you staying around to watch another game," Kian asked.

"Part of me thinks I should get Katie back to the house and find out what all that girl talk was about."

"You saying you don't trust me," Mia asked.

"To be honest, no. Not to mind your own business anyway."

"We were just talking about how you two really met." Katie's hand slid to Ronan's upper thigh and his hand clamped over it.

"And just what did she tell you?"

"That you two met at some hotel lounge and you seduced her on the damn spot."

"With one of those fancy Bailey's espresso martinis. I'll admit to that much," Ronan said.

"And what else happened," Mia asked.

"Why? She wouldn't tell you?"

"She just said you two ended up talking and you tried to make a move," Mia said.

"That I did."

"She never went any further than that," Mia said.

"Good." Ronan took the last gulp of his pint and Pat brought over another.

"Are you gonna tell me the rest of the story," Mia asked.

"No. At some point you have to mind your own lass. I get being over-protective and all, but that's between us." Katie's hand slid up his thigh until he stopped her.

"What was so different about Katie," Mia asked.

"I don't know. There definitely was something though."

He thought back to that night. Her moaning his name, her begging for more. That sound that always turned him on even more. The fact that he couldn't say no to her. That they'd done it more than once and she never once complained or expected anything but sex from him. The sex. The sex that drove him crazy and had him thinking about her for days. He remembered his reaction when he'd found out she was on the foundation board with him. How it was the perfect excuse to see her again.

His hand slid up Katie's thigh and right up under her skirt, pushing the lacy panties to the side. First it was one finger teasing, then two, then one sliding inside her as he could feel her getting wet.

"Ronan," Katie whispered.

"Mm." He took another gulp of his pint.

"What was it about her," Mia asked.

"Everything. She dared me to date her even after I warned her I'm horrible at dating."

"Nice move," Mia said.

"Agreed," Kian joked.

"Can you two stop meddling now or are you going to keep asking a million questions," Ronan asked.

"There are things I could ask," Mia said.

"And you can keep them to yourself. After this pint I'm heading to the house." Two fingers slid inside her and Katie tried not to show a reaction. It's when the fingers started sliding in and out faster that she slid her hand over his.

"There's another game on at half one," Kian said.

"Have something I need to do."

"Which is? Folks making you come over," Kian asked.

"Nope. Something else," Ronan said as Katie's hand slid in the front pocket of his jeans, and he felt her hand graze him. He shook his head. She whispered in his ear. "Bathroom." He shook his head. Katie smirked and he shook his head again.

"You two talking in code now," Kian asked.

"Something like that," Katie replied.

"And?" Katie finished her drink, Ronan finished his pint and got up, pulling his hand away, paid for the drinks and they said goodbye to Mia and Kian.

They walked towards the door and Ronan saw his ex. Alone. He slid his hand in Katie's and pulled her to him as they walked outside.

"What," Katie asked. He leaned her up against the wall and kissed her, devouring her lips.

"Don't start that in front of them."

"Don't start what," she asked. He looked at her and shook his head.

"Bad. So very bad."

"And you love It," she replied. He kissed her again and walked her back to the house.

"Are you telling me that I wore a skirt for nothing," Katie asked.

"Not for nothing," Ronan replied as he smirked.

"Meaning what?"

"Meaning I'm finishing what I started."

"Where? Stairs?"

"If you don't get up the steps fast enough, yes."

"Promise," Katie said as he unlocked the front door.

"Now that's what you want?"

"You, yes."

"You do realize what sticking your hand in my pocket did right?"

"Should've done it in the pub."

"Oh really lass."

"Yes, oh really," she replied as she stood in front of him and slid her boots off.

"You better start running lass."

"Who says I'm running?"

He shook his head and kissed her walking her up against the wall in the hallway. "Kick them off."

"Kick what off?"

"You know what. Off."

"Take them off yourself," she said with a grin. He kissed her and kneeled down, sliding her lacy panties off and tied her hands with them.

"Ronan."

"You want to misbehave, you get bent over the sofa."

"Then I'm misbehaving more often."

"Bend over the sofa."

"Or what?"

"Katie."

"Or what?" He took her hand, walked her to the sofa and bent her over it then undid the zipper of the skirt and pulled it off. "Ronan."

"What?"

"I want you."

"You'll get me when I say."

"Meaning what," Katie said not seeing what Ronan was doing.

She felt his tongue slide over her wetness and her breath hitched. "Ronan."

"What?" His warm breath had her even more turned on.

"Ronan."

"Mm." He licked and teased then slid two fingers deep inside her until her breath hitched again then kept going until he could feel her wetness double. "Shit Ronan."

"What? Give up?"

"I need you."

"Which part?"

"Funny Ronan. Now."

"Now what?" He started going harder and faster until her legs were giving way.

She moaned. "I need you inside me."

"I am."

"Ronan, please." He undid his jeans and stood up, leaning up against her. His fingers continued to tease until she was trying to reach for him and couldn't.

"Ronan." He slid his jeans and boxers off and threw them onto the sofa. "Please," Katie said as he licked his fingers.

"You taste good."

"Shit." Katie went to turn around and he stopped her.

"Ronan."

"Behave." He bent her back over the sofa and slid deep into her until her breath hitched again.

"Ronan."

"Damn you feel good," Ronan said.

"Because you got me all wet and turned on first?"

"Because you should always be that way. Ready for me."

"Ronan."

"Yes love," he said as he slowly started to slide in and out, hard and deep.

"Mm."

"More?" She nodded and her back arched as he slid in deep all over again. "I'm gonna taunt you."

"You already did."

"I'm gonna have your legs begging me to stop."

"Ronan." He kept going then went harder and a little faster. "Aah."

"Good."

"Please," she begged. His hand slid around her hip and teased her as he slid in and out. "Ronan." "Mine."

"Yes."

"Only mine."

"Yours."

"Nobody else touches you."

"Just you."

"Good girl."

He kept going, harder and harder until he was pounding into her over and over again and she was crumbling around him with every thrust. When she climaxed once, then twice, then three and four and five times, he kept going until she was begging then exploded into her. "I can't even move."

"Good. No more teasing me."

"Ronan."

"What love?"

"Mine."

"What's yours?"

"You."

"If that's what you want."

"Nobody else."

"Never thought about it."

"Good," she replied. He kissed the back of her neck, and she stood up with shaky legs. "Now, go upstairs."

"Why," Katie asked facing him and leaning her back against the edge of the sofa.

"Because I said so," he replied as she smirked.

"And if I said make me," she teased. He pulled his jeans and boxers up, zipped his jeans and picked her up, flipping her over his shoulder. "Ronan."

He walked up the steps to the bedroom and leaned her onto the bed. "What are you gonna do now," Katie asked. He walked over to his dresser and grabbed something from the drawer. All she could hear was the buzzing.

"Hands."

"Ronan, what are you doing?" He pulled her shirt off and grabbed her hands.

"Taking advantage." Handcuffs clicked around her wrists and when she went to move her hands, they wouldn't move.

"You handcuffed me to the bed? Seriously Ronan."

"Now don't move."

"Undo them."

"Nope." When she felt a blindfold go over her eyes, she knew that she was at his mercy. "Now are you going to tell me what you told her about us?"

"I just told her that we were good together."

"And?"

"When she asked about us sneaking into the ladies room you mean?" She felt the buzzing slide up her inner thigh. "Shit."

"And what did you tell her about the ladies room moments?"

"Nothing." She felt her bra slide off and the buzzing ran over the peaks of her breasts. Intense was an understatement.

"Tell me."

"I just told her that we had fun. That we're still in the playful stage," Katie said as the buzzing ran over and between her breasts all over again until she moaned.

"And what else?"

"Nothing."

"No telling her about me and you in bed?"

"She asked."

"And?"

"I told her it was between us." The buzzing intensified and got stronger. "Aah."

"Katie."

"She asked if I had been another one-night stand."

"And what did you say?"

"I told her that it was more like a 3-month stand. That I dared you to date me." The buzzing grazed her hip and almost made her jump as she pulled at the handcuffs. "Undo them."

"No lass."

"Ronan."

"And tell me lass. What else did you mention about us?"

"That we were having fun and enjoying each other. That you told me you loved me." The buzzing went up her inner thigh and grazed her wetness. "Shit Ronan."

"That's all," he asked as he nibbled at her breasts and licked as the toy buzzed and teased her into an orgasm.

"Aah. Ronan, please."

"Oh I haven't even started yet lass."

"Meaning what," she asked.

"I'm in control, not you." He slid the toy deeper between her legs until her toes were curling and smirked.

"What are you doing?"

"Making you beg for more."

"Aah."

"You're not allowed to come."

"Ronan, move the toy."

"Nope."

"Then you're intentionally torturing me."

"Don't."

"Ronan." He kissed her and grabbed the other toy from the drawer and turned it on, watching it glide up and down. "What's that noise?" He smirked and turned it onto vibrate, teasing each nipple with it. "Mm."

"Say you want it."

"Want what?"

"Say you want it."

"I want it." He parted her legs, still teasing her with the buzzing wand then slid the other inside her and flipped it onto thrusting. "Shit." He turned it on low as he kept teasing. "Ronan."

"Yes lass."

"How?"

"Open your mouth and put your head back."

"Why?"

"Do what I tell you." She did and he kicked his jeans off, slid his boxers off and slid himself into her mouth as she instantly started to lick and suck him in deep. He could hear her moans around him. "That what you wanted?"

"Mm." She took him deeper and bent over, pushing the toy in deeper as the other wand teased each nipple until she was practically grinding against the toy.

He shook his head and watched her fight against the handcuffs and suck him in as deep as she could. Hell. That exact moment was hot as hell, and he'd pulled it off. "Mine," he said. He could hear her moaning all over again and turned the intensity up even more. When he felt himself starting to lose control, he pulled away much to her disappointment.

"Where are you going?" He slid the wand back up to her nipples and made her moan again as he saw her body throbbing around the toy.

"Say mercy," he teased.

"Aah."

"Just give up and beg for mercy," he said as he felt the toy move with her orgasm.

"Ronan, I need you. No more toys."

"Come for me."

"I want you inside me."

"One more," he said. He watched and slid the toy deeper as her stomach started to shake.

"I give up."

"Calling mercy?"

"Mm."

"Good girl." Just as he said it, he heard her moans. The one she made when she'd had an intense orgasm. He slid the toy out and slid deep inside her, pounding into her over and over until she was almost begging. "Ronan."

"Yes love."

"More."

"More of me or the toy?"

"You." He kept going, feeling her body throbbing around him as he took her through three more intense orgasms then couldn't hold himself back anymore and exploded into her. "Shit," Katie said.

"Had enough or do you want more," Ronan asked.

"I can't even move. Come up here for a second."

"Nope. None of that lass."

"Please."

"Nope." He kissed up her body, nibbling at each breast until she was moaning again.

"Good girl."

"Ronan, undo them." He licked and teased his way up her chest, then her neck, then her chin, then devoured her lips.

"I think those are the ones I lost the key to," he joked.

"You aren't funny."

He kissed her again and got up. "Where are you going?"

"To get the key." He walked into his closet, grabbed fresh boxers, went and cleaned up, had a quick shower, then came out and undid the handcuffs and slid the blindfold off, putting them into his drawer.

"You seriously went and showered and got re-dressed instead of undoing them?" He nodded and kissed her. She went to get up and her legs were so shaky, she fell back onto the bed.

"Much better," he teased.

"I can barely move."

"That was part of my plan love."

"While I enjoyed that little plan, you aren't playing fair and you know it."

"I let you get what you wanted."

"Then come here and let me do it again."

"No," Ronan said as he slid his jeans on.

"You do realize that you don't ever play fair." He nodded and leaned over and kissed her.

"Now, if you wanted more, I can do something about that," Ronan said.

"Where did that other thing come from?"

"My drawer of tricks."

"I bet it did." He kissed her and went and pulled a shirt on.

"And where are you going?"

"Was thinking we could go for dinner. Somewhere not with Kian and Mia there."

"Name it," Katie said with a smirk.

"I'll find someplace. You get dressed. I'll meet you downstairs."

"I need my skirt back."

"You really want to tempt fate with a skirt again," he asked.

"Yes."

"Then be prepared. I may have to carry you into work tomorrow."

"Ronan."

"Yes love."

"Were you really that worried that I was gonna tell her everything we've done?"

"I just like to keep my private life and all the fun we have private. That's all lass."

"And if I ever did tell anyone about the insane, mind-blowing sex that we have. What would you do?"

"There wouldn't be anymore."

"Why?"

"Because I don't need our sex lives shared with the world lass. Dublin, even if you don't realize it, is like a little town. Everyone knows everyone else's business. If they don't know, they find out. I don't need my personal life being put into that." He kissed her and walked downstairs, got her skirt and brought it up, handing it to her, then made his way downstairs to get something to drink.

When Katie came downstairs, she could barely walk. "You okay lass," he said almost with a laugh.

"Fine. My legs are a little sore. Like you didn't do that intentionally."

"I could make it worse love, but you really wouldn't be walking. Maybe tonight you just sleep in the bed with me instead of trying to make a move."

"Maybe."

"The pub is just down the way. Maybe a 10 minute walk. You alright with that?"

"You're hilarious Ronan. You really are." He pulled her onto his lap and kissed her.

"You wanted more, you get more love."

"Only one thing that I'm surprised you didn't try."

"And what's that?" She looked at him as if he could read her mind. "See, if you're saying what I think you are, that's a conversation to be had."

"You haven't?"

"Oh I have. Fact is, that's a you decision."

"Can we talk about it after we get food?" Ronan smirked and kissed her. She stood up then straddled him on the chair.

"You sure your legs can handle that lass?"

"No. But I need you." He pulled her to him and was about to slide the lacy panties back off when his phone buzzed.

"Yep."

"Do you think the two of you can make it out of that love nest and come meet up for dinner," Kian said.

"We were actually just heading out."

"I doubt that. I promise. No more Spanish Inquisition," Mia said from the background.

"Honestly, we're gonna have a quick dinner then I'm taking her out."

"Ronan."

"She's there Kian. Not happening."

"She came down and sat with Mia and I."

"All the more reason to avoid her. Not happening. I'll see you during the week."

"Fine. I guess I'll watch the last game with Mia."

"Enjoy my friend." He hung up with Kian and Katie devoured his lips. "You saying you want to stay home?"

She nodded. "All I have in the fridge is chicken and curry sauce."

"Then we have chicken."

"Hot curry."

"I can maybe cook something," Katie said.

"You and your shaky legs can sit down on the sofa."

"Only if you're sitting with me."

"I have to cook." Katie kissed him again and he picked her up and leaned her onto the sofa, leaning into her arms. "Fine. Takeaway it is."

Ronan made two calls. One to order the food and one to his driver to pick it up at the other pub. "You do realize we could've just gone and had it there," Ronan said.

"Like the idea of you eating on the floor with me instead.

"Why do I get the feeling that there's more to that thought."

"You shirtless and without the jeans."

"And you lass?"

"Naked."

He shook his head and kissed her. "You're insatiable."

"One of the million and one things that you love about me I think," Katie teased as she went to slide his shirt off.

"We're still going out love."

"Where?"

"You know that they're gonna ask. There's another game at 6."

Katie shook her head. "Mine."

"Oh really." She went to undo his jeans, and he stopped her.

"Food is coming."

"Then you can answer it."

"Lass, stop." Her hand slid down the front of his jeans and he shook his head.

"Don't go starting something that you can't finish."

"I can finish it."

"No lass." He removed her hand and kissed her sliding his hands up her arms until he had both wrists in his hand.

"Ronan."

"What?"

"Let go." He shook his head and smirked.

"Stay here."

"Why?"

"Because I told you to. Stay."

He walked upstairs and grabbed the buzzing wand, slid it in his back pocket and grabbed the silk scarf. If she wanted to do it all over again, she'd get it double time. He walked down the steps and went into the sitting room, seeing her in the same spot he'd left her in.

"Now what were you planning," Katie asked. He tied the scarf around her eyes then tied her hands so she couldn't move. If she did, the scarf tightened on her face.

"Ronan." He slid the lacy panties off, sliding them into his back pocket, then undid her shirt and slid it over her

314

head, covering her hands. He slid the bra off and nibbled at each breast as she moaned. "You do realize that you aren't playing fair right?"

"And I also know that you asked for it." He kept licking and nibbling at each breast until her back arched.

"Good girl."

"Ahh."

"More?"

"I want you."

"I bet you do," Ronan teased as he kept going until he could hear her breath hitch. "Katie."

"What?"

"Mine," he replied as he slid the vibrating toy from his pocket and turned it on, sitting it against the tender nub between her legs.

"Shit."

"You can't until I say so," he whispered.

"Ronan."

"No."

"Please."

"No. Don't make me take it away."

"Mm. Aah."

"You come before I say and I'm sleeping alone tonight."

"Ronan." He kissed her and he could tell she was trying to hold back. "Please."

"You need to?" Katie nodded. He kissed her and took it away before she could reach her climax.

"What happened?"

"Food is here."

"Ronan." He slid the toy into his back pocket and took the food, taking it into the kitchen and plating it.

"You do realize that I can't move right?"

"Open your mouth."

He fed her one of the mussels from her dinner. "Mm."

"Good?" Katie nodded. He slurped back one of his oysters.

"What was that?"

"My dinner."

"You didn't seriously get oysters."

"Do you want one?"

"Rather be tasting you."

"Good answer." He fed her two more of her mussels and slurped back two of his oysters.

"You're teasing intentionally."

"And you're way past being insatiable." He gave her a few more then went for one of his own. By the time they finished eating, he had a smirk ear to ear, and she was still immobile.

Chapter 9

"Now, where was I," he asked.

"Torturing me."

"Oh yes." He pulled the toy back out and slid it over each breast, teasing until her back arched then moved back down her body.

"Ronan, put it back where it was before dinner."

"Nope."

"Please."

"You mean here," he asked as he rubbed it hard against that perfect spot.

"Mm."

"Not until I say," he said.

"Then I want you inside me."

"Again lass?"

"I need you." He kept going and then slid the toy inside her, rubbing it against the perfect spot.

"Please," Katie said.

"What?"

"I need to."

"Beg."

"Ronan."

"You do it I'm sleeping in the bedroom and you're in the guest room."

"I need..." He kissed her and put more pressure on it. She moaned and he whispered.

"Come for me." She exploded a minute later and kept going until the toy vanished from inside her and went back into his back pocket.

"Ronan."

"Yes lass."

"I need something."

"Nope."

"Please."

"Making you explode like that was enough for me love." Fact was, he was past being turned on to the point that his jeans couldn't hold him.

"Take them off."

"Nope." He walked upstairs and charged the wand toy then grabbed the thruster again and walked back downstairs.

"Ronan, please."

"Please what," he asked.

"Jeans off and come here." He smirked and slid his hand over her, teasing with his fingers until she was moaning again. "Tell me what I have to do," Katie said. He kissed her and she moaned as he slid two fingers deep inside her and teased even more. "Shit."

"You wanted more. I did hear that right."

"Ronan." He turned on the thrusting toy and slid it to the hilt inside her as Katie's toes curled and her legs were even twitching.

"Aah. Shit...Mm...Ronan."

"Not until I say you can."

"Ronan."

"I'll take it away."

"Mm. You aren't being fair."

"Mine."

"Please."

"Not yet."

"Ronan, turn the speed down then." He turned it up.

"Aah. Ronan, please. Please."

"Not yet."

"Please." He nibbled at her breasts, and he could tell that she was trying.

"Okay," he said.

"Please."

"You can." She crashed around the toy, and he smirked. That toy was relentless. The perfect thing he'd bought and never used with anyone...until her. It kept going until he turned it to high and left it there. "Shit." He licked her and teased as the toy did its job. It just made everything more intense, that was until Ronan flipped her onto her stomach. It made it even more intense.

"Ronan."

"Yes love."

"I'm calling for mercy."

"Why?"

"Because I can't take any more." He got up and walked over to her, sliding himself into her mouth. She was moaning around him but kept going deeper and sucking and licking more until she climaxed again. He slid in and out of her mouth over and over again, going deeper until he could feel his release coming. She wasn't stopping and he was determined to make her stop. "Katie."

"No. Aah." He slid out of her and grabbed the toy, flipping it off. He leaned her against the arm of the sofa and slid deep into her again, over and over until he could feel her crumbling around him in her release. That was enough to do him in, and he knew it. He exploded into her and leaned up against her. "Shit," Katie said.

"Had enough have you," Ronan asked.

"I need a soak in the tub."

"Sore?"

She giggled. "A little." He slid his boxers back up, zipped up his jeans and pulled her onto his lap, undoing the blindfold and the scarf from around her hands. Katie looked at him with a smirk ear to ear.

"What love?"

"I don't think I can move."

"Good. By the way, guest room," he said.

"You said..."

"I know you love. I knew you couldn't hold back until I said."

"I tried."

"Oh, I know you did. You managed to do it the second time."

"I can't sleep without you in bed with me."

"Then learn love." He kissed her and devoured her lips.

"Please stay in bed with me." He shook his head.

"Punishment for not doing what I asked."

"And if I sneak into bed with you in the middle of the night and wake you up by doing that again?"

"Then you're sleeping in there two nights." Katie shook her head.

"So, this is what this is now? You telling me what to do?"

"Little game for the weekend."

"Then I want a do-over." He kissed her.

"Thank you for not telling her everything."

"Not that she didn't ask a few things, but it's between us."

"Correct."

"And by the way, she did ask what you were like in bed."

"I've known her for years. She's practically like my sister. Why?"

"I told her that half the time I can't even move after." He slid her off his lap. "Ronan."

"Katie, not appropriate."

"She said her and Kian were the same at the beginning."

"I don't need to hear this."

"And I told her the best part is falling asleep in your arms." Ronan took a deep breath.

"Upstairs." Katie grabbed her clothes and walked upstairs with him two steps behind her.

"Where are we going?" He walked into the bedroom, slid the toy into the sink and drew Katie a hot bath.

"Are you coming in with me?"

"All things considered, you couldn't handle if I did."

"Party pooper."

"May need to rinse my mind out with soap for thinking what I was thinking just when I flipped you over."

"Why didn't you?" Ronan looked at her.

"Are you saying what I think you are?"

"I trust you. I know you wouldn't let me get hurt intentionally."

"Just get in the tub."

She slid into the hot water and closed her eyes. "Ronan."

"Yes love."

"Were you really gonna do it?" He shook his head.

"Tempted, but no."

"Why?"

"Meaning what?"

"Meaning why didn't you?"

"Because I told you we would've needed to talk about it."

"You can next time."

"Katie, that isn't happening until we discuss it. Not you saying to do it."

"If that's what you want to do..." He kissed her.

"Stop talking and just relax." Ronan kicked his jeans and boxers off and slid into the shower, cleaning up, then went into the bedroom with a warm towel wrapped around him and slid fresh boxers on and laid down on the bed. When Katie finished in the tub, she wrapped a towel around her and walked into the bedroom. "How was your soak?"

"Relaxing and lonely."

"Not enough room for two of us love."

"Were you serious about me sleeping in the other room?"

"You didn't do what I asked." Katie shook her head, slid the towel off and threw it at Ronan then walked into her closet and pulled on pajamas.

"Tell me you weren't being serious."

"You're gonna end up sneaking in here anyway."

"Then?" He grabbed his phone and started going through emails. She slid her phone off the charger and walked into the guest room to see rose petals on the bed and a glass of Jameson on the bedside table.

"You really are a party pooper," Katie said.

"And if you end up in here, you're in there another night."

"And if I come in tomorrow morning before you wake up?"

"That's up to you if you want to wake up that early."

Ronan relaxed and got a few emails done when one came in from Katie:

> *Am I allowed to ask for a reprieve since you intentionally taunted me to make me explode when you said not to? Next time I promise.*

He replied a few minutes later:

> *Miss me already lass? One night won't kill us.*

She sent a reply:

> *Can I at least stay in there with you until I get tired enough to sleep?*

He smirked and put his phone on the charger, then walked into the guest room. "Miss me already?"

"Since when were there punishments?"

"Since I said so."

"And if I said that you couldn't punish me?"

"I sleep better with you too love. One night."

"Ronan."

"Next time you're staying in here complaints or not."

"Then you can't use that toy anymore."

"I have others."

"Ronan."

"Worse."

"No more pushing until I explode if you don't want me to."

"So now you're making rules?"

"You want to tease without toys then fine, but with you can't tell me not to."

"Interesting."

"And about that thing that you used."

"What about it."

"I need to borrow it."

"Why?"

"Because if you make me stay in here alone, I'm gonna need it."

"That's part of the punishment."

"No toys."

He shook his head. "And if I catch you playing with yourself, I'm tying your hands."

"Bossy."

"Like I said. Mine."

"You weren't like this before today."

"I just didn't say it."

"Why now?"

"Because you two talked about you and me all morning and I wanted the truth out of you. I don't share my private life with anyone Katie. Most of all them. All they should know is that we're dating. Period. Mia now knows everything."

"Am I allowed to come back to bed with you?"

"Depends on whether you plan on keeping your hands to yourself."

"And if I run my nails up and down your back?"

"Katie." She could see he was getting turned on again.

"Well?"

"No."

"And if I slid your boxers off in the middle of the night and had you in my mouth when you woke up?"

"Katie." He was getting more turned on.

"Or I just slid my backside tight against you intentionally."

"Then you wouldn't be getting any sleep."

"What would you do," she asked. He shook his head.

"Leave you in here to sleep alone." Ronan got up and walked into the main bedroom, sitting back down on the bed and slid a blanket over him.

Katie got up and walked back into the bedroom. "What," he asked.

"Am I allowed to get in bed with you?"

"That was a warning."

"Okay," she said. She slid into the bed and intentionally took the silky nightgown off.

"What are you doing?"

"Getting in bed with you."

"Clothing."

"Optional. My new rule."

He shook his head. "Katie, I know what you're doing. You can't handle more."

"What time is it?"

"Almost 9."

"Then we should probably get some sleep." She flipped her light off and saw him flick his light off.

"Phone." She handed it to him, and he put the phones on the charger. When he rolled over, Katie's arms slid around him.

"What are you up to lass?"

"Nothing." He slid his arm around her, and she smirked.

"What?"

"Want me to take care of that?"

"I want you to stop teasing. Sleep." Her fingernails ran across his chest and got him even more turned on.

"Katie."

"What?"

"You can't handle this."

"Oh yes I can," she replied.

"Roll over."

"Meaning what?"

"Back to me."

"And what are you gonna do Ronan?" She did as he asked and his boxers slid to the floor.

He curled his arm around her and pulled her tight to him. "What," Katie asked.

"No more teasing. Deal?"

"Meaning what," Katie asked. He slid deep inside her and his hand slid over her hip and started teasing her.

"Aah."

Her breath hitched. "This what you wanted?"

"Mm." Her version of yes. He took his time, slowly sliding in and out until she met his pace then turned her face down and took over. It was more intense, deeper, harder and even a little hotter as his body pounded in and out, over and over again until she was begging. "Please."

"Please what," he asked.

"Can I?"

"Not yet."

"Ronan, please." He kept going until he could feel her almost throbbing.

"Please."

"Come for me." She exploded around him as he felt warm and wet surrounding him. He kept going, each time making her wait a little longer to find her release until he couldn't stop himself and his body melted into her. When her body clamped around him, he shook his head.

"Ronan."

"Yes love."

"Still in trouble?"

"You always will be," he teased as he fell to his back on the bed.

Her leg slid around his and her head rested on his beating chest. "Better," she joked.

"Insatiable."

"Addictive." He kissed her then kissed her forehead.

"I need sleep love."

"Honestly, so do I." He got up and grabbed his towel, cleaned up and pulled his boxers back on then slid back into bed.

"Put the pajamas on."

"Why?"

"Because if you don't, I'm gonna end up between your legs in the middle of the damn night."

"Still can."

"Katie."

"I'm just saying," she teased. He watched her perfect backside get up and slide the satin teddy back on and turn to look at him.

"Who's insatiable now Ronan?" He shook his head.

"Sleep." She slid back into the bed and curled up with him. "Goodnight love."

"Goodnight handsome." He closed his eyes and was out cold within a matter of minutes.

The next morning, Ronan woke up with Katie in his arms and her backside up against him. He shook his head and gently got up. He smirked, got changed into workout gear and went and freshened up quietly. He snuck out of the bedroom and went down to the gym and started his workout. Fine. The woman exhausted him to no end. He'd never met a single woman who could have ever kept up with him and now she was tiring him out completely. He finished his workout and looked up to see Katie watching him. "You woke up."

"You left me in bed alone."

"Workout."

"By the way, you may need to carry me into work."

"Legs a little sore?"

"Yeah," she replied as he walked over to her and backed her up against the wall. He picked her up and wrapped her legs around his hips then carried her downstairs to the kitchen.

"What," Katie asked. He kissed her, devouring her lips and sat her on the kitchen counter.

"You do realize that you could've stayed in bed this morning."

"Had to get my workout in. Long day today."

"So you aren't gonna let me come with you?"

"Katie, unless there's a reason, no. You have work. You like the people at work. Why would you want to come sit in my office all day?"

"To tease you."

"And I told you no funny business in my office."

"Still say that whole idea of sneaking in before anyone else gets there and christening your desk would've been fun."

He kissed her. "I love you too Katie." He grabbed eggs from the fridge and started on an omelet for them both.

"Why don't you ever let me make breakfast?"

"Because you're too damn distracting." He kissed her and handed her a knife.

"For what?"

"Chop up the fruit." He handed her the fruit from the fridge, and she turned it into an oversized fruit salad then plated some for them both as he plated the omelet. He made his protein smoothie and sat down with her. "Coffee," he asked.

"Please." Ronan got them each a coffee, handing one to Katie, finished his protein drink and ate with her. "What did you put in the omelet?"

"Cheese and spinach. Why?"

"I thought you had no food?"

"Dinner, no. Food yes." They ate and when they were done, Katie got up and started to do the dishes. Ronan smirked. "You realize you just have to rinse them and put them in the washer, yes?"

"Yes," Katie replied. She finished doing the dishes when she felt him kiss her shoulder. "And what was that for?"

"Dishes." She turned to face him, and he picked her up, leaning her body against the edge of the counter.

"And what do you want?"

"It's almost 7. You're up early."

"I was planning on teasing you this morning if that's allowed," Katie joked.

He kissed her again, devouring her lips. "Shower first." He picked her up and carried her upstairs, sitting her on the bathroom counter. She slid his shirt off and went for the waistband of his joggers when he shook his head.

"What?"

"Nothing love." He kissed her, turned the water on in the shower and stepped out of his boxers and joggers. He threw them into the laundry and stepped into the shower. Katie slid her satin teddy off and threw it into the laundry with his things, then stepped in behind him, sliding her arms around his torso.

"Katie."

"What?"

"Don't start that."

"I'm not starting anything," she replied as he turned to face her and kissed her.

"Just don't."

"Why?"

"Because we both have work."

"And?"

"Katie, it's half seven. We both have to get ready."

"We have an hour and a half." He shook his head, kissed her and washed his hair as she watched the water trail from his hands, down his rock-hard body, to the one spot that she wanted.

"Don't even think it lass."

"Need me to wash your back for you?"

"Not when I know that you are up to something." He rinsed out the shampoo and slid her under the water.

"Ronan."

"Shower." He washed up and when she stepped out of the stream of water, he rinsed off.

"You sure we don't have time?"

He kissed her. "Shower." He stepped out and wrapped his warm towel around him.

"Ronan."

"I'm getting dressed." He freshened up, trimming his beard and when he felt her arms around him again, he laughed. "You done," he asked.

"Missing something."

"And that's waiting until later."

"And if I say no?"

"Then the toy is going to work with you."

"You wouldn't."

"Want to make a bet?" He walked into the bedroom and grabbed it from the drawer, walking over to her. "Ronan." He flipped it on and pulled her to him.

"It's on and you can't touch it unless you ask me."

"And if I say that I want to go without it?" He kissed her and she felt the soft toy slide inside her.

"You're mine love. You're wearing it all day. I can tease you as much as I want to."

"And if I say no?"

"You're still doing it." She shook her head, and he kissed her. "And when you get home, if it's where I left it, you might get what you want."

He walked into his closet and Katie shook her head.

"And if it's not where you left it?"

"Guest room. Alone." She shook her head and walked over to her closet, intentionally picking out a dress that would make him horny in 3.2 seconds. She slid sexy lingerie on and slid the dress on then came out of the closet and sat down on the bed, sliding on heels. He came out of his closet in all black and saw her.

"Katie."

"What?"

"You're not seriously wearing that." She nodded and got up, walking over to him and kissed him.

"Like it?"

"Something tells me it's gonna be on the floor."

"Wearing it anyway." She went and did her hair, put on some perfume and he came in behind her, sliding his arms around her waist.

"What," Katie asked.

"You aren't gonna be walking tomorrow."

"That mean we aren't going to the pub tonight?"

"It means that the door is gonna be locked and we're gonna be on the stairs with you screaming my name."

"You sure about that?"

"More than sure."

"Good. That's what I was hoping you'd say." He let go and walked into the bedroom, flipping his phone to the app that controlled the toy and held his finger on the screen until he heard her moaning.

"Shit Ronan."

"Don't tempt me."

"Stop." He let go and slid his phone in his pocket.

Katie shook her head and finished getting ready. When she walked downstairs and saw him going over emails, she smirked. "Are you ready to go?" He slid his laptop in his bag and got up.

"Had to wear the sexiest dress you have."

She smirked. "And here I thought you'd like it."

"Leave it at if I could work from home today, you'd be tied to the damn bed."

"Promises, promises." He shook his head and pulled her to him, devouring her lips. He slid the bag over his shoulder and slid his hand in his pocket as he teased her again with the toy.

"Ronan, stop."

"Then stop teasing."

"By doing what?" He kissed her again and pressed the button of the phone to intensify the teasing. When she moaned, he broke the kiss.

"You sure we don't have time?" He nodded and they headed off to work, locking up behind them.

"You sure you don't want me to come to your office with you?"

"You have work. Actual work love."

"Still though."

He kissed her forehead. "You're going to work."

"Still think you need to do something about that office."

"Such as?" Katie smirked. "No." She nodded. "I said no and I meant it."

"Christening your office."

"Answer is still no." He ran his finger over the screen intentionally and saw her squirm in her seat. Her hand slid to his thigh, and she squeezed.

"Then quit teasing," Katie said.

"Or what," he asked. Her hand slid up his leg and found its target. He stopped her and removed her hand.

"You sure you don't want company at the office?"

"I'm sure lass. Besides. We're here." She shook her head, and he hopped out, helping her out of the SUV.

"You sure," Katie asked. He nodded and kissed her.

"I'll see you tonight." Katie nodded and went inside. Ronan left with the driver and headed to his office.

When he got there, he walked into his office and saw a package on his desk.

"Sir," his assistant said.

"What's with the package?"

"The courier said it was a back order that you'd ordered." Ronan nodded and put it aside. She handed Ronan his messages and papers for the day and left him to work. He opened the package and saw the one thing he didn't expect – another toy. It'd slide into her lacy panties and he could control it with the little remote or on his phone. He smirked and slid it into his bag. Just as he did, his phone buzzed with a text from Katie:

Just got an email. We have a foundation meeting on Friday night.

He replied back:

Guess we'll have to have a little fun while we're there. Should I make you wear it again?

Katie: *And here I thought you wanted me to behave.*

Ronan: *No fun in that lass. So many things I could do to make you squirm. Have one here in fact.*

Katie: *Don't tell me that you bought more.*

Ronan: *Was gonna get what we were playing with last night but bigger. See how long you lasted on high.*

He knew it'd make her squirm. He also knew exactly what that toy would do to her.

Katie: *Don't start. If you lock me in that guest room tonight, I hereby request that toy to come with me.*

Ronan: *That toy stays where I put it or else.*

Katie: *Then I get the other one. You.*

Ronan got a smirk ear to ear and shook his head.

Ronan: *Then do as I asked. Don't touch it or you'll be in that guest bed all alone. No toys.*

He put his phone down and went through the messages when his phone buzzed again. Instead of answering, he flipped the app on and ran his finger over the screen just enough to make her squirm in her seat. His phone buzzed a second time:

Katie: *And if I said that I wasn't? What would you do?*

Katie: *Ronan please.*

Ronan: *I'd walk you in there and tie you to the bed and leave you there all night.*

Katie: *I'd rather you do that in your bed.*

Ronan: *Get back to work Katie. For once, behave.*

He got some work done and his phone buzzed:

Katie: *I want you tonight as soon as I get home. On the stairs if need be.*

He smirked. That was part of his plan. He went through the paperwork, signing off on this and that and when another text came in, he half-expected it to be from Katie. When it was from his ex, he shook his head:

> Devil: *I know you miss me Ronan. Meet me at the house tonight. I have something for you.*

Ronan deleted and blocked the number.

He got some work done and was just about to walk into a meeting when his phone rang. "Yes."

"What are you doing?"

"About to walk into a meeting," Ronan said as he could hear the wanting in Katie's voice.

"Ronan." He slid his AirPods in and ran his finger over the screen.

"Miss me," he asked.

"Need."

"How much," he asked as he ran his finger over the screen again and heard a quiet moan.

"I'm coming to the office."

"No."

"I told them that I was working from home. That's the other option. I can't."

"Katie."

"I can't stop thinking about last night."

"I have a meeting this morning and one at 1. I won't be back until 3."

"Then I'm coming there."

"Katie, it's almost 11. Stop."

"Ronan."

"Get work done. When I finish my meeting, I'll let you know."

"Ronan." He ran his finger over the screen, holding it there and making the buzzing even more intense to her.

"Tonight. I'll come and get you myself."

"Mm."

"I'll take that as a yes."

Ronan finished his meetings, had a quick lunch, and headed to his last meeting when his phone buzzed again:

>   *Craving you.*

He took a deep breath and went into his meeting. He managed a reply behind the paperwork he had:

>   *You, me, handcuffs, and you begging for more.*

He finished his meeting and his phone buzzed:

>   *More.*

He shook his head and grabbed his paperwork and laptop. "Sir, you have a visitor," his assistant said.

"I was just about to head...."

"Ronan," the Devil herself said.

"I have other places to be. Second, you aren't welcome here. Third, go back to the hole you crawled out of and stay there." Ronan grabbed his bag, walked her out of his office, walked her back to the reception desk and told security to remove her.

"I'm heading home," Ronan said.

"Yes sir." Ronan walked out, walked downstairs and got in the car, texting Katie:

More starting now. Blindfold.

Katie replied back almost instantly:

Where are you?

He replied:

On my way. Be outside in 20.

The car made its way to Katie's work and when he pulled in, Katie was there waiting with her laptop bag in hand. She slid in beside him and kissed him. "And how was your day," Ronan asked.

"Home."

"That bad?" She looked at him and he shook his head.

"What excuse did you give?"

"Headache," she teased. He kissed her and they headed back to the house.

When they got back to the house, he walked her inside, put his laptop bag down and kissed her, pinning her against the front door. He locked it and slid the hem of her skirt up.

"Ronan."

"You wanted stairs you get stairs." She kissed him and felt her lacy panties sliding off.

"Here?" He kissed her, devouring her lips. He picked her up and slid her legs around his hips as his hands slid to her bare backside. "Ronan." He kissed her and leaned her onto the stairs.

"No."

"You really think that I'm letting you get away with teasing me?"

"Meaning what," Katie said as she started trying to ease her way up the steps.

"You heard me."

"You mean the texts," she teased as she regained her footing and backed up to the top of the steps.

"Katie."

"What?" She got up and ran for the bedroom. He caught her hand and pulled her back to him. He pinned her against the wall of the hallway and pinned her hands above her head.

"What," Katie asked. He slid the toy out and slid it into his pocket.

"Really trying to run away?"

"Teasing." He kissed her and picked her up, carrying her to the bed.

"Ronan."

"What?" He kissed her, devouring her lips and unzipped the dress, sliding it off.

"You're overdressed." He slid his suit jacket off and threw it onto the chair. "Ronan." He slid the shirt off and threw it into the laundry. "Take it all off," he said.

"Ronan, I just..."

"Just what?"

"I was teasing." He walked around the bed and grabbed something out of the drawer.

"I wasn't," Ronan replied.

"Meaning what?" He looked at her, completely naked on the bed and slid the blindfold over her eyes.

"Ronan." He handcuffed her to the bed.

"What are you up to?"

"Like I said, begging for more." She shook her head.

"Kiss me." He devoured her lips and broke the kiss just as she was starting to fight the handcuffs. "Undo them."

"Nope."

"Ronan." He undid his dress pants and got up, hanging them up with his suit jacket.

"What are you doing?" He grabbed the other item from his drawer that she'd said no to. He walked back over to her and Katie's toes curled. He slid his boxers off and kissed her neck.

"Ronan."

"What?"

"You know what." He kissed down her neck then nibbled and licked at each breast.

"Mm."

"What," Ronan asked.

"You know what I want."

"And if I said that you don't get what you want?"

"Ronan." He kissed and nibbled at her hip until he felt her leg wrap around his.

"Please." He kissed her inner thigh, and he saw her toes curl.

He kissed and licked and teased her then nibbled his way up to her wetness. "Shit."

"Mine," he said. He kept going until he pulled her legs over his shoulders.

"Ronan." He licked and teased then slid two fingers inside her, teasing as he licked. "Shit."

"And I'm just getting started love."

"Just want you. I need you." He grabbed the toy and slid it inside her, turning the thrusting on. "Shit Ronan."

"And if you come before I say, you're in the guest room."

"Not fair. Not fair at all."

"Then don't."

"Aah."

"Don't do it love."

"Then stop it."

"Not on your life."

"Aah."

"Don't."

"Ronan, I want you."

"Not yet lass."

"Mm."

"Not yet."

"I can't take anymore." He turned up the intensity and Katie shook her head.

"Stop."

"Nope."

"Ronan, please."

"Please what?"

"I need you instead of that."

"Meaning what?"

"Mm."

"Ask me," he said.

"Please."

"Come for me." She did and he turned the intensity up even more.

"Shit. Not fair Ronan."

"Oh, it's staying there until I decide it's my turn."

"I need you."

"Which part," he teased.

"I need to taste you." He kissed her hip.

"Mm."

"You're gonna keep going until I say that you're stopping."

"Ronan, please." He kissed her and slid the toy in deeper until he could almost feel her throbbing around it.

He got up and walked around to her and kissed her. "You sure this is what you want?" Her mouth opened and he slid himself in as she licked and sucked. "Shit Katie."

"Mm." He shook his head, and she took him deeper. She fought the handcuffs, and he smirked. Just as he was starting reach his max, he pulled away from her. "Ronan."

"Nope."

"Aah."

"Don't do it."

"Ronan, please." He pulled the toy out of her and slid deep into her until he could feel her starting to throb.

"Not yet."

"Aah," she moaned.

"Katie."

"Ronan, please." He pounded into her over and over again until he felt her starting to throb again and then whispered to her.

"Come for me." She exploded around him and held on tight around him.

"Good girl," he whispered. He kept pounding into her harder and deeper until she climaxed again. When he followed, he had her pinned.

"Mine," he said.

"Back at you," Katie joked.

"You aren't done yet love."

"Meaning what," Katie asked as he slid out of her and slid the toy back in on high. "Ronan, you aren't fair."

He slid it in deeper until her legs were shaking. "Ronan, please stop."

"You begging for mercy?"

"I need to."

"Again," he teased.

"Please." He slid it out and licked and teased until she was exploding again.

"My girl," he said.

"No more."

"And?"

"I can't. Undo them." He kissed her and undid the handcuffs and slid the blindfold off.

"You promised me that was staying in the drawer."

"And you behaved."

"You can't keep doing that."

"What? The part where I tell you that you can't come?"

"The part where you use that toy to make me beg for mercy." He kissed her.

"Oh, that toy is gonna come out when I say it is lass."

"And if I said no?" He shook his head.

"You have no choice love."

"Ronan, you aren't playing fair."

"And you teasing me all day when I'm at work was fair?" He got up and walked into the bathroom and cleaned up, stepping into the shower. Katie went to get up and her legs almost gave out.

Just as he was stepping out of the shower, she sat down on the counter. "And what do you want love?"

"No more toy."

"I have others."

"Ronan."

"You want me to stop making you do that?"

"I want it to be the way it is without them."

"Then you're not gonna be walking."

"Meaning what?"

"I can make you come over and over again until you beg me. You know I can."

"Ronan."

"You did one good thing," he teased. Katie's legs slid around his and pulled his soaking wet body closer. "Katie."

"This mean we're curling up in bed tonight?"

"This means that if you behave, you get me all to yourself tonight."

"And if I pounce on you instead?" He kissed her and picked her up, pulling her legs tight around him and leaned her onto the bed.

"What," Katie asked as he pinned her arms above her head.

"You do realize that the more you tease, the less sleep you're gonna get, yeah?"

"I want you. That not allowed?"

He kissed her and shook his head. "You can wait," he teased. "Meaning what?"

"I have to log into work." He got up and grabbed his shirt. He slid it on, pulled on a pair of jeans and walked downstairs, logging into his work email. When he opened his email up and saw that he had a call-in meeting in a matter of 15 minutes, he shook his head and walked into his office.

Chapter 10

Katie slid his other dress shirt on and walked downstairs, seeing his office door closed. She smirked and went and got a bottle of water from the fridge and walked into his office. He shook his head. He was already in his meeting. She nodded and he looked at her. "The process needs to be made easier to do," Ronan said as Katie looked at him. She walked over to him, and he shook his head. She got down on her knees and went for the button of his jeans. He shook his head and kept going with his meeting. She unzipped his jeans quietly and he stopped her. "Understood, but we still have to make it easier. If it's going to be accessible to everyone, it has to be easy to use." Katie slid her hand into his boxers, and he shook his head. Katie nodded. When he felt her mouth on him, he did his best to concentrate on the call, but when she kept going even when he tried to stop her, he needed the call to be over. "Mm," Katie said as he silenced her. "We can work on it. I'm hopping off," Ronan said as he hung up.

"Aah." She kept going until his fingers slid into her hair. "Katie, stop."

"Mm." She took him deeper, and he shook his head.

"Get up."

"Mm mm." She sucked harder and he pulled her away from him and pulled her to her feet. He bent her over the desk and slid deep into her, pounding into her over and over again, harder then deeper until her knees were giving out. He felt her throb around him and exploded into her. "You are never gonna behave, are you?"

Katie kissed him. "And you love it."

"Next time I say no, I mean it."

"And what were you gonna do Ronan?" He shook his head and got up, towering over her.

"Upstairs."

"No."

"Katie, go."

"Why?"

"Because I said to go."

"And I'm going upstairs why?"

"Go." She walked out of his office and walked upstairs.

"Why," Katie asked. He kissed her and pinned her onto the bed.

"Ronan."

"When I say stop, I mean stop." She kissed him. "Katie."

"I'm not allowed to get you back?"

"No." She smirked. "And you stole a shirt?"

"Yep."

"Katie, I love you but stop."

"Stop what? Getting back at you for taunting me? Doing the one thing I told you that I was gonna do?"

"Katie."

"What?"

"Meeting. Important meeting."

"I still get to tease you back. You started this Ronan."

"Not when I'm in an important call-in meeting. Agreed?"

"Only if you promise that toy stays in the drawer."

"I have others lass."

"That one stays in the drawer." He shook his head. "Then you're not getting your way. If you're on a call and you say no, I may think twice, but I get my way." He shook his head and walked downstairs.

When Katie heard the front door slam, she took a deep breath and looked out the window, seeing Ronan walking down the street. She slid on her jeans and a shirt, slid on her boots and grabbed her keys, purse and phone. She locked the house up behind her and walked down to where she knew Ronan was. She walked into the pub, and he was ordering himself a drink. "Add on an espresso martini for her."

"I'll bring it over," Pat said as Ronan went and sat down. Katie went to slide in beside him and he shook his head.

"Seriously," Katie said. Pat brought the drinks over and Ronan was quiet.

"What," Katie asked.

"I said no. I meant it."

"Fine. I was having a little fun with you."

"And next time I say no, you're not gonna like what's gonna happen."

"Is that a threat?"

"Promise."

"And what are you gonna do Ronan?"

"Don't dare me." She took a sip of her drink and Ronan was silent.

"What would you do?"

"The guest room would be the least of your damn worries."

"Meaning what?"

"I said no. That was an important meeting."

"I gathered that."

"And so is the one on Friday. I'm not playing games with you."

"Meaning what?"

Ronan shook his head and glared. "What do you want me to do Ronan? Read your mind?"

"Move."

"So you can walk off again? No."

"Move to the other side."

"No."

"You don't understand, do you? Work is work. Play is separate and they aren't crossing over."

"Meaning?"

"Guest room."

"I did what you asked."

"No, you didn't."

"Ronan, you promised me." He shook his head.

"What do you want me to do? Beg? We were having fun. We both got carried away."

"You disobeyed what I said."

"And before that I didn't. I'm not gonna sit here and have a damn fight about it."

"Then go home."

Katie looked at him. "Not without you, smart ass."

He finished his pint, and he watched Katie slowly sip her espresso martini. "Katie."

"I'm not moving."

"When I have a meeting I have to do, you can't start that. Deal?"

"Fine."

"I have a question."

"Ask away Ronan."

"Hotel suite or home?"

"After the meeting?"

He nodded. "Depends on what you're doing in the hotel suite."

"Same thing we always do. Make you explode over and over again until you pass out from exhaustion."

"So, sorta the same thing you did the first time that we were alone in one."

"Is that a yes?"

"Depends on whether you're doing what you just did when we were in bed."

"Even better. I could tie your hands and your feet," he whispered as she got goosebumps head to toe.

"Not exactly the part I was talking about, but I am almost worried about what else you're coming up with to taunt me so I can't move," she whispered.

"Oh, there's worse I could do love."

"I bet there is."

"As long as it doesn't involve including anyone else, fine."

"Now that's something I never considered."

"Don't even go there Ronan. And that thing is staying at home."

"Nope. For what I have planned, you'll need it."

"Meaning what?"

"That thing that you hadn't done," he whispered as her goosebumps got goosebumps.

"No." He nodded. Her entire body clenched. She shook her head.

"Or I could just tie you to the bed and make you come over and over again until I decide it's my turn. Then use it somewhere else," he whispered.

"Ronan."

"Or make you keep it in there all the way through the meeting."

"How," she asked.

"Because I got you one that you can wear."

Katie looked at him. "You got what?"

"You heard me."

She looked at him again. "You wouldn't do that."

"I take it that's a yes." She shook her head.

"Then you're wearing it during the meeting. The big one comes to the hotel room and stays on until I say it's off."

"Ronan."

"What?"

"You're kidding right?" He shook his head. "Ronan." He slid his phone out of his pocket and texted his assistant to book the suite at the hotel where the meeting would be.

"What," he asked.

"You aren't really planning that are you," she asked. He nodded. "Ronan." He kissed her and she shook her head.

"Move over lass."

"No."

"Why?"

"Because you're just gonna walk off again."

"Katie." She shook her head, and he took a deep breath.

"I need to get up and get another pint."

"Pat, can you grab us another drink," Katie asked.

"Sure lass," Pat said as Katie smirked and slid in closer to Ronan.

"Katie."

She kissed him. "Tell me what you want love."

"Do you want a hint?"

"Not happening."

"Then meet me in the ladies." He shook his head. "Then we go home."

"Katie."

"Something."

"I needed to get out of the house. You just automatically think that everything is free game. It's not. You're not the one in control Katie. Sit where you want, but you don't get to do that. Just stop."

"And I'm supposed to just let you control everything?"

"I have since day one lass. Leave it alone."

"So, me doing what I did set you off, but you did enjoy it."

"You start that again, I swear Katie. When I say no, I mean no. I don't mean do it anyway."

"Ronan, it won't happen again unless you say it's okay. That work?" He nodded.

"Tell me what I need to do." He looked at her.

"What?"

"Move over to your side of the table."

"Nope," Katie said as she leaned into his arms. Pat brought the drinks over and smirked.

"What," Ronan asked.

"Glad to see you two made up," Pat joked as he went back to the bar.

"Katie." She wrapped his arms around her and kissed him.

"What," she replied. He shook his head.

"You're sucking up."

"I'm getting you to stop being in a bad mood."

"You aren't wearing a skirt lass."

"Meaning what?"

"Meaning the bathroom thing isn't happening. We finish these drinks and head home."

"What are we doing for dinner?"

"Reservation. You can't wear jeans and either can I."

"Where are we going?"

"Bull and Castle."

"The new steakhouse place?"

He nodded. "Ronan."

"What?"

"What time is the reservation?"

"6."

"Then we should go." He took a gulp of his pint.

"You have a drink to finish lass." She drank it and smirked. He took another sip of his pint and Katie looked at him.

"What?"

"Are you coming to dinner with me or am I going alone?" He drank down the pint and they headed off after paying.

They got back to the house and Katie went and got changed into her sweater dress and sexy lingerie while he changed into dress pants and a dress shirt. "You ready love," Ronan asked as he sat down on the edge of the bed and checked over work emails. Katie walked out of her closet in heels and a sweater dress with a thigh-high slit.

"Katie."

"Like?" It hugged every curve and was almost too sexy to take her out in.

"Had to right?" She smirked and walked over to him.

"Just for you," Katie said.

"Then let's go do this dinner so I can rip it off of you."

"Really. So, you aren't adding anything to it?"

"Good point. Bend over. He got up and grabbed the item that he'd shipped to his office and turned it on.

"Ronan."

He slid it inside her and smirked. "Mm."

"Good. Now stand up."

"Ronan, don't do that in the middle of the restaurant." He slid the remote in his pocket and pressed the button to start it. "Shit."

"No complaining either," he teased as they made their way downstairs.

"Had to go pulling that out of that damn drawer."

"You love that drawer." They headed out and he locked up behind them as he walked her to the waiting SUV. They slid inside and he intentionally turned the toy on as it went in and out in a slow grueling pace. "Mm." He shook his head.

"Not yet."

"Then turn it off." He shook his head. He left it on and her hand gripped his.

"Katie." She looked at him. "Not yet."

"Then turn..." He turned it up. "Shit." She gripped his hand, and she looked at him, almost begging him to let her come.

"Mine," he whispered in her ear.

"Please."

He slid her to him in the back seat and whispered, "Come for me." She did almost silently, and he turned it up even more. All it took was one look from her and he got a grin ear to ear.

"Tell me you're mine."

"All yours," she whispered. He kissed her and flipped the toy off.

"Aah."

"Good," he teased. They pulled up to the restaurant and went inside, getting a booth in the back, away from anyone else.

"You are so not fair," Katie teased as he ordered them drinks.

"Don't make me turn it back on."

"Ronan."

He smirked. "Yes lass."

"Not in here." He smirked again. The waiter brought over the drinks and they ordered dinner.

"So, what's the special occasion Ronan?"

"Meaning what," he asked.

"Fancy restaurant. It's not the weekend."

"Decided that we needed a real night out love."

"And what else? Wanted to try out your new toy?"

"That too," he replied.

"Promise me that it stays off during dinner."

"That what stays off," he asked as his hand slid in his pocket and he turned it on low.

"Not fair Ronan. I can't do anything."

"Good." He turned it up and Katie looked at him.

"Mm."

"Good."

"Not here." He took a sip of his drink and Katie looked at him.

"Have your drink lass."

"Turn it off and I will." He turned the intensity up.

"Ronan."

"Tell me when."

"When what?"

"You know what."

"Aah."

"Are you?"

"Bathroom." He shook his head. "Ronan." He turned it up even more and she gave him that look. The one that said not to deny her because she was about to explode. He flipped it completely off.

"What did…"

"Nope."

"Why?"

"Because I said so."

Dinner showed a few minutes later and they both ate and finished their drinks. "I can't believe you," Katie said.

"Do you want to get another drink?" Katie nodded. He ordered a second drink for each of them and leaned back in his seat.

"Why did you flip it off?"

"Because I didn't want you coming all over the seat." She took a sip of her martini, and he looked at her, taking a gulp of his drink.

"Stop staring at me like that."

"You do realize that you're gonna have to hold back all the way home right?"

"Then don't turn it up."

"Finish your drink." She took another sip, and he drank down the rest of his drink. She took a gulp of her drink and finished it. He paid, took her hand and walked her outside.

"What," Katie asked. He kissed her, devouring her lips. As soon as the kiss broke, they got into the SUV and headed back to the house. He slid his hand in his pocket and turned the toy back on. Her leg slid to his and he looked at her. "Tell me when you're close, but don't come," he whispered.

"Mm."

"Don't," he said quietly.

"Not fair."

"Yeah, it is," he replied. He turned it up just as they were coming around the corner to the house.

"Ronan."

"Don't."

"Turn it off," Katie said. He flipped it off and her hand clamped down on his leg.

"Shit."

"What," he asked.

"Upstairs."

They got back to the house and headed inside. The minute they were through the door, he turned it back on high. "Aah."

"Not yet," he said.

"Ronan," she moaned. He picked her up and carried her up the stairs. He leaned her onto the bed and flipped the toy off. "Aah."

"What," he asked.

"That's twice." He kissed her and slid the dress off, seeing the black lace lingerie.

"And you thought that you could really get away with this," he teased.

"Sorta hoped you'd bend me over the bathroom counter," Katie teased. He shook his head and slid the toy out, throwing it on the bed beside them.

"Now what?" He peeled the lacy thong off and undid his dress pants, kicking them aside and kicking off his boxers. She still had her heels on.

"What were you saying," he asked as he flipped her to her stomach and pulled her backside against him.

"What? No handcuffs?" He tied her hands with the belt from his dress pants and slid deep into her.

He pounded into her over and over again until she was moaning his name. "Ronan, please."

"Not yet." He kept going and felt her body clench around him.

"Please." His hand slid around to her wetness and stroked her until she was about to completely crumble then he let her have her release. "Aah."

"I'm not done with you," he said as he kissed down her neck and kept pounding into her. He went harder, deeper until she was moaning all over again then went faster until she was throbbing all over again.

"Ronan, please." He kept going harder until he was nearing his release and said the words.

"Come with me," he said as he kept going until he exploded into her and her body throbbed tight around him.

"Good girl," he teased as he undid his belt from around her hands.

"That what you wanted?"

"I can't even move." He walked off into the bathroom and Katie caught her breath, sliding out of the lingerie.

"Leave the heels on."

"Ronan." He cleaned up and came back into the bedroom, grabbing boxers.

"Am I allowed to take the lingerie off?"

"No."

He walked in and grabbed the other toy from the drawer. "No."

"Oh I'm nowhere near done with you."

"Ronan." He kissed down her neck and flipped her onto her back.

"What are you doing?"

"Nothing." He walked around the bed and grabbed a tie from his drawer and tied her hands to the bed.

"What are you doing Ronan? Untie them."

"Not until I decide you've had enough."

"Meaning what?" He spread her legs apart and licked at her inner thigh, nipping it and licking his way up to her core.

"Ronan."

"Yes love."

"Please don't." He flipped the toy on and slid it deep into her as he continued to lick then flipped the thrusting on.

"Aah."

"Good."

"Not fair."

"What isn't? The fact that you're gonna keep going until you beg me to stop or the fact that you might get me too?"

"Mm."

"That's what I thought." He turned the intensity up and she moaned.

"I want you to come over and over again until you can't take anymore, then I get my way with you."

"Aah."

"I want to taste you." He kissed and licked, making the sensation even more intense. He could feel her throbbing and turned it up even more. "Ronan." He teased until she was climaxing over and over again, then flipped her back onto her stomach and slid it in deeper. "Shit."

"Tell me what you want love."

"Mm." His hand slid across her backside and she slid closer to him, backing up and arching her back so it was against him.

"Not doing it."

"Yes." His thumb slid inside her and it made it even more intense.

"Aah."

"More," he asked.

"Mm. Yes."

"Katie, I'm not doing it."

"I need you inside me." He slid the toy in and out harder until she was moaning again.

"Aah." Hell. It was turning him on. She came over and over again and finally, was begging him. He left the toy in place and walked around in front of her, sliding his boxers off. She looked up and opened her mouth as he slid himself in and she sucked and licked.

She took him deep into her mouth and kept licking and teasing until she found her release again. She was moaning around him. "My good girl," he said as he slid himself deeper into her throat. She kept going and sucked harder and faster until he completely pulled away. "Aah."

"Beg," he said.

"I need this toy gone and I need you. Now."

He slid the toy out and threw it onto the bed beside her then slid deep into her as her body throbbed tight around him. "This what you wanted," he asked as he went hard, deep and fast into her until she was throbbing all over again. "You don't get mercy tonight until I say you do."

"Ronan."

"Mine." He kept going until he knew he was almost at his breaking point and felt her body explode around him.

"More," he almost growled.

"Please. I can't take any more." He kept going until he exploded into her and her body crumbled. He undid the tie around her hands and slid onto the bed beside her.

"I can barely move."

"Good." Her heels slid to the floor, and she curled up to him.

"Sore," he asked.

"I may have collapsed completely if we hadn't..."

"Good."

"Meaning what?"

"Sated."

She kissed him. "Understatement. I need to get up."

"Why?"

"Pajamas. Take all of this off." He kissed her and undid the bra, then nibbled at her breasts. "Mm."

"What," he asked. Katie smirked.

"I like."

"I know you do lass." He kept going until he felt her arms sliding around him.

"And here I thought you were spent."

"Mm." He licked and nibbled at each little peak until her back arched.

"Tell me what you want."

"More." He kept going until her hand slid his between her legs and felt her getting wet all over again.

"Insatiable."

"You started it," she said.

"Katie."

"What?"

"Not happening lass. You need sleep and I need a shower." She slid his fingers inside her.

"Mm."

"Katie." He shook his head and leaned into her arms.

"Determined to have your way I see," he teased.

"I want you." He slid deep into her and her legs wrapped around his hips.

"Mm."

"Katie, you can't take much more." Her hands slid to his backside, and he shook his head. He slid deep into her and her knees slid up his ribs so he could go deeper. "Aah."

"Not sore," he asked as he slowly slid in and out.

"I need you." He pounded into her, and she held on tighter.

"Mm." He kissed her and kept going, fast and hard until he could feel her throbbing.

"Mine." She moaned and he kept going hard, deep and fast until she was almost trembling in his arms. He exploded into her and she throbbed around him, holding onto him.

"You are going to bed," he said.

"In here with you." He nodded and she kissed him again, all but refusing to let him go.

"I have to get up love." She shook her head, and he untied her legs from around him and got up. He walked into the bathroom and had a quick shower, stepping out and wrapping a towel around him. He pulled on fresh boxers and looked over to see Katie out cold on the bed. He slid their phones onto the charger and saw a text message on hers:

When you want a real man, let me know.

He looked at the number, texted security to do a search on it and went to go to sleep when he got a reply:

> *Let her know she should block it or notify the police. It's from the guy she has the protective order against.*

Ronan shook his head and went into her phone, blocking the number it came from and deleted the text. He put his phone down and saw two texts. Both were from women he'd known in what he felt was another life. Life before Katie. He deleted both the texts and blocked them. He walked downstairs and got a drink, grabbed a bottle of water and headed upstairs. He curled up on the bed, flipped the light off and before he knew it, Katie's naked body was coiled around him, and her head was on his chest. He nodded off a few minutes later and smirked. Walking was gonna be a challenge for her the next day.

He woke up the next morning, got a workout in and went downstairs to make breakfast. When she didn't appear, he put her breakfast on a tray along with his and two mugs of coffee, grabbed his after workout shake and walked upstairs to eat with her. "Why are you up so early," Katie asked.

"Making you breakfast." He put the tray down, taking his breakfast off and taking a few gulps of his protein shake.

"My legs are a little sore."

He smirked. "I can't imagine why." He kissed her and they both ate. When they were done, he moved the tray to the counter and kissed her again.

"What time is it?"

"6:40."

"Meaning you're coming back to bed?"

"Meaning we're getting up and I'm heading in early."

"Nope." He kissed her and got up.

"Where are you going?"

"Shower and getting ready for work."

"It's not even 8 yet."

"You really want to have to be carried into work?"

"Something like that." He shook his head and walked into the bathroom and flipped the shower on to warm up the water. He kicked his workout clothes off and threw them into the laundry and stepped under the stream of hot water. He washed his hair and rinsed and felt arms slide around him.

"Katie." She came around in front of him and kissed him.

"What? Something I need." "Still not happening love."

"Why?"

"Because I'm going in early. I have to be in the office by 8:30."

"It's not even 7. We have time."

"For what?"

"Want a hint?" He shook his head, and she kneeled and took him in her mouth. "Shit Katie."

She sucked and licked and teased until he shook his head and stared down at her. "Katie, stop."

"Mm." She took him deeper, and he pulled her to her feet and flipped her so her face was against the cool tile of the wall.

"You are so bad."

"And that's why you love me."

"Because you always get what you want?" She nodded with a smirk ear to ear. He shook his head and pulled her to him, sliding deep into her. "This what you wanted?" Katie's hands braced her against the wall, and he pounded into her over and over again until she was throbbing around him.

"Shit Ronan."

"Oh, I'm not even close," he teased as he kept going harder and deeper until he exploded into her.

"Aah."

"Don't ever start something you can't finish," Ronan teased.

He slid her under the stream of hot water and washed her hair for her. "Mm."

"What," he asked as she smirked.

"Now that's how the morning should've started."

"Insatiable." She nodded and he rinsed her hair out. "Finish your shower."

"Ronan." He kissed her and stepped out, wrapping himself in a towel. He freshened up and walked into the bedroom, grabbing his clothes for work and laying them on the bed. He slid into his clothes, and she stepped out of the shower. She walked into the bedroom and saw him shirtless in her favorite cologne.

"You smell good," Katie said.

"Well thank you lass. How was your shower?" She walked up to him and kissed him.

"Take the boxers off and the pants."

"Nope. I have a half hour to get ready then I have to head out."

"Ronan."

"Do you want to go in early and leave with me?"

She smirked. "What if I just went to work with you?" "Somehow that dirty mind of yours wouldn't survive a day in my office. Not when you're gonna have to behave."

"And if I came to your office without panties in a skirt, what would you do?"

"Tell you that you aren't coming into my office."

"And why not?"

"Because you're too tempting, especially when you're doing it to get me to do something that I'm not doing in my office."

"And if I talked you into it?" He shook his head and slid his dress shirt on.

"Katie, no." She kissed him and walked into her closet. When she came out, she was in a skirt and a top that he knew would be almost too tempting not to rip off of her.

"You aren't coming to my office."

"Sorta already emailed my boss."

"Katie."

"I'm coming with you today." He shook his head.

"If you're coming with me then you're wearing it."

"Wearing what?" He bent her over the bed, slid her skirt up and slid in the toy he'd teased her with over dinner.

"No."

"You want to be in my office, then you're doing what I tell you to."

"You are so not fair."

"You want to do this?"

"This mean we're having fun in your office?"

"This means that you may not last all day." She stood up and slid her skirt down, stepping into her heels.

"You aren't playing fair. You realize that right?"

He kissed her. "I'll meet you downstairs."

By the time they got into his office, Katie had a smirk ear to ear. "Nothing is happening Katie. You do realize that." They got into the office, and his assistants weren't there yet.

"Perfect timing," Katie said.

"No." He walked her into his office and set up his laptop. She put hers on the table by the sofa and closed his office door.

"Katie." She locked his office door and walked back over to him. "You are never gonna behave."

"I want you. Not a toy." She slid his laptop back and sat on his desk.

"Katie, I said not in the office." She slid her heels off and slid her skirt up. He shook his head.

"No."

"I want you, not the toy."

"Not here." She slid him closer to her, and he shook his head.

"Never ever gonna behave."

"Nope." He flipped the toy on and started the teasing.

"Aah."

"At some point you have to learn to behave lass."

"Toy out."

"Nope."

"Ronan, I want you."

"So, you only came here to try and seduce me in my office."

"Partially...aah."

"And what else did you want to do," he asked as he turned up the intensity of the toy until she was almost moaning. She went to slide off the desk when he stopped her. "What," he asked.

"If you're gonna do this, I'm getting payback."

"Can you even consider the word no?" She shook her head.

"I either have you or take you." He shook his head.

"Take the toy back or I'm on my knees with you in my mouth."

"Katie, not here." She looked at him as if it were a challenge that he couldn't find a way to win.

"Take it out." He shook his head.

"No." She got down on her knees and undid the zipper of his dress pants, then the button.

"Katie." Her hand slid under the waistband of his boxers and before he'd even had time to say no, he was in her mouth. She was sucking and licking and deep-throating him. "Shit, Katie stop."

"Mm."

"Katie."

"What," she asked with a full mouth.

"Stop." She shook her head, and he turned the toy up to high. She kept going until he exploded into her mouth and she climaxed more than once.

"Off."

"Shit." Katie licked her lips and looked up at him as he flipped the toy to low.

"Aah," Katie moaned.

"You aren't getting off that easy lass." She stood up and kissed him.

"Something else you wanted to do?" Katie smirked.

"Had to be bad today."

"Yep. That was part of my plan," Katie teased.

"And what else was part of that plan?"

"Lunch with you."

"And," he teased. Katie smirked. "No."

"You really are a party pooper. You're seriously just gonna do work and nothing else."

"It's called work love." He redressed and got up, unlocking his office door then went and sat back down, grabbing the air freshener and spraying.

"Ronan."

"What?"

"Come here for a minute." He walked over to her and sat down with her.

"What," he asked.

Katie kissed him. "I love you."

He shook his head. "I love you too. Just promise me no more distractions." Katie nodded. When she got a smirk ear to ear, he shook his head. "If you're so determined to have your way, we're going home at lunch."

"That a promise?"

"That's called you not behaving. We go home at lunch and you're staying home."

"And why is that," Katie asked.

"Because you won't be walking."

"That a promise or a threat," Katie teased. He kissed her, devouring her lips and when the kiss broke, he smirked.

"What do you think?"

Katie smirked. "Looking forward to lunch then." He shook his head.

"You're just determined to get your way." Katie nodded. "Just remember who has control over that little toy."

"And you aren't gonna leave it on, right?" He slid his hand in his pocket and ran his finger over the screen as it thrusted in and out.

"Ronan."

"You really think you're gonna do what you did and not get it back ten-fold?"

"Ronan, stop."

"Nope."

"Ronan." He turned the intensity down and saw her slide her heels off.

Just as Katie was about to get up and walk over to Ronan, there was a knock at his door. "Yep," he said.

"Your messages and coffee. Oh. Katie, did you want a coffee as well?"

"Please," Katie replied.

"Thank you for this."

"You're welcome, sir," his assistant said as she left the room. Katie smirked.

"I swear you are intentionally trying to taunt me until I take you home."

"I may need to take full advantage of you when we get home," Katie said.

"You kind of already did love."

"Then the other thing that you're teasing me with can go into my bag."

"Touch it and you're in the guest room."

"Ronan." He looked over at her and she shook her head.

"You're intending on taunting me all damn day, aren't you?"

"It's only fair love. You started all of this when we got here."

"I started all of this when we were at the house. All it would've taken was you curling back up in bed with me."

"Lass, if I'd done that, I wouldn't have got anything done and either would you. We'd still be home in bed."

Katie got a grin ear to ear. "And what would be so bad about that?"

"Work."

She smirked. "Ronan."

He shook his head. "Don't start teasing. We both need to get work done love. I have almost 500 emails to go through."

"Fine," Katie said as she logged into her work email and started getting work done as his assistant came in with her coffee.

"Thank you," Katie said.

"Most welcome. Sir, your 10am meeting was pushed to 11. The one this afternoon is gonna be a call instead."

"Thank you," Ronan said.

"Meaning you can do the call from home." He looked at Katie and she smirked.

"Without interruption."

"Not even a tiny distraction?" He shook his head.

"Not even a small one lass. It's an important meeting. I have to get it finished today."

"Party pooper," Katie joked.

"Meaning you aren't gonna be in the room."

"Fine. We can work today, but lunch is still mine."

"And what exactly did you have planned for lunch?"

"You and me in bed."

"Katie."

"You said we were going home for lunch, did you not?"

He shook his head. "Don't tempt me Katie."

"I'll take you with a toastie on the side," she joked.

He shook his head. "You're bad. You realize that."

"And since we're going home for lunch, tell me what you want."

He looked at her. "Can't wait that long," he teased.

"You can't or I can't?"

"You. I have to get this meeting done then we can talk about lunch." Katie nodded and went through emails.

"I still can't believe you aren't wearing anything."

"And I can't believe what you brought out to tease me back with," Katie replied.

"Speaking of."

"Ronan, don't you dare start that."

"Start this," he teased as he ran his finger over the screen and her toes curled in her heels.

"Mm."

"Then don't tease."

"You keep doing that and I'm going to pounce," Katie said.

"Behave." She shook her head, and he ran his finger over the screen again as the toy slid in and out.

"Ronan."

"Meeting then lunch. No interrupting. Deal?" Katie looked at him.

"Fine, but I get you first," she teased. He shook his head and got going through his emails. By the time he went to his meeting, he was almost finished going over the emails he had. When he sat down to the meeting, he got a text from Katie:

>   *Can't wait to get you home.*

He shook his head and replied:

>   *No distracting me. Get work done. You may be tied up this afternoon.*

Ronan had his meeting without a single distraction. As soon as he was done, he ran his finger over his phone screen and teased her as he walked back to his desk. He went in and Katie was gripping the edge of the sofa.

"Ah. So, you got my message," he teased.

"Stop."

He lifted his finger from the screen. "Can we leave now," Katie teased.

"It's not even 11 yet love. An hour and a bit and we can go." Just as he said it, his assistant knocked and came in.

"What time is that meeting this afternoon," Ronan asked.

"Just got moved to 2pm. Are you working from home this afternoon?"

"I believe so," Ronan said as Katie smirked.

"Probably heading out in an hour. That alright," Ronan asked.

"Yes sir. Just keep in mind you have 4 meetings tomorrow. First one is 10am, then 12 then 2 then last one at 3:30."

"Thank you," Ronan said.

"Did you need anything before you head out," his assistant asked. Ronan nodded.

"I need the paperwork for that meeting this afternoon so I have it. I'll let you know if I need anything after the meeting."

"Yes sir."

His assistant left the room and Katie smirked. "What are you doing," Ronan asked.

"Working like you said. I just finished all of the emails I had. How was the meeting?"

"Luckily that one is done and the papers are signed. Now to get the last one finished before the mess of meetings tomorrow."

"I gather that means that I'm not coming to work with you tomorrow."

"Not unless you want to sit in here alone." Katie looked at him.

"So, now that you're done your meeting, what do you have left to do before we head to the house?"

"Get papers together for the meeting this afternoon then I can take you home. Why?"

"Because I want this thing out. You've teased enough."

"Oh, I haven't even started yet."

Ronan smirked and had that look that he always had when he had something dastardly on his mind. "Oh really," Katie said. He nodded and his assistant came in with a folder containing the notes and documents he needed.

"We're going to head out. If anything comes up, let me know please," Ronan said.

"Will do sir. Let me know when you're available and I'll forward calls to you if they come in."

"I will," Ronan said as he looked over at Katie. Ronan put his papers and his laptop into his bag and Katie slid hers into her bag.

"You ready to head out lass?" Katie smirked and nodded.

They got into the car to head to the house, making a quick stop to grab lunch on the way back, then pulled up to the house and hopped out. "Sir, are you heading back this afternoon," his driver asked.

"Working from the house. We're good. Thank you," Ronan said as he closed the door, and they went into the house.

Chapter 11

"Ronan," Katie said as he slid her jacket off.

"What?"

"You can turn it off." He slid his hand in his pocket and ran his finger over the screen as she almost fell to her knees.

"You decide to taunt me in my office after I specifically said no."

"Mm."

"Up."

"Where," Katie said as she gripped the handrail of the steps.

"Upstairs." She slowly made her way upstairs almost crumbling with each step.

"I'd move faster if you'd cut it out."

"You want to tease me, I'm getting you back for it lass."

"Aah." She made it up to the bedroom and he pulled her to him.

"Ronan, stop."

"Lay down."

"Not until you stop with the toy." He stopped and had her pinned to the bed in a matter of a few minutes. He slid her skirt off then went for her top.

"See, I knew this was what you wanted," Katie said. He undid her top, sliding it off then slid off the lacy, see-through bra.

"You are so bad."

"I wore it for you." He kissed her and pinned her arms above her head, reaching into the drawer. He pulled out the handcuffs and locked her hands in place.

"Ronan, not fair." He kissed her and ran his finger over his phone screen again until her legs were shaking.

"I'm not even close to getting warmed up with you," Ronan said.

"Mm." He slid his phone onto the charger and slid the toy out.

"Thank you," Katie said. He got up and walked into the bathroom, washing it off and came back into the bedroom, grabbing the other toy from his drawer.

"Ronan."

"What?"

"No."

"No what," he asked as she felt the toy slide inside her and start to vibrate and thrust.

"Shit."

"That's what happens when you disobey me."

"Aah."

"Don't even think about it."

"Then turn it down."

"Nope. You have to stop yourself."

"You aren't being fair."

"Want me to turn it up lass?"

"No, down." He turned It down a little but turned the vibration up.

"Shit."

"What?"

"Please. You know that this thing makes my insides go crazy."

"Ask."

"Please."

"Just a little longer."

"Ronan." He kissed her, devouring her lips.

"Now." She crumbled in place and took even more.

"Off." He shook his head.

"You aren't spent yet."

"I want the real thing."

"I'm sure you do," he said as he turned the intensity back up.

"Aah." She was moaning his name, and he slid his dress shirt off, sliding it gently onto the chair, slid his dress pants off and placed them on top then kicked his boxers off, throwing them into the laundry. Watching her climax over and over again was a turn-on. Watching her beg to come was even more intense. "Ronan, please. I need you."

"Do it again," he said as he kissed up her leg.

"Mm."

"Good girl," he replied as he kissed her hip and felt her grinding against the toy to try and wriggle it out. He slid it back in deeper and kissed and nibbled at each breast as she panted and moaned.

"Mm." He kissed her, devouring her lips and then nibbled back down her neck.

"Aah. I can't Ronan."

"Then come for me love."

"Aah." He could feel her heart racing and her body almost shaking. He kissed back down her body and slid the toy out just as she was grinding all over again. He slid deep into her, pulling her legs over his shoulders.

"Aah."

"Mine."

"Ronan." He went deeper, harder, faster until she was throbbing around him.

"Mm."

"Katie." She looked up at him and exploded around him.

"Ronan." He kept going, slowly going harder and deeper until she was throbbing around him again.

"Tell me you want me," he said.

"Aah."

"Do you want me?"

"Ahh yes."

"Then come for me. Now." He kept going until she couldn't hold herself back. She crumbled around him, and he kept going over and over until he was spent and so was she.

"Shit." He undid the handcuffs, and she shook her head.

"I can't even move."

"Good. You won't be taunting me during my meeting."

"That's what all of that was for?"

"Partially," he replied. He kissed her and slid to his side.

"I can't even move Ronan." He pulled her to him and kissed her.

"What am I gonna do with you," Katie asked.

"Just what you did a few million times over," he replied with a smirk.

"Ronan, we need food."

He got up. "Relax. I'll bring it." He kissed her and got up, cleaned up, got redressed and went and warmed up lunch, bringing it upstairs with two bottles of water. When he walked into the bedroom, she was out cold on the bed. He put the toastie on the bedside table and walked downstairs and had his while he went through emails. He messaged his assistant that he was in his office at home and within a matter of minutes, she called him.

"There are a few messages. The meeting at 3 was moved to 1:30. Should be done by 3. The first meeting tomorrow is at 9:30."

"Then I'll be in early. Katie is going into the office tomorrow. Just have to drop her at work then I'll be on my way in."

"Yes sir."

"Any mail come in for me?" He went through the papers and mail with his assistant then logged into the call for the meeting while he finished his toastie. He texted Katie that he couldn't be disturbed and that the call was moved up just in case she thought about making a move. Within a matter of 15 minutes, the call had started, and he closed his office door.

Katie woke up around 2, slid her jeans and t-shirt on and went downstairs. She warmed up her lunch, grabbed the water and her laptop and sat down on the sofa to get some work done. She saw the text from Ronan and smirked:

> *Going into meeting early. Hope you had a good rest. You'll need it for later.*

Katie spent the next two hours getting her work done and when Ronan opened his office door and looked at her, she shook her head and got a smirk ear to ear. "And how was the meeting," she asked.

"Finally got the contract resolved. Just have to go through some emails and that kinda thing. How are you doing?"

"Good lunch you picked by the way. Exactly what I needed to get my energy back," she teased.

"Did you want to go out tonight?"

"Where?"

"Pub or that restaurant you were looking at down the way. Up to you. Both have music tonight."

"Can we go to the restaurant?"

Ronan nodded and made a quick call. "Table reserved."

"Good."

"Now, did you get that work done?"

"Almost. A few more emails and I can clock off since I started early." He kissed her and went and made them each a drink. He handed one to her and took a sip of his drink. "Ronan."

"Yes lass."

"Thank you."

He came and sat down with her and went through the last of his emails while she finished up work. He watched her and smirked. "What," Katie asked.

"Nothin love."

"I can see it all over your face. Just say it."

"You may want to get dressed."

"And what else are you intending on adding to the outfit?"

"The pink thing."

"Shit Ronan."

"Go. We have a reservation in a half hour."

"Ronan."

"Go."

She went upstairs and he came up 10 minutes later and kissed the back of her neck. "No." He bent her over the bed and slid the toy in place, flipping it on. "You are so not being fair." He smacked her backside, and she slid her shirt on. He slid his suit jacket on, and she slid her heels on. "You ready," he asked as he sprayed on her favorite cologne.

"Ronan." He turned and saw her in a sexier top with that same way too sexy skirt.

"Are you ready love?" She nodded. He walked her downstairs, helped her with her jacket and they headed off.

They walked into the restaurant, and it was packed. The host walked them back to their private booth in the back and Katie smirked. White tablecloth and all, she slid into the booth and Ronan slid in the other side, so they were side by side. They ordered drinks and Ronan smirked. "What," Katie asked.

"Nothing," he teased. He slid his hand in his pocket and ran his finger over the screen, teasing Katie into a frenzy. Her hand gripped his thigh, and he nuzzled her neck.

"I like it," he teased.

"I know you do, but you need to quit it."

"And why is that," he teased as their drinks came, and they ordered dinner.

"Because we're gonna end up being the center of attention."

He smirked. "And?"

"Ronan, stop." He kissed her and Katie smirked.

"I love you too," he said. She shook her head and leaned her head on his shoulder.

"Cheers," Katie said lifting her Baileys espresso martini to his pint.

"Slainte." Katie smirked and sipped her drink, and he took a gulp of his pint.

"And what else did you want to do tonight," Ronan asked.

"Something that involves less clothing."

"Something like what we just did at home?"

"More."

He shook his head. "What kind of more?"

"The fact that I can actually walk right now is kind of shocking."

"Oh, I know. Next time when you beg for mercy, I'm gonna keep going."

"Ronan."

"What?"

"How was your meeting?"

"Change of topic I see. Meeting was good. Thankfully, that part of the contract is handled. Tomorrow I have 4 major meetings. You're gonna have to go into your own office tomorrow."

"Are you gonna drive in with me at least?"

He nodded. "I have to go in for half 8. I want to get a few emails done before the meetings start."

"Then it's a good thing we're having dinner early."

He kissed her neck. "Now about that plan you have for when we get home." His hand slid into his pocket, and he ran his finger over the screen as the toy buzzed and teased. He slid his other hand to her leg as he felt it tense. He smirked and Katie shook her head.

"Enough," Katie whispered.

"You keep hinting at what we're doing when we're home and it'll get flipped on high."

"Ronan."

"What?"

She shook her head. "Please."

"Please what?"

"Stop," she whispered as his hand slid up her thigh.

"On one condition," he said.

"Ronan." He lifted his finger from the screen and

Katie exhaled. "What's the condition," Katie asked.

He kissed up her neck. "I get my way at home."

"You sure you don't want me to have a little fun first?"

He looked at her and the waiter showed with their dinner.

They ate and she shook her head. "Determined to make me at the table."

"Make you explode? Yes," he said quietly.

"You succeeded." He smirked and had his steak.

"Good. That won't be the last time tonight."

Katie almost choked on her food and shook her head. "You're so bad," she said.

"Just another reason why you love me lass." Katie smirked and they finished their dinners.

"Dessert," he asked.

Katie smirked. "Two crème brûlée and two baileys Irish coffees please."

"Ronan."

"We're having a nice night out lass. Walking distance."

She smirked and shook her head. "Delaying heading home?"

"Not a bit. Having a nice night with my girl."

"Ronan." He kissed her.

"Just relax and enjoy. You wanted to go out somewhere nice and we are. No pub tonight."

"Still looking forward to going home." He smirked.

"Oh, I know you are love. Delayed gratification." She kissed him. The dessert and coffees came and he smirked.

"And we're leaving after these yes?" Ronan nodded.

She had her dessert and sipped her coffee. "Worth it," Ronan asked.

"Almost," Katie replied. He kissed her. They finished their dessert and coffees, Ronan paid for dinner, and he walked her back to the house hand in hand.

"And," he asked as they stepped inside, and he locked up and flipped the alarm back on. She kissed him and he slid his hand in his pocket, flipping the toy back on high again.

"Shit."

"You wanted to go out to dinner lass. You. We could've gone and had fun at the pub, but you wanted a fancy dinner."

"Ronan." She leaned against the wall, and he kicked his shoes off and walked towards her, pinning her against the wall.

"Upstairs." He kissed her neck and undid the top she had on.

"Ronan, please."

He smirked. "Sofa."

"Stop."

He stopped and Katie went to slide her heels off. "Leave them on."

Katie ran up the stairs and he was one step behind her. He unzipped her skirt. "Ronan."

"Take it off." He leaned her onto the bed, peeling her clothes off and smirked.

"You're still dressed."

"Staying that way."

"No." He slid the toy out and put it on the bedside table.

"What," she asked. He kissed her and peeled her lace bra off, then the lace thong that was soaked through.

"Damn," he said.

"I told you." He walked around the bed, and she rolled over and went for the waistband of his dress pants. "Katie."

"I want mine first."

"Katie, hands." He tied her hands with a piece of rope from his drawer and tied her hands to the bed, immobilizing her.

"Ronan." He kissed her and went around the other side of the bed. "I know what you want lass. You don't get your way."

"Says who?" He smirked and walked over to his drawers, sliding the one toy out of his drawer that would drive her wild and use up every ounce of energy she had left.

"I want you."

"I bet you do." He kissed her, devouring her lips, then kissed down her neck.

"Aah." He went lower, licking and nibbling at each little peak of her breasts until she was almost moaning.

"Mm. Ronan, come here."

He smirked. "Tell me what else you want," he said as he licked his way down to her hip, then her inner thigh and her warmth. He licked and teased and pulled her legs over his shoulders.

"Aah."

"Mine," he said.

"Yes." He kept going until he could feel her reaching climax and slid the toy in making it go deep inside and thrust and tease through her climax.

"Shit."

"Oh, I know you're not holding back love. I want you to come over and over again until you can't stand anymore."

"I want to taste...mmm." He slid the toy in deeper and teased her a little more. "Shit." He smirked and undid his dress pants, watching her writhe and grind against the feeling of the toy. "Ahh." He slid his dress pants onto the chair, slid his shirt off, throwing it into the laundry, slid his socks off and threw them into the laundry then walked around to her and kissed her. "Ronan."

"It's gonna keep going until you beg me to turn it off, then I'm leaving it on until you can't move."

"I need to taste..."

He kissed her. "I know what you want. Not sure if you'll get it or not."

"Undo my hands."

"Nope."

"Then come here." He kissed her.

"What do you want Katie?"

"Mm. You in my mouth." He was so turned on that his boxers barely held him.

He slid himself out of his boxers and gave her what she wanted. The toy was still going, and he could feel her climax every time. She took him deep down her throat and sucked and licked until he pulled away. "Ronan."

"Not happening lass. I'm nowhere near done with you." He kissed her then watched her grind against the toy again.

"Ronan."

"Tell me what you want love."

"You. Come here." He shook his head and turned up the intensity of the toy, watching her body react and her toes curl.

"You have no idea how hot this is," he teased as he kissed her inner thigh.

"I want you. No more stupid aah...toy." He smirked. He slid the toy out just as her body was throbbing around it.

"Ronan." He slid deep into her and her legs curled around his ribs.

"Ronan." He kissed her and went hard and deep into her slowly going at a slow pace then speeding up until she was exploding around him like fireworks going off on a holiday. He kept going with her moaning his name. "Katie."

"Aah."

"That's my girl."

"Shit Ronan." He kept going until he exploded into her.

"Aah."

"More?"

"No."

"Yes?"

"Ronan." He kissed her and slid the toy back inside her, flipping it on high. "Shit."

"No mercy for you lass."

"Ronan, stop."

"Not on your life." He watched her as her body throbbed around the toy and saw her climax again then watched her stare at him. "Please Ronan." He slid the toy out and kissed her. "I can't even move my legs." He smirked.

"Good. Then you won't sneak into the shower with me." He walked into the bathroom and turned the shower on, cleaning up then walked back into the bedroom to see Katie trying to undo the rope. "Did you think that I was gonna let you get out of that," he teased. "Undo it." He shook his head.

"Ronan, no more toys."

"Says who," he asked as he kissed her back and pulled on boxers.

"No." He licked and kissed her lower back. "Ronan."

"Tell me what you want."

"Undo it." He smirked.

"Seeing you try to get out of that is almost appealing."

"Meaning what," Katie asked.

"No ahead and try love." He walked downstairs and got them each a drink and walked back upstairs to see her still trying to undo the knot that he'd tied the rope with.

"Give up," he asked as he put the drinks down.

"Undo it." He untied the rope, and she shook her head.

"You are so not fair."

"And why's that lass?"

"I literally can't move."

"You did start this all by yourself."

"I wanted you. Not the stupid toys."

"You got me. Tell me what you want love." He sat down on the bed, and she coiled around him.

"Just you. No toys, no games, no rope. Just you." He kissed her and she slid into his lap, leaning against his chest. Her legs slid around him and his hands slid to her backside.

"Katie."

"What?" He shook his head and kissed her.

"You are addictive love."

"Meaning what?"

"All mine."

"Always," she replied.

"Good. You'd better be."

"Ronan."

"What?"

"No more toys."

He looked at her. "And why is that?"

"Because I just want you."

"You need more than that."

"Ronan."

He kissed her. "You do love."

"No, I don't. All I want is you."

He shook his head. "You think that's all you want."

She kissed him and slid her arms around his neck. "You really think after all of this, that you aren't enough for me? I'm the one that was worried that I wasn't enough for you Ronan." He shook his head.

"Hush lass. So far from it."

Katie looked at him. "There's nobody else you would even want to be with?"

"Katie."

"What? You aren't even tempted?" He shook his head.

"Get up."

"Ronan, you aren't getting up and walking off."

"Move." She shook her head. "Katie."

"I'm not moving and either are you Ronan. I don't want to lose you because you need more. If what goes on with you and me isn't enough, we figure it out. I'm not walking away Ronan."

He tried again to get her to move and she wouldn't. "Katie, please." She shook her head and kissed him. He slid her to her back and got up. "Where are you going?" He took a gulp and finished his drink and went back downstairs.

He poured himself another drink and went and sat down on the sofa, sipping it slowly. When he heard her walking down the steps, he shook his head. She walked over to him and sat down on the sofa beside him with her drink.

"Tell me what's wrong," Katie asked.

"I'm right here with you. You. Nobody else. You know that right?"

Katie nodded. "I want us to just be together instead of the other stuff. I don't need to have my legs die just to be satisfied Ronan. I just want you inside me."

He pulled her onto his lap. "Don't second-guess things. Promise me."

"Are you sure that I'm enough?"

He kissed her, devouring her lips and slid her glass from her hands. He put it on the side table and pulled her tight to him. "Don't even think it."

"After all of those one-night stands you had, none of them are trying for another chance?"

"I wouldn't care if they did. I have my lass. There isn't another woman I even want Katie."

"Nobody even tries to win you over?"

He kissed her, intentionally getting her off the topic with a distraction. "Do you want me or no?"

"Always," Katie said.

"Then don't ask that again. Nobody is replacing you. There aren't any messages with anyone wanting to take your place love. Not one." He kissed her again, devouring her lips and her hands slid down his body. "What," he asked.

"I want you." He shook his head and leaned her onto the sofa.

"You're overdressed lass." She slid his t-shirt off of her and he kissed her.

"How badly do you want me?"

She reached for the waistband of his boxers, and he stopped her. "Don't start that."

"Don't start what?"

"Upstairs. You can't be trusted down here."

"No rope." He shook his head.

"And what else?"

"No tying my hands."

He got up. "Get your drink and follow me love." He grabbed his, handed her glass to her and walked her upstairs. She smirked and followed him.

He put her drink down on the table and kissed her, leaned her onto the bed and kissed her. "What," Katie asked.

He shook his head. "I don't know how you can even think that there's a replacement for you somewhere."

"I can't believe that you don't have other people trying to get you back."

He kissed her. "You know I love you," he said.

"Of course," she said.

"Then stop wondering who else is trying to replace you." She kissed him and he pulled the blanket over them and curled up among the blankets with her, making out like teenagers. "We need sleep love."

He slid to his back and finished his drink. Katie slid into his lap. "And if I said I wanted you?"

"You're sleeping."

She kissed him. "Still want you."

"Come and lay down love." She curled up in his arms and he kissed her again.

"Ronan."

"Yes love."

"I get all of you."

"For as long as you want me."

Ronan nodded off a little while later and Katie curled up in his arms and was almost asleep when she heard the buzz of a text. When a second and a third came in, she got up. She looked at her phone and there were no texts. She looked at his and saw text messages from three different women. When she read them, she shook her head. She looked at Ronan and took a deep breath. She was right to assume that women from his past were coming back in droves. Seeing the explicit texts and photos they'd sent was past upsetting. She put his phone down and went back to bed and tossed and turned all night.

The next morning, Ronan woke up and she wasn't in bed. He grabbed his phone and saw the texts and deleted them, blocking the numbers. He walked over to the guest room, and she wasn't there either. He walked downstairs and saw her asleep on the sofa. He picked her up and carried her upstairs to their bed. Just as he put her down, her eyes opened.

"What," Katie asked.

"You gonna tell me why you ended up downstairs?"

"Couldn't sleep. Texts woke me up." He shook his head.

"Katie."

"Just go do your workout."

"Katie."

"You didn't have to lie to me."

"I just delete messages like that."

"So, there were more."

"Katie, ignore them." She shook her head and got up. "Katie." She walked into the bathroom and washed up, stepping into the shower. He kicked off his boxers and stepped in behind her.

"Ronan, don't." He slid her underneath the stream of hot water and kissed her.

"Tell me what you want me to do."

"Don't lie to me. I asked you and you lied. You don't think I guessed that women you once knew were trying to contact you? Wasn't bad enough when you bumped into that woman you knew at the hotel when we were there, but now you're hiding texts? I mean, the pictures they sent."

"Katie, it doesn't go anywhere. If I get messages like that I just delete them. I'm never seeing them again."

"So, there were more."

He looked at her. "Past. Not now."

"And I'm supposed to be able to trust you. You hid..."

He kissed her and leaned her against the wall of the shower. "History. Period."

"You hid it from me."

He shook his head. "What do you want me to do?"

"Stop lying to my face." He kissed her and picked her up, wrapping her legs around his hips.

"And you..." He kissed her and they had sex against the wall of the shower.

"Mm." He kissed her as she moaned and writhed against him. When he couldn't hold himself back anymore, he exploded into her.

"History. Period." She nodded and slid to her feet.

"I couldn't sleep last night." He slid under the water to rinse off and looked at her.

"Katie."

"Don't lie to me Ronan. I don't want to show up in a pub to meet you at some point and see you with someone else. I don't want other women sending messages like that to you. I knew that you were keeping something from me."

"Katie, they're the past love. I can't do anything about the stupid texts except blocking and deleting them."

"I don't want them coming to your phone at all."

"I can't fix that. All I can do is delete and block. It's not worth fighting about."

"Then let me finish my shower."

"Katie."

"Just go." He pulled her to him and kissed her.

"I'm going to get a workout in. Come down when you're done." She nodded and washed her hair as he stepped out and changed into his workout gear and went down to workout.

He finished and walked upstairs to see her gone. He shook his head and walked downstairs and saw her making breakfast. "Katie."

"Figured I'd cook since I had time." He walked over to her and leaned her against the counter. "Ronan, the bacon is gonna burn." He flipped the element off and flipped the omelet.

"I thought you were coming into the gym with me."

"I was hungry." He kissed her and devoured her lips.

"You mad at me?"

"Way beyond mad."

"Katie."

"Did you think the sex in the shower was somehow going to give me amnesia?"

"They're history. You're the only future I want love."

"Then fix it."

"How?"

"No more messages in the middle of the night." He kissed her.

"Fine." He changed a setting on his phone so it would be on silent from 10pm to 6am.

"What else?"

"Don't ever lie to me."

He kissed her. "Fine."

"You had to realize that's why I was asking last night."

"Lass, you're all I could ever want. I don't want someone else."

"I'll remember you said that." She went to move and he stopped her.

"Katie."

"What?"

"I'm sorry." He kissed her again and she pushed him away.

"Just leave it," Katie said. She turned the element back on and finished making breakfast. Ronan got them each a coffee and sat down with her.

"I can't stop them from texting Katie."

"I know."

"Then why are you getting mad at me for something they did?"

"Because it's happened more than once. For all I know it happens every night."

"So, you're gonna get mad at me over my past again."

"All I asked was for you to be honest. I asked and you lied."

"Fine. I get those texts and delete and block them the minute they come through. I have what I want." She was silent through breakfast and when she got up to clean up, he stopped her. He put the dishes in the washer and took her hand, walking her upstairs.

"Ronan, just stop."

"Tell me what you want love. You want me to proclaim it from the rooftops that we're together, I will. You want me to message them back saying I'm taken, fine. Just say what you want me to do to fix this."

"I don't know what to do Ronan."

"Then think about it while I get ready."

"I'm gonna drive myself."

"Katie, no."

"Why?"

"Because we're going in together." He took a deep breath and kissed her. He had a quick shower, dried off and got dressed, putting her favorite cologne on.

"Ronan, I can drive myself."

"We're going together love. I can't concentrate if we're in the middle of a damn fight."

"Next time I ask if there are still texts, don't lie to me."

"They're gonna come whether I like it or not love. All I can do is delete and block."

"And when one is too tempting for you?"

"I have what I want."

"That wasn't an answer."

"None of those texts are tempting Katie. You're the only temptation I have."

"I'm still mad."

"I don't understand why people think those texts are gonna get a response from me."

"Because they would if you were single." Katie got up and went to walk out of the bedroom when he took her hand and pulled her back to him. He kissed her and held her until she hugged him back.

"And I don't see me being single anytime soon."

"Good. I just couldn't get those messages out of my head last night. I didn't want to wake you up with all my tossing and turning."

"Do me a favor alright? Next time wake me up. I don't want you stressing over stupid crap from my past."

She nodded. "You do realize that it's not even 8 yet, right?"

Katie looked at him." "And just what did you have in mind," Katie asked looking up at him. He kissed her and leaned her onto the bed.

"Ronan." He kissed her again, devouring her lips.

"What," he asked as he let her up for air.

"I thought you had to go in early."

"As in 9, not 8, love." She looked at him as he slid her legs around him and slid her skirt up her thighs.

"What are you up to?"

"Nothing. Just getting you comfortable." She shook her head and felt his hand slide under her lace panties.

"Shit."

"What?"

"I know what you're up to."

"Good. Kinda better that way," he teased as his fingers started to tease her and get her turned on.

"What are you doing," Katie asked breathless.

"Making up."

"No toys." He shook his head, and she looked at him.

"Then you're overdressed."

"Just for you."

"Then you're still overdressed. I want you." He kissed her and teased, sliding two fingers inside her until her breath hitched.

"Ronan."

"This is all I want Katie."

"Aah."

"Mine."

"Ronan." He kept going until he could feel her body throbbing around his fingers.

"I need you inside me."

"I am."

"Ronan."

"All you love." He kept going and teasing going faster until her body crashed around his fingers.

"Mm. Shit Ronan."

"Good. Just what I wanted."

"Your turn."

"Nope."

"Ronan, please."

"Tonight."

"Ronan."

"What love."

"Your turn." He shook his head, and she kissed him and tried to flip him onto his back.

"I know what you're doing."

"I know you do."

"Still not happening lass. Just needed to remind you of something."

"Which was what," Katie asked as he started teasing all over again.

"Yours."

"Mm."

"I'm gonna keep going until you beg me to stop."

"I want you inside me. No more mm...teasing."

"Come for me," he practically purred into her ear. Her arms wrapped around his neck and pulled him to her.

"Aah."

"Good girl."

"I need you." He shook his head, and she started throbbing all over again.

"Ronan, please." He kept going and Katie throbbed even more.

"You sure," he asked. Katie nodded. He kicked his dress pants off, slid off his boxers and pulled her legs around him, sliding deep into her.

"Aah."

"Mine," he said as he pounded into her over and over until he could feel her throbbing around him. He kept going deeper and harder over and over until he could feel her body crashing around him.

"Not yet love."

She tried to hold herself back. "Ronan."

"Not yet."

"Aah."

"Please." He kept going harder and faster and then said the words she wanted to hear.

"Come for me." She crashed around him, and he came right after.

"That what you wanted lass," he asked.

"Yes," she said.

"You do realize at some point that shot or whatever is gonna run out."

"Shit."

"What?"

"I knew I had to do something." He looked at her.

"Seriously?"

"It's fine."

"Katie, it's not."

"Then I should probably make an appointment." He shook his head and got up.

"What?"

"When are you due for it?"

"Next week."

"Katie."

"It's fine. I have time today. She can do it while I'm at work."

"Please."

"Ronan, are you saying that you don't want kids?"

"I'm saying not right now. We just got together Katie. Neither one of us are ready for something like that right now."

He got up and walked into the bathroom and cleaned up then came back in and got dressed. "Ronan."

"You saying you are?"

"I'm covered. I see her every day at the hospital. I can get it while I'm there."

"Please."

"Okay," Katie said. She went and cleaned up and got redressed for work.

"Ronan, what would happen if I did get pregnant?"

He looked at her. "First you dared me to date you and now you're asking that after that fight?"

"I'm just asking."

"It'd be something we had to figure out. Leave it at that."

"Would you want to keep it?"

"If we were, yes."

"I kinda have to do a test before she'll do the shot anyway."

"Just promise me that you'll tell me if you are."

Katie kissed him. "I wouldn't hide something like that."

"Are you ready to go," he asked.

Katie smirked. "Are you, is the question." He kissed her and they headed out.

"I may be finished early today."

"Do you want to meet me at the pub," he asked.

"I could," Katie said.

"Or here."

"I'll let you know." He nodded and walked her downstairs. He grabbed his laptop and her laptop bag, and they headed out not long later. He took her to work, and after a kiss goodbye, he headed into his office with just enough time to get a coffee and his emails done.

Ronan got through his meetings, but the nagging feeling that she might be pregnant was bugging him all day long. What the hell would he do with a kid? He hadn't planned on one for a while. At least until he knew he'd found the one that he wanted to marry or something. When it got to the end of the day, he looked at his phone and saw a text from Katie:

> *Heading home. Going to meet up with a friend for a drink. Come meet me.*

Ronan took a deep breath and finished up some emails when he got a text from the driver that he had arrived. Ronan went down to the car, hopped in and headed straight home. When he got there, she'd already headed over. He changed into jeans and a t-shirt and grabbed his wallet, phone and keys and locked up, walking over.

Just as he was walking over, he bumped into one of his one-night stands. "Long time no see Ronan," she said. "Me blocking your phone number wasn't enough of a hint?"

"I know you miss me."

"I actually have a girl now."

"She can join us."

"Hard pass. She's not that kind of girl."

"When you get tired of being with her, let me know."

"Pass on that too. Have a nice life," Ronan said. Her name completely escaped him. He went to walk into the pub and saw Katie running for the bathroom. He went and sat down at the bar and Pat gave him a pint.

"Thank you," Ronan said.

"She was waiting here and kept watching the window for you."

"Who?"

"Leona," Pat said.

"So that's her name." Pat shook his head.

"What happened to Katie," Ronan asked.

"She was watching that lady and overheard her talking to someone about you." He shook his head and saw Katie come back to the table. When he saw her sitting with a guy, he shook his head again. He finished his pint and watched her. When Katie didn't get up and come over to him, he almost snapped. He got dinner to go and went back to the house.

He had dinner, poured himself a drink and got work done, turning in around 10. When Katie hadn't come back, he called her. No answer. He texted her that he was turning in and still got no answer. He took a deep breath and walked over to the pub and saw her sitting with that same guy.

"Katie."

"Hey."

"Can I talk to you for a minute?"

"Ronan, this is Carter. He's an old friend."

"Nice to meet you. Please."

"Give me a minute," Katie said excusing herself.

"Ignored my texts?"

"You were supposed to come and hang out with us."

"After what happened this morning, I thought you would be coming home."

"I will. We're just finishing our drinks."

"Katie."

"What Ronan? You can talk to other women, but I can't talk to other guys?" He shook his head and walked out, going back to the house. He walked in, grabbed himself another drink and walked upstairs. He slid out of his jeans and slid into bed. He took a gulp of his drink and tried to calm his system down. He finished his drink and curled up in bed alone for the first time in weeks. Months.

The next morning, Ronan woke up to an empty bed. He walked into the guest room and saw her out cold. He shook his head and went and changed into his workout gear and did his workout. When he came back upstairs, she was still asleep. He walked into the guest room and kissed her.

"Hey," Katie said.

"Why didn't you come to bed?"

"Because I didn't. Who was she?"

"Ex. Who was the guy?"

"A guy I used to date when I was in high school." He looked at her.

"And you spent that long with him."

"You didn't come sit with me."

"After this morning, I thought we were gonna talk."

"We can. I just wanted to hang out with him for a bit."

"Had nothing to do with her showing up at the pub."

"Maybe a little."

Ronan shook his head. "I told her that we were together. That I wasn't interested in whatever she was trying to do."

"That's good." Katie looked at him. "You're waiting for something."

"You could've come and sat with us." He shook his head.

"Your plan didn't work." Ronan walked back into the main bedroom and went and hopped into the shower.

Chapter 12

Ronan washed his hair and Katie slid in behind him. "You're actually mad," she asked.

"Proving a point? I got it."

"Ronan, he's a friend from school."

"One you chose to drink with at the pub until 10. He could've taken advantage of you."

"He's not interested in me."

"And that's why he was looking you up and down." Ronan rinsed off and stepped out of the shower, wrapping a towel around him.

"Ronan, come here." He walked out of the bathroom and got dressed. Katie finished her shower and stepped out, wrapping a towel around her and walked into the bedroom, seeing Ronan putting his tie on.

"So seriously, you're gonna get mad that I was talking to a friend when you were talking to an ex before you came into the pub."

"I told her to leave me alone and walked away Katie. Different. I wouldn't have invited her for a drink."

"Ronan, he wasn't looking me up and down."

"I could see him from the bar. He was. And you just sat there and had a few drinks with him. Did you even talk to the doctor at the hospital?"

"First off, I had a soda. Second, yeah, I did."

"And?"

"She did bloodwork."

"Meaning what?"

"Meaning she wanted to do bloodwork because I'm not due for the shot until next week."

"Did she do the test?"

"Yes."

"And?"

"Inconclusive." Ronan shook his head, grabbed his phone, and walked downstairs. He put breakfast on, and Katie took her time getting ready.

When she came downstairs, her breakfast was on the table. "You were drinking with him."

"I had a drink or two, then I drank soda."

"If you are Katie, you can't go and do that."

"Which part are you mad at? Me having a drink with a guy you don't know while you claim he was looking me up and down, or the fact that the test was inconclusive?"

"Both."

"Are you gonna tell me who that woman was?"

"I couldn't even remember her name. Your exact words were to make sure they knew that I was with you. I did. Hope you had a great time with whoever he was."

Katie looked at him. "You're seriously getting mad."

"Then you don't come to bed."

"Ronan."

"What," he asked as he finished his food and got up to clean up.

"Are you seriously mad that I slept in the guest room?"

"You were pissed that I even suggested it when you didn't do as I asked. Now you voluntarily did it? Come on Katie. You don't want me to smell his cologne on you, fine."

"Meaning what?"

"You two looked all cozy when I showed last night."

"You think I slept with him?" Ronan closed the dishwasher and sat down on the sofa with his laptop in hand and went through emails. She walked upstairs and finished getting ready, checking her sweater. She did smell like him.

She came back down a few minutes later and he was still pissed. "He wanted to meet up for dinner tonight. Are you gonna come with me?"

"No."

"Then I won't go."

"Do what you want to Katie. By all means, do whatever the hell you want."

"Then come get me at work when you're heading home."

"You sure you don't want to leave early to see him?"

"I'm not fighting about this. I'm not going to dinner with him."

"I might go out."

"Can we talk about this?"

"No. We both have to get to work."

"Ronan."

"Just leave it."

"What if we had dinner at the pub just us."

"Kian and Mia are coming."

"He's not worth fighting over Ronan."

"That's for sure. You don't want to see that he was making a move on you, that's on you Katie."

"We can talk about it after work." He nodded and they headed off to work. For the first time in forever, there was no holding hands, no teasing and not even a kiss goodbye. He'd turned his feelings off like he'd done a million times before with one-night stands. He got his meetings finished and when he headed home, he was still mad. He got to the house, and the driver went to pick Katie up. Ronan went and called Kian.

"What's up my friend," Kian asked.

"Need you and Mia at the pub tonight."

"For what? You two having a date night?"

"She was there with an old boyfriend and I'm trying to convince her that he thinks she's available. I saw them. I saw how he looked at her. He had the balls to ask her out to dinner. Don't tell me that she doesn't see it."

"Ronan, breathe. We'll be there and I'll make her see it."

"I can't deal with her," Ronan said.

"Meaning what? You're pushing her away like you do people that betray you?"

"Her on a damn date yesterday proved my point. There's no point in me dating."

"Ronan, let me handle it."

"Whatever," Ronan replied.

"Meet you over there."

Ronan went and got changed and went over to the pub, texting her that he would meet her there. Ronan walked over and Kian was just coming in.

"Where's Mia?"

"Coming. She's just getting changed from being at work. Don't you two have some big meeting thing on Friday?"

"It'll be handled."

"Ronan, are you sure you weren't just seeing red last night?"

"Watch." Kian nodded and Pat brought over two pints.

"May need a shot," Ronan said.

"If you do, let me know."

Ronan nodded. "I swear, if that idiot shows up here to see her, I'm gonna lose it."

"Ronan, breathe. If he makes a damn move tonight, you can crash at the house with Mia and I," Kian said.

"Hotel."

Kian shook his head. "You do realize that you can't just take off and disappear on her."

"I'm not standing in the way of her getting what she wants."

"And if she said she wanted you?"

"Not with that guy around."

Katie showed the same time as Mia. "I didn't know you two would be here," Katie said.

"He called and asked us to come. I know he was pissed last night. That much I got from Kian."

"He's overdoing it. It was nothing."

"What was," Mia asked.

"I bumped into a guy I used to know back in high school, and he came for a drink. We ended up talking until late."

"Alone?"

"We were here."

"And Ronan saw you two."

Katie nodded. "That's when what's her name was here waiting on Ronan."

"I don't even know what that woman wanted with him."

"She's a pain in the backside. She was when Ronan went out with her that one time. She practically stalked him from that night on," Mia said.

"He talked to her."

"Probably told her to screw off. He only has eyes for you Katie. We both know it."

"Right now he's mad at me," Katie replied.

"Let's just hope that guy doesn't show up here or Ronan may be mopping the floor with him."

They walked in and went and sat down with the guys. Ronan just looked at Katie.

"What," she asked.

"Nothing."

Ronan drank his pint and Pat brought over the martini for Katie and a drink for Mia. They all made small talk a bit and Katie tried to get Ronan to react towards her, but it was like he was shut off. Just like he had been that morning.

"Ronan."

He shook his head and looked at Pat. Within a few minutes, 4 shots of Jameson were on the table. Ronan drank two of them. Katie shook her head. Kian drank one and Ronan grabbed the third and drank that one too.

"Ronan."

He shook his head. Katie motioned for him to come with her, and he shook his head. "Please." He took a gulp of his pint.

"So, are we doing Sunday this week," Kian asked trying to get Ronan out of his bad mood.

"Not sure. May do it somewhere else."

Kian shook his head. "Ronan, can you come here for a minute," Katie said, intentionally making a point.

"I'm good," Ronan said. She grabbed his hand and pulled him to her and walked outside.

"What," Ronan asked.

"So, you're just gonna completely ignore me."

"I'm fine."

"You aren't acting fine Ronan. Fine. You're mad that I went for drinks with him. I didn't do anything and he isn't interested in me. We're friends."

"Right."

"Ronan." He walked back into the pub and sat back down. Katie walked in and finished her drink. Pat brought everyone something to eat and as Ronan was on his third pint, Katie looked up and saw Carter at the door. Ronan looked at Pat and he shook his head. Ronan nodded. Pat brought over another round of shots and the minute Katie got up, two of the shots were gone. When she got closer to Carter, Ronan had the third one.

"Ronan," Kian said. Even Mia shook her head.

"Can we talk for a second," Carter asked as he walked Katie to the other side of the bar.

Ronan took a deep breath. "Right. He's not into her at all."

"Ronan, she's a pretty lass. Let it go," Mia said.

"I couldn't do dinner tonight. Ronan's all mad. He thought that there was something going on with us last night and he's not impressed," Katie said.

"Well, see, that's what I wanted to talk to you about. I realized after we talked last night that I missed you. Honestly, I think you leaving town when we were finishing high school about killed me. I want another chance," Carter said.

"And she's just soaking it all up. Watch. He'll make a damn move on her next," Ronan said as Kian traded spots with Mia. Ronan finished the last shot on the table and finished his pint.

"You do know that Ronan and I are together right?"

"I just want a chance. One dinner. One date," Carter said. His hands slid in Katie's and she looked at him.

"I told you," Ronan said as he got up and paid the tab for the drinks and got another shot.

"You don't need one," Pat said.

"One last shot before I leave." Pat gave him the shot, he drank it and Kian pulled him back to the table.

"Just chill," Kian said.

"If he kisses her, I'm walking out," Ronan replied.

"Carter, I'm with Ronan."

"I just want a chance," Carter said.

"I can't do that to..."

The minute Ronan saw Carter kiss her, he got up and went to walk out.

"Don't you dare," Mia said. Kian looked at Ronan and shook his head. Ronan got up and walked out of the pub, went back to the house, packed up clothes for a few days and his laptop bag and got his driver to take him to the hotel where the event that Friday was gonna be. He checked into his suite and went down to the bar, getting a double Jameson.

"I can't Carter. I am in love with Ronan. I can't do this," Katie said as she walked back to the table and saw Ronan gone.

"Where did he go," Katie asked.

"He walked out when he saw the kiss," Kian said.

"Shit." Katie went to walk back to the house and saw the car leaving. "Shit." She walked back into the pub and Kian shook his head. "He's gone."

"He wasn't doing well all damn day Katie. When he shuts off like that, it's not a good thing. He was like that after the breakup. He said he was leaving."

"To go where," Katie asked.

"A hotel. He has been acting up all day long Katie. He was pissed last night. I thought I could stop him from taking off, but when that guy kissed you, he snapped. I couldn't stop him."

"Can you call him and find out where he is," Katie asked.

"How did you not know that guy had a thing for you," Kian asked.

"Kian," Mia said.

"I would lose my crap too if some guy ever made a move on you," Kian said.

"Just go call him," Mia said as Kian got up and walked outside.

"Carter," Kian said as he saw the guy who'd caused all the drama.

"Do I know you?"

"Just a suggestion. When a lass tells you that she's taken, it doesn't mean make a move in front of her boyfriend," Kian said.

"He doesn't give her what I do," Carter said.

"Nah. He gives her more," Kian said.

"Obviously not what she wants or she wouldn't have been out with me last night."

"You're lucky my fiancée is here or I'd beat you down myself," Kian said.

"Right. Wouldn't get far," Carter said as Kian nailed him in the face. Carter left and Kian called Ronan.

"What," Ronan asked.

"She's asking where you are."

"Doesn't matter. I'm sure she's having fun with what's his name."

"You mean the guy that I just punched in the face for making a move on your girl? He's gone. Katie's losing it."

"Then let her."

"Where are you staying," Kian asked.

"A hotel."

"Grafton?"

"I don't want her anywhere near me."

"You do realize you're gonna see her on Friday or Saturday at that event right?"

"Then I'll change hotels."

"Ronan."

"I can't."

"Then I'll come meet you. Let the ladies talk."

"No."

"See you in 20." Kian hung up with him and walked back into the pub.

"Did you find him," Katie asked.

"I'm going to meet him. You two stay," Kian said.

"I need to talk to him," Katie said.

"Leave it at he's on mute and it is gonna be like pulling nails to get him to snap out of it. He was already 6 shots of Jameson and 3 pints in when he showed. He's not in a good place Katie. I'll try to talk to him for you, but I don't know that you're gonna get anything out of him tonight," Kian said.

"I need to see him," Katie said.

"Not tonight. You don't want to." Kian got up and paid for the last of the drinks then got in a cab and went straight over to Ronan's hotel.

"I need to know where he is Mia."

"I've seen Ronan like this. It took a long while to snap him out of it Katie. He's in off mode. It's not good."

"We're living together. How am I supposed to stay in the house alone?"

"Just breathe. I mean, unless you want to stay with us until you two figure this out," Mia said.

"I need to talk to him."

Kian got to the hotel, walked into the lounge and saw Ronan with a Jameson in hand. "You realize that's the last thing that you need right," Kian said.

"I said not to come."

"You do realize that she's losing her mind, right?"

"Good."

"Ronan."

"She kissed another guy Kian. She sat and had drinks with him and came home like it was nothing. He kissed her right in front of me."

"And got a black eye and probably a busted nose for it," Kian said.

"Don't tell me he had a snarky comeback when you told him to back off."

"He said that you don't give her what he does. That's when I knocked him one."

"Good."

"You still shut off when it comes to her?"

"She was on a damn date with him when she told me to come have a damn drink with them. I couldn't even sleep in the damn bed last night."

"Ronan."

"I can't," Ronan replied as he sipped the drink.

"Don't do something stupid and start over with someone else that isn't worth it."

"Meaning what," Ronan asked.

"No one-night stands. Just give yourself a breather. She's still living in your damn house." Ronan sipped his drink and finished it, ordering another.

"She needs to move out."

"Ronan, this is the first damn girl that you even liked enough to give her a real chance. Hell. She comes to sports Sunday. You aren't walking away from her."

"She kissed him."

"Correction. He kissed her and she pushed him away."

"I can't Kian. I just can't."

"You know you need to talk to her right?"

He looked at Kian and shook his head. "Not doing it."

"Talk to her. Flip the damn switch back on and talk to her."

"Meaning what?"

"You turned off every damn reaction we all thought you'd have. You flipped a damn switch, and you know you did. You're talking to her."

"No."

"Yeah you are."

"Kian."

"Pay for the drinks. We're going to your room so you can talk and have some privacy."

Ronan paid for the drinks and walked upstairs to his suite. He went and poured another glass and sat down on the sofa. "Call her." Ronan took a sip of his drink. Kian grabbed his phone, dialed Katie's number and handed it to Ronan. He leaned back on the sofa and put the phone to his ear.

"Ronan, where are you?"

"Staying somewhere tonight. I just need some space."

"Ronan, come home."

"No."

"I should've listened to you alright? He went too far. I pushed him away and you were gone."

"You have history with him Katie. You deserve history."

"And I have history with you too. You're mine. I'm yours. That's all I want. I just want you."

"I can't."

"Then tell me where you are."

"No Katie."

"I need you."

He hung up. "What the hell," Kian said.

"I can't," Ronan said as he drank down the Jameson.

"You need to go home and be with her."

"Kian, I'm in no shape to be around her right now. Not after that."

"You do realize that Mia is gonna get involved in this right?"

"Meaning what," Ronan asked.

"That girl loves you Ronan. I knew the day I saw you two together. You finally let yourself feel something. Fine. Some guy made a move, and she realized it. It was a little late, but she realized it. She needs you."

"I could've sworn that you were supposed to be my friend Kian."

"I'm being your friend. You need her just as damn much as she needs you. Just say it."

"I can't do it. She wants to be with him, let her. I was fine on my own. I can do it again," Ronan said.

"You were shit on your own and you know it."

"Kian."

"I get you being mad. You're pissed, knock the guy on his backside. Katie was blind to it. I get it. Either you do something, or you lose any chance of getting that girl back in your life."

"I want to be left alone."

"You aren't gonna be until you go home and talk to her."

"Then it can wait." Ronan got up and grabbed another drink.

"You do realize that the answer isn't in the bottom of the damn bottle, right?"

"She kissed him."

"He kissed her, and she pushed him away and walked back over to where you were."

"I'm not going back there."

"You know that the two of you are gonna be face to face this weekend, right?"

"And? I can avoid that situation."

"And you're just gonna hide here? Ronan, she loves you. We'll take the car back to the house, you go inside and talk to her. One on one. Emotions raw and everything. You want to leave after that, leave."

"No." Ronan took a gulp of his Jameson.

"Do you realize how damn stubborn you are," Kian asked.

"Still staying."

"Then I'll drag your butt to the damn house. She's with Mia."

"I don't need this. I gave her what she wanted, and she did this."

"She was blind to it. Just like she's blind to whatever the hell you did to get her in the first place. She loves you even when you're a stubborn pain in the butt. Deal with it instead of shutting down. You always shut down and go back to the bad side. Back to the pointless hookups. That's why I'm here. Making sure you don't do something stupid."

"Like what? Hookup with someone in the bar like I did when I met Katie?"

"I knew. Thing is, she's the only one you ever held onto after. Like it or not Ronan, you love her. You're not walking away. You're pouting."

"Kian, don't."

"You're sitting here shutting down because an idiot made a move on your girl. You didn't beat the crap out of him you just walked away."

"She told me she didn't want me fighting."

"You're going back to the house."

"No."

"Finish the drink. You're going or I'm bringing her here."

"Kian, leave it."

"You can't live without her. You've had more to drink tonight than you have since that idiot devil bitch did what she did. Katie's a good girl." Ronan shook his head and drank down the glass.

458

Ronan went to get up to get a refill and Kian stopped him. "You need a few bottles of water not another damn drink," Kian said.

"I'm not going."

"Then talk to her tomorrow night."

"No."

"Then I'm calling her and telling her where you are."

"Kian, I swear."

"You have two choices. Either you go there tonight and talk to her until it's out of your damn system and flip the damn switch back on, or I'm bringing her here."

"Not happening."

"Do you love her?"

"Kian."

"Do you love the damn girl or not Ronan?"

"She has the guy with the history. She doesn't need me."

"That's not an answer. Do you love her?"

"Of course I do."

"Then flip the damn switch back on and go home to her."

"No. I'm not going tonight."

"Tomorrow."

"I don't know."

"Meaning what Ronan?"

"Meaning I'm not ready to turn that damn switch back on."

"Do you want her?" Ronan gave him a look that told everything. "Then do something about it."

"Go home to Mia. I'm sleeping it off here tonight."

"Then talk to her tomorrow."

"No."

"Fine. Meet me at the pub tomorrow and you two can hash it out over there."

"Great. So that little shit can show up and cause more drama?"

Kian looked at him. "He's not coming near her again. Not with me there to knock his ass out."

Ronan took a deep breath. "Go home to Mia."

"You promise you'll be there?"

"Fine."

"Then I'm having a drink with you then heading out. You didn't even offer me one," Kian joked.

"Mia, what am I supposed to do?"

"Just go back to the house and try and get some rest. If I know Kian, he'll talk some sense into Ronan. It took months last time he just flipped the damn switch and turned all the feelings off. He loves you. We both know he does Katie. He'll come to his senses."

"We have a damn event on Friday. That's in 48 hours. How am I supposed to be in a room with him when he's avoiding me?" Mia gave her a hug and got a text from Kian:

> *Talked to him. Meeting at pub tomorrow. That idiot shows, I'm taking care of him. I tried love. I know where he is. He's drunk and safe. No stupid replacements in sight. See you soon. Meet you at pub.*

"Well, he came up with a ceasefire between you two. Meeting at the pub tomorrow. I swear, if I have to nail him to the bench I will," Mia said.

"I can't sleep without him."

"Just get some rest. He'll get past it if it takes all three of us to do it." Katie nodded and within 10 minutes, Kian was back.

"I'm walking Katie back to the house then we can head out yeah," Kian said.

Mia nodded and Kian walked Katie. "I can't sleep without him." "He's out cold. He's at a hotel downtown. In his suite. Just let him sober up and tomorrow you two can talk."

Katie nodded and gave Kian a hug. "Thank you for trying." He nodded and Katie went inside, locking up and flipping the alarm on. Kian walked back to Mia and took her home.

Katie flipped the lights off and walked upstairs. She got changed into pajamas and sat down on the edge of the bed. She tried to come up with a way to get him to say something to her, then looked at the drawer. The one that held the toys that he'd teased her with. She went into the drawer and found the one he had made her wear at the restaurant. She flipped it on and instantly, a message went to his phone:

Activated

He looked at his phone and saw the word on the screen. He shook his head. He logged into the app and saw which toy it was and ran his finger over the screen.

Katie felt it moving in and out and knew he'd got the message. When it intensified, she was moaning. She was about to explode, and the toy stopped. "What the hell?" It started again and took her to the edge then stopped. It paused for a moment or two then went slowly and sped up. Just when she was about to come, it stopped again. She called Ronan and he didn't answer, but the toy started again, taking her to the edge and stopped.

She called him again and slid her earbud in. "What," Ronan asked.

"You're not being fair."

"Really? Me not being fair? You went on a damn date with him last night then let him kiss you today and I'm not fair?"

"Then be mad. Don't take it out on me."

"Because you want that toy going so damn badly?" His finger ran over the screen making it even more intense then stopped again.

"Ronan."

"That's how you make me feel. One minute you say you love me and the next you're with an old flame from school. You don't want me, Katie. You want someone to make you feel good." He ran his finger over the screen and made it so intense that she exploded and moaned his name. "Now you got what you want." Ronan hung up and closed the app. He wasn't playing games anymore.

Katie slid the toy out and cleaned it off, sliding it back into the drawer. She laid down on the bed and cried herself to sleep. The only thing she could do was to curl up with his scent on the pillow. She'd screwed up bad. Really bad. She should never have gone to drinks with Carter without Ronan. She shouldn't have let Carter get that close. Now she could lose Ronan. Something she couldn't stand to do.

The next morning, Ronan woke up with the hangover from hell and went to do his workout. Just as he was finishing up, his phone buzzed with a text from Katie:

*I miss you. Please just talk to me. I get it.
Meeting up with him at all was a mistake. Just
talk to me.*

Ronan stared at the message the entire way up to his
suite. When he walked in, he ordered breakfast and had
a shower. By the time he was out of the shower, there
was another message:

*You can't just avoid talking to me. We live in the
same house Ronan. Please.*

He got dressed and just as the food was coming in, his
phone rang. One look at the call display and he shook his
head. "What do you want Katie?"

"I want you back in this house. It's your house. Come
home."

"I'm just sitting down to breakfast."

"Ronan." His emotions were teetering on a limb. He
didn't want to feel the hurt, but he didn't want to hurt
her either.

"Katie, I can't. I have to go to work."

"Then come home tonight. We can talk about it. I'm
sorry. I didn't realize what he was doing."

"Now you do. Hope you two are happy."

"Ronan."

He hung up and had his breakfast, still irritated. He finished breakfast and finished getting ready for work when his phone rang again. "Katie."

"Come home tonight alright? You don't want me here, fine. I'll go stay with a friend."

"I'm fine here."

"Ronan."

"We can talk later. I have to get into work."

"It's not even half 8. Talk to me."

"What do you want me to say Katie? You went out with someone else. You let him kiss you right in front of me. Am I supposed to say that was alright? It wasn't."

"And you avoiding being near me isn't alright either."

"It was either that or I completely snapped and made it an even bigger fight."

"Then fight. I'm not losing you because some idiot guy from my past tries to make a move. That woman tried something with you."

"And I told her that I had a girlfriend, and I wasn't interested. I told her that was why I blocked her text then I walked into the pub."

"I just thought that he wanted to catch up like friends Ronan. I didn't know what he was really doing. I told him that I was with you."

"And that's why you stayed there past 10 alone."

"Ronan."

"I have to go Katie. I can't talk about this right now."

"Then just come and meet me so we can talk."

"I'll think about it," Ronan said as they hung up.

Ronan got to work early and was still pissed. He popped a Tylenol and guzzled down a bottle of water when his assistant came in. "Good morning," Ronan said.

"Did you want me to grab you a coffee?"

"Please. And another bottle of water if you can."

She nodded and within maybe 10 minutes, she came back in with the water and coffee. "There weren't any messages for you last night. A package came in for you though. Did you want me to bring it in for you?"

"Please," Ronan replied as she went and got the package and brought it in. When she put it on the desk, he shook his head. He knew exactly what it was. He slid it in his bag and shook his head. He got a few emails done and then saw one from Katie:

> I get that you're mad. Hell. I'm mad at myself for even going. I should've stayed home with you or made sure you were with me. I'm sorry. I should've stayed with you. I don't know what I can do to fix this, but I don't want to lose you because of it. It was a mistake. You aren't and

> *you never will be. Please just meet me so we can*
> *go home tonight and fix this. I don't want to*
> *sleep alone again. I need you.*

Ronan shook his head and stared at the screen, reading the message over and over again. The flip got switched back on even though he didn't want it on. Re-reading the words did it. Fine. He missed her, but he was still mad as hell. Luckily, he only had one meeting that day. One. One that would take up half the damn day. He got his emails done then went back to the one Katie had sent. When he found himself replying, he shook his head:

> *I knew the minute I saw you two talking that he*
> *wanted something. You didn't listen to me. I told*
> *you that he was gonna make a move and he*
> *made more than one. If that's what you want,*
> *there's no point in me coming back to talk. You*
> *have a choice, Katie. You can either be with*
> *screwed up me or be with someone who's*
> *playing games with you and will just hurt you in*
> *the end. I can't see that again. I can't.*

He pressed send and got up, drinking down his entire mug of coffee then drinking the water. When his assistant knocked to tell him his meeting was starting in 10 minutes, he grabbed another bottle of water, grabbed his papers, and went down to the meeting, doing his best to ignore the email that he knew he was going to get.

He got through the meeting and went back into his office, knowing the email would be there:

I don't know what you need me to say so we can get through this Ronan. I should've listened to you. Honestly, I shouldn't have gone at all without you there with me. I thought it was just a friend thing. I want us. Screwed up or not, I want you and me and only you and me. Please just talk to me.

Ronan took a deep breath. He couldn't have asked for anything else. The fact was that the emotional light switch wasn't back on. It was still off. Until something made him crack and let it go back on, he wasn't having any emotions at all. She wasn't gonna like that side of him. Nobody did. He had some lunch and tried to relax for a moment or two when Kian called him.

"And what do you want," Ronan said sarcastically.

"Are you still coming to the pub tonight?"

"Nothing's gonna change."

"Something already has. Just come and meet her and talk this crap out so you can stop being a damn robot. She told Mia that she emailed you and called. At least you sorta talked."

"Kian, while I appreciate the assistance, you aren't a therapist, and you can't fix this problem."

"I can drag your butt there. Don't forget. I know where you're staying."

"Leave it alone."

"Then come to the damn pub. Pat even offered his office so you two could talk in private."

"Kian."

"You realize Mia will have my head if you don't show."

"Fine, but I'm coming back to the hotel after."

"If that's what you want."

"And you aren't changing my mind."

"Unless you two make up and end up going home together."

"Still coming back to the hotel."

"Stubborn mule."

"Wanna be therapist."

"See you at 5."

"Can't even eat first?"

"I'll buy you dinner. Just get down here."

"Fine."

Ronan hung up with him and saw a text from Katie:

> *Please just come meet me. We can talk this out Ronan. Nobody interfering. I didn't even tell Mia anything. Kian knows what's going on because*

he got to talk to you. I didn't. I need you home.
Promise me you'll hear me out.

Ronan didn't reply. He was still determined to stay unemotional. He was safer that way. It was easier. He'd treat it like a negotiation. One that meant getting his heart broken for the millionth time, but still a negotiation. He took a deep breath and went through the rest of his emails, delegating a few and getting through the rest before he left. He left around 4, heading to the hotel. He slid into jeans and a shirt and walked around the room, trying to get the guts to do what he needed to. She hadn't slept with the guy. She'd been pulled into a kiss that she didn't want supposedly. He tried to negotiate his feelings in his mind over and over again. She voluntarily went with him for drinks. She actually thought Ronan would want to meet him. He shook his head. He knew what was going on in Carter's head when he was with Katie. He finally had his chance that he'd never had before. What Carter didn't know, was that Ronan had seen it all. Katie didn't even know. He grabbed a drink, slowly sipping the Jameson. If he was gonna have to do it, he wasn't about to be sober.

Katie got back to the house and got changed into the skirt that Ronan liked. Even the shirt he liked. She put on his favorite perfume. She said a quick prayer hoping that somehow that would fix what had happened. She locked up and went over to the pub, seeing Mia and Kian.

"I talked to him. He'll be here," Kian said.

"I tried all day to get him to talk to me. All he did was get mad. How am I supposed to fix this," Katie asked.

"Let him say what he needs to say. Pat said he'd give you his office to talk. Whatever you do, don't get mad. It'll just piss Ronan off. He loves you and he knows he does. He's not gonna leave you and walk away," Kian said.

"And what happens if we can't fix this?"

"Then you have Friday night for your second chance. That meeting you said you two had," Mia said.

"I could barely even sleep last night. I got too used to being beside him."

"Leave it at he had Jameson to curl up with last night. A lot of Jameson," Kian said. Just as the words came out of his mouth, Katie saw Ronan walk in. He walked right past all three of them and went to the bathroom. Katie gulped down the lump in her throat.

"Pat, three pints and a fancy drink for Katie please."

"Probably not a good idea on that one," Pat said.

"Please," Mia said.

The drinks came to the table and when Ronan came out of the bathroom, Kian got up and handed him a pint. "Talk to her."

"I'm here because you asked me to. Nothing is getting solved. Not the way she wants anyway."

"Mule." Ronan shook his head.

"Sit down."

"I'm good at the bar."

"Ronan, don't make me push you into the booth."

"I'm not doing this," Ronan said.

"Pat, can we get the keys?" Pat threw him the keys to the office and Kian walked him back there.

"Nothing is getting resolved," Ronan said as soon as the door shut.

"You're gonna talk to her and stop being a damn mule. Talk. Make out. Do whatever to get past this stupid thing so we can have dinner."

"I'm not staying," Ronan said.

"You are staying. I don't want you two fighting. Mia gets all cranky at me because I can't fix this for you two. Drink your damn pint and hear the woman out." Ronan shook his head and sat down in the desk chair.

"Still not happening."

"Stay here."

"Kian."

"Either you two talk or I'm not letting you out of the office." Kian walked out and sat back down with Mia.

"Well," Mia asked.

"He's a stubborn mule. You two talk. We're not letting you two out of that room until this is fixed," Kian said.

"Nothing like interfering in their lives," Mia joked.

"He's a pain in my backside Mia. Stubborn. Determined to have the world bow at his damn feet."

"So he's still shut off," Katie asked.

"You're the only one that can get him to stop. Go."

Chapter 13

Katie got her drink and walked back to the office, walking in and seeing Ronan's empty glass. "Are you gonna talk to me," Katie asked.

"What is there to talk about Katie?"

"I prefer what you called me before this."

"Fat chance of that."

"He showed up at my work that day. He had a meeting with his mom's doctor."

"And? Didn't think to tell him that you had a man?"

"Ronan, I told him that we were together."

"Still went out for drinks with him alone."

"I asked you to come and you didn't."

"I saw you two together, got takeaway and left and went back to the house."

"Then you should've come and sat down with us."

He shook his head. "This isn't on me Katie. You agreed to drinks. If I hadn't said something, you would've gone to dinner with him too. If you don't want to be with me and you'd rather be with that, fine. Just say it."

"I don't want him. I want you."

"You let him kiss you."

"Ronan, I pushed him away. Don't do this."

"What do you want Katie? Tell me so I can leave and get out of here."

"I want you home. I want us home. I don't want anyone else. I want you."

"You went out with him."

"Ronan, stop. I made a mistake alright? I can't go back and undo it. I just want us to be okay."

"We're not."

"I know. Tell me what I have to do to fix this." He looked at her and could feel himself crumbling.

"I can't unsee that."

"I'm yours Ronan. Nobody else's. I don't want to be anyone else's."

He looked at her and Katie got closer to him, backing him up against the edge of the desk. "Katie."

"I need you."

"You don't."

"Ronan, I want you. Tell me what I have to do."

"Nothing."

"You want to push me away."

"You basically went on a date with someone else while we were together. You didn't come home until late. Then actually thought that I would go out for dinner with the two of you when I knew he was planning another date. When he showed up, which I knew that the loser would do, you let him kiss you. With me in the room no less. Did you really think that I was gonna sit there and take it?"

Katie kissed Ronan. It was the only thing she could think of to do. She refused to let him break the kiss until she could feel him kiss her back. She slid in tight to him and he pushed her away.

"Don't."

"Don't what? Make you feel something?"

"You let him kiss you."

"And I want you. Not him. I never wanted to be with him."

"Katie, just stop."

"I'm not walking out that door until you forgive me."

"Then we're gonna be in here a while."

"Ronan, I made a damn mistake."

"And?"

"You were getting emails from all of those women. I forgave you."

"Not really."

"Meaning what?"

"You saw her waiting. You saw me talking to her and you saw me walk in. Notice there was no hug, no kiss and no contact? That's called being faithful."

"Ronan."

"You still sat there with him. Who knows what time you got back. You didn't get into bed with me."

"Ronan, I got back at 10. Nothing else happened."

"And I'd know that how?"

"Drinks and I ended up drinking soda after the first two."

"Katie, just don't." She kissed him again.

"I promise you that it's never happening again. Please."

"I can't do this."

"Ronan."

"I'm not doing this Katie. I'm leaving."

"You promised that you would hear me out. You promised we could talk."

"And you promised a lot more crap that you just destroyed in 48 hours."

"I'm not losing you over a stupid drink."

"Kiss."

"I pushed him away."

"Still happened."

She kissed him again. "Don't do this Ronan."

He went to walk out and couldn't open the door. "Kian, stop and let me out." He tried again and the door wouldn't open. Ronan walked past her and sat down on the chair.

"Talk to me," Katie said.

"And what do you want me to say Katie? That I forgive you for being an idiot when it comes to him? That I forgive you for letting him think that he was going to date you when we were together? What?"

She looked at him. "That you forgive me for being a fool. I should've stayed at the house with you instead of coming here. I shouldn't have even agreed to a drink."

"He probably figured if he got you drunk, he could get his way."

"You seriously think that? It was a drink Ronan."

"One is all it takes Katie. You know that as well as I do."

"You're the only man I want. What else do I have to say to make you see that?"

"Katie."

She kissed Ronan again. "These are the only lips I want to kiss. Just you. I promise you that."

He tried to push her away, but Katie wouldn't give up. "Just stop," he said.

"No. I'm not losing you over this."

"What would you do if I'd done what you did?"

Katie looked at him. "I'd be mad, but I wouldn't have walked away. I wouldn't have avoided you and pushed you away like you're doing right now."

"If I'd gone for drinks with another woman. Kissed another woman. You wouldn't be sitting here right now if it were me that did it."

"I'd fight to fix this either way Ronan."

"Katie, I need time."

"You had time."

"Just leave it be."

"No."

"What the hell do you want me to do? Beat the crap out of him for touching you? Taking back my possession? What?"

"Fight to keep me in your damn life instead of turning off every damn emotion. I'm fighting for us. You're fighting against it."

"Katie."

"I'm yours. Is that what you want?"

"Obviously you aren't." She walked closer and he shook his head and backed away.

"Yours. All yours."

He shook his head again. "I can't do this Katie. I just can't."

"Why?"

"Because I can't get the visual of you and him kissing out of my damn head. Half a damn bottle of Jameson couldn't either." He'd cracked.

"I want you. Just you. Only you. I don't want anyone else Ronan." He looked at her like she was about to pour water on the wicked witch of the west.

"Say something," Katie said. He shook his head and ran his fingers over his head. "Ronan."

"What am I supposed to say?"

"That you love me. That you forgive me. Something."

"I can't forget that. I can't turn it off."

"Then just forgive me. Forgive me Ronan. Please."

"Katie."

"Please."

He shook his head. "I can't keep doing this. Katie, I can't get past that you kissed someone else. I'm sorry. I just can't. Especially when I damn well warned you that he was gonna try something. I told you over and over that he was trying to make a move and you didn't listen. What else do you want me to say?"

"That you forgive me."

"I don't know that my mind can." She walked over to him and wrapped her arms around him. "Katie, please."

She held on until she felt his arm wrap around her. "Let go."

"I can't lose you Ronan. Please just come home."

"Katie, I can't. I can't even wipe the kiss out of my head." She kissed him again and that kiss turned into making out. He backed her up against the wall and pinned her hands. When he stopped, he shook his head. "I can't."

"Ronan."

"No."

"Come home. We can talk alone."

"No."

"Ronan." He shook his head again and Katie kissed him.

"We're going home."

She opened the door, took his hand and walked him out of the pub and down the street to the house. She walked him inside and locked the door behind them. "Katie, why?"

"Why what?"

"Why did you even go in the first place?"

"Because I thought you'd show up and be there with me." He shook his head, and she sat him on the sofa.

"Katie, just don't." She slid into his lap and straddled him.

"I just want you." He shook his head again and she kissed him, leaning into his arms.

"Katie, this is ridiculous."

"Please." She kissed him again and he deepened the kiss, pulling her tight to him.

"Tell me what you want."

"You." He picked her up and walked upstairs, leaning her onto the bed in the main bedroom.

"Take the skirt off," he said.

"Ronan."

"Off. The shirt too." She looked at him and did as he asked. He peeled his shirt off and his jeans and reached into the drawer. "What are you doing?"

"Bra off."

"Ronan."

"Do it." She did and he tied her hands to the bed.

"Ronan." He kissed her then nibbled down her body, nibbling and licking each breast then kissing his way down her body. He got up and went to grab something from his drawer and she begged him not to.

"Please, no toys. Just you."

He shook his head. "Katie."

"Please." He shook his head and then walked back over to her, licking and teasing from her hip to her inner thigh. "Mm." When he licked her wetness, she thought that maybe she'd finally broken through. He kept licking then his fingers slid deep inside her and teased until she exploded around his fingers.

"Aah." He shook his head and kept going until her toes were curling. When he got up and slid deep inside her, she was moaning. He kept going over and over, harder and deeper, faster until she came again and again until he was spent.

"Undo my hands." He shook his head. He hadn't said a single word. He undid her hands and walked off into the bathroom, grabbing his clothes on the way in. When he came out 10 minutes later, he was fully dressed.

"Where are you going?" He shook his head. "Ronan." She grabbed the silk robe from her closet and got up. "Ronan, don't leave." When he walked out the door, she shook her head.

He walked down to the pub and sat back down with Kian and Mia as he waited for the SUV to pick him up. "What happened," Kian asked.

"She got what she wanted."

"Then what the hell are you doing here?"

"Waiting for the car to pick me up."

"Ronan," Mia said.

"I can't wipe the picture of them kissing out of my head alright? I can't." He got a shot, paid and within maybe 5 minutes, he was in the SUV on the way back to his hotel.

Katie showed up 15 minutes later and Ronan was gone. "Where did he go," Katie asked.

"He left. He went back to the hotel," Kian said.

"I thought that maybe he might..."

"Come and sit down," Mia said. Katie sat down and shook her head.

"It's not like I slept with Carter."

"Might as well have in his eyes lass," Kian said.

"I can't fix this can I," Katie asked.

"What happened," Mia asked. He finally let me in a little then we went back to the house, and we were okay. He got up and walked out after and it's like he'd tuned me out." Kian shook his head.

"I did all I can do lass. He's shut down," Kian said.

"I'm not losing him," Katie said.

"Give him tonight to calm down. Best bet is Friday," Kian said.

"I'm not waiting that long. There are other things we need to talk about."

"Katie, leave him be."

"What hotel is he at?"

"Katie," Mia said.

"Tell me."

"The Grafton," Kian said.

"That's the hotel we were at when we met."

"Just leave him be lass. He's in no shape to deal with anything if he stormed out of the house. He came in here, got a shot and left. He barely said two words to us," Mia said.

Katie looked at her. "I can't do this. I can't pretend that this isn't killing me to be fighting about something like this with him."

"Then let him decompress," Kian said. Katie shook her head. "I'm going over there."

"Then he's just gonna end up leaving and going somewhere else." Katie called him and there was no answer. Kian tried and got no answer. "He's not answering," Kian said.

"What am I supposed to do? Wait until he calms down," Katie asked.

Ronan got to his room and sat down on the sofa. He broke down in tears. So much for turning his emotions off. When his phone went off again, he looked at the phone and ignored the call. When Kian called, he ignored it. He couldn't handle another tough love moment with Kian. When he got a text from Katie, he couldn't even look. She deserved better than him. He'd screwed that up for her too. Now, he was stuck in a hotel suite and miserable. He went and got the bottle of Jameson and poured himself a drink. Not 10 minutes later, his phone rang again. This time, it was a call that he really didn't need – another ex. He ignored the call and blocked the number. He'd lost Katie. She wasn't his anymore. It didn't matter what she'd said.

He had a few more drinks and his stomach started growling. He ordered dinner to the room and downed the rest of his drink. When there was a knock at the door, he figured it would be room service. When he was face to face with Kian and a bottle of Jameson, he let him in.

"Thought you were room service," Ronan said.

"You gonna tell me what happened?"

"No."

"Ronan, the girl came back in tears. What happened?" Ronan walked into the bedroom and splashed his face with cold water. "What," Kian asked.

"She deserves better than me."

"She wants you. Even I know that. I've known that since the day you introduced her to us."

"Maybe she's better off with him."

"Ronan, do you realize that I had to talk her out of hunting you down in every hotel in town?"

"I can't do this Kian. I just can't."

"You two left the damn pub and you show up 45 minutes later even more pissed off. Whatever the hell happened just say it." Ronan shook his head and there was a knock at the door. He opened it and his food showed. "Thank you," Ronan said. Kian looked at him.

"What?"

"Waiting."

"She thought that she could fix it. She couldn't. She wants to be with him then great for her. Hope they're happy," Ronan said.

"She loves you."

"And?"

"Has it been that long since you had someone other than your friends give a crap? The woman is in love with you. Not that stupid loser. You."

"She doesn't."

"Ronan, don't make me drag you to that house. She wants to be with you. She was crying at the damn pub. What do you want her to do? Get in a Time Machine and undo it?"

"She doesn't want to be with me. If she did, she wouldn't have gone in the first place."

"You just have that stuck in your damn head because of the devil bitch. She wants you. Get that stuck instead. She wants to be with you. You won't go back to the house because you don't want her near you. You haven't got past it. You know how many disagreements I've had with Mia? A million. None of them resulted in me disappearing and vanishing on her to a random hotel. I sat down and worked through it even if we were sleeping in separate rooms for a night or two. You can't just avoid her." Not two minutes later, his phone rang again. It was Katie. Ronan shook his head and Kian grabbed his phone and answered.

"Ronan?"

"It's Kian. You okay?"

"I need to talk to him," Katie said. Kian put her on speaker.

"I put you on speaker. Say what you want," Kian said.

"You just walk off again and disappear? Ronan, come back to the house so we can finish this." Ronan ate in silence. "Please Ronan. I get you're mad alright. I'm mad at myself for going and even talking to him at work. I shouldn't have. I have what I want. I have you. That's all that I want. You aren't screwed up. You're the man that I love even if you won't see it. Please just come home," Katie said.

Ronan stopped eating and shook his head, putting his burger down.

"Are you with Mia," Kian asked.

"I'm at the house. Mia came with me."

"Go ahead. He's listening lass," Kian said.

"Come back to the house Ronan. Please. I'll sleep in the guest room. Please. I blocked him from contacting me. I don't want him anywhere near me. He disrespected us and our relationship. I drew the damn line. Please just come home."

Ronan got up and got himself another drink. Kian went and took it away from him. "Talk or you don't get it back," Kian said. Ronan grabbed a second glass and poured himself a drink and tossed it back.

"I'm not coming," Ronan said.

"Then let me come there."

"No."

"Ronan, you can't hide at a damn hotel just because we're in a fight."

"I'm not hiding. I'm avoiding doing something that I can't take back," Ronan said.

"What do you want to do Ronan? Tell me."

"Beat the crap out of him."

"Kinda already told him off and did that for you," Kian said.

"Ronan."

"If you loved me that damn much, how the hell do you do what you did and think nothing of it? That's not love Katie. I tell you not to and you do it. I tell you that he has ulterior motives and you let him get away with what he did. If you'd slapped him or something, I might be able to get past it, but you did nothing."

"Ronan, please just tell me where you are. We can talk this out alone. Please." Ronan shook his head. Kian looked at him.

"Ronan," Kian said.

"No," Ronan replied.

"Katie, if he doesn't tell you where he is, I will. Give me a half hour."

"Ronan, please just come home." Ronan finished his burger and Kian hung up with Katie.

"Get your crap together."

"Kian, this has nothing to do with you or Mia. I'm handling it my way."

"Your way as in not handling it at all and taking off on her," Kian said sarcastically.

"I can't go back to the house. I just can't."

"You're not staying here, or I swear I'm going to get her and bring her here myself," Kian said.

"You can't just butt out and leave this alone."

"Ronan, you're acting like an idiot. You're blowing a gasket over a kiss. She didn't sleep with him. Nothing even close to that."

"That's what she wants."

"Then why the hell is she fighting so hard to get you back? Did you think about that?" Ronan took the drink away from Kian and drank it. Kian got up and got a bottle of water, handing one to Ronan and drinking the other.

"You're going."

Ronan shook his head. "I'm staying tonight. I'll go on Saturday."

"Then she's staying here with you. Those are your two choices. Either you go home tonight, or I'm seriously bringing her here."

Ronan shook his head. "You never just butt out do you?"

"Not when my girl is getting just as damn mad at you as you are mad at Katie." Ronan shook his head and sat down. "I tried to sleep at the house, and I couldn't alright? All I saw was the two of them kissing and what would've happened if I hadn't been there. I just can't Kian."

"Shutting yourself off doesn't work."

"I need to be away from her."

"You need to sit down and let it sink in that you don't have a choice right now. You disappeared yesterday. You only showed today because I asked you to."

"She only wants me there because she's horny."

Kian shook his head. "The woman begged Ronan. You're going."

"Or what?"

"She already knows what hotel you're at." Ronan shook his head.

By the time Kian called Katie back, he'd got Ronan and his things into the SUV on the way to the house. He went with him to make sure that Ronan didn't find a different hotel. "I can't do this," Ronan said.

"Just for tonight. Give it a damn chance." When they pulled up to the house, Ronan shook his head.

"I can't do this. Just take me back to the hotel," Ronan said.

"You're getting out of the car and you're going in. Go," Kian said. He got out and got Ronan's things out of the back, handing them to him and gave him a look.

"You do realize that you can't make me do this right?"

Kian nodded. "Making you flip the damn switch back on? Yeah, I know. You're going in there. Go," Kian said as Ronan shook his head and walked into the house.

Katie looked up and saw Ronan. "Are you gonna talk to me?" He walked upstairs and put his bag up in his closet and repacked for the next 48 hours, including his suit for the event. When he heard the bedroom door close, he turned around and saw Katie standing in the doorway of his closet. "What?"

"You can't just disappear because something happened. Cut me off like I'm nobody."

"You chose him Katie."

"I choose you. I always choose you. I'm not losing you because he's an idiot. I want you. I have since the day we met. I should've listened to you when you said he was up to something."

"Even when I was there, he still made a damn move."

"Then tell him off. I didn't know. If I'd known when he showed at the hospital that he was planning something I would've put a stop to it." He walked downstairs and got himself a drink. Katie took it out of his hand and put it down. "That isn't gonna solve it Ronan." He took the drink back and walked back upstairs.

"Ronan, please just stop."

"What do you want Katie?"

"Sit and talk."

He sat down on the chair in the bedroom. "Talk."

"What do you need me to say so we're over this?"

"There's nothing you can say Katie."

"Please. I can't change it. All I know is that I love you. I'm not gonna stop loving you." He took a gulp of his drink.

"I'm not staying."

"Why?"

"Because I can't sleep in this bed and not think about it."

"Then sleep in the guest room. Sleep on the sofa. Just don't leave."

"Why? Because you want to get some?"

"Because I can't sleep when you aren't near me. I need you."

He shook his head. "I'm going."

"Ronan, please just stay. i don't know what else to say."

"I have to get it out of my system Katie. Takes a couple days."

"Then stay here."

He looked at her. "And that thing you did last night, not fair."

"Back at you," Katie replied.

"Tell me what you want Katie." She walked over to him and grabbed his hand.

"What," he asked. She walked him over to the bed and sat him on it.

"I need you to sleep beside me."

"He..."

"Ronan, I shouldn't have ever talked to him. Period. No conversation would mean no drinks and nothing else. I have what I want right here right now with you. I don't want him. Period. What else do you want me to do?" He shook his head and finished his drink.

Katie walked over to him and slid her arms around his neck. When she felt his arm wrap around her waist, she was almost nervous to move. "Ronan."

"What?"

"I'm sorry."

He nodded. "I know."

"I just want you with me. I don't care about anything else."

"I know."

"Will you forgive me?"

"I'm trying to." She looked at him and knew making a single move would scare him off.

"What do you need me to do?"

"I don't know."

"Do you want to kick his butt?"

"More than anything."

She slid her heels off. She took a ragged breath and felt his arm tighten around her. "Tell me what to do Ronan."

"Listen to me when I say not to do it." She took a deep breath.

"I promise I will." She wanted to do something to try and pull him to her. She knew better. She wasn't about to ruin it. "Ronan."

"It killed me."

"I know it did."

"I thought you wanted that."

"I want you, love. I only want you."

"You sure that you don't want that guy?"

"I just want you." She could feel Ronan crying.

"You sure you don't want him?"

"I only want you Ronan. I only ever want you." He took a deep breath. She didn't know what else to do. She looked down at him and saw him looking at her. "Tell me what you want me to do Ronan." He went to get up and she didn't let go.

"I'm not letting go." He kissed her.

"I know you aren't."

"I'm not letting you leave Ronan." He kissed her again and she snuggled in tighter to him.

"I know you aren't. I just need to calm my mind."

"Then calm it here."

"I used to be like him Katie. Who cares about her man. Who cares if she has someone. I was a damn wrecking ball to anyone that got in my way. I ruined relationships."

"And now you're not."

He shook his head. "I need to clear my head."

"Then we go for a walk. Sit outside. I'm not leaving your side whether you're mad or not," Katie said.

"I need to be out of here."

"Not without me."

"Katie."

"Not without me Ronan. Not after you took off."

"I can't get the image out of my head."

"Then stay here and let me try and blur it a little."

"I can't."

"Then I'm coming with you." He shook his head.

"Katie, please."

"I couldn't sleep last night without you here. I don't care if I'm sleeping in the guest room." He shook his head.

"Fine."

"You'll stay?" He nodded. She looked at him. "I love you Ronan."

"I know," he replied. He hugged her to him.

"Tell me what I need to do."

"Just lay down with me." Katie was almost stunned that he had even said it. Katie nodded and they curled up together on the bed.

"Ronan."

"What?"

"Please stay tonight."

"I can't promise that I'll be here in the morning. If I can't sleep, I'm going back to the hotel."

"Just don't shut me out." He took a deep breath and Katie looked up at him.

"What," he asked.

"I love you," Katie said.

"I know you do. I just need to get past this."

"You know that I pushed him away, right?"

"Katie."

"Okay." He felt her head on his chest. He shook his head and tried. He tried not to react. He tried not to push her away. When she moved closer, he took a deep breath.

"Katie." She kissed him. One kiss turned into two then making out. Then him on top of her and pulling her legs around him. "Katie."

"Tell me what you want." He kissed her, devouring her lips and pulled her shirt off.

"Ronan."

"Off." She slid it off and he pulled his shirt off. He undid her bra.

"Ronan."

"All of it off."

"I'm not..." He kissed her again and pulled her skirt off.

"Ronan." He undid his jeans and kicked them off. "You sure," Katie asked as he leaned in and kissed her again. "What do you want Ronan?" He kissed her, devouring her lips and peeled his boxers off. He pulled her legs back around him and kissed down her neck. "Aah." He didn't say a word. He slid deep into her as Katie moaned. He kissed her again and went slow and hard into her over and over again. He pounded into her until she was moaning again. "Shit," Katie said. He still said nothing. He devoured her lips and kept going until he felt her throbbing around him. He exploded into her, and Katie kissed him. He didn't move. "Ronan." He kissed her again.

"Don't leave."

"Katie."

"Don't leave. Please."

"I have to move." He leaned onto his back, and she curled up with him.

"You okay," Katie asked. He gulped and shook his head.

"Ronan." He got up and walked into the bathroom. Katie heard the water running in the shower and slid the satin robe on from her closet. She slid back into bed and when Ronan came back out of the bathroom in a towel, he slid boxers on and sat down on the side of the bed. "Come lay down." He took a deep breath.

"Katie, I need to go."

She shook her head. "No."

"I need to."

"Then I'm going with you."

"No." She got up and walked over to him.

"Katie."

"You aren't leaving. Just stay here. We'll just get some sleep. I'll sleep..."

"Katie."

"I don't want you to go Ronan." He got up and pulled on boxers.

"I can't sleep here," he said.

"Please." Ronan shook his head. He went to slide his jeans on and she stopped him. "Get into the bed Ronan. Get some sleep."

"I can't."

"Try. For me." He laid down on the bed and she curled up with him. "Just get some rest."

"Katie."

"Please. I need you here tonight." He put his phone on the charger beside hers and flipped the light off. "Goodnight Ronan."

"Goodnight," he said as he attempted to close his eyes and sleep.

The next morning, Katie woke up and he wasn't in bed. His phone was gone. She walked into his closet, and his bag was gone. She walked downstairs and saw a note by the coffee maker:

> *Couldn't sleep. I'll meet you for dinner before the event tomorrow night.*

She shook her head and looked at her phone, seeing a missed call from Ronan. She called him back and he answered. "I was wide awake at 1am. I just couldn't sleep."

"That's what the guest room is for Ronan."

"I know. I don't know what's wrong with me, but I just couldn't."

"Can I come meet you somewhere tonight?"

"Katie."

"I'll come to the hotel. Maybe you'll sleep better."

"I'll think about it."

"I love you."

"I know you do. I'll talk to you later. I'm just getting breakfast and heading into the office." Katie took a deep breath, walked upstairs and packed a bag for two nights plus her outfit for the event. She got showered and dressed, made breakfast and cleaned up and by the time she walked outside with her overnight bag in hand, the car was waiting for her. "Did you want me to drop your bag off at the hotel," the driver asked.

"Please. I'm staying there with him tonight."

"Yes ma'am."

By the end of the day, Katie was determined to get to the hotel as fast as she could. She got to the front desk, and they gave her a key to the suite. When she looked at the room number, it was the same room they'd been in that first night they were together. She got to the room and saw Ronan's suit hanging up in the closet. She breathed a sigh of relief and sat down. When he came in 20 minutes later, he was almost stunned to see her. "What are you doing here?"

"We're having dinner."

"How did..."

"Ask your assistant." He took a deep breath and walked over to her and hugged her.

"What time did you leave?"

"Around 1. I tried Katie. I did. I just couldn't sleep. I came back here, had a few and conked out."

She looked at him. "Can we have dinner alone?"

"Like up here?"

"So we can finish talking."

"I finally got it out of my head."

"Good. Now let me in." He kissed her and went and changed out of his suit.

"Katie, I get that you want to fix this right now, but..." She kissed him. His arm slid around her and pulled her to him. "Tell me what you want," he asked.

"Time with you."

"Katie."

"I'm staying with you tonight."

"You realize I came here because I couldn't sleep with you beside me, right?"

"I'm not sleeping in that house alone. Besides the fact that tomorrow we both have to be at that event."

"Katie, you should..."

"Don't."

"Fine."

"I thought we were okay last night."

"Katie, I can't get the visual out of my head."

"Then figure out how. I'm not losing you over a mistake."

"Katie." She looked at him, completely standing her ground.

"Dinner."

"Katie, I get what you think…" She kissed him again and he shook his head. "Determined?"

"I'm not letting you push me away again." He kissed her.

"Okay," Ronan said.

"Good." He shook his head and Katie sat down on the edge of the bed. "Why this room?"

"The suite I usually stay in when I'm here."

"Our room." He nodded.

"Are you mad that I'm here?"

"Just surprised." He finished getting changed and Katie watched him.

"What?"

"Come here." He walked over to her shirtless.

"What?" Katie stood up and looked up at him.

"I know what you're doing."

"Good. Thought you might need a reminder."

"Katie."

"Sit." He shook his head and sat down. She slid into his lap.

"Katie."

"What?"

"I know exactly what you're up to."

"Good," she replied as she slid her arms around his neck. He slid his arms around her waist.

"Tell me what you want."

"I want to hear you call me love again. I want us. The way we always were after work until this." He kissed her. His arms tightened around her.

"You're sure you wouldn't rather..."

"I chose you. I always will choose you. She kissed Ronan and he shook his head.

"What," Katie asked.

"All of this stupid stuff with him screwed me up."

"I know it did. I don't want it to anymore."

"What do you want me to do Katie?"

"Forget about it. Like it never happened." She kissed him and when she felt his fingers slide to her scalp, she slid in tighter to him. He kissed down her neck and she got a grin ear to ear.

"You're way too tempting."

"And yours." He held on tighter and kissed her with a deep, intense kiss that had goosebumps popping up everywhere.

"Ronan," she said when he let her up for air.

"What?"

"I don't want to be without you." He kissed her again and picked her up, leaning her onto the bed

"Good thing you don't have to be."

"This mean that you're coming home?"

"I just needed to get it out of my head. That's all Katie."

"Then I want us back. All of it." He kissed her again and Katie slid her heels off. He slid the sweater dress off and saw the black lace lingerie under it.

"Nice," he teased.

"Your favorite."

"Had to tempt me."

"Part of the plan." He shook his head and leaned into her arms.

"You're overdressed." He shook his head and undid his jeans.

"Off."

"Katie."

"I need you."

"Here I thought you wanted dinner."

"In bed."

He shook his head. "Katie, if this is the only reason you're here, you could've just told me you wanted me to come home."

"And you wouldn't have come."

"So, you're only reason for coming was because you were horny."

"Ronan, I missed you."

"Katie."

"I don't want to fight about this anymore."

"I don't even know what all of this was for." He did his jeans back up and pulled on a shirt from his bag.

"Ronan." He shook his head.

"You're seriously going to walk away right now." He took a deep breath and sat down on the sofa. She shook her head and walked back over to him.

"Ronan, I don't want us fighting about this anymore. This is ridiculous. I didn't sleep with him. It was a mistake. I thought we were okay," Katie said.

"I know it was Katie. I just..."

"What Ronan? Yell at me. Do something other than shut down."

"You went on a date with him. You literally sat at the pub where we go together and sat with him. You almost went out to dinner with him. Next thing I know, he's kissing you in the pub. I'm supposed to just get over that?"

"Come here."

"No. You don't get to just brush it under the damn carpet like it was nothing. You let another man kiss you."

"And I slapped him. I walked out and saw you taking off. You walked away from me. You up and left and I had no idea where you were. Not until today anyway. You don't get to run away from me because I made a mistake even if it was a big one."

"And what do you expect me to do Katie?"

She walked over to where he was sitting. "Get up."

"What," he asked.

"Get up." He did as she asked.

"Do you know who I want Ronan? You. I want you in my bed, in my life, kissing me, sitting at another stupid sports day together at the pub. I want us. I've wanted us since the first damn time we were in this room together. I dared you to date me. Now I'm daring you again. Give me another chance. I made a mistake that I wish I could go back and delete. I can't get a Time Machine. All I can do is tell you that I want you. That I need you. I'm sitting here begging you to take me back Ronan. You needed time to clear your head, and you got it. Now it's our time. I want you. I want you more than anything right now. I'm standing here in your favorite lingerie. I'm asking you to forgive me for the idiotic mistake I made. Please just stop pushing me away and kiss me."

"It's not that easy lass."

She walked towards him. "Then make it that easy." She kissed him. "You want to tie my hands, tie them. You want to use the stupid toys, fine. I just want you. I want your heart. I want your soul Ronan. I don't want to be pushed away again. Please." She went to kiss him again and his head bent down and devoured her lips. The kiss went on until she felt him pulling her tight to him.

"Don't ever do that again. Promise me."

Katie nodded as he undid the bra. "I promise you."

"Next time I say stay away from someone, do it." Katie's legs almost started shaking.

"I just want you," Katie said.

"I know."

"You don't want me?" He picked her up and carried her to the bed, leaning her onto the blankets and pulled off the lace panties. "Ronan." Her heart started racing.

"Don't ever make me second guess this. Promise me." She nodded and just the feel of his body against hers had her turned on. She undid his shirt and slid it off.

"Take them off," Katie said as he kissed down her neck.

"Nope," he replied.

"Ronan." He licked and nibbled at her breast. "Mm."

"You don't get to say a word," he said. She smirked and he kissed down her torso, kissing and nibbling at her hip. "Aah."

"Don't move."

"Kinda hard to do," Katie teased. When he licked her inner thigh, she shook her head.

"Teasing," Katie said. He licked and sucked and nibbled at her until she was soaked in his hands.

First his fingers started to tease, then his fingers and his tongue. "Shit."

"I'm gonna keep going until you beg for me."

"I already have." He licked and teased even more until she was grinding against his fingers.

"Mine," he said. The words were almost too much. The words she'd been wanting to hear since this entire problem started. The one word. The one that meant more than anything. "Always," she replied. He kept going until she was throbbing around his fingers.

"Ronan."

"What?"

"Please."

"Please what?"

"Take the jeans off." He kicked his jeans off, slid off his boxers and he was beyond turned on. She'd flipped the switch back on and he wanted every inch of her shaking in his arms.

Chapter 14

"Ronan please."

"Please what?"

"Come here. I need you." He kissed his way back up her body as his fingers continued to tease and probe her body.

"What do you need?"

"You. Inside me. Now." He slid his boxers off and kissed her neck then her lips.

"And what else do you need?"

"Please." He pulled her towards him and wrapped her legs around him as he slid deep inside her. "Aah."

"That what you wanted?"

"Mm. Yes."

"Good. Just remember what you promised."

"What?"

"Mine and only mine." He slid deeper into her, going in and out, over and over until he started to speed up.

"Ronan." She was getting closer to her climax, and he didn't let up for even a minute. "Shit."

"Not yet."

"Ronan."

"Not yet Katie."

"Please." Her body tightened around him. "Please." He kissed her and kept going harder, deeper, faster until she was throbbing. "Please."

"Come for me."

"Aah." He didn't stop. He made it even more intense as he slid his hand over her and teased with his fingers as he pounded into her. "Shit Ronan."

"Not done with you lass." Her heart was racing and he kept going. When her legs started shaking again, he went harder and deeper.

"Mm. I want you."

"Good thing I'm here then lass," he whispered as he kissed and nibbled down the side of her neck.

Just as he was about to explode into her, his phone buzzed. "You touch that phone and I swear..." He kissed her and ignored it. He came and devoured her lips until she was a mess in his arms.

"Mine," he said.

"About time," Katie joked. He shook his head and slid to his back.

"I swear, if you get up right now, I'm tackling you back to the bed."

"Katie."

"Please just stop. I want the rest of it. I want you calling me love again. I don't want to fight about any of this anymore. Please." She snuggled in close to him, wrapping her leg around his.

"All of this because you missed me calling you love?" Katie nodded. "You're bad."

"And yours."

He kissed her again. "I can't go through that again. You know that right?"

She kissed him. "You'll never have to."

"I mean it Katie."

"So do I. I don't want anyone else. I want us."

"Promise me." She kissed him again and he snuggled her to him.

"I promise." Katie's head rested on his shoulder.

"We're staying tonight." She nodded.

"And after the event tomorrow?" He kissed her forehead.

"Up to you."

"And if I say I want us to stay?"

"Then we leave Saturday morning."

"I just don't want to be going home alone."

"Too quiet?"

Katie nodded. "And lonely."

He snuggled her to him. "I just needed time. You know that right?"

Katie nodded again and kissed his shoulder. "Just promise that you won't disappear again."

"I promise," he said.

Katie breathed a sigh of relief. He pulled up the blankets and snuggled her to him. "I miss you calling me love."

"Oh really," he asked. Katie nodded. "It'll come."

"Ronan."

He kissed her. "What?"

"Promise me that those texts aren't what I think they are."

"Don't care."

"Ronan."

"They just get blocked and deleted lass." He grabbed his phone and saw messages from Kian.

"Like I said, don't care."

"And what did he want?" Ronan looked at the screen:

You realize that she's gonna find out where you are and show up right? You need to throw the lass a bone.

Ronan replied:

Busy. Katie's here.

When there was no return text, Ronan smirked. "What," Katie asked.

"Nothing. He was just getting ready for round 4 of trying to be a relationship therapist. When he reads the reply, he'll be dead silent. Watch." When there was no return text, Katie almost laughed.

"He was really on my side wasn't he," Katie joked.

"He was seeing both sides. Trying to make me go home though."

"I know why you couldn't be there." Ronan looked at her.

"I just don't understand why he made a move when I was clearly there."

"He had some sort of plan. Thank goodness I have you instead."

"Second choice?"

"First. Always."

"And why's that," Ronan asked as he teased.

"The first guy who made me dare him to date me."

"Made you now?" She nodded. "Made you dare me? Lass, I just wanted you warned ahead of time. I didn't know that you were ready for me."

"After that first night, I didn't think I was either." He nuzzled her neck.

"Oh really."

Katie nodded as he leaned her onto her back. "Ronan."

"Mm."

"And here I thought we were just having dinner."

"Food could be ordered."

"Or what," she asked.

"Dessert first."

"You already had dessert."

"Seconds."

"Ronan."

"Mine."

He kissed her and devoured her lips until her toes were almost curling. "Katie."

"Mm."

"Food. What do you want?"

"You." He smirked and kissed down her neck.

"Real food."

"Don't care. I want you." He nibbled on her earlobe.

"Mm."

"Ronan."

"Yes lass."

"More."

He kissed her. "Food first."

"You first." He kissed her and got up. "Where are you going?"

"Ordering dinner." He ordered dinner for them both and walked back into the bedroom.

"Bed."

"Dinner will be up here in a half hour. Get dressed."

"And if I said no?"

"Don't make me get my tie out of my bag."

"You wouldn't." He nodded. "I'd still be naked."

"Mm." She smirked. "Still need to get up lass."

She got up and slid his dress shirt on, buttoning it. "Better," she teased as he pulled his boxers and jeans on.

"No. Have to steal my shirt?"

"Yes. You want it off me, undo it." He shook his head.

"Tempting."

"How tempting?" He walked over to her and undid the first button. Just as he did, there was a buzz from his phone. He looked and shook his head.

"What?" He showed her the text:

> *About time. You two aren't allowed to fight anymore. That's from me and Mia.*

Katie smirked. "I agree. No more fights."

"You mean since you got me back."

"Ever."

He shook his head. "There are gonna be disagreements."

"And? No more disappearing on me."

"Katie."

"I know. Just no more disappearing. I don't want to sleep in that bed alone anymore."

"I needed to clear my head."

"You needed to remove yourself from it so you could understand it."

"Something like that."

"Then next time, fight it out. No more shutting me out."

He kissed her. "How about no more causing a problem."

"Would it be a problem if I did this," Katie asked as she undid his jeans.

"Katie."

"Would that be a problem?"

"Yes."

"And if I did this," she asked as she slid her hand around him and slid her hand up and down until he was hard in her hand.

"Starting a problem."

"And what problem would that be," Katie asked. His heart started pounding.

"Katie, you start it, you're finishing it."

"Then sit." He shook his head and pinned her against the wall, sliding deep into her again and kept going hard and fast and deep until she was moaning his name. "You are so bad," he teased.

"And yours." He poured himself into her and leaned against her.

"You..."

"What," she asked as her legs got shaky.

"Get in the bed."

"Thought you said that dinner was coming."

"You can't be trusted."

"Says who?" He shook his head and pulled his shirt off her.

"Ronan." He kissed her and was just about to make a move when there was a knock at the door.

"Stay here." He zipped his jeans up and went and answered.

"In here," he said as the room service attendant brought in their dinners. "Thank you." The attendant left and he walked back into the bedroom.

"Dinner?" He nodded.

"Put your dress on."

"Only if you promise to pull it back off." He shook his head.

"You're just bad," he teased.

"That mean you're pulling it back off?"

"That means you're gonna be tied to the bed tonight and I'm not letting you get up until you beg."

"I missed that."

"I bet you did."

She slid the sweater dress back on and walked into the living room to see steak dinner waiting for them. "How'd you know this is what I wanted?"

"Because you're gonna need your strength for tonight."

"Why? What's tonight," she said sarcastically and laughed.

"The one thing you said you hadn't done."

"Ronan."

"You wanted all of me. I get every inch of you."

"Ronan, you aren't doing what I think you are," she said.

"What of it?" She looked at him. "Eat your dinner lass. You'll need the energy." She smirked and had her dinner. "What," he asked seeing the look on her face.

"You are kidding right?"

He looked at her and she knew her answer. "If you say no, fine. Still gonna tease you until you beg."

"Shit." He nodded and had his dinner. When he poured them each a glass of wine, she smirked.

"What?"

"Memories of this room."

"If I remember correctly, it mostly took place in that bed."

"But bent over that sofa wouldn't have been bad either."

"Or the chair."

"Or the table for that matter." He was starting to get turned on all over again.

"Or against the wall." Katie smirked.

"Tempting."

"Very," he replied.

Katie finished her steak and looked at him. "What?"

"All mine." He shook his head.

"About time you said it." Katie got up and walked over to him, straddling him in his chair.

"What?"

"Did I ever tell you that you're sexy?"

"Hungry for dessert?"

"Something like that." When her hand undid the button of his jeans, he stopped her.

"No."

"Ronan." He shook his head. "Why not?"

He kissed her. "Up."

"No."

He looked in her eyes. "Katie, up."

"Or what?" He got up and picked her up.

"About time," Katie said. He walked into the bedroom, peeled her dress off and grabbed the tie from his bag, tying her hands to the edge of the bed.

"Ronan."

"Now you're gonna behave."

"Come here." He kissed her and walked back in and finished his dinner, watching her squirm in the bed. "You realize you aren't being fair right?"

"Be done in a minute or two." He finished his dinner and saw her still squirming, trying to get her hands free.

He finished his glass of wine, refilling both their glasses, brought the glasses to the bedside and kissed her. "Ronan."

"Lass."

"Come here." He walked over to the end of the bed. "Ronan."

He smirked. "You don't get your way tonight."

"Jeans off." He shook his head. "Then undo your jeans."

"Nope."

"Ronan."

"What?"

"I need you to come here." He smirked.

"I'm right here."

"And if I said closer?"

"Because you want dessert."

"Yes."

"Answer is no."

"Why?" He kissed the edge of her calf.

"Because I'm having dessert first."

"You had dessert."

"And I get seconds, and thirds and fourths. You can't do a darn thing about it."

"Ronan."

He kissed her thigh. "What?"

"You're teasing."

"Intentionally." He kissed her inner thigh.

"Mm." One lick and her toes were curling. "Shit."

He licked and sucked and teased then slid two fingers inside her, teasing her even more. "Aah."

"Mine."

Katie nodded. "Yours." He made it more intense. "Mm. Ronan." He licked and teased even more. "Aah. Please."

"Please what?"

"You know what. Please."

"Not even warmed up yet lass."

"I need you." He shook his head, and his fingers kept teasing. When she started throbbing around his fingers, he got a grin ear to ear.

"Good girl."

"Ahh."

"Keep going," he said.

"I can't." He kept teasing. "Shit Ronan." He licked and nibbled until he could see her toes curling.

"More," he said.

"Mm." He slid his jeans off quietly, then slid his boxers off. He was beyond just getting hard. He was turned on. Watching her grind against his hand was getting him even more turned on.

"Ronan, I need you." He slid his fingers out and slid deep into her. "Aah."

"That what you wanted?"

Katie nodded. He pounded into her over and over until he felt her throbbing around him again then flipped her onto her stomach. "Ronan." He slid back into her, pulling her backside against him. "Shit."

"What," he asked.

"Aah."

"Mine."

"Ronan." He pounded into her harder and faster until she crashed around him.

"Not done with you."

"Shit." He slid his hands across her backside, sliding a thumb inside her and kept pounding.

"Mm. Ahh."

"More?"

"Aah." He kept going, harder, deeper and faster until he couldn't hold back anymore and exploded into her. "Hands," she said. He untied her hands and slid to his side.

"You're so bad," she said.

"You liked it."

"Yes," she replied.

"You sure you wanted dessert?"

"Still do," she teased. He shook his head.

"You're gonna have to give me a minute."

"I don't know that I can take anymore."

"You start something, I'm finishing it."

"Ronan."

"What?"

"I love you."

"I know."

"Ronan."

"What lass?"

"Please."

"Please what?"

"You know what." He kissed her.

"I love you too."

"About time," Katie joked. He shook his head.

"So determined." When he got up, Katie almost laughed.

"What?"

"Not allowed to leave the room."

"I'm not." He kissed her and got up, cleaning up a little, then came back to bed, pulling his boxers and jeans on.

"Ronan."

"What?"

"Can we just curl up in bed for a bit?" He nodded and still hadn't taken his jeans off. She went to unbutton his jeans, and he stopped her.

"What's wrong," Ronan asked.

"Jeans off."

"And here I thought you were tired."

"I am. Jeans off."

"Why?"

"Because I don't want you in jeans if we're curled up in bed." He shook his head and slid the jeans off.

"And the boxers." He shook his head.

"I know better."

"Party pooper."

"I know you lass. I know exactly what you're gonna do."

"Which is what?"

"Lick."

"And? My dessert."

"No Katie." She slid into his arms.

"No what?" He shook his head and Katie kissed him.

"I know you're up to something."

"Waiting."

"For what?"

"That word."

He kissed her. "I know you are." She kissed him and he deepened the kiss until she was in his lap.

"You are teasing." He shook his head.

"You're the one crawling into my lap all naked." She smirked.

"Intentionally."

"And what do you want lass?"

"Say love."

"Katie."

"Say it."

"What do you want love?" She kissed him.

"That's what I wanted."

"Why?"

"Because it means we're okay."

"You do realize you're not staying in the room tomorrow right?"

"Work. I know."

"And I have meetings."

"And I'll be your treat when you get back." He shook his head.

"You're bad."

"I'll beat you back here."

"Probably," he joked.

"Then we get to go to that thing tomorrow night."

"You know where I'll end up."

"Honestly, if you hate those events so much, why do you even go?"

"To show off the sexy lass of mine."

"And vanish in the middle of the event."

"And take my sexy lass up here and have my way with her instead of standing around for hours."

"That what you're planning?" He nodded. "Ronan."

"Just enough time tomorrow to go to the house and pick up a few things from that drawer."

"Ronan."

"Some of them might involve you wearing it."

"Not at a business event."

He nodded. "The little one."

"Maybe the other one that makes your toes curl."

"You wouldn't."

He nodded again. "Ronan."

"The one that pounds into you."

"Not when we're at that event."

"Or the one that makes your toes curl."

"Ronan, don't."

He smirked. "Or the other one that does both." She looked at him.

"New?"

He nodded. "Perfect timing to try it out."

"And where is this magical thing?" He kissed her. "In my laptop bag." Katie shook her head.

"You do realize those toys are slowly piling up."

"Just get to randomly choose one to taunt the hell out of you with."

"Ronan." He smirked.

"Kinda liking the idea of that new one."

"Ronan."

He kissed her. "What?"

"You do realize that I don't need the toys, right?"

He nodded. "They tend to be fun," he joked.

"You sure you really want to do that tomorrow?"

"Honestly, I want to tonight, but someone is determined to stay in bed." She kissed him.

"Because I don't feel like being that far away from you."

"Katie."

"I just got you back. No more fight, no more stress, no more drama."

He looked at her. "That's why you are determined not to leave the bedroom." Katie nodded.

"I don't want us fighting ever again. Not like that. I can't go through that again."

"Probably didn't help when Kian and Mia got involved."

Katie nodded. "I just don't want us like that again."

Ronan kissed her. "Still going to get a few things from the house tomorrow. If you really want to stay, we're gonna need clothes."

"Sorta brought mine," Katie teased.

"And what would've happened if I didn't let you stay?"

"I was staying regardless handsome."

"Oh really?" She nodded. "And what would've happened if I'd said no?"

"I wasn't planning on going anywhere until we resolved it."

He leaned into her arms on the bed and pinned her hands. "What am I gonna do with you," he asked.

"Take the boxers off and find out."

He shook his head. "No." "Then we're probably sleeping, unless you have other plans."

He kissed her. "I always have plans."

She smirked. "And what are your plans?"

"Depends on what time it is."

"It's not even 7 yet," Katie replied. He made a call and smirked.

"Did you bring a swimsuit?"

"Yeah," Katie said. He smirked and told whoever it was that they'd be down in a few minutes.

"What," Katie asked.

"Saltwater pool. Grab your swimsuit." He kissed her and went and slid his swimsuit on, pulling on a shirt with it and his water slippers that, somehow, he'd remembered to pack in that rush.

Katie slid her sweater dress over the bathing suit, and they went down to the spa and went swimming in the giant pool alone. Katie slid in and Ronan dove in beside her. When he came up for air, he was right in front of her.

"Hey," Katie said.

"Hey yourself. Thought we needed to get out of the room before you tired me out completely." Katie smirked.

"But tiring you out is part of the fun." He shook his head.

"I know it is for you lass." She kissed him and he leaned her up against the side of the pool.

"What," she asked.

"Ever done it in a pool?"

"Not here Ronan. No." His hands slid to her backside.

"No what?"

"You know what." He slid her bathing suit to the side of her and slid his fingers inside her.

"Shit."

"We have the pool to ourselves."

"Mm."

"Good." He kissed her and Katie's legs wrapped around his waist.

"You want it," he whispered. She shook her head, almost daring him to make a move. He slid his swimsuit down and slid himself out of it and into her. "Shit."

"Shh." He pounded into her quietly under the water so there was no noise and kept going until her nails were digging into his back. "Not yet," he said.

"Ronan."

"Not yet love."

"Mm," she moaned. He went deeper into her and Katie's eyes closed.

"Look at me," he said. Katie opened her eyes, and he nodded.

"Come for me." He exploded into her as her body throbbed hard around him.

"Ronan." He kissed her.

"What," he asked as he slid out of her and slid his swimsuit up.

"Not fair."

"No. This isn't fair," he said as his fingers slid inside her again until she climaxed again.

"Shit." He slid his fingers out and slid her bathing suit back over her.

"So that's why you wanted to come down here." He smirked.

"One of the reasons."

"And what was the other reason," Katie asked as he pinned her into the corner of the pool.

"Needed to cool off."

"Ronan."

"And always thought it'd be fun to do it in a pool."

"Something you haven't done." He nodded and kissed her. "Out of all the people…"

He kissed her. "Leave it. I know what you're gonna say."

"You're bad. You just come up with all of these ideas randomly, don't you?"

"Second option was the hot tub, but we'd be on video."

"We need a hot tub."

"And I have a few ideas of what to do to you in there."

"Then tell me."

"Up and in the hot tub." He got up and stepped out of the pool, followed by Katie and went and walked over to the spa manager.

"Sir."

"Are the cameras necessary if it's just the two of us in there?"

"Company policy." He nodded.

"But we are closing up in about a half hour."

"Thank you," Ronan said as he saw Katie stepping into the hot water of the hot tub. She slid in and he followed, sitting opposite her.

"Come," he said. Katie slid across and into his lap, straddling him.

"No fun for you in the hot tub tonight."

"Just have to be careful," he teased.

"Meaning what?" He pulled her towards him, and she felt his fingers inside her again, teasing and making her insides melt.

"Shit," Katie said.

"You're on top. Don't make any big moves."

"Meaning what," Katie teased. He smirked and slid his bathing suit down, sliding inside her as her body clenched around him. "Shit Katie." She grinded her hips slowly as she leaned against him. He teased her as she kept going, turning her on even more.

"Tell me when you're gonna come," he whispered.

"Mm."

"Mine," he said.

"Ronan." He pulled her tighter to him as she kept going and felt her tighten around him.

"More," he said.

"Mm."

"One more lass." She kept going and crumbled around him.

"I can't." He slid deep into her, sliding them into the deeper section of the hot tub. He kept going, not letting anything be seen and then when he felt her come, he slid back into his seat and pulled his bathing suit up.

"Shit," Katie said as his fingers kept teasing then slid inside her to make her come again. She shook her head and kissed him as she moaned quietly. "Good," he said as she climaxed.

"You realize you're gonna have to carry me upstairs, right?"

He shook his head. She didn't move from his lap.

"Katie."

"What?"

"What are you up to?"

"Your turn."

He shook his head and Katie nodded, sliding him out of his swimsuit.

"No." She nodded. Her hand slid around him and started sliding up and down. "Katie."

"Mine." When he slid up in the water and Katie smirked, he shook his head.

"Don't start."

"Then we're going upstairs." He nodded. He pulled his swimsuit up and stepped out of the hot tub, drying off. Katie dried off and walked into the ladies change room and slid the bathing suit off. She slid her sweater back on and came out, walking to the elevator with Ronan.

"And what did you do," Ronan asked.

"Nothing on under the sweater dress." He shook his head.

"Good. You'll be tied to the bed faster."

"What was that?" He kissed her and pinned her in the corner of the elevator.

"You heard me."

"So, you're back in the mood."

"Then we're going to sleep. If I have to leave you tied up I will." The elevator stopped and they went down to their suite. The minute they were through the door, he pulled her sweater dress right off.

"And," Katie asked. He picked her up, wrapping her legs around him and walked into the bedroom, grabbing the tie from earlier and tied her hands to the bed. He slid out of his swimsuit and threw it into his laundry bag, then walked over to Katie.

"Undo them," she asked. He shook his head and kissed her.

"Ronan, it was your turn."

"And now it's yours."

"Then I want to taste you." He shook his head and Katie nodded.

"Katie."

"Mine." He got up and walked around to her, giving her exactly what she had asked for. She slid him deep into her mouth and sucked and licked until he was trying to hold back from exploding into her mouth. "Mm."

"Katie, stop."

"Um mm," she said as she licked some more. He pulled away from her and after protesting for a half second, he was deep inside her, pounding her until her body was throbbing around him. He kept going harder, deeper and faster as he neared his climax. "Aah.Mm. Ronan. Please."

"Say you're mine."

"I'm ahh yours."

"Say it again."

"I'm yours. Mm. Please." He looked at her.

"Then come for me," he said as he exploded into her, and she found her climax almost simultaneously.

"Shit," he said.

"Aah."

"You are insatiable," Ronan said.

"And yours." He slid to his back and Katie fussed with the tie trying to undo her hands.

"Undo it." Ronan reached over and slid one hand out of it so she could untie the other and got up.

"Where are you going?"

"Clean up. Back in a minute." He came back in 2 minutes later and she was curled up under the blankets.

"Come to bed," she said. He pulled on boxers, went and locked the door and drew the curtains then slid into bed with her as her leg curled around his. "We need a hot tub and a pool," Katie joked. He smirked.

"Or going somewhere that we can have our own for a night or two." Katie nodded and kissed his neck.

The next morning, Katie woke up to an empty bed and a cup beside her bed with her latte that she always liked. She slid her satin robe on and gingerly walked into the living room area to see Ronan going through emails in his joggers and no shirt.

"Why didn't you come back to bed?"

"Had to get a few emails in. I was waiting for the breakfast to show."

"You did your workout already?" He nodded and smirked. "What?"

"Thought you'd like a latte to be different."

"Thank you for that," Katie said.

"Welcome lass." He finished another email and sent it then put his laptop on the table and got up, walking over to her. "How are the legs today," he teased.

"Not funny."

He smirked. "What?"

"Put the latte down." She put it down and he walked her back into the bedroom. "What are you up to," Katie asked. He undid the belt of her robe and bent her over the bed.

"Ronan." He tied her hands with the belt and slid his joggers down. "You want morning sex, you get morning sex."

"I get to taste you first." He slid deep into her.

"Aah." "You don't get your way this morning lass." He pounded into her hard over and over, deeper and deeper until he could feel her building to her climax.

"Not yet."

"Ronan."

"Not yet love." He went harder. "Aah."

"Katie."

"Please." He kept going, intentionally making her wait. It just made everything more intense. "Ronan."

"Come for me." She crashed around him and turned around and got on her knees.

"No."

"Mm." She took him in her mouth and sucked and licked and took him deep into her mouth until he came. "Much better," Katie said as she licked him clean.

"You are never..."

"Never what," she asked as she stood up.

"Bad."

"Because I got what I wanted?"

He nodded. "And here you thought all that time that I was yours to tease. Once in a while I get to tease you back."

"That was a lot more than teasing."

"You started it downstairs Ronan." He shook his head.

"We need sleep."

"Because I drained all of your energy?" He kissed her.

"Sleep."

The next morning, Katie woke up to Ronan snuggling back into bed with her.

"Good morning," Katie said.

"Hey there," he whispered as his arm pulled her tight to him. His hand slid between her legs and started teasing.

"Ronan."

"What?"

"Teasing."

"And," he asked as he kissed her shoulder and his fingers slid inside her.

"Aah."

"Yes or no?"

"Mm." She leaned up tight to him and nodded. He pinned her to the bed and pulled her backside towards him as he slid deep inside her.

"Aah."

"Mine," he said as he started slowly sliding in and out, harder and deeper with each thrust.

"This what you wanted?"

"Mmm." He kept going then started speeding up as she throbbed around him. "Aah."

"More," he asked. Katie nodded and he kept going. Hard, fast and pounding into her over and over again until she was moaning his name.

"Shit Ronan."

"Not yet."

"Ronan."

"Don't come yet."

"Aah."

"Not yet."

"Mm. Please."

"Not yet." He kept going until he was almost at his breaking point then he told her to come. He pounded deep into her and exploded into her as she reached her climax. "Oh my goodness," Katie said.

"Good." She collapsed to the bed, and he slid to his back. "Was that what you wanted," he teased. "Yeah. It was," she said.

"Good. You may just get that every morning."

"Promises, promises." He kissed her. "Now, come get up and eat."

"What time is it?"

"Almost 7:30."

"What were you doing up so early?"

"Getting my workout in."

"And cardio."

He smirked. "Come on love." He pulled his boxers on and walked into the living room area, taking the lids off their second last breakfast in the hotel. Katie walked in with her satin robe on and walked over to Ronan.

"What," he teased. Katie kissed him and he pulled her into his arms.

"Come eat." She kissed him again and he undid the belt of her robe, sliding it off.

"Ronan."

"Mine for after."

"What do you mean after?"

"Eat and find out for yourself." She slid into the chair, letting the robe slide open as he looked her up and down. She had her omelet and fruit, and he smirked. "What?" He shook his head and motioned for her to finish eating. He finished his food and had his coffee then she got up and slid into his lap.

"Tell me what you're thinking."

He slid the satin robe off and tied her hands behind her back. "Ronan."

"At my mercy."

"And what are you planning to do with me?" He picked her up, wrapping her legs around him and leaned her against the wall.

"Ronan."

"What?"

"Hands." He kissed her and carried her into the bedroom.

"I want you," Katie said.

"I know you do."

"Ronan."

"No. Not happening."

"Then take the boxers off." He pinned her down on the bed and slid his boxers off.

"Lick," Katie said. He shook his head. He untied her hands as she went to reach for him.

"Nope."

"Ronan." He covered her eyes with the belt and tied her hands.

"Not fair." He kissed her and kissed and nibbled down her body.

"Ronan." He licked at her core and kept going until she was trying to wriggle free.

"The more you move, the tighter they'll get."

"Mm." He licked and teased and got up. "Where are you going?"

"Grabbing something."

"Ronan, no toys." He slid the toy inside her and pressed the button on the phone to activate it. It started thrusting into her over and over again and she shook her head.

"Shit. Ronan, take it out."

"Nope."

"Ronan." He made it more intense. "Aah."

"I'm thinking you should be stuck with this one all day."

"No." He smirked and kissed her.

"Open your mouth." She did with a smirk ear to ear.

"Aah." He slid himself in her mouth and she licked and sucked and took him deep in her throat.

"Katie."

"Mm." He pulled away from her and Katie shook her head.

"Tease." He slid the toy out just as she was nearing climax. He slid deep into her from behind her and slid the other end of the toy against her to tease.

"Shit." He pounded deep into her and kept going until he felt her exploding. The toy didn't stop and either did he, just positioning her so he was hitting just the right spot. "Shit."

"Mine."

"Aah."

"There?"

"Oh my god." He went harder and faster until she was almost shaking in his arms.

"Ah. Ronan. Ah." He kept going until he could feel her reaching her max.

"Don't come yet."

"Please." He kissed the back of her neck and kept going until he was almost there then told her to come. Her body tightened around him as he exploded into her, and she crumbled around him.

"Aah." He kissed her shoulders and untied her hands, sliding the blindfold off.

"Happy," he teased.

"I can't even move." He smirked.

"That was part of my plan lass." He slid to his back and Katie rolled over and kissed him.

"What," he asked.

"I like how I woke up this morning."

"I bet you did lass."

She kissed him. "Shower?"

He nodded. He got up and went and showered and Katie slid in behind him.

"Lass, we have to get ready."

"I don't think I could start something right now," she teased. He finished his shower and washed her hair for her.

"Lass."

"What?"

"The red one." Katie turned and looked at him.

"Red one what?"

"The red one that you called me to turn on when you were at the house alone."

"Or?"

"The one that I just had out."

"Not when I'm at work."

"Under the sexy dress."

"I brought the emerald green dress." He looked at her and shook his head.

"Finish your shower. I'll go hang the dress up."

By the time they got back to the hotel after work, Ronan had everything he needed. He had the extra toy that he was missing and changed into his suit for the party. When Katie came in, she smirked. "Nice suit."

"Just until I can sneak out of there with you."

"Still think we should stay tonight."

"Because you're wanting round 3?"

"And 4 and 5 and 6." He shook his head.

"Might want to get into that sexy dress lass. We have to be down there in 45 minutes." She walked into the bedroom and saw the lingerie laid on the bed beside the dress.

"And what's this?"

"Just put it on." She got undressed and slid the lingerie on then came into the living room.

"Well," she asked. He kissed her and bent her over the table. "What," Katie asked.

He slid the toy in place, and she shook her head. "Determined to make me squirm."

"Not going all out unless we're up here."

"So, when you're ready to get out of there I'll know." He nodded and kissed her.

She walked into the bedroom and slid the dress on, touched up her makeup and when she came out, he smirked. "What," Katie asked.

"Need to check something."

"No, you don't." He ran his finger over the screen, and she shook her head.

"Mm. No more of that."

"And if my finger gets itchy?" She shook her head. He kissed her and they went down to the party.

When she slid her hand in his, he smirked. They walked around the party, had something to eat and just as the conversation was starting to get stale to Ronan, he looked at his watch and buzzed the toy. He saw her almost jump. He snuck out and went into the bar where he'd been the night they'd first met. He ordered a pint and a Baileys espresso martini and waited. He intentionally sat down at the same chair he'd been in when they met, and when she came in, she sat down in her chair from that night.

"You got my hint," he teased.

"You do realize that your hand has been on the screen of your phone off and on ever since you did that little tease."

"Good." Katie shook her head and took a sip of her drink.

"You've only been there two hours."

"And?"

"People are gonna wonder where we went." He shook his head.

"I'm not staying while they do a million speeches. I made sure neither of us would be missed." She kissed him and took another gulp of her drink.

"Trying to finish it rather fast," he joked.

"Determined."

"For what? What's waiting for you upstairs?"

"Depends on what's waiting." He finished his pint, and she smirked.

"Ronan."

"Finish your drink and you'll find out." Katie finished her drink, and he got a grin ear to ear, taking her hand and walking her to the elevator.

"I have an idea," he said.

"Depends on what it is," she replied.

He walked her onto the elevator and smirked. "What," she asked. He looked at her and Katie slid her body up against his.

"Press the elevator button."

"The stop one or our floor?"

"Either one." Katie smirked and pressed the one for their floor. He slid his hand in his pocket and ran his finger over the screen to activate the toy and make her knees crumble.

"Ronan, you are so not fair."

"No, this would be unfair." He held his finger on it as it pulsated and thrusted in and out of her.

"Stop." He did and smirked.

"And I can't do anything to get you back for it."

"Depends on what you're thinking." She slid her hand down his torso and felt him through his dress pants.

"Not in the elevator Katie." She looked at him.

"And why not?"

"Because it has cameras." She kissed him and felt him again, rubbing up and down.

"Katie." The elevator stopped and they made their way down the hall to their suite. When she walked in, the bed was made, and roses were beside it.

"What's all of this?"

"No idea what you're talking about," he joked. Katie slid out of her heels and walked over to him.

"I liked the heels on."

"And I like you better naked."

"Katie." She slid his suit jacket off and slid it over the back of the table chair.

"And this off," she said undoing his dress shirt.

"And I think that you need to show me that lingerie again." She slid the dress off, laying it on top of his suit jacket.

"You look sexy as hell in that. You know that right?"

"With the toy?"

He slid it out. "With or without it."

"And here I thought you were leaving that in to tease me with." He pulled her to him and kissed her, devouring her lips. "Shirt off," she said.

He pulled it off, throwing it onto the chair and she went to undo his dress pants. "Katie."

"Mine."

"Not now." She nodded and undid them, pulling him out of his boxers. She slid her mouth over him, and he leaned back with a groan as she took him deep.

"You aren't starting that again lass."

"Say it or I'm going to."

"Meaning what?" She looked up at him and he smirked.

"Shit Katie. Stop." He pulled her to her feet and leaned her back against the window.

"What," she asked. "The first time we were in this room, you told me that you never did this."

"Never had before you." He kissed her and undid the bra.

"And then you begged me to date you."

"Rather proud of that moment." He undid the garters and threw them to the floor.

"And what do you want now?"

"You to call me love again."

"Katie."

"That's all I want." He picked her up, wrapping her legs around him and slid deep inside her. "Aah."

"And you know what I want," he asked.

"Me." Katie kissed him, and they had sex against the window for the world to see.

"Now everyone can see that you're mine."

"And?" He kept going until she was crumbling around him and he followed, leaning her onto the bed in the bedroom.

"Say it Ronan. Please."

"Yes love."

"What?"

"Yours. All yours love." She kissed him and they curled up in the blankets together.

"Say it again," she asked.

He kissed her. "Yours."

THE END

SUE LANGFORD

ABOUT THE AUTHOR

When Sue started her writing career, she was determined to write books with strong female characters, and stories that you wouldn't ever forget. Now, after her Charleston Series and now her new Ireland series, she's gone from sweet romances to the spicy and sultry end of the romance world. The second-chance and small-town romances can take place anywhere in the world, and she's determined to write the stories from our favorite vacation locations, and a few of the locations from her dream bucket list. Now, her newest series takes place in the beautiful Isle of Ireland and will no doubt be the top of her favorites, and the spiciest that she's ever written.